With
Blood and Scars

B. E. Andre

PebbleStone

With Blood and Scars

Copyright © 2014 by B. E. Andre
Cover Design: Phil Wagstaff
Cover Layout: www.coppermedia.co.uk
Editor: Sarah Dobbs
All rights reserved.
Paperback ISBN 978-0-9931472-0-3
Kindle ASIN B00Q9AK9VA

Published 2014 by PebbleStone

For Jadwiga Wiśniewska and Andrzej Brzęczek and for those who came
with them and before them

Glossary of Polish Words and Phrases

Armia Krajowa – arm-yah kra-yovah: Underground Army, Partisan Army

Babcia (n fem) – bab-cha: granny, grandma

Barszcz (n masc) – barsh-ch: clear beetroot soup

Bigos (n masc) – bee-goss: Polish hunter's stew

Cholera jasna (interj) – holler-ah yas-nah: English equivalent – bloody hell

Czuwaj (v imperative) – tchoo-vay: be prepared, be vigilant

Dupa (n fem) – doo-pah: arse

Dziadzio (n masc) – jaj-oh: grandad

Dziecko (n neut) – jets-koh: child

Dziękuję bardzo (interj) – jen-koo-yeh bards-oh: thank you very much

Dzień dobry (interj) – jeyn dob-ree: good morning

Fakultet (n masc) – fak-ool-tet: faculty

Gaj (n masc) – gah-y: grove

Góral (n masc), górale (pl) – goo-ral: highlander from the Carpathian mountains.

Gówno (n masc) – goov-noh: shit

Herbatka (n fem) – herr-bat-kah: tea

Katarzynka (n fem), katarzynki (pl) – kat-ah-zhyn-kah: chocolate-coated honey cakes

Kiełbasa (n fem), kiełbasy (pl) – kee-eh-w-basah: Polish sausage

Kolacja (n fem) – kol-ats-yah: dinner

Kolonia (n fem) – koh-lon-yah: brownie/cub camp

Kominek (n masc – koh-meen-ek: indoor singsong around a fire

Kotlet (n masc) – kot-lett: minced pork burger

Krótko i węzłowato – ktrut-koh ee venz-woh-vatoh: in brief, short and sweet (colloquial)

Krówka (n fem), krówki (pl) – kruv-kah: Polish fudge

Kurwa mać (interj) – koor-vah mach: English equivalent – fucking hell

Lalka (n fem) – lal-kah: doll

Mały (adj) biały (adj) domek (n masc) – mah-wee bee-ah-wee domek: little white house

O mój Boże (interj) – o moo-y boh-zheh: Oh my God

Obiad (n masc) – ob-yad: lunch

Pan (n masc) – pan: Mr

Pani (n fem) – pan-yi: Mrs

Piekielne szczury (phrase) – pyeh-kyel-neh shchoo-ree: hellish rats

Pierog (n masc), pierogi (pl) – pee-eh-roh-gee: Polish version of ravioli

Psia krew (interj) – pshah kref: dog's blood (swearing)

Rosół (n masc) – raw-soo: bouillon

Sernik (n masc) – sehr-nik: cheesecake

Śniadanie (n neut) – shnyah-dah-nee-eh: breakfast

Solidarność (n fem) – solid-ar-noshch: solidarity, fellowship

Sopocka (n fem) – sop-ots-kah: type of cured meat

Srebrzysty (adj masc) – sreb-zhee-stee: silvery

Sto lat (saying) – stoh lat: a hundred years

Surówka (n fem) – soo-ruff-kah: salad of finely diced or grated vegetables

Święty Mikołaj – shfyen-tee meek-oh-wah-y: Saint Nicholas

Szacunek (n masc) – shats-oo-nek: respect

Tata/tatuś (n masc) – tat-oosh: Dad

Uśmiechnij się (v imperative) – oosh-myeh-h-nee sheh: smile

Warszawiak (n masc) – varsh-a-vee-ak: person from Warsaw

Wesołych Świąt (interj) – ves-oh-ee-h shfyont: Merry Christmas

Wigilia (n fem) – vee-gee-lyah: Christmas Eve

Zasrane (adj) – za-sra-neh: shitty, shit-covered

Złoty (n masc) – zwoh-tee: unit of Polish currency

Think about it…

How do you think
I got here? Blown in
on a yellowing leaf? Do you think

we seeped into your cities
or your suburbs with the rain?
How do you think it happened?

Do you think we rode
the backs of waves, shattering –
flotsam jetsam against white cliffs?

Or did we spring out of the earth
from seeds you'd sown
and then forgotten.

Every one of us came here
for a reason. Ask
your ministers, your generals.

Ask them what treaties they signed
ask what they bartered and stole
what game they used us for.

Or will you go on thinking
we simply fell out of the sky
and that is why we smoulder still?

Maria Jastrzębska, M. (2004). *Syrena*. Bradford: Redbeck Press

CHAPTER ONE

DAY ONE: NOW

Not much for his little life – ten lines in the *Manchester Evening News*.

I stare at the report, wishing it away. It mentions the Moors Murderers, a speculation that couldn't be more off-beam. It won't be me who informs the police. One of the others can call. Their version will be simpler.

I'm phoning about the child's remains found on the building site. In 1966, this happened, followed in 1967 by that. No, I'm sorry. I don't recall anything further. Case closed, date-stamped.

But nothing is ever that simple, is it? Assuming one of them sees the report, of course, which they might not; they could be anywhere for all I know. Only another ten minutes' drive and I'd have been in Altrincham instead of these services, oblivious.

"Is it all right?" The man's voice interrupts my thoughts.

I lift my gaze from the inside of my cup. "Sorry?"

"Do you mind if we...?" He indicates the three free chairs at my table. His wife and child dawdle behind him, both holding trays, waiting for my reply.

"No problem. Go ahead."

I filter out the family's chatter. Couldn't it all have waited? This, and Dad. I'd nearly managed to put my feet up; mortgage paid, the kids educated, independent. No more arguments, apart from Rachel's "Mum, stop *liking* all my comments on Facebook – you're so embarrassing." Thank God for Sam.

I've had less than two months without some form of anxiety or other; a fleeting instant when China and India seemed more than a pipe dream. Unlikely, but at least possible.

"You said you *wanted* chips," the man barks at his daughter; inside I wince, but I pretend not to hear the harshness in his voice, continue stirring the froth in my coffee. He even looks like Dad back then.

No, for the moment I can forget the photo status-update of me in a

1

rickshaw or sitting on an elephant, proof I haven't yet ossified into crippling oldfartdom. I'd settle for calm. No niggling, unidentifiable worries, or dithering over unimportant choices. No more crises. Or being in the wrong bloody place at the wrong bloody time.

Suddenly they're breaking free – those twelve months I'd filed away for good, up through the corner of my eye, back deep in the recesses of my brain. Sleep at night, get up in the morning, sort the kids out, go to work, days to weeks, into decades; nothing to trigger open the memory store.

But that's not what it's like, is it, history? It's never gone, like the *Shoah* documentary. Wham. I could have been listening to Radio Four, sewing my patchwork, same as every other night that week. Why did I even switch on the TV? The man standing by the tracks said, "Let me put it this way. When you cut your finger, does it hurt me?" He demonstrated how he warned the Jews by raising a hand to his throat and making a slitting motion. Then he smiled. Realisation spread like a gigantic boil, weighing me down, growing heavier. It wasn't about regret or sorrow, nothing as noble as that, just Dad's guilt. He was another person then, but it didn't lessen the disgust when I looked in the mirror.

I lick the last of the froth from the spoon then stand to go.

"Have a good journey," the man says cheerfully. "Sorry if we disturbed you. Kids, eh? More trouble than they're worth," he adds, winking at the girl.

I dash through the squall to the car park. The windscreen mists up as soon as I turn on the ignition. I won't wait for it to clear. Squinting, I inch towards the slip road leading to the motorway. The lights of the other cars come into view through the frantic rhythm of the wipers.

Focus. 1966 – concrete events, proper happenings, dotted among the humdrum go-to-school, be-scared-of-Dad, eat-*kolacja* canvas of existence. Victory over Germany in the World Cup. The Beatles everywhere like some kind of infestation. Vietnam.

Meanwhile, those Manchester Poles had nothing but the past. Saigon was irrelevant. The only conflict of significance occurred in Europe over twenty years before. A jumbled collage of images even now. Loose threads, chunks missing, overlapping, glued ad hoc with no pattern. No continuity or harmony or big picture to stand in front of and say, "I get it."

And smaller glowing moments; Whitsun half term and the summer holidays. When did we sit in the round bellowing 'Paperback Writer'? In August, or just before it happened? I see Stevo, laughing, face up to the sun, mouth open wide, two small black holes in his back teeth like trapped poppy seeds.

Did I make that up?

It plays tricks, the memory, I know. Whether the frames rolling by are happy or sad, they breed exaggeration made truer by repetition. Babcia told me she had eleven brothers and sisters. Several times. The year before she died she changed her mind and said there were twelve; she'd mislaid a brother blown to smithereens in 1916. How can you forget a sibling who sat at the same table for the first ten years of your life? That's memory for you, unreliable.

I ought to let it go, pretend I never saw the paper, block it out. Or at least put it aside for the moment. I've Dad to think about now. How much time does he have left? How much time do I have to ask him?

The downpour eases at the traffic lights. I turn right on to the A556, lighten up on the accelerator and crawl past the cameras.

Presumably, if they've found Stevo, the police have the box too. What the hell did we put in there? Nothing to suggest our identities, I'm sure. Nor his either since the report didn't mention it.

A mess of shredded, white tissue paper tumbles through the desert of my brain, no substance.

THEN

Ten a penny we were, us Anias – me and Ania Tarczak, Ania Skokowksa, Ania Kubek, et-cet-era, et-cet-era. Except I was the only one who was ten. The others were all younger or older. I only ever met them down there in Polska Land which was to the left of our gate on Upper Chorlton Road. But first, next door, Mr. and Mrs. Nasmith from Ghana, who were usually nice apart from when I played two-a-ball right next to their window. Then, the 81 and 82 bus stops. After that, Kombo's, Brooks's Bar and the Polski deli. Then, the number 53 bus, the stinky Hyde's Anvil brewery, Alexandra Road, Polski church and Polska School.

The right side was miles better. First, in the house attached to ours, Ossie, which was dead good because his bedroom was right next to mine. Then Granny and Grandad further up, and down the road the doctor's surgery and Chorlton library. It was the best library in the whole universe because a very rich man called Mr. Andrew Carnegie said it had to have a domey thingy built on top of it, like a cathedral. It was probably his favourite library too, even though the lady who stamped our books told me he'd built hundreds of them. When you went past the library and turned left, Quarmby's was on the other side of the road – another good thing about to the right because they sold the best pens and pencils and everything.

Round the corner of Ossie's house on the avenue was the rest of my gang – Dermot, Gianni and Manuela, plus those other boring kids. Then, spreading out, the Candy Box, Ayres Road and Seymour Park Junior and Infants School.

Across from our road there was nothing interesting, just more houses with people I didn't know and the Territorial Army base. So that was that.

But our back garden was great because it had a swing, a pear tree, a fab place to hide behind the garage and an escape route. My *best* thing was hanging by the backs of my knees on the top of our swing, even after Granny made me tuck my skirt into my knickers because I was a shameless heathen communist. Sometimes when I was upside down counting Groucho's poos on the grass, I heard the cheer from the Stretford End, when Georgie Best scored a goal for United. Not always, just if the wind was in the right direction and if it wasn't raining. Mum wouldn't let me go that far though. And Maine Road was also off the map, not that I cared, somewhere beyond the frontiers of Polska Land. I never did hear a peep from over there because Manchester City were rubbish. It was a well-known fact.

Granny and Grandad's back garden was another brilliant place. A bit like a farm except smaller. Well, exactly the same size as our garden probably. But they grew loads of vegetables and fruit, because of "in Siberia when we were slaves and only ate water soup" blah-blah. And Granny had her three fat chickens who talked to her when Grandad didn't feel like it. Which was nearly always.

CHAPTER TWO

DAY ONE: LATE AFTERNOON

The usual anxiety fills my chest as I enter Altrincham and count and curse the traffic lights on Washway Road. The after-spray of my thirty-five miles an hour in a thirty zone soaks the feet of a pedestrian in a furry-hooded parka. I glance in the rear view mirror, lift my hand in apology and the male or female – whatever it is – gives me the finger back.

Welcome to Manchester. My dad's dying. Sorry I drenched you.

The bungalow is lit up as if in denial; the tacky faux-candles twinkle in front of the curtains. The paint is cracking under the window frame of their little white house, and for some reason Mum's displayed the Christmas wreath way in advance. I park up behind their cars, take my mac from the back seat, put it around my shoulders and open the boot; there's only the tiny Ryanair suitcase, my make-up and wash things. I don't know how long I'll be staying. Psiuńka barks in the hall as the suitcase wheels scrunch across the gravel drive.

Above the letterbox is a label with ragged corners. It says *Christus + Mansionem + Benedicat* and then, in Polish, a few words about God bestowing His blessings here, asking the angels to visit and keep the house from danger.

Mum opens the door. There are heavy grey bags under her eyes. Her silver hair sticks out like feathers on a white baby dove. I don't suppose she's had time for a haircut what with all of this. I'll do it for her tonight if I can find Dad's trimming scissors. If she'll let me.

"Tatuś is watching television," she says in a whisper. "He's tired. I'm so glad you're here. Thank you." She hugs me as if she hasn't seen me in five years. Actually it's two weeks.

In English I ask, "Is Evie – sorry – Iwonka coming over tonight?"

She replies in Polish, "No. She was here earlier. She'll come in the morning."

Dad sits in his Lazyboy in his navy dressing gown. Underneath it, navy blue brushed-cotton pyjamas with a design of tiny golf-balls, clubs and tees. He's never played golf in his life. The leg-rest is up and his feet are motionless in ankle-high blue and green tartan slippers; the right foot is zipped-up, the left not. The slippers have pristine soles, new, probably from one of those old people's 'gizmo to get you into the bath, out of the bath, open a jar, trim your nasal hair' catalogues that litter the house. The Zimmer frame is on his right. I glance at the screen and see a moustached John Wayne wearing a US cavalry uniform. Maybe *Rio Grande*. Cowboys, Indians and musicals, as always.

Dad looks at me. "You're here, child. Hello, favourite eldest daughter." He smiles into hollow cheeks and lifts his face to receive my quick kiss.

"Yes. I've come. Hello, favourite only father. Taken some leave. *Eco Crafting Monthly* can manage without me for a few days. They all want my job, so they'll do their best." Did I just use the right declension in Polish? Will he correct me?

He lets my failings pass him by as if he's floating in a boat, carefree. "Mama could do with some help. Wanda, tea. Please." The please sounds like an afterthought, as if he's learning manners where Mum's concerned. Only took him sixty years to get there.

She scuttles off to the kitchen, telling us both that *kolacja* will be ready in about half an hour. Dad says, "Not for me," then "thank you." Another afterthought.

Mum throws me a pleading look. "Perhaps Ania can make you some Complan?"

"I don't want Complan." He huffs, and sighs.

He can't weigh more than nine stone, probably less, and his eyes have a sort of milky opacity, no longer the burnt amber that used to bore into me. I ask how he's feeling. He says, not long now. I fidget on the sofa and wonder what to say next. There's no point in contradicting, pretending this isn't happening, mainly because he'll tell me off. Absolutely no change there. Will he ever acknowledge that I'm middle-aged? I've brought up two children quite successfully, know to switch the lights off at night and I'm perfectly capable of deciding when to shift gear in the car. 'Ever' no longer exists.

"Can I get you something that's not Complan? What else do you fancy, Tatuś?"

"Nothing," he says, sees my disappointment, then has a think. The depth of the frown lines between his eyebrows suggests he's racking his brain, as if grappling through some gigantic mathematical equation. I wait. Finally, he says, "Gorgonzola."

I almost laugh but stifle it. "Gorgonzola?" Since when has he liked Gorgonzola? "Won't that make you ill? Isn't it too rich?"

He looks at me as if I'm deranged, so I say nothing further. I know what he means; he means: "I'm dying. I want Gorgonzola," like a man facing the firing squad wants a last fag. I sit back and rest my hand on the arm of the sofa. Dad reaches for me at the side of the Lazyboy; his hand covers mine, squeezes it, strokes it, then he draws little circles, like he used to when I was a child and he twiddled my hair round. Below his knuckles the skin is yellowy-white like tea-stained crêpe paper, yet the texture is soft, as if he's never done a day's work in his life. The wedding ring which used to dig into his flesh is loose now and ridges run along short, clean nails I barely recognise. These are my father's hands.

He pats his fingers, one after the other, on my wrist, and gives further instruction. "Gorgonzola on a Ritz biscuit." He's distracted by a conversation in the film. "John Wayne was the best," he says, nodding at the telly. Then, "I want something…" he rolls his tongue around his mouth, "…tasty. Something with flavour."

I agree. "Yes, he was." John Wayne was crap, wooden, a rubbish actor. God knows how he ever made it in Hollywood. Maureen O'Hara comes on the screen – it is *Rio Grande*. "I'll go to the Co-op in a minute."

Mum brings the mugs in. I drink the tea – he doesn't touch his – and watch the end of the film with him. Then I drive to the Co-op where I walk up and down rows selecting Gorgonzola, Cambozola, Brie, Camembert, St. Augur, Dolcelatte, Stilton, Ritz biscuits, TUC crackers, Marr's Melts, Jacob's cream crackers, oat biscuits.

Dad's lost three and a half stone at least. I only lost two, but that was the chemo. I put a tub of Müller Rice vanilla custard in my basket, perhaps he'll eat that. And buttermilk. And four individual pots of crème brûlée – he's always liked crème brûlée – that should tempt him. And a giant bar of Cadbury's Fruit and Nut.

The boy at the counter – he can't be more than eighteen – opens a plastic bag, drops the groceries in, giggles and says, "That's a lot of cheese. Got some fancy foreign mice coming, have you?" I want to say, why don't you shut the fuck up? My dad's dying. He wants cheese. I don't say it, of course. He's only being friendly. And I'm not given to swearing. Ordinarily.

I put my credit card into the machine to pay the sixty-four pounds and forty-two pence it's asking me for and tap out the same pin I've always had – the last four digits of our phone number in Old Trafford.

The *Manchester Evening News* is stacked up in an orderly pile next to the entrance, reminding me, taunting me that there's something else to sort out. I'll find Ossie on the internet. He'll know what to do.

No. Shake it away. Concentrate on Dad.

THEN

Manchester United had beaten Benfica 5–0, Dad was in a brilliant mood, and Georgie Best had come back to England wearing a sombrero. It was on the telly. That was the day when everything changed. March was it?

All wrapped up we were, warm as possible in gabardine coats, scarves and mittens.We were playing rounders in the avenue with the other kids from down the road. Our team was losing, mainly because Ossie hadn't arrived yet. Dermot had wandered off in disgust, saying Ossie would never be opening batsman for the West Indies if he didn't show up soon.

When Ossie bounded up, panting and waving his arms, his brown face gleaming from the exertion, he summoned the gang into the drive behind his back gate. Gianni, Manuela and I sprinted over leaving the other kids to play on their own and hung about waiting for Dermot, who was doing acrobatics on the sticky-out bars on top of the lamp post outside Mrs. Czaplińska's house.

Ossie yelled, "*Psha kreff!*" imitating Granny. "Come on, slowcoach. Speed it up, you div."

Dermot jumped and landed on his scrawny bum with a loud ouch. Manuela rolled her eyes at me.

Ossie said, "You'll never believe it! I've found us a den. A proper den. Where we can go even when it's raining."

Manuela pulled her thick, black plait over her shoulder, smoothing it down to her waist. "And have meetings?" She wove her fingers through the hair beneath the toggle while looking at Ossie from under her eyelashes.

"Yes, everything. It's a mansion. Huge!"

"Where?" Gianni asked.

"Whalley Road. Behind the barracks."

Whalley Road. Quite a risk. I wasn't allowed to go that far, but what the eye didn't see, Mum couldn't know about.

"Who lives there?" I asked.

"That's it," said Ossie. "Nobody. It's empty."

"What do you mean, 'empty'?"

"No furniture. No people. By the looks of it nobody's lived there for years. It's proper tatty."

"So what's so good about it?"

"It's gigantic…like…" He was scrambling around for some pitch to persuade us into something stupid, not for the first time. "Like Buckingham Palace!"

Dermot said, "How long will we be there?"

Ossie tsked. "Not long, you donkey. Come and have a look."

It seemed like a chance worth taking. We crossed Upper Chorlton Road further along by the bus stop, so that if any familiar grown-up was passing we wouldn't be spotted, scooted down Sylvan Avenue and turned left into Whalley Road.

"Hurry up. This way." As Ossie directed us through two massive, ivy-covered gateposts, we entered a jungle of sycamores, oaks and horse chestnuts with long, drooping branches, and scores of bushes, brambles and weeds. But then, a few steps in, the building itself came into view – and was Ossie ever right! We stood in front, mouths agape. How come we didn't know about this place?

The entrance was an imposing dark oak door reached by five wide steps bordered with iron railings, now flaky with rust and dried crumbs of white paint. Two-thirds up the door, in the middle, hung a black cast-iron knocker in the shape of a football trophy.

On the right of the door, recessed a little, was a room with a circular bay as wide as my entire house, containing three sash windows. On the other side of the door, a veranda jutted out, its roof supported by six white columns, and, at the far end of it, two more huge windows and a glass door. The roof of the veranda was a balcony where I imagined breakfasts eaten in the morning sunshine by posh people in velvet dressing gowns. Above the second storey was yet another floor set into the slate roof where smaller arched windows stood proud, like shrines waiting for a statue of Our Lady.

"Come on, you lot," Ossie said. "It gets even better. Look at this." He dragged back the tangled shrubbery which stretched like a green moat right round the mansion and invited us in. Neither Manuela nor I fancied it much. Gianni and Dermot leapt down. After a moment, we heard "Wow! Wow! Wow! Come and see!"

Shielding our faces with our hands, Manuela and I pushed through and jumped, following the boys. They were rubbing the muck off the windows, making plans.

As with all of Ossie's great schemes, it was only fabulous on first viewing. When we climbed through one of the broken windows and Manuela saw the cadavers of the millions of creepy crawlies and a few decomposing mice, her enthusiasm waned. "I'm not staying unless you get rid of the dead things."

Ossie said, "What? Don't be such a daft 'aporth. They're dead. Can't do you any harm now."

"Don't care. I hate dead things."

"What are we going to do then?"

"She dun't have to go in every room," Dermot said to Ossie. "Suppose we just clear out the rooms we want."

While Manuela returned outside, sat on the steps and sulked, we investigated the house from top to bottom, gingerly manoeuvring round floor boards that were either missing in parts or starting to crumble with the smell of rotting mushrooms and dirty toilets. Many rooms contained nothing but cast-iron fireplaces – all the grates were gone. But some, like the kitchen, still had remnants of warped shelving and sagging cupboards. Even so, the place was grand. And apart from the central staircase, we discovered two smaller ones at opposite ends of the house. Ossie said that was because in the olden days ladies couldn't breathe because their corsets squashed their rib cages and flattened their lungs, so they didn't like to walk all the way to the main staircase because "they'd get puffed out and hyperdentilate."

Choosing our den was simple. We had to be at the back, so that if anybody wandered in off Whalley Road, just as Ossie had done, the likelihood of being seen was reduced, and we'd have time to escape if necessary. We decided on a room on the left of the house with a wide bay window that had a seat underneath it. Gianni struggled to lift any of the four parts forming the seat's cover. Between the three of them the boys heaved, pushed and shoved until the sections came loose. When they were open Gianni looked inside and said the box was big enough to hide some of us in the event of snoopers.

Dermot cheerfully added there was enough space for two grown-up dead bodies. He knew that for a solid fact because when his great Aunt Concepta died, his family went to her house, where he'd seen her laid out in the coffin in her front parlour.

Dermot closed his eyes, sucked in his freckled cheeks and crossed his hands on his chest. "She were all yellow and waxy. That's what happens when you die, in't it?"

Was it?

"Aw, shut it. Let's clean up and let Manuela in," Ossie said. There wasn't really that much to do. The boys weren't squeamish, and I preferred dead insects to live ones. Using bits of wood we'd found, we swept everything into one corner of the room. The boys picked the bits up and went to throw them outside on the rockery next to the steps where Manuela had been kicking her heels all the time we explored.

Ossie bowed. "Please enter, Your Majesty. Your palace is ready." After she'd inspected if we'd done it all properly, she pronounced the den satisfactory. "Let's give it a name."

"Baskerville Hall?" Gianni suggested.

"Ooh! Baskerville Hall? Where've you got that from?" Ossie said.

Gianni reddened. "It's a book I'm reading. Sherlock Holmes."

"Nope. No Sherlock Holmes here. Something else."

We sat on the floor and went through a few ideas and decided upon Spooky, which quickly became Old Spooky.

Soon after, we brought our own stuff over which meant it was almost like being at home, except without parents and annoying brothers and sisters. Between us we cobbled up a random stash of jacks, marbles, an Exacto knife, Cluedo and other odds and ends. We stored everything in the back of the remaining cupboards in the basement and filled the fronts with scrunched up newspapers as a disguise.

It was such a superb adventure, such a marvellous wheeze. No grown-ups knew about it. We were going to have a great time. Forever and ever.

*****

It was Ossie's eleventh birthday so we arranged to meet in the afternoon. We trickled in over the course of an hour. The den was more homely now the floor wasn't covered in muck, and the April sun did its best to shine through the dirt-mottled window panes. While the boys wafted smoke signals up the chimney, I lay on the window seat sunbathing through the glass.

The boys started one of their farting contests just as Manuela turned up. She poked her nose round the door to say "Hi" and went down to the basement. A moment later she marched back in, looking chuffed as a pig's head on a butcher's hook.

"Who's had my Rolos? I was saving them." Her eyes accused the back of Dermot's head.

Gianni tried to calm her down. Was she sure she'd brought them in? His Hotspur comic had disappeared the day before yesterday, he said, but then he thought he might have lost it at home, so didn't mention it.

Dermot, still unaware he was under suspicion, carried on ripping bits of newspaper in the fireplace. Without turning round, his voice almost a whisper, he said, "Maybe it's back."

Manuela glanced at the grey beads and the blue amulet wrapped around the door handle.

A few days after we'd found Old Spooky, a crow had flown into the den through the broken window. It had flapped and slapped its wings, smacking back and forth from the walls to the ceiling, cra-krawing so loud I'd thought my ears would burst. Manuela screamed and screamed until Ossie jammed his hand against her mouth to shut her up. Berserk, that crow was. Dermot squashed into me, him and his cabbagey smell, and we huddled into the corner, cowering to keep out of its way, praying it would find the way out again. My heart pounded as I remembered a film where vultures jab-jab-jabbed at a cowboy's eyes until there was nothing left but dried up holes.

When the damn thing finally got out, and we dared drop our hands from our faces, everyone slumped back and breathed. What a flipping hoo-hah!

Dermot was pulling at his fingers, making them click. "You know what that were, dun't you?"

Ossie grimaced. "Eh?"

"The Devil's Ghost."

"The devil doesn't have a ghost, you great 'nana."

"It's his spirit, in't it? Come to collect evil souls," he whispered, as if demons were a regular occurrence in O'Donnell world.

The boys had scoffed, but Manuela didn't speak for ages and refused to budge from the corner. Dermot didn't bother me though. I'd cottoned on to him yonks ago – he didn't half spout drivel at times. Like when he boasted he'd be emigrating soon. As if. Because Old Trafford was only his parents' stopgap between Limerick and Chicago. And his dad would buy him a horse. He'd claimed that when we were five, and here he still was, having gone absolutely flipping nowhere and not so much as a gerbil in sight. So I wasn't about to fall for evil spirits, was I?

Dermot had brought rosary beads after Crow Day and looped them over the door handle. They were a present from Father Maloney for serving at mass. And because they were blessed with holy water, we'd be safe now, Dermot said. Nothing bad would happen at Spooky again. Manuela also contributed a scary eye on a bit of blue glass with a black cord. She coiled it round the back of Dermot's beads. The crucifix dangled against the background of the eye and clinked whenever we opened the door. So that was three things we had to protect us, if you counted Ossie's lucky rabbit's foot.

But now we had to find Manuela's Rolos. It wasn't us, so she must be mistaken, Gianni decided. We trooped downstairs to the kitchen to double-check they hadn't fallen behind the shelving when she'd pushed the newspaper back.

*****

A sound on the landing stopped us in our tracks.

"D'you hear that?" Gianni said.

"Yeah." Ossie cocked his ear towards the ceiling. "Something's up there."

I already knew what he was going to say next.

"Who's coming?"

No way was he going to convince me to go, no way. I didn't believe in all the devil rubbish, but still…Manuela didn't look keen either.

"You go. That's your job," she said to the boys, allowing no back-answers.

"Aw, come on – you're such a sissy," Ossie said.

With his sleeve, Dermot swabbed away the snot-lines sludging towards his mouth. "If we go together," he smeared his cuff against his trousers, "it'll be safer 'coz there's more of us." He'd obviously been taken in. How I hated being put on the spot like that – it kind of made you have to go. And we weren't sissies anyway – we just weren't as stupid as Ossie. Well, not me, anyway.

Manuela's elbow poked me in the side. She glared at me. "We're coming."

Ossie headed up the narrow basement stairs. "Don't get your knickers in a twist. It's probably just a cat," he whispered.

Manuela grabbed my hand, dropped it when Dermot turned round and saw us, and linked my elbow instead.

The hall was dark and gloomy and the staircase seemed much longer, wider, noisier than it ever had before. Halfway up we heard another skitter, then the tread of hasty footsteps. Whoever or whatever it was had reached the third floor, up in the eaves. No place left for the human, animal or Devil's spirit to escape other than the roof. A piercing horn beeped outside making Manuela and me jump and catch our breath. She clenched her elbow round mine, tight as a vice, put her mouth to my ear. "Let's go back, Ania. Please.

12

Something horrible's going to happen."

I wasn't going to be a coward now that we had got that far. "Too late, twit." This was her fault.

We stood behind Ossie as he hesitated. Then he puffed himself out and straightened his back, like John Wayne getting ready for a shootout. He turned round, looked at us and turned back. Under his breath, he said "It's only a cat. It's only a cat." He faced us again, "It's only a cat. That's all. Come on," and walked on. A cat wearing shoes.

Gianni, who'd been quiet so far, as if in a trance of some kind, kept parallel to Ossie, but Dermot, Manuela and I dithered. The creaking stairs were bound to give us away – I really wanted to slap Manuela.

We crept up to the top floor, gradually becoming a huddle.

"Shush, listen," Ossie said. "Here's the plan. Me and Gianni will go in first and you three stay behind the door. If it gets past us two, grab it." Manuela and I abandoned the link and clasped hands. As Manuela tried to do the same to Dermot to form a line of defence, he swiped her away with a "Get lost" and inched up behind the boys.

The two doors of the attic rooms were shut. The only glimmer of light from a tiny glass porthole in the ceiling cast freaky shadows on the wall. Ossie opened the first door. Through the crack I glimpsed something move.

"Watch out!" I shrieked.

Ossie tripped and crumpled to the floor, followed by something else, followed by Gianni launching himself on top. A confusion of arms, legs, screams, grunts, then Dermot pulled his wits together and also leapt on the writhing mass. The skirmish lasted couple of minutes until eventually, between them, our boys dragged up a scruffy, dirty, stick insect of a lad. The smell of him – stale, sweaty-sock biscuits – made me gag.

"Fuck off! Gerrooooff!" he wailed, jerking like a bucking bronco. Gianni and Ossie gripped his hands behind his back in a double arm-lock while Dermot stomped for all he was worth on the lad's feet. I felt obliged to contribute something, so I punched him one in the stomach and grabbed a fistful of his hair. Meanwhile, Manuela didn't lift a single finger to help, just stood there chewing the bottom of her plait, doing absolutely nothing of any use *what-so-ever*. As flipping usual.

I don't know why he held out for so long; we were hardly going to kill him. Defeated, he moaned, "All right, all right." His body flopped in the boys' grasp. "I give in. Don't hit me any more. Please."

Manuela piped up. "Was it you who took my Rolos?"

"Ya what?"

"Did you take my Rolos?"

"Oh. Yeah. Sorry. I'm starvin'. Haven't had any food for ages."

After motioning to Dermot to take charge of the double arm-lock, Ossie, chest spread and eyes narrowed, said, "Down to the den." It was like he'd

13

suddenly become the Sheriff of Apache Junction or something.

*****

With Ossie and Gianni going first and facing the lad, the boys negotiated each step backwards down the stairs and we arrived at the den without further to-do from our prisoner. Gianni pushed him down into the middle, and we sat cross-legged in a circle surrounding him.

"Who are you?" Gianni asked. "And what are you doing here?"

The lad examined us. "If I tell ya, ya can't tell no-one else."

"Maybe, maybe not," said Gianni. "Depends."

I wanted to hold my nose, but it seemed impolite. The stench had grown worse and I really did think I would throw up. Plus the glob of creamy stuff in his overlapping front teeth was giving me the heebie-jeebies. Everything about him was revolting.

"I'm Steven Corders. Stevo." His green eyes flashed. "I've run away from home."

Wow! How brave to run away from home. We'd talked about it among ourselves before, usually after we got a clip round the ear or when our mums gave us unreasonable chores, but no-one seriously considered doing it. Ossie told him our names, and then Manuela said, "Why did you run away?"

Stevo folded his arms and looked down at his thighs. "Ya won't tell?"

For a brief moment, I thought of a film on the telly where two sisters and a brother found Jesus in their barn and looked after him in secret because if they didn't he'd be crucified all over again on a Lancashire hilltop. Stevo didn't look holy to me though. Not a bit.

He told us, his voice flat like someone reading the times tables, that there was never any food at home, so he sneaked into other people's houses, neighbours' further up the street. He'd wait in the backyard behind the bins, and when they went to the front parlour, he'd nip in the kitchen, whip whatever was available and sprint back down the alley. Or he'd walk by a greengrocer's and pinch fruit from the crates on the pavement.

"Aren't you scared?" Manuela asked.

Stevo raised his eyebrows at her as if she was bonkers. "Give over. 'Course I am. It's not funny when yer starvin'. Yer belly squeaks and ya can't think of nowt else. Just gotta get summat in there."

"What about your grannies and your aunties?" said Dermot who was blessed with seven million on both sides of the Irish Sea.

"Not got none."

Manuela asked why his mum never went to the shops. His mum, he said, spent nearly all day lying in bed and only got dressed in the evening – that was when his dad was around. And when his dad went on one of his trips, which was for stretches at a time, she didn't bother with anything, which meant Stevo didn't go to school much. He enjoyed school, just didn't like the other kids there. They made fun of him.

Ossie asked where his father went, and Stevo, who was scratching at the floor boards with a nail he found, said, "Dunno. Don't care. Hate 'im." When his dad was there, he said, all he did was drink cider, sleep and clout Stevo. The last thing he'd done before Stevo took off was to whack him across the head with his shoe for sneezing and waking him up.

We sat in silence for an age.

Dermot shifted around on his buttocks. "Me too. I had the slipper from me mam *and* me dad after I put Mrs. Brennan's cat in the dustbin."

Ossie scrunched his mouth up and started to say something, but then he didn't. He glanced at Dermot, who seemed to nod his head. What was going on with the boys? They were being kind of weird, as if Manuela and I were invisible, like they had a secret code. Gianni sat bent forward, his fingers making a church steeple in front of his mouth, and observed Dermot and Ossie.

Ossie said, "I got my dad's belt when I cut up our Melinda's exercise book. My bum was on fire."

When Ossie finished talking, Gianni stroked his chin as if he'd grown a beard.

Stevo looked at the floor. "Want to see summat?" He didn't wait for a reply. He stood and lowered his trousers down to his bum crack. "See that?" He turned round in a circle making sure we all saw it – an angry, red, raised welt about six inches long. "Hot poker," he said.

Ossie gasped and moved nearer to study the scar. He peered into it, like he was looking down a microscope. "Can I touch it? Does it hurt?"

"Not now."

"How long was it there? The poker?" Ossie applied his finger to Stevo's back. Why was Ossie touching it? Another bubble of sick rose in my throat. I swallowed it back.

"Not long – just whacked me with it. Straight outta the fire. Burnt through me kecks."

"Blimey – what'd you done?" Gianni asked.

"Dunno. Breathed. Got in his way. Dunno…" His voice tailed off. "Wanted a shilling for summat to eat. There's more." He lifted his shirt and jumper up his stomach to his chest. His skin, all tight against his ribs, looked like a watercolour wash – blues, greens, purples, dirty tea-stain browns. Horrendous. Manuela groaned.

"What're ya gonna do? Gonna help me?" Stevo asked.

Ossie said, "What *can* we do?"

Dermot was picking at a scab on his knee and testing the flakes for texture. "Men of faith can achieve great things…"

Flipping heck! Where'd he get that from? St. Ally's probably. But his matter-of-factness made the rest of us sit up a second, made us wonder if it

15

might be possible. Maybe we did have a solution.

"I could ask Mum if you can come and live with us," Gianni said.

Stevo gnawed at the inside of his bottom lip, pressing it into his teeth with his thumbnail which along with his other fingernails housed a thick layer of black grime beneath it.

"No," he said, "I know the game. Yer parents'll tell someone and they'll come and get me."

Maybe Stevo could hide in Granny and Grandad's garage. At least he'd be closer, more easily feedable. Then it dawned that there'd be no space for him what with the old sofas, three-legged chairs, cupboards and boxes of unknown gubbins left by lodgers who'd broken into the electricity meters and done a moonlight flit.

After we'd mulled over the possibilities we reached the conclusion there was nowhere to go except Old Spooky, so he'd just have to stay there, and we promised to provide him with food just like the kids in that Jesus film.

Gianni said we should 'pact' it to secrecy. We shuffled in on our backsides to tighten the circle. Gianni took out the pact pin from his tin box, jabbed it in his finger and pressed out a tiny bubble of blood. He passed the pin to Ossie who did the same, and Dermot and me. Manuela pretended. As usual.

"You too." Gianni nodded at Stevo who seemed glad to accept it. Gianni smacked his hand on the floor. "I promise!" The rest of us slapped our hands onto Gianni's, one after another, into a six-hand indestructible clump.

*****

Gianni now addressed the practicalities of the situation. How was Stevo going to survive at Old Spooky? We made a list of what might be necessary – blankets, a pillow, a torch, a knife, food. It was like playing the add-another-and-say-them-all-again game. Gianni offered to bring in more comics, pencils, and a sketch pad. I was already visualising how we'd go about it, what I could bring, where I'd get it from. The day had taken a thrilling turn and, instead of just Manuela's meetings, there'd be a bigger purpose, something important to think about and organise every day. And as secrets went, it was a humdinger.

"Don't you think your parents will come and look for you in the end though?" Manuela said.

"No. They don't care about me. Feelin's mutual. They can kiss me *dupa*."

Dupa? My stomach clenched.

Dupa. A Polish word. How did he know that? "What did you say?"

His reply was dull and dry as cardboard. "They can kiss me arse."

"No, you didn't. You said *dupa*." Thoughts were scrambling in my brain, bashing against each another.

"Same thing."

"How do you know *dupa*?"

"Me dad's Polish."

"Polish? Like from Poland?"

"Yeah, Polish." He paused. "Bastard." He paused again. "They're all bastards."

The others were mute. Why were they suddenly staring at me like that? Like Stevo's dad was somehow my fault. Like I was responsible for all bad Polish people in the world. It felt as if slugs were crawling over my face leaving trails of hot slime. I put my hands on my cheeks to stop them. My insides were squirming. I mustn't, mustn't cry in front of the gang. "But you said your name was Corders," I said.

"Not Corders. Kardasz."

Dermot, the only one who hadn't stared, sniffed the snot dribble up his nostril. He was hunched up over his knees, curling his sock up and down his calf. "Could've just as easily been Irish." Slowly he rolled his sock back to his knee. "Or Jamaican." He lifted his head and eye-balled Gianni. "Or...anything. It's true, in't it?"

The others gazed at the floor.

"Yeah," Gianni finally said. "Or Italian..."

Why had I asked how he knew *dupa*? Why couldn't I have let it go? Me and my big mouth.

For some moments we all sat still, hearing nothing but our own breathing. I waited for a miracle. For somebody to do or say something.

Stevo spoke first. "It's just the way it is. Yer all right, Ania." He gave me a rueful smile and shook his head. My face cooled a little. Not much.

Gianni said, "Oh well, look... Never mind. Let's go home now. Who's coming back later to bring something?" I volunteered first, mainly to get out of there as quickly as possible. Ossie and Gianni said they'd return, too, with provisions.

Ossie tossed out one last question. "Blues or Reds?"

Stevo looked as if he'd been caught in headlights. "City."

Ossie and Gianni exchanged glances.

Gianni sighed. "We'll sort him out later."

On the way home I realised I'd never seen Stevo at Polish School, church or the club, and you simply couldn't be Polish if you didn't do those things. That was the order of life. His nose didn't even look Polish, sort of tilting up at the end like a ski jump. Plus, his dad sounded like no Polish person I'd heard of, not of our ilk and so, in my opinion he didn't count. Perhaps he was half Russian or German, pretending to be Polish. I stashed it in the back of my mind, behind everything else jumbled in there, convinced there'd be a logical explanation.

I forced myself to remember the film again. How did those children look after Jesus before they discovered he was a murderer?

17

CHAPTER THREE

DAY ONE: EARLY EVENING

At the house, I go round the side, enter through the utility room and smell burning. Mum's left something on the sodding cooker. Bloody potatoes for God knows who. I turn off the heat. She's also left the CD player on. Oh Lord, *Tosca*, 'Vissi d'arte'. I can't be doing with this. Bring back Jim Reeves.

Mum calls out, "Ania, is that you? Come here." Then to Dad, "Why are you always so stubborn?" The three Co-op bags huddle together on the surface by the cooker. What's in them apart from the Gorgonzola I went for?

I go to the sitting room where Mum stands by Dad's side as he pulls himself up, teetering within the frame. "Time to lie down," he says.

"Shall I bring you the biscuits?" I ask.

"Biscuits? What biscuits?"

"Ritz? With Gorgonzola?"

He nods. "Only two." Mum and I move aside as he lifts the frame a fraction, inches it forwards and gingerly steps into it. It takes him several minutes to get to the bedroom. I prepare his biscuits and come and stand behind Mum as she pushes the door open. Since he's been ill, Mum's slept in the larger guest room. I'm in the smaller one. Dad tells me to wait outside and I watch through the crack in the door. He lowers himself on the side of the bed, Mum removes the dressing gown, empties his leg bag, fat with brown piss, attaches a fresh one. Kneeling in front of him, she tugs his slippers and socks off then lifts his feet up onto the sheet while he attempts to swivel round.

"I can't…No washing tonight, Wanda," he says, then moans when she covers him. She's blocking my view, doing something on his face, when he mumbles, "No. I'll leave them in while Ania's here. Tell her she can come in now."

Bugger – he knows I've been spying on them. I enter with the plate held

18

aloft in my right hand and say in Polish and French, "Here you go. And tonight's feast, prepared by Mr. Walewski's very own chef – voilà des petits biscuits couverts de fromage italien."

I've smeared a delicate layer and cut the flesh of a tomato into tiny pieces to add extra appetising colour. Dad looks at them, thanks me and says tomatoes don't agree with him these days. I get a cocktail stick from the kitchen, come back and pick the red bits off the cheese. He nibbles at the edges and then leaves it, saying it's not how he imagined it would taste when he decided he wanted it. I offer him crème brûlée instead. He says perhaps later. He asks me to turn the radio on; it's tuned to a crackly Polish station on medium wave, around 647 kHz.

Something is choking me, draining me of energy, and I have no idea what it is; maybe the sourness in the air. Does cancer have fumes? He wasn't this sad little old man same time last year, nor even two weeks ago. How quickly it happens. There are still things to do.

"Will you sit with me a while?" he says. I want to forget I have questions to ask. And he's going now – what purpose would it serve? He looks so exhausted; God, how he liked parties, and now it's just me sitting there, being dumb. Someone ought to write a book on the etiquette, *How to be with a person about to peg it. Ten top tips for a pleasant demise.* I love you, Dad. I *love* you, Dad. I love *you*, Dad. I do love you, Dad.

I have to ask you and you've got to tell me. Did you do it? Nothing but the truth, Dad. I know you've never forgotten, that it's always haunted you. I found out and I need to understand why.

A car drives up, the outside light switches on automatically.

Fuck it. I stand to see who's arrived.

He says, "It's been a good life, Ania."

I turn round and look at him. His eyes are closed. How can he say that?

THEN

When I got home, Mum was ensconced in our new black PVC armchair, legs curled beneath her on the fake fur orange cushion. Groucho was snoozing, tucked in next to her like a raggedy black mop. Good sign. I checked out the book Mum was holding in front of her face. *Angelique and the Sultan* by Sergeanne Golon. The cover picture was of a blonde lady with long curly hair cascading to her balloon bosoms and a gold dress ripped off her shoulders. A man in a peculiar pointed hat stood behind her, glowering and twirling a whip.

"Is that the Sultan?" I said. "Don't they wear turbans?"

Mum made a high-pitched 'Mm?' sound, and stopped reading. "What? Yes, they do. Do you want something?" She tripped her fingers across the cigarettes to count how many were left in the Kensitas packet, pulled one out and put it to her mouth.

19

"Pass me the ashtray, please. Where have you been?" she said as she struck a match and placed the ashtray on the wide arm of the chair.

I said, "Nowhere. Outside," and attempted a nonchalant smile.

She inhaled slowly, blew out the flame with the smoke she exhaled and returned to her book. She'd stopped reading Polish paperbacks, and now the bottom layer of the bookshelf was filled with Georgette Heyer, Jean Plaidy and this Sergeanne person. The more Mum read, the more I got away with. Most handy for nabbing stuff now that I needed to. She'd be here for some time, I reckoned.

In the kitchen I fastened the buttons of my cardigan and opened the guest-food cupboard. Peanuts, two bags of pretzels, three packets of biscuits. I tucked the unopened pretzels in my skirt waistband underneath my cardi.

Janek appeared from nowhere. He seized his chance.

"Gonna tell on you," he squawked. "Mama! Ania's stealing!"

She didn't hear him straight away. From the moment she'd brought the weasely snitch home from hospital, I'd hoped he was adopted and his real parents would take him back one day, but they seemed to be taking their time. I thumped him twice – once for dobbing me in and again for good luck.

When Mum came in, he was writhing on the floor. She blinked her bleary eyes. No shouting, just the look. I stood sideways to disguise the pretzel-packet-shaped lump sprouting above my left hip, while Janek wailed as if Cassius Clay himself had biffed him with a right hook.

"She bashed me. Make her go to her room."

With all the squealing and fuss he forgot what the whole episode was about. I might get away with it. I sidled towards the back door.

"Ania – whatever you are hiding, take it out now," Mum said, lips pursed. I removed the pretzels and gave them back to her. Janek poked his tongue out while she wasn't looking, and continued sobbing for her benefit. She said I had to sit at the table with my hands under my bum for half an hour, told Janek to shut up and went back to the Sultan.

When my half hour, which I was sure was twice as long, was up, Mum said I had to tidy our room, on my own, without Iwonka. I hoped Manuela and the boys had had better luck. Easter was round the corner, which meant being stuck at home from morning till night either doing jobs or eating. Stevo would be starving by the time I got round to fulfilling my part of the deal.

*****

On Good Friday, straight after *śniadanie*, I was busting a gut to know what was going on at Old Spooky. So when Ossie came out into his garden, I leaned against our picket fence to hear the latest developments. They turned out to be nothing much – Ossie had gone back to Old Spooky with a torch and cream crackers for Stevo. He'd not get fat on that, would he?

"Is that all? Couldn't you get anything else?" I asked.

"Oh, he'll be okay," he said. "Did you do any better?" he added in a tone implying I'd shirked my responsibilities. I told him what had happened with the pretzels and promised to get some more supplies. I'd hand them to him via our bedroom windows later on – if I got a chance between my gigantic list of chores.

By eleven o'clock, millions of eggshell chips lay scattered before me on the yellow Formica of the table and also all over Iwonka's colouring book.

Iwonka flicked them back to my side. "Stop doing that! You're ruining it." Her mouth was all mucky from the raspberry jam sandwich she'd wolfed. She was crayoning in a red-tiled roof on Hansel and Gretel's house. She was too young to etch eggs, Mum said. But she wasn't, not really – six was old enough – she was just too cack-handed.

I had two perfect eggs, two disasters. It wasn't going well. Granny had brought the eggs, saying there weren't enough because Serafina hadn't laid for three days, and if she didn't make a concerted effort, she'd find herself in the *rosół*. That wasn't true – that was just Granny – she'd never make soup out of Serafina. Genowefa and Leokadia maybe, but never Serafina.

Ever since Grandad had removed the door and knocked out a wall chunk between the kitchen and breakfast room, it was miles easier to earwig and lip-read when Mum and Granny dropped their voices right at the juicy bit of whatever they were talking about. The downside of the renovations was now apparent – Mum and Granny had an equally good view of me. How was I going to nick anything without them seeing? And they were bound to be in here all day.

Plus, if I didn't sharpen up and get on with it, Mum might tell me to go tidy my room again. Good Friday was grim enough already, what with having to eat nothing but fish all day – oily herring for dinner, trout with scaly heads and slimy eyes for *kolacja*. Almost as bad as Christmas and flipping carp. Except nothing on earth could be worse than that.

While Mum, tears rolling down, peeled the onion skins off to use as dye, Granny adjusted the floral kerchief permanently glued to her hair, pushed up her glasses, and began kneading the dough for the pierogi. Four small pans of water were boiling on the stove – one in preparation for the skins and the rest for red, blue, and green tints.

Had Stevo ever eaten *pierogi*? Or any Polish cooking?

Mum and Granny talked normally for a while then changed to whispered mouthings. I pretended to be engrossed, so they'd forget me and Iwonka were there. With the needle pinched tight, I ground the tip into the North Pole of Egg Number Five.

Granny muttered, "Did you see her? The Wróbelska woman was in confession for twenty minutes with that dead animal of hers." She made a funny noise through her back teeth. "We all know what—" she lowered her voice further and faced Mum. Ears on rubber bands would have been handy.

Mum was on to it. "Stop it! Children…" she said, sniffing from the vapours. Using a spoon, she let the first egg float off into the water.

Granny walloped a ball of dough onto the rolling board and swore, "*Psia krew!*"

I'd chiselled through the North Pole without collapsing my work of art and was attacking the South. Here was news! Mrs. Wróbelska, her of the inch-long fuchsia nails and jet and gold clip-ons, up to shenanigans Granny didn't approve of. I loved that fox whose head flopped over one side of Mrs. Wróbelska's shoulders. One day, if I ever plucked up courage, I'd ask to look inside its mouth to count the teeth.

I waited for more gossip, and when nothing came offered my own contribution to the grown-ups' conversation. "She probably has lots of sins, Babcia."

Mum spun round. "Anka! Mind your own business."

Granny's rolling pin thwacked into the wood and splatted the ball into two. She grunted as she glanced at me and Iwonka, archly adding, "She held everybody up. I'll say no more."

When my two holes, top and bottom, were big enough, I took a deep breath and blew. Nothing emerged. No matter how hard I ballooned my cheeks, cross-eyed with trying, I failed in the attempt.

I must have dislodged some internal blockage through all the effort because that was the exact moment when the *stupendous idea* pinged into my brain. Stevo might not be able to live in Granny's garage, but there was bound to be stuff in there he could use, we could all use, at Spooky. I'd do better than just bringing him food.

But how to get the key to the padlock? It required stealth and careful planning.

I pricked the needle deep into the hole and tried again, third time lucky, remembering not to grasp the shell too tight or push hard with my mouth, as I'd done with previous catastrophes. The goo dripped out, yolk and white merging in the bowl.

Mum removed the boiled eggs from the pan, cooled them under running water and asked which colours I wanted. I chose red and onion-skin bronze. She handed mine to me then smeared a knob of butter into her palm and flopped the remaining eggs between her hands, making them shine like Smarties, after which she washed her hands and went to the garage to unearth our manky Easter basket.

I now had three blown eggs and two ready to become *pisanki*, just like the wooden ones my other grandparents sent us from Poland. Since my earlier brilliant hard-boiled designs had run the length of the shell and the failures round the girth, I started at the top again, scratching out a white groove into the colour, all the while planning my next move. What could I steal for Stevo? Everything currently available on the kitchen surfaces seemed to be an ingredient, not a proper thing you could eat. Mum hadn't put the pretzels back in the cupboard, but I couldn't take them now because she'd know it was me. But I didn't want Ossie thinking I'd done nothing. The only item of any use was a box of Sugar Puffs still out after *śniadanie*.

My moment came when Janek let out a wail. Granny pelted to the sitting room.

Granny shouted, "*Cholerny pies*," – bloody dog – and we heard a resounding slap and a yelp. Iwonka pulled a "here we go" face, grinned and left her crayons to have a gawk. While Granny was oy-ing and kissing Janek's wounds, I took out the inner packet of the Sugar Puffs carton. It was about a third full. It would have to do. Granny was still going on in her only-for-Janek voice, "My prince, my angel – one more kiss should make it better." It was funny, that. Neither Iwonka nor me were ever elevated to royalty.

Through the window I saw Ossie tying up bits of wood with string in his back garden. I opened the window, checked Mum was still in the garage, beckoned him to lean over the fence and lobbed the Sugar Puffs to him. Quickly I told him my plan. I'd try to get the key to Granny's garage and would he help me when the time came? Ossie said he had just the idea for how to shift any useful gear we found there. Great! I closed the window and chucked the carton into the cellar. I'd get rid of it later.

*****

Granny returned, dragging Groucho by the collar, and then slung him out. Maybe he *was* the scruffiest poodle in Manchester like Ossie said, but he certainly didn't deserve *that*! She came back and stood by my side. She lifted my bowl and, in the silence, dipped and swirled a fork in the eggy mixture. How she saw anything at all baffled me. Her pointy glasses were filmy with face powder because she never used a mirror. Dab chin, dab nose, dab-dab cheeks, close eyes, dab-dab lenses and forehead.

"Not so dear these days," she said.

Ossie waved at me through the window, put his thumbs in his ears and waggled his fingers. He pointed to the avenue to make me jealous that I was stuck indoors, and put his tongue out. I returned the compliment.

Granny had said something, hadn't she? "What?" I asked.

"Eggs."

"What about them, Babcia?"

"They used to cost more. Life or death."

Had I missed something? For a moment I sat back in my chair wondering what she was bibbling on about. Eggs – a matter of life or death. Perhaps she was going batty like Mrs. Jeleńska – she'd be hoovering her lawn next.

"After the amnesty in '42, in Kazakhstan," she continued.

I'd never heard of it. Maybe this story might be more interesting than the usual ones she spouted when we refused to eat something growing mould that she'd scraped off in secret. "If you had been in Siberia…" blah-blah. Yes, but I wasn't, was I? I was in Manchester.

She stopped mixing and moved over to the cooker to stir the mushroom and sauerkraut stuffing for the pierogi that Mum had put on a slow heat.

"Your mama and Kasia were starving. And Kasia, so ill."

She added some salt then pepper, lifted the wooden spoon to her mouth and gingerly pinched her teeth on the edge to take a mouthful. After transferring the stuffing from one cheek to the other, she seemed to park it between her lips and teeth. She dropped several whole peppercorns into her hand then flung them into the pan.

I'd never heard of this Kasia person. "Who's Kasia?"

"Your mama's sister. Never any trouble." I had an *auntie*? A real one, not a Polska Land add-on? This was the first I'd heard of it. Where was she? She couldn't have been very nice – I'd never so much as had a birthday card or Christmas present from her.

The sun sloped off behind the clouds, so I switched on the light to see what I was doing. I hoped I didn't need glasses – please not that. A ponytail, two cowlicks *and* being a speccy-four-eyes – the worst nightmare ever.

Granny was still talking. "Only three, my baby. The man promised me four eggs if I made him happy." Granny was back-circling figures of eight with the fork, staring into the bowl, as if she were watching some film in there. The groove between her eyebrows deepened.

"Mm hm," I said.

"The train stopped and Dziadzio went to find some food. A few minutes later, with no warning, the train started up. I was sure I would never see him again."

Granny balanced the fork against the bowl's edge and came and stood beside me. She petted the top of my head from the bunch of my ponytail forwards, flattening my fringe with annoying granny-pats, and went on. "We travelled four stations and it stopped again. For two whole days."

"Mm hm."

I was concentrating so hard, my *pisanka* wasn't living up to my expectations, and the stroking was getting on my pip. I tried not to show it because she seemed very sad. I'd miscalculated the number of vertical lines on my egg. If I'd been methodical, started in one place, then scratched exactly opposite and found the centre of both halves, the design would have been even. Instead, I'd estimated and made one panel much thinner than the rest. I waited for inspiration to improve it. None came. Flipping infuriating. Perhaps I could give the hopeless ones to Stevo – after all he wouldn't be bothered if the shell looked rubbish. Except who likes cold hard-boiled eggs?

I wondered how to manoeuvre Granny to speed up the story and finish the cooking so we could go to her house. I abandoned my pisanka and started colouring the blown ones.

Granny said, "Kasia was sick with typhus. I had nothing to trade and no food. I did what had to be done. By the time Dziadzio found us she was dying, so we got off the train. After she passed, he begged for planks in the village to make a coffin. But no-one had any."

Oh, my goodness. Kasia died – *that's* why I'd never got any presents from her. Granny stood over me, still fiddling with my hair, watching me as I outlined daisies and stars. It was a very sad story. Very sad. I'd be very sad too if Iwonka died, even if she did get on my nerves.

"We buried her in a pillow case on a hillside, three of us, your Mama, Dziadzio and I. We couldn't even make her a proper cross for her grave. Nobody would ever know my baby was there. Mama was stronger, older – I cut off her plaits and shaved her head. She survived." All the while Granny had been talking, even though she was still messing about with my hair, she seemed to getting further away, like she was disappearing behind a black fog. I wanted her to get back to normal. Maybe talking about nice things might do the trick.

"And what about that man? The one with the eggs. Did you make him happy?" I asked as I licked my dry felt tips to squeeze out some colour.

Granny undid the knot of her kerchief and retied it under her chin, giving it a hefty yank. "Yes, my dear. I made him happy all right." She thrust her hands on her hips, elbows forward like spikes. "Not as difficult as I thought," she added, suddenly alert.

"What did you do, Babcia?"

She didn't answer immediately. Then, with a shiver, she replied, "I sang a song." Her voice spat shards. "*Jeszcze Polska nie zginęła.* I'll say no more."

No way! I perked up. *What* a liar! She *must* have sung something more cheerful. Why on earth would somebody give you a gift for the dirgy Polish National Anthem? It was horrible. And besides, I knew she'd made the story up. Anyone who heard her trilling *Boże Coś Polskę* in the fourth pew would be happy to part with a hundred chickens, just to shut her up. Especially Grandad.

*****

"I'm going to see if Babcia wants me to help her with something," I lied to Mum and scarpered out of the house before she had time to ask me what with. The key to the padlock was becoming an urgent matter since I'd promised Stevo I'd be back two days ago.

Along with all the others, tens of them, mainly old door keys to tenants' bedrooms, the padlock key was kept in a carved wooden box on the Singer machine in Granny and Grandad's bedroom. I knew what the key looked like because she often asked me – and any random stranger who might be passing the garage – to help her cart stuff in and out of there. I knew which one it was because it had a piece of blue card attached to it by a loop of red plastic-covered wire.

As soon as I entered through the back, I heard the rhythmic lull of her feet on the treadle. The pong of mothballs hit my throat as I opened the bedroom door just as the needle snapped. She hissed *"Psia krew,"* rearranged the fabric under the presser foot and opened the little drawer beneath the sewing table. She was taking up the hem of curtains for one of the lodgers' rooms, I guessed, and the key box had been put out of the way on the counterpane. It would be a cinch.

She sifted through the buttons, thread and other paraphernalia. "Yes – what is it? What do you want? Are you going to stand there all day?" Somewhat unfair since I'd only just arrived. Definitely a bit tetchy. Sewing was not her favourite occupation – slapping paint onto walls was better. She pulled the kerchief off her hair to around her neck and wiped her forehead.

I said, "Nothing really. I came to see you."

"Why? Are you hungry?"

"No, thank you."

"Money?"

"No, thank you." It was most unkind of her to suggest the only reason I ever went there was to wheedle something out of her.

She found the packet with fresh needles and took out a tiny screwdriver from the drawer. After fiddling about for ages – probably because her glasses were covered in powder – she tsked. "Go on – you try it."

She stood over me as I got to work.

"You know this machine came from Uganda, don't you?" she said. I hoped it wasn't going to be the usual Granny stuff about how all the starving mums and children in Siberia had to go to India and Africa to wait for the war to end. I'd seen some of the places she mentioned in my encyclopaedia, weird names like Krasnovodsk, but they didn't look very interesting. And anyway, she'd probably remembered it wrong because those people seemed to go back and forth all over the place, like they couldn't make up their minds. Why didn't they just go in a straight line?

I squashed the needle up into the hole and twisted the screwdriver.

Breathing the smell of pear drops past my ear, Granny said, "I bought it with Dziadzio's army pay. I nearly had to leave it out there in Africa, but I had a few words with the ship's captain and he let me bring it with us. Good machine."

I was expecting her to tell me she sang the National Anthem for him too, but she just watched.

I turned the screw one more time – dead easy, leaned back in the chair and smiled at her. "Done."

"You would like a reward perhaps?" Well, I hadn't come for pocket money, but if I accepted, she'd have to root about in the wardrobe with her back to me. It made sense to take up the offer. I perched on the edge of the bed while she unlocked the wardrobe door with a key from the ring she kept in her apron pocket. She bent over, giving me a full view of her flesh-coloured bloomers and her white- and blue-coloured thighs. As she dug deep at the bottom, rearranging shoes, handbags, hats and whatever else was there, I flipped the lid of the box, found the blue tag and stuffed it down the back of my sock.

With a little groan, Granny hoiked out a black rigid-framed handbag that contained all the shillings and sixpences collected from the lodgers' electricity meters and hefted it on the bed.

"You know the rules," she said as she unclasped it and ran her hands over the embossing. I'd known them for years, but she always checked. I must never tell anyone this handbag existed or where it was. Not anyone. Ever.

As she spread the sides wide, hundreds of bits of silver jostled up and jangled against each other. She picked out a sixpence, taking care to choose a shiny one, and handed it to me.

"Thank you, Babcia."

"Hm. May God reward you," she replied dryly, as if she meant something else.

And then I was gone. I couldn't get on with the plan yet because I needed Ossie, and he'd driven off with his family earlier in the morning. When I got home, I bunged the key under my mattress for safe-keeping. Nobody would find it there.

*****

In the afternoon we went to Kombo's for the traditional blessing. Just about everybody from Polska Land thronged in the hall of the Polish Ex-servicemen's Club with their Easter baskets, the significance of which I could never remember. New life, Jesus's shroud, accepting the bitter and sweet in life, all that kind of curious symbol stuff. The congregation arranged the baskets on the tables, and the mums and grannies split off into gossipy huddles waiting for the priest.

Mum chatted to Auntie Teresa while I looked at our basket, compared it to the others and found it miserably lacking. As usual. All the others were splendid, loaded, lined with brilliant white napkins draped artistically over the edges. I swear Mum had put a tea towel under ours. New, possibly – but still a tea towel. And our scraggy bit of *kiełbasa* wouldn't feed two termites. Some ladies had even baked sheep-shaped cakes and covered them with butter icing. Meanwhile, our decrepit sugar lamb made me cringe, excavated as it was every twelve months, and browning at the extremities, as if he'd been gnawed by rats. Except it wasn't rats. It was Iwonka who'd had a good old suck at it last year before Mum had caught her and hidden the manky thing back in the garage depths.

Why didn't Granny and Mum ever try harder? Why was I always the *only* one to put in a proper effort? We had enough *pisanki* at home to open a warehouse – they should have all been in there. I shared my observations with Mum who, for no reason that I could work out, told me to stop blithering on, and then totally ignored me while she talked to Auntie Teresa. So when Mrs. Wróbelska arrived, I decided to get my own back, both for the disgraceful basket and that suspiciously long half hour I'd spent staring at the wall on Thursday.

"Mama, Babcia," I said in a loud voice. "Look, there's Pani Wróbelska. Why don't you ask her why she spent so long in confession last week since you were so interested?" Auntie Teresa snorted then giggled behind her hand. When Granny pinched me at the wrist, her nails almost piercing through to the bone, I knew I'd scored a victory. It flipping hurt.

But I didn't care – I had the key.

CHAPTER FOUR

DAY ONE: LATE EVENING

I pull back the curtain and peer into the drive.

Iwonka's here wearing a furry scarf and the beanie hat I gave her after my hair grew back. She's carrying a casserole dish. It's what she does when she doesn't know what to do with herself – cooks; cooks, feeds, freezes, cooks some more. I hear the door open and her voice directing Mum to divide the goulash into smaller containers.

The beanie, scarf and puffa coat are gone when she comes into Dad's room. She's dyed her hair a walnut colour, presumably to hide the grey at the temples she was complaining about. Looks good.

She says, "Hi, sis. Okay journey? Hi Tata."

Dad swallows on nothing and wipes his mouth. "Hello, favourite youngest daughter." Iwonka kisses him first on the forehead, then me on the side of my nose; the icy cool of her cheek feels refreshing in the musty room.

I wait for Dad to carry on about his good life while Iwonka pulls up a chair on the opposite side of the bed. Lying there in that broad bed he reminds me of the last anchovy left in the tin with no Mum or Psiuńka to fill the extra space. Iwonka lifts him by the shoulders and tells me to raise the pillows so that he can sit up better.

"Iwonka, sh, sh..." He curls his finger at her then puts it to his lips. Iwonka bends over, puts her ear to his mouth, and he whispers, "Don't tell your mother. I can't manage the Zimmer any more. Get me a wheelchair from somewhere."

"No problem. You'll have it tomorrow."

"Don't pay good money though," he adds, pursing his lips into an expression of distaste and straightening his finger to wag it at her.

Iwonka winks in my direction and says, "I'm too clever for that, Tata. Have I ever paid over the odds?"

"Do it then. Don't take..." He motions with his head towards me. "You know what she's like." What does he mean? Why doesn't he trust me?

"So, you going to eat this?" Iwonka points at the one intact Ritz, and when he shakes his head she flicks it whole into her mouth, her tongue catching a random crumb off her lips. "Janek phoned. He'll be round tomorrow. Why's it so gloomy in here?" She swirls the dimmer switch round and the ceiling lights up with the pretend sunshine she's created.

We chat about nothing. Dad says Psiuńka is looking skinny; Iwonka says she'll take her to the vet. Dad says he thinks the weather vane on top of the house is loose; Iwonka says she'll get Janek to fix it. Dad says his watch has stopped; Iwonka says Michael has six watches, she'll bring one round.

I look at my watch. Five hours and thirty-two minutes have gone by since I arrived. Iwonka tells Dad it's time for his medication, rummages among the pile of little cardboard boxes on the window ledge, reads from lists on pink, yellow and green post-it notes stuck to the sill and takes out various pills. She sends me to get a fresh glass of water. As I get up, she strokes Dad's forehead upwards, smoothing over the few remaining wisps of hair as if he's a baby, her pink-Vaselined smile glowing with plump-cushioned kindness.

She doesn't know. I've never told her.

THEN

On Easter Sunday I woke to the smell of mushroom soup wafting up the staircase. Mum was already in the kitchen, finishing off the preparations for *obiad*. Almost as soon as my eyes snapped open, I thought of my mission and was itching to get going, but then remembered I'd have to starve for hours. Flipping church. None of us, apart from Iwonka, who wasn't a fully-fledged Roman Catholic yet, was allowed a single thing to eat. Not a morsel. With it being a Holy Day of Obligation we had to go to communion, which meant three hours fasting beforehand.

I planned ahead. Once we finished the Easter meal all the family would end up watching telly or lounging about, gorged out on eggs, cold meats, salads, soup and *bigos*. And if that didn't sink them, the final round of cakes would. Three hours to go till *obiad*, five – probably – till escape.

Granny came to our house alone at 9.30. Grandad, she said, was going to St. Ally's for the service, which I suspected wasn't true.Whenever I asked if to go with him, he looked horrified and said: "Not this time. Maybe next week." Except next week never came. And he was always back in their kitchen, fully kitted out in his navy-blue overall and black leather-trimmed beret, by the time we got back from Polska mass. But if Granny then mentioned something needed fixing round the house, he reminded her the Sabbath was a day of rest as laid down by the Lord. Which was weird. Because he still went into his tool shed for hours.

Then I had a super idea – I'd get out of going to church. Dad might carry on sleeping, and, if everybody else left, I could have a sneak preview of what was in the garage, or get Ossie to come over immediately. We'd have approximately two to two-and-a-half hours all told from Mum's departure to her return. So I pretended to be afflicted with the most terrible headache. Mum put her hand on my forehead and pronounced me healthy. Even when I swore on Groucho's life that it was the truth – I felt a bit guilty about that – she was having none of it. She instructed me to put on the red dress handed down from Auntie Teresa's daughter, Danusia. Which I did. But she hadn't issued any orders regarding accessories, had she?

I stayed upstairs until the last minute and quadruple-checked the key was well hidden between the bottom sheet and the underside of the mattress. When Mum called up that it was time to get into Dad's delivery van, I ran out while she was doing something in her handbag and clambered in via the driver's seat to the back with Iwonka and Janek. Granny, all tarted up in her Sunday best, pink hat, pink suit, cream gloves, already sat bolt upright in regal splendour at the front.

Good! No-one had noticed.

On the way, beneath rain-filled clouds, we drove past less fortunate Catholics standing in a line at the number 53 bus stop beyond the deli, also making the pilgrimage to the Church of Divine Mercy. Her palm flat and open, Granny waved like the Queen, showing her gleaming gold tooth to the queue and turned round to us at the back:

"What a shame we can't take Pani Jeleńska. I hope the weather holds." It was the Christian thing to do, she said. Luckily for Janek, Iwonka and me, the back of the van had no room for other Christians or old Polish people. Now *that* was a blessing.

Because Mum launched into chatting with acquaintances at the front of the church while us three loitered on the steps waiting, it wasn't until we were in the aisle en route to our pew that she registered my protest.

"Ania!" she whisper-yelled and grasped my shoulder. Mrs. Jeleńska, whose bus must have come soon after we drove by, craned her neck from the pew in front.

"What?" I'd already forgotten I'd done it.

"What do you think you are playing at?" Mum pointed an accusing finger at my legs.

I suddenly remembered. "I couldn't find the other one," I said, already wondering what to do about communion in view of such a whopper beneath the nose of Our Lady.

Mum's left eye almost closed as she peered into me and shoved me in the kidneys. "Oh Lord – your feet! Make them look even. Now." It wasn't really going to help. Rolling down the white knee-length sock to match the ankle-length beige one would still look daft, and by that time I couldn't think why it seemed like such a good idea. And what could I do about the odd shoes

31

anyway? I nearly opted out of communion, just in case, but my stomach was gurgling so much that food of any kind, even a penny-sized wafer, seemed like a feast. Although when the priest put it on my tongue, it didn't help much.

We suffered our way through the interminable mass and the endless parish notices from the pulpit, and endured Granny's extremely loud, soprano-warbling of the hymns while people on the balcony grimaced down at us.

When the opening notes of 'O Lord! Who through so many centuries surrounded Poland with the brilliance of power and glory' sounded from the organ behind the altar, we were at last on the home straight. Only a couple of hours left until I could raid the garage. My stomach squeaked with hunger during those yawning sections when the choir and congregation dragged on, dirging as if they'd walked a million miles. Thank goodness for the last two lines. Even Janek and Iwonka joined in with 'At your altars we beseech you, return a free motherland to us once more, O Lord.' That was the only good bit in the song. Actually, in the whole mass.

When we got home, Dad was up and about and Grandad had already turned up in his suit. In the porch, Mum told me to go straight upstairs to change my shoes and socks and said if I ever did anything like that to her again, I'd pay for the rest of my days. "And don't..." she wagged her finger at me, "let Tatuś see you."

After everyone had kissed and hugged and wished each other whatever good fortune was appropriate, we shared the pieces of boiled egg – the eggs I'd spent flipping hours colouring for no good reason other than not being mortified by having the most pathetic basket at the blessing in Kombo's.

In addition to her usual wishes for me – maybe as a result of the shoes and socks – Mum muttered a new one. "And may you always be a good girl and make your parents proud."

I had a feeling that might not be immediately possible.

*****

After *obiad*, when Mum, Granny and I were clearing away in the kitchen and transferring the left-overs to smaller containers – Grandad had snuck off home already – I saw Ossie in the back garden. I intensified my domestic efforts so it would look as if I'd been really helpful and taken her wishes to heart. He'd gone by the time we'd finished, but my ruse paid off. When I asked her if I could go out to play, she said yes. I rang the front doorbell of the MacDonalds' and Ossie answered.

"I've got it." I showed him the key. "And the coast looks clear."

We had much to catch up on. He'd been over to see Stevo on Saturday.

"See that space over there?" He pointed across the road. "Just wait till I tell you!"

They'd played in the garden, exploring every nook and cranny, squeezing behind all the bushes and trees, and they'd discovered the walls around the garden were intact, except for two places – one on the right, that didn't have a useful purpose, and the other at the very back on the left. Here the cement had crumbled and the bricks were disintegrating. They'd climbed over to see what was on the other side and found a path wide enough to act as a short cut from Upper Chorlton Road to Old Spooky. From the road, it looked like nothing, merely a gap between the waist-high front garden wall of the house opposite mine and the six-foot wall of the Territorial Army base. Handy, that. I'd seen it thousands of times from our hall window upstairs. Not a route we could march through together everyday though because we risked the house owner seeing us. It was good to know it existed, but we couldn't use it now.

Ossie was ready and on standby to help with transport. "Pram's sorted," he said.

We walked across Knutsford Avenue to the drive. I checked out the back and, to my dismay, saw Grandad's beret bobbing about in his shed. He'd changed from his suit into his overalls and was ignoring not only the third commandment but also Easter. So much for the Lord putting his tools down on the Sabbath. It was touch and go. Should we abandon the whole thing for now or hope for the best?

"Aw, come on," Ossie said. "He won't see us. He's busy." He was at it again – goading me into something I might regret.

I inserted the key in the rusty padlock, struggling to twist it open. My heart raced.

Ossie nudged me aside. "Give it here."

"I can do—"

"I'll be quicker."

He couldn't turn the key immediately either, and his pride was offended, so despite wanting to snatch it back off him, I let him get on with it, while I darted back and forth, keeping a simultaneous look-out at the shed and beyond the gate. The avenue was empty, apart from a ginger cat asleep on Mrs. Czaplińska's wall.

"Got it!" He yanked at the loop which released itself. We slipped inside, pulling the door to behind us to be greeted with an overwhelming smell of turpentine and wet wool, and dusty, dead-fly-infested cobwebs. When I saw them hanging in menacing curtains, I nearly fainted. If there were cobwebs, there must be live spiders somewhere, ready to crawl into my hair. Dead insects were okay, live spiders – not. Why had I suggested this?

The garage was crammed to the ceiling, the windows covered by piles of loosely stacked cardboard boxes and wooden crates. Below the roof Grandad had created rope hammocks which extended from rows of hooks from one end of the garage to the other. Across these lay wooden planks of various lengths, spare copper piping and yards of hose. Thank God for Siberia and Kazakhstan and all those weird places – if they'd never had the war, they'd surely have chucked all this stuff out. What use was it?

The settee (which had stuffing bulging out of a hole where the threads had split) and the two wing-backed chairs would have been great in the den. Too bad we had no means of taking them.

"You start there," I said, pointing at the Welsh dresser which was dumped because one of the number 76 lodgers – Madeleine from Liverpool – had painted it lime-green and added heart-shaped bits of sticky-back plastic.

Ossie tugged at its drawers, warped by damp, and I scrambled over the boxes as quietly as possible to the far end in order to be systematic in my rooting. In a mahogany cupboard I found an uneven stack of fabrics, mainly old sheets and raggedy curtains, but also a heavy pink bedspread, two thick blankets and a huge grey towel.

Ossie kept up a running commentary as he opened and closed drawers and doors, "Plugs, iron, plates—"

"Take two plates," I said, "and shut up or someone'll hear us."

He jerked a drawer, jangling the contents. "Tools. Nails. Hammer—" he whispered.

"And that."

"Saw—"

"That too."

"This thing." He held up an item that looked like a wide screwdriver.

"And that."

These things would all come in handy for something. It was good to be prepared. I knew that from Brownie camp.

"What's this?" Ossie pulled out a square, flattish box. "Heyeeeee," he squealed.

I'd have to thump him. "Shut up for God's sake!"

He said it again, except quietly, "Hey," and grinned at me. "Monopoly."

I was about to call it a day when tyres rolled up slowly in front of the gate. We froze exactly as we were, me bent over an orange box containing rusty tins of Dulux, and Ossie crouched down, balancing on the balls of his feet, squashed between the dresser and the armchair. Then the engine switched off. Right in front of the gate. It was all over. Done for. Plan gone for a Burton. We waited for the car door to open, for footsteps. None came. Ossie's breathing, short little intakes through his mouth as if he'd been running, were freaking me out. Why couldn't he breathe through his nose like normal people? God knows how long we remained in those positions. Any longer and my fingernails might have actually grown. The car stayed and stayed and nobody came out.

In the distance a yappy dog barked three times, then another deeper-voiced one joined in. They continued their duet while traffic rumbled past on Upper Chorlton Road. When my stomach gurgled, loud as a faulty drain, Ossie teetered backwards.

"What the hell was that?" he whispered.

"Sorry."

Ossie see-sawed back and forth on his haunches, trying to maintain his balance. In the end, he too had had enough.

"I'll see," he said.

"No, don't. We'll get—"

"I'm going." He stood up in degrees as if his legs had been cemented in that crouching position, inched towards the door, opened it a fraction and peeked through the gap. I straightened up, ready for whatever was coming. To my horror, he just walked out and closed the door behind him. Walked out! Leaving me alone inside!

I negotiated my way to the dresser and crept after him. Standing sideways for what seemed like forever and a fortnight, I peered through the thin white line of light. All I saw were the holly bushes. Where was he?

The door flung open, Ossie's face suddenly in mine, grin as bright as the whites of his eyes.

"We're safe," he said, then manoeuvred past me and picked up the Monopoly set.

"Who is it?"

"Nobody."

"Nobody who? Where are they?" Why was he talking at normal pitch? Idiot.

"In the car," he said. "Ha-ha!"

"Shut up, will you?" There we were, inside my grandparents' garage, stealing, actually stealing their things. You never saw burglars on telly chatting and laughing as if they were passing the time of day on a park bench. Boys were so stupid. I could never in a million years actually marry one.

"*You* shurrup. They don't know us," he said.

"Who don't?"

"The people snogging in the car. He had his hands on her titties. Haha! And she was all moany, like this…" He did an impression for me, with sound effects, his eyes closed and rubbing his chest in circles.

I tried to ignore him. "Shut up! We'll get caught!"

"Nah. Let's get out of here. I got the pram. Walked straight past them. We'd better get our skates on or it'll be dark when we get back."

I double-checked round the side of the garage and could just make out Grandad still in his shed. I made sure the pram was empty then leaned against number 76's gate to see if the car had gone. It hadn't. The two people were sitting and talking. I didn't know whether to believe Ossie or not now. He must have been lying. The lady in the passenger seat was Mrs. Wróbelska, except she wasn't wearing her fox this time. When she saw me, her face clouded over. Then she nodded and smiled. The man, someone I'd never seen before – was it her husband? – looked in front of him, switched on the ignition, and drove off.

*****

Into the pram we piled a hammer, saw, tins of paint, string, two small knives, paintbrush, screwdriver thing, the pink candlewick bedspread, two thick blankets, a towel, Monopoly, draughts, cushions, and an orangey fur coat, half-bald where the hairs had been rubbed away. Enough to be getting on with, anyway. With all this squashed in, the pram bulged and the cover wouldn't go on properly. We couldn't afford return trips but, just in case, I adjusted the catch of the padlock as far as it would go without clicking it back in. Left at an angle, nobody would notice it wasn't locked. Ossie ran up the avenue to get Dermot to give us a hand, and Dermot brought his mum's shopping trolley and took charge of the games and smaller items.

Me and Ossie had taken Marguerita for a walk in the pram before when she'd cried so much that Mrs. MacDonald declared "that chile need a change o' scenery." Then, though, it was at a leisurely pace and with permission. This time we practically ran – Ossie had to get the pram back before his mum discovered it was gone. We crossed the road at Sylvan Avenue, Dermot dawdling behind us, and strode down Whalley Road.

At Old Spooky, Ossie pushed the pram round the back, the wheels crunching along the path. We unloaded it and also Mrs. O'Donnell's trolley and then Ossie legged it back home. Dermot and I went inside the hall.

"Hello!" Dermot called up to the ceiling. "It's us. Are you there?"

After a couple of thuds and some shuffling, Stevo plodded down the staircase.

"We got you these," Dermot said. "Where d'you want them?"

"I was freezin' last night." Stevo's tone was sharp as if we personally could have altered the weather or his predicament. "Why did it take ya so long? I've only got this." He tugged the zip of his brown anorak up to his neck and put his hands in his pockets.

Well, honestly! The flipping cheek! I'd been so excited about doing all this for him, risked life and limb, nearly got caught and this was the thanks.

I bristled. "I had to get the key for the garage. It wasn't easy, you know."

He didn't look any happier. If he was going to carry on being a pig, I'd withdraw my labour. He could get lost. I'd expected a thank-you at least. I almost felt like telling him to go home to his dad if it was so horrible here. But I didn't.

Stevo examined the pile of goods. "Sorry. Yeah. Help us take this, this and this upstairs." He indicated all the bedding. "And this." He pointed to the screwdriver thing. "Might be good for protection."

The bedspread had unfolded between the garage and Spooky's stairs, so I carried it in a pile until it fell apart completely halfway up. I pulled it around my shoulders, trailing it behind me. Meanwhile Dermot bundled up the cushions and other bits of linen into the towel.

In his tiny cupboard-room, not much more than the size of a pantry, Stevo arranged his bed into some kind of order. Both blankets and the bedspread were double so with help from Dermot and me, he folded them in half, one of the blankets acting as a mattress. The two psychedelic cushions added a nice touch. We stood back and surveyed our handiwork.

"You'll be all right here," Dermot said. "I fancy it meself."

Stevo curled up between the covers, lay his head on the cushions, turned to one side then the other and decided, "It'll do for now." He stood up. "Let's see what else ya got."

*****

Downstairs the three of us put the remaining gear, apart from the games, in the basement cupboards and came back up into the den. Dermot had to go because he'd told his mum he'd be back in half an hour. I knew I ought to go too, but what Stevo had said when we found him troubled me. It jarred and I didn't want to discuss it in front of the others.

Because after all, Polska Land wasn't the type of place where people could be anonymous. Everybody knew everybody else and if they didn't know them, they knew somebody else who did. Well, that's what if felt like anyway, especially when complete strangers congratulated you on the school play, or asked whether Granny was going on the pilgrimage to Lourdes.

And I also wanted a proper apology from Stevo. He'd been rude.

"I can stay a bit longer if you like."

"If ya want."

A crank-up in sincerity would have been nice. We sat on the window seat, shifting about not knowing what to say to one another, and looked at the garden where nothing much was happening at all except grass, trees and bushes growing and dots of yellow at the far end. So many questions but where to begin. I mean, you couldn't just come out with it and call someone a liar, could you? And he wasn't saying anything to me of his own accord. I wondered why *he* didn't have questions to ask. But no. Nothing. Maybe he just wasn't keen on girls.

"Want a game of draughts then?" he said eventually.

"If you want..."

We arranged the counters on the board. One of his was missing. Probably why the lodger left the box behind. Stevo picked up a bit of ceiling plaster, tore at it until he had a vague circle shape that he placed where the counter should be.

"Polish or English?" I asked.

"Yer what?"

"Polish or English? Rules?"

"What's the difference?"

"Polish rules are more difficult. It's what champions play." I'd stepped up to a higher plane. "You can take forwards and backwards. And a King, except it's a Queen, can go right across the board if none of her pieces are in the way and capture anywhere she likes. And if you're in the way, that's the end of you." I emphasised the last syllable, so's he'd pay attention.

"English then."

After three moves each, I formulated a plan. The only way to get at the truth was to sneak up on him sideways, lull him into it.

"Do you think you'll like it here?" I asked.

"It's okay." He was taking an age with move four. Ossie and I would have been chasing one another round by now, jumping, and setting cunning traps. Perhaps Stevo was a bit thick? He pushed his counter onto another square.

"I'm huffing you." I blew on the piece he should have moved to take me. Scratching around, I was. "We were dead happy when we found it."

"Mm. Yeah. It's a good place. Ha!" he said in triumph as he took one of mine.

"Yes... It'll be fun having you here. You can keep an eye on things. We'll visit every day." I put on my winning beam expression, the one that rarely worked with Granny. A smile flickered across his face.

Now was the moment, I judged. "Is your dad really Polish?" I heard my voice rising to a note on the far right of piano keys. Squeaking almost. The breath he drew made his nostrils widen. With the round of his thumb, he dragged upwards against his nose, as if rubbing out a stain. His eyes bored into me. "Said so, didn't I?" It was obvious what he was up to and I wouldn't let him off the hook.

I persevered. "Is your mum Polish, too?"

He looked back down at the board. "Nah. She's from Eccles. English, like me."

"But you're not English. You're half Polish if your dad's Polish."

He snapped, "No, I'm not." I wasn't sure whether he was just rubbish at arithmetic or he meant something different. He took another of my counters. Why was he being like this?

"Did you ever go to Polish school then?" I said.

"What ya asking me all this for? No. What's Polish school?"

"It's where you go to learn Polish and stuff."

"No. Never been." He didn't even ask me where it was.

"I could teach you some more Polish words if you want."

He was looking at the board. "What for?"

"So..." Trying to form the right questions was difficult, "So... what's your mum like?"

"Like? I told ya already."

"No, I mean what does she look like?" Perhaps if I let him win, he might talk more.

"Like a mum." His eyes narrowed when he raised them to glance at me, then he immediately looked out of the window. I followed his stare. Still trees and bushes and bits of yellow, a squirrel on the wall, fascinated by something in its paw. This line of enquiry was going nowhere fast. I took another of his counters and asked, "Does she really lie in bed all day?"

Stevo slammed a draught at my end of the board with a sneer. For a second I thought he was going to overturn it – the whole kit and caboodle.

"Go on then," he said, waiting for me to put a counter on top of his and king him. It looked as if he might beat me after all.

My question hung between us, thick as a brick wall. Had he forgotten I'd asked it?

"Does she?"

"Does she what?"

"Lie in—"

"What's it to *you*?" His voice was slow and deliberate. "Can't ya just leave me alone? She lies in bed sometimes. All right?" The conversation was closed. I'd have to try later with a different approach. Maybe I'd find out from Granny. She knew everything about everyone in Manchester Polska Land.

CHAPTER FIVE

DAY ONE: NIGHT

Ossie, Manuela, Gianni, Dermot and I are sitting in a noisy Starbucks. We all look about eighty. The *Manchester Evening News* is on the circular table, open at the report.

"He's dead," Ossie shouts above the racket. My eyes flip open from the dream.

I've been sleeping with the door ajar. The house is quiet as a grave. I lie staring at cold blackness above me, plucking up courage to go into Dad's room. This is it; I know it is. I can't hear him. He's gone. I don't want to be the first to find him like that.

Now I'll never know the truth about Yankel.

Come on, Ania, sort yourself out, woman. You can't leave this to Mum.

The clock says 4.56. I move the covers aside.

The clock says 5.15. I sit on the edge of the bed.

The clock says 5.27. Stand up, Ania. Go in there.

The clock says 5.29 and I hear Dad mumbling. I let myself exhale normally at last. I'm freezing so I put on my dressing gown and go into his room. At the foot of his bed, in the dim glow of the night light, I watch his face, contorted as if he's arguing with someone. What's in his dreams – the now, the not-so-long-ago or the distant past? Maybe it's the future. Maybe he's arguing with God. He settles and I wait for his breath, for the snores that used to make the whole house rumble when we were little. It's not what you'd call snoring now – more like gathering, vibrating mucus, a toxic brew churning in a conical flask. When he lets out a groan at 5.38, I say, "I'm here."

"Can I have more painkillers yet?" he asks. Iwonka says he always leaves it until he's already on the road to agony. Why is that? He's such a stubborn mule. He reaches out and switches on the bedside lamp.

I say, "I don't know," and check the post-it lists. It's stupid. Of course, he can have painkillers – what would too many matter now? "If you want, Tatuś." I slide my arm behind his neck, tense the muscles, heave him into an upright position, give him a couple of scheduled, mega-strength paracetamol, hand him the glass of water. He concentrates on swallowing, doesn't achieve it first time, swallows repeatedly, with resigned eyes-shut frustration, as if the pills are the size of gobstoppers. Desperation is carved into his features as he tries to crunch them between the dental plates he's wearing for my benefit. Honestly, Dad, I know your teeth went years ago, you twerp. I could mash the pills with a pestle and mortar, but they're supposed to be slow-release. Fucking paracetamol – bloody useless.

When the pills finally go down he says, "Go back to bed, child. I'll be fine now." 5.50 on his clock.

I return to my room. I despise myself for needing to be sure about what he did, what I am, who I am. He's still here though, and I must pick the moment, the right words. I need him to still love me when he dies. When he's gone, there'll be no-one to ask.

THEN

I'd bribe it out of Stevo. He'd tell me everything if I made him trust me. I'd start off with a donation of one of my Easter eggs. I had three. One I could spare.

On Easter Monday, Manuela called at my house on her way to take some food to Stevo. She leaned against the porch door jamb, raised her eyebrows and looked sideways, definitely smug.

"I've got something else, too, but we can't let the boys see it. It's a secret. Show you when we get there."

I wasn't expecting much. I thought maybe she'd stolen some lipstick or leased a piece of her mum's jewellery for the day. I dashed back up to my room and took the smallest egg. We knocked on Ossie's door. He was still in his pyjamas and said he'd be over shortly.

We called out for Stevo as we entered the den and, to our surprise, were met with a new design feature. The hopscotch grid we kept restoring with bits of pebble because our pilfered school chalk had run out was now a permanent lime-green, the same colour as the Welsh dresser in my grandparents' garage. Stevo must have painted it in for us. I can't say that it was perfect, but for a boy, all things considered, he'd done quite well. Kind of him to go to the trouble.

In addition he'd roughly traced the shape of the circle we sat in on the day we found him. He'd painted another circle around it, and within the two, spaced all around, were the initials of our names. Groovy! His S was there too, next to the G, like he was officially one of us. In the centre his daubs resembled a spider or a sun, with twisted legs or beams.

Manuela and I were admiring his efforts when he sauntered in.

"Like it?" he said. I gave him the egg.

His face brightened. "Ta."

"It's great. Thanks!" Manuela jumped from the number 2 to the number 8 and back again, chanting, "The dear departed went and farted, to his grave he fast was carted." I stopped myself from asking about the peculiar shape in the centre – it might hurt his feelings, and I'd probably done enough damage with my previous questions. I wanted him to like me.

"What d'ya think of the campfire?" he said. "Wrong colour, I know."

Now he mentioned it, the wiggly things could be flames.

"It's very nice, thank you," I said politely.

He flicked the tip of my nose and laughed. "Don't sit on it or ya'll get yer arse burnt."

Where was my witty comeback? I felt flustered.

Manuela undid the paper round the several bricks' worth of baklava brought from her dad's night club, gave me a piece, and passed two packets of halva to Stevo. The baklava stuck my jaws together, so I gave up. Dermot would eat it. It would make a change from the potatoes and cabbage he claimed they only ate at their house.

He and Gianni turned up soon after, Gianni carrying his contribution to the food bank – two salami sandwiches and a Tupperware container full of his mum's cake neatly cut into squares. Gianni said Signora had made it for God-knows-who since there were only three of them, and his step-dad didn't eat cake. The bag of notebooks, biros and pencils Gianni brought – surplus stock he called them – were also thanks to his step-dad who worked at a printers.

There was still no sign of Ossie. As we installed ourselves on our letters, Gianni put the box on top of the campfire. He opened the Tupperware and – all Italian now – said, "*Signore e signori, vi dono questa...Torta di Mele Genovese!*"

"*Torrrta di Mellay Jenno Vazay,*" Manuela repeated, larking about, exaggerating Gianni's rippling R. Dermot's tried to do it too. Hopeless. He couldn't mimic the R which was weird because he knew whole chunks of mass in Latin.

Manuela took a bite. "How do you say delicious in Italian?"

"*Delizioso,*" Gianni replied.

Manuela pretended to be St. Bernadette of Lourdes, all holy, and looked up to the ceiling as she sank her teeth into another piece. "*Torrrta day-leats-yoh-zo.*" Then she launched herself backwards, holding her knees into her chest and cackling like a demented rooster. Stevo laughed too.

As we scoffed the cake I was mildly concerned that Ossie would miss out. I nabbed two squares and put them aside for him.

When the boys went out to play, Manuela offered me some gum. "Do you want to see it then?"

"See what?"

She blew a pale pink bubble, popped it and stretched the gum out in front of her as far as it would go. "The secret?"

I'd forgotten all about the secret.

"Let's go to another room. They might come back here," she said.

We went to the basement where she opened her bag and slowly inserted her hand, keeping her eyes on my face. "Are you ready?" Inch by inch, she revealed the two magazines she'd *borrowed* – this time from her dad, not her mum. She'd found them under her dad's side of the bed when her mum sent her to get her slippers.

On the front cover of the first – *Parade* it was called – was a lady with shoulder-length blond hair pushed back behind a royal blue Alice band. She wore a navy bikini covered in red and white stars. On the cover of the second, called *Spiced*, on a background of palm trees, stood a lady with chestnut hair that hung in loose coils and covered her chest – good job too because she wasn't wearing a single stitch. Nothing. *What-so-ever.* At the top of her legs, with both hands – her nails were painted bright tangerine – she held a pineapple the size of a dinner plate. And her orangey lips had squashed in an "oo" as if they'd got stuck after sucking spaghetti.

Manuela discarded the *Parade* and flicked open *Spiced* at the first page. "Look inside." She grinned. "Go on. It's from America."

I turned the pages, photo after photo, no more pineapples, horror mounting with the dawning realisation that this might be what lay ahead for me. Deep brown nipples sticking out like marbles, beards sprouting from private parts. I thought of the painting of Jesus that hung near the confessional at Polski church. The one where he was distributing loaves and fishes to the people of Galilee, who all had *foot-long beards*. It didn't bear thinking about. How would you keep it all inside your knickers?

"These aren't real," I said, convinced she was having me on.

"Course they are. Alex says so. It's all real. Big brothers don't lie."

"This?" I pointed to a ginger beard on a lady lying on top of a dead bear in a four-poster bed. "Has your mum got one?"

Manuela said, "I suppose so." Ha! She didn't know really, she was acting. Manuela put her hands together and rolled her thumbs round and round. "Hasn't yours?"

Obviously a trick question. Like when she'd told me there were special men in Turkey who sucked goats' milk through rubber pipes and spat it into buckets which were driven to England. That's why school could afford to give us milk. That's why it had a peculiar taste. I'd passed this nugget onto Grace Hitching who started crying. Then Mrs. Deptford threw me out into the corridor until I learned to be 'less of an ungated nole'. Gianni later insisted I'd heard wrong. Mrs. Deptford probably said 'unmitigated know-all'. That sounded quite posh really.

Should I answer Manuela honestly now or not?

"Don't know. I've never seen her with no clothes on."

When Stevo rapped on the window we almost jumped out of our skin. Manuela hastily shoved the hairy ladies into the bag. With his nose flat against the pane, he called:

"What yer doing? Come out to play." Manuela dumped the bag in the cupboard and I decided to get a proper look at Mum before she sausaged up into her roll-on girdle. Manuela had to be lying, as usual. I knew I shouldn't ever trust her.

*****

Later that week we played hide-and-seek around the house and garden, then tag, which was a bit dull because Ossie wasn't there. When a drizzle interrupted outdoor play, Manuela went home, leaving just me and the boys.

I sat beside Stevo who pretended to give me a Chinese burn, so I pretended to give him one back.

Gianni kicked my foot for no good reason. "Come on. Let's play the alphabet game. I'm sick of football teams, let's do…"

I was sure he'd pick a topic I knew nothing about. Football teams were hard enough. If we weren't forced into watching the results on telly every Saturday because there was nothing else on, I'd not have the vaguest idea beyond United, City, Liverpool and Benfica. I'd even remembered a team beginning with P when the boys were clueless because it had been on the previous Saturday. "Hibernian – Three," the telly announcer had said. "Partick Thistle – Two."

"Partick Thistle!" I'd yelled during that game. My suggestion was disallowed on the grounds the club wasn't English. Gianni and I squabbled for several minutes, me saying that a football team was a football team, him saying this alphabet game was English football teams, me saying it was on English telly, so that made it English. We fell out and didn't speak for two days.

With dread I waited for him to say constellations or caterpillars or something else equally Gianni-like.

"… fruit and veg," he said. "Me first. Apple."

Dermot said, "Banana."

I said, "Carrot."

Stevo said nothing. He was stumped for something beginning with a D.

"Not got all day," Gianni said.

As Stevo's pupils flitted from the coving to the ceiling searching for an answer, I half-wanted to give him a hug because I couldn't think of anything either. Dermot began clicking his knuckles, then folded his arms tight around him and hunched over.

Gianni slapped the floor. "Damson, you div!"

"What's one o' them?" Stevo asked.

"You don't know what a damson is? It's like a plum. You *have* seen plums, haven't you?"

Dermot skew-whiffed his mouth at me, as if to say 'let's get out of here.'

"What's got into ya?" said Stevo, voice louder. "I was only asking."

Gianni shrugged. "Don't know what you're talking about."

We heard Ossie shout, "I'm here!" He bounced in, sweaty like he'd run all the way over. Dermot's face lightened and I breathed a sigh as my elbows loosened.

Ossie vibrated his lips, purrupping like a wild horse. "My mum got mad and made all of us clean the house. Every bit of it. *Psha kreff!* She made me clean round the bottom of the loo with a toothbrush." He plonked himself down and, with his legs stretched out in front of him, did a perfect impersonation of Mrs. MacDonald while pointing at his shoes. "Me puttin' me feet up," he said in a Jamaican accent, "Me restin' me chilblains." The peculiar atmosphere had gone. Thank God for Ossie. Everyone giggled. Everyone apart from Stevo who, nostrils flared, sat chewing his thumbnail.

*****

When Dad asked me if I wanted to go to the factory with him, I immediately said yes. Even Spooky came second to that. We drove past Manchester Cathedral, then Strangeways. I was thinking about the stock room. What would I bring home today? And would I find anything in there for Stevo?

Dad parked the van at the back of the factory. All the loading bays were still closed. While we walked round to the front, he told me his building was more than a hundred years old and the bricks weren't really black. Manchester was like Łódź in Polska, and that's why soot covered everything. This was built in the time of Queen Victoria who, Dad said, was the ugliest woman he'd ever seen. Which I knew already because there was a picture of her with her hooky nose in my encyclopaedia.

We went up the oak staircase then past Mr. Cohen's raincoat factory, Mr. Rogoff's umbrella factory, and Mr. Gottlieb's shopping bag factory. Nobody was there because it was Shabbos and they had to go to synagogue which was Jewish church. Poor things.

Dad went straight into his office, saying I wasn't to bother people or interrupt them working, but if anybody did ask me to help, I could put an apron on. I put one on just in case.

Today, my first port of call was the packing room to visit Mr. Edzio and Mr. Widzowski.

"Ania – welcome!" Mr. Widzowski said as I breezed in, togged up ready for work. "Edek, wake up, old man. Our assistant is here."

Mr. Edzio looked up from checking the poppers on the wallets and pushed up his tortoiseshell glasses. "*Ausgezeichnet!* Excellent. We could do with some expert help."

"Indeed. Indeed," Mr. Widzowski said. "We must take advantage of this opportunity."

The first time Dad let me come to the factory, I asked if they were twins. Mr. Edzio laughed and said he came from Olsztyn, which was now in Polska, but had been in Prussia. His father, he said, liked to get about but probably not as far as Wilno. Which was where Mr. Widzowski came from. And Wilno, Mr. Edzio said, used to be in Polska, but was now in Russia.

I hadn't understood any of that, but I pretended I did.

Now Mr. Widzowski suggested a race to fill one layer of a carton. While Mr. Edzio found some boxes and laid out the black wallets for me (they were called WT 959), Mr. Widzowski tied a knot in the neck loop of my apron because it was so low the hem was flapping around my ankles. Then he took off his watch and placed it on the table.

"So, let's see if our future boss can put us to shame again." He waited for the second hand to reach the twelve. "Ready... go!"

The boxes were flat, already glued at one edge. I folded the first box back against the crease, straightened it up, inserted the top flap, shoved the wallet in a cellophane bag, put it in the box, closed the top flap. I glanced at the watch – two minutes. Not good enough.

As I picked up the pace, Mr. Edzio seemed to get his tubby fingers stuck in all the flaps, and he kept saying, "It's not going at all well today. I don't know what's the matter with me," and Mr. Widzowski, struggling to sharpen the creases, said, "Hurry up, Edek, we'll be thrown out if we lose." By the fifth one, I was zooming through.

They were still smiling when my layer was three-quarters full, as if they thought they'd beat me, but I was way ahead of them. Sliding the last box into my carton, I proclaimed victory.

"Thirty-one minutes!" Mr. Edzio said. "You are your father's daughter. You'll put us out of a job. Come now. Apron off." He stood up and beckoned.

Mrs. Markham was busy typing when we went through her room, but I said hello anyway because that wasn't really interrupting someone, that was being polite.

Mr. Edzio knocked on the door to Dad's office and we went in together. Dad was sitting at his desk, smoking his pipe and cutting out a pattern for a new handbag. Leaning back in his chair, he put down his scalpel then swivelled to face us.

"Ania did a good job," Mr. Edzio said. "Twenty-four boxes in thirty-one minutes." One eye was blinking as if he'd got some cardboard dust in it. "If you don't mind, Pan Witek, could you arrange for her to leave school and come and work full-time with us? We could do with improving our piece-work rates."

Dad whistled. "Twenty-four? Not bad, child. Is it open, Edek? Let her in. Only one item, so take your time, and choose carefully."

I'd been waiting for this. The best place in the world. It smelt gorgeous. Long and narrow, the stock room stretched to a window at the far end covered with black plastic, so you could only see in there if you switched the light on. On the left hand side lay rolls of brightly coloured leather, plastics and linings tight up against each other like sticks of rock, gold and silver frames for purses and spectacle cases, and then threads, rivets, rolls of gold-blocking foil that Dad said was genuine gold and cost a fortune.

On the bottom shelf stood bottles and containers of glues, leather dyes, solvents for cleaning machinery, and huge tins of coffee, tea and sugar. On the right, all the way down to the window, cardboard boxes of completed products were stacked ready for dispatch.

And, in front of these, on the floor, my special cartons, the reject boxes. Heaven.

I sat on the floor and took the products out, lining them up in categories, and examining what was wrong with them. A stitch missed here or there, a slightly wonky frame on a purse, a cock-eyed, gold-blocked 'Real Leather. Made in England' on a wallet.

It took ages to decide. Then I found a cherry patent leather handbag with gold trims. I sniffed the inside and the outside, tried the strap on for length, zipped and unzipped the inner pockets, made sure both the top and bottom of the poppers fitted together. I also found a spectacle case that looked okay and slipped it inside. I'd tell Stevo it was for his pens and pencils.

I took the bag back to Dad's office.

That patent leather was so gorgeous. Manuela would be so jealous. Positively green.

*****

Dad and I strolled through the ladies' production area. There were three gluing tables against the wall on the left, with four ladies in tabard aprons sitting at each. In front of them, the ladies had their tools – a marble block for working on, coloured plastic clothes pegs holding folded squares of foam, an ivory thingy that looked like a paper knife with which they smoothed edges, and two discarded tins each of Dad's Gallagher's Rich Honeydew Tobacco, one filled with PVA that smelled sweet, the other with latex that was as bad as cat wee.

Dad wandered in and out of the tables, saying good morning and looking at their work. The radio blared Nancy Sinatra's 'These boots are made for walking' and whenever the sewing machines stopped, the gluing ladies bounced on their bums and used their tools in time to the music. It was so good to be in the glue room – it seemed like everyone was always happy there. Then Dad stopped to chat in English to Mrs. O'Hanrahan and Mrs.

MacGrath and look in their crates.

We went through to the men's area. He must have forgotten I was following because I wasn't usually allowed in there. In the middle of the room were two giant cutting tables, piled high with linings and layers of foam, and around the walls of the room were the dyeing counter, presses, creasers, gold blockers and framing machines.

I was just congratulating myself on being there instead of at home with Iwonka and Janek when Dad stopped to inspect a crate full of purses. I stood right beside him.

Bright lemon yellow they were.

With a lilacy-purple enamelled clasp.

The man next to the crate was carefully sliding a purse into its frame, and I wondered if I'd get another chance to come to the workshop before the end of the school holidays. I couldn't wait to get my mitts on one of these when they turned up in the rejects box.

As soon as Dad stood next to him, little beads of sweat bobbled up on the man's receding hairline and his mouth moved, though no words came out.

I don't know what happened – one minute everything was nice, normal, the next, a roar burst from the depth of Dad's throat. It felt like an earthquake.

"What the hell are you doing?" he shouted, eyes bulging, the whites breaking out in spidery red veins. "Look! Maniek, look! The stitching – all on the outside, not under the frame. What is the matter with you, you cretin?"

He jabbed the purse up under the man's nose. The man's face filled with horror as he uncurled his fist and Dad slapped the purse into his hand.

"P- Pan Witek," he stammered, examining it for himself. "Please forgive me. Sorry. I didn't—"

Dad cut him off, sharp as an axe. "Sorry?" His spit drops landed on the bloated patch under the man's eye. "Up my *dupa* with your *sorry*." He was so deafening that I jumped back again.

Dad bent over and rooted through the box. "Will sorry make up for the money you cost me?"

The man dabbed the spittle with his thumb.

"More!" Dad bellowed, as he straightened up and slammed another purse onto the press. "And again! These won't last a minute."

The man stepped back, bent his head and looked down at his shoes. He seemed small as Janek during a table rant about eating with your mouth open. I knew the feeling. Eyes, ears and tongue inching back, groping for blackness where you wouldn't have to be part of what was going on.

Dad picked twenty-three faulty purses out of that box. Counted them all out at the top of his voice so that everybody heard. I wished I'd never got excited about them. It was as if I'd brought it on the man myself, like I made it happen by wanting there to be some faulty ones to end up in the rejects box.

Finally, Dad said, "*Kurwa*!" grinding his teeth with an R like machine-gun fire, whipped round and strode back to the office, his limp more pronounced than ever, leaving me standing there.

On my own.

In the blue and green dress Mum bought for me last week, with the short sleeves and the box pleats in the skirt.

Everyone on the shop floor had stopped working. What should I do? My feet refused to move, they'd grown into the ground. Wherever I looked there were gawping eyes with no faces.

Then the Maniek man, whose own eyes were swimming now, patted me on my head.

"Don't worry. It's fine. You can go now."

I said sorry, trying my best not to cry, turned round and went after Dad. If ever I wished I could be a woodlouse, crawling and hiding in the floorboard cracks, that was the moment.

*****

Mrs. Markham must have heard the fracas from her office.

As I shuffled in, she muttered something, crumpling her eyes as if she'd just cut herself, and nodded. "You going in? Sure? Be quiet, love, eh?" There was no need to tell me that. She only saw Dad at work, I had to live with him.

Dad was hunched over his desk with his head in his hands when I deposited myself on the scruffy armchair behind him. I looked at my cherry bag. It didn't seem so beautiful now.

He stayed there not moving, while I sat and fidgeted. I looked in a triangle from the back of his zip-up suede cardigan, above him to the wall at the picture of the white eagle wearing a crown, and to the framed document about T.W. Whitcher Ltd. Then I did it again, over and over. There was nothing else to do because I'd forgotten to bring a *Chalet School* book for office-sitting.

He picked up a piece of paper from his desk, read a few words and shouted, "Dorothy! How many times have I told you? Suppliers on the left, customers on the right. Come in, go out."

Mrs. Markham murmured, "Yes, Witek," and resumed typing.

I couldn't stand it anymore.

"Tatuś," I ventured, "if he makes all those mistakes why don't you sack him or send him to work for Pan Kulik, like Pani Kwiatkowska when she sewed the flaps the wrong way round?"

The office was shrinking round me. I waited for him to reply, but he just picked up a pen and scratched calculations on a piece of squared paper.

"Of course I'm not going to sack him," Dad said, with a heavy groan. "Never. He can't help it." He turned to face me. "Didn't you see his arm, you

49

silly, silly girl? The rest of them want me to get rid of him, but I will *never* sack him."

What had I said? I'd forced the tears back earlier, but now they were collecting again. I wouldn't let him see. I crept out of the office and went to the stock room where I huddled between the rejects and seconds' boxes and had a good bawl. Anyway, I *had* seen it, a long number on the inside of his forearm. It looked as if he'd scratched it in with a pen. What did that have to do with anything? And why did that make me silly? It was Dad who was silly. Silly and stupid. Stupid and horrible. And cruel, just like Stevo's dad. Why couldn't he just die?

After half an hour, I decided he didn't have to die completely because then who would look after us. But it would serve him right if somebody was as mean to him as he was to me and that poor man. And Mrs. Markham. And everyone.

*****

While no-one was looking I sneaked to the washroom and splashed my face with cold water until the puffiness went down a bit. Then I went back to Mrs. Markham's office. She stopped typing and turned her chair round.

"Sit down, love. Your Dad's gone on a delivery to Frankel's. How are you?" She opened a drawer. "Want some?" She offered me a piece of treacle toffee and slipped one into her mouth too. She took out a mirror and brush and backcombed the top bit of her hair.

Maybe Mrs. Markham could explain. She was always kind to me and never went crazy, not even when I asked if I could have a go on her typewriter when she was on her dinner break. How should I start?

"The man that Dad shouted at…"

"Maniek?"

"Yes. Mr. Maniek. He has a number on his arm…"

Mrs. Markham put her elbow on her desk and cupped her cheek with her hand. Three crinkles appeared on her forehead. "Yes, love?"

"Is it important?"

Mrs. Markham stopped chewing. "You want to know what the number means?"

"Yes, please."

She didn't seem to know the answer because she had to think about it for a long time. "Well…hm…have you heard of a place called Auschwitz?"

I thought I might have, but I wasn't sure. "Is it on the telly?"

Mrs. Markham smiled a little smile. "Oh dear… yes. Sometimes." She sighed and continued. "Auschwitz was a kind of prison."

"Like Strangeways?"

"No. Not at all like Strangeways." She swallowed and rubbed her eyebrows. "Auschwitz was a very bad prison. Oh dear. I mean it was a prison

50

run by very bad people."

"Yes?"

"And the bad people took Mr. Maniek there when he was eleven."

"Why? Did he steal something?"

"No. It was because *they* were bad. You've heard of Nazis?" Of course, I'd heard of Nazis. Hadn't everyone? I heard about them all the time it seemed to me. Non-flipping-stop.

"Yes."

"The Nazis created Auschwitz."

"Oh. What about the number?"

"Yes, the number…"

Something was stirring in my memory. I knew where I'd heard of Auschwitz. It *had* been on the telly. On *All Our Yesterdays* that time when Dad told me to leave the room even though I'd done absolutely nothing wrong. A picture was forming in my mind. I remembered lots of very thin people, even skinnier than Dermot. Soldiers were holding them and helping them to stand up. Some of the thin people were in pyjamas with grey stripes that went up and down, others were lying on the ground with no clothes on.

Mrs. Markham seemed to have forgotten she was talking to me.

I reminded her. "Mrs. Markham? The number? Mr. Maniek has a triangle as well."

"What?" She swallowed again. "The numbers are tattooed. They'll never come off. You see, the Nazis needed a system to remember the prisoners…"

She was looking at an envelope that had been ripped open and on top of it a brown wallet. It must have been a return. She picked up the wallet by its gold corner.

"Do you know what this is?" she asked.

"I have to look inside." I knew most of the products from when I was packing with Mr. Edzio and Mr. Widzowski. Sometimes the wallets looked exactly the same on the outside, you just couldn't tell them apart, but they had different insides, a bit like Mr. Edzio and Mr. Widzowski. Sometimes it was the other way round. She flipped the wallet open. It had a pocket on the left, three paper-money dividers and a tab for stamps. I said, "It's a WT 745."

"Right. Well, that's called a serial number, love. All factories have to have serial numbers so that they can identify the goods." Then she stopped again. "Oh dear. I mean…Well, any road, that's how they knew who the prisoner was. They gave them a number. Do you want another toffee, love?"

*****

"Come here, treasure," Dad said, patting the sofa between his knees. I wasn't expecting this after the commotion at work.

Treasure. I hadn't been so precious earlier on. I'd been silly then. But I wasn't so silly now that I knew what the numbers were. Maybe I'd be a detective when I grew up.

Dad was wearing his straight-from-work smell, plastics, leathers, dyes, latex, PVA, cleaning fluids, oil, much better than the Kombo's whiff, so I sat down on the floor between his legs.

He stroked my hair. "So, shall we ask Mama if you can stay up for the film tonight?" He gave me a conspiratorial wink. "Marx Brothers? Just you and me?" Janek and Iwonka were already upstairs getting ready for bed.

I leaned my head back on the edge of the sofa, looked at his upside-down face. "You ask her then."

He twiddled my hair, and by the time the Metro Goldwyn Meyer logo appeared on the screen, I was number one child. Exactly as it should be.

Dad could never be like Stevo's dad. Not really.

*****

The damson incident wasn't the first in which Stevo showed his ignorance about everything. Even though he narked me, I felt oddly protective towards him, his half-Polishness and lack of brains seeming like my responsibility. We could tell that he hadn't been to school much – that part of his story was definitely true.

I brought him my *Alpha Book of Facts for Girls* and *The Children's Comprehensive Encyclopaedia* and said he could borrow them for as long as he wanted. A huge sacrifice because I dipped into those books all the time. My other favourite, the *Oxford Concise Dictionary*, which Mum had bought when I was struggling at school, stayed at home. Mrs. Deptford had said I ought to do a *Five New Words a Day* list to improve my English vocabulary. C was the best letter – there were some dead brilliant words like contemporaneousness – nineteen letters. And excruciating and obnoxious were good too.

Stevo had only had the books overnight when he set me a challenge. He proposed we have a quiz on the capitals on the blue side of Europe which I already knew back to front so that wasn't much of a competition for me. I suggested writing down fifty other countries' names and learning their capitals.

"Easy!" he said. He opened a notebook Gianni had brought, threw me a pencil and, copying from the *Alpha* book, we agreed on and wrote down countries from the red side of Europe and everywhere else in the world, starting with Algeria. The contest was set for the following day.

The next day when Manuela and I crossed Spooky's threshold, she called out, "*Torta di Mellay Jenno Vazay*" to get Stevo to show himself.

He bounced in, looking very pleased with himself. "Ya ready? I'm gonna beat ya." Had he been learning all night? That torch battery wasn't going to last long if he wasn't careful. I'd have to see if there were any candles in the cellar. Manuela asked what he was talking about.

He replied, "I'm gonna beat the pair of ya at capitals. Take this." He ripped out a few pieces of paper and handed them to us. Manuela said she wouldn't play because she didn't have an *Alpha* book and only knew some of Europe, so Stevo made her the referee. He told me to fold my page in half and write out just the countries first, copied from the previous day's labour.

"Now the capitals. On yer marks, get set. Go!" he shouted.

We sprawled facing downwards on the floor and began scribbling.

The other boys arrived, took one look at us, and said they were going into the garden.

I'd forgotten the capital of Ecuador and wasted too much time trying to remember it. He didn't look up at all while he wrote, fierce with concentration, the tip of his tongue poking out on the side of his mouth. When I gave in because I'd also forgotten half of Asia and the only thing that came to mind for Paraguay was Spam, I sat up upright. He raised his head and grinned at me. Why was he so pleased with himself? It was only a stupid quiz yet he looked like he'd just received a gold medal. He carried on in his babyish writing while I watched. His sandy fringe, which he kept brushing away, flopped over to the right, halfway down his cheek. He needed a hair grip. Some of his words were properly joined up, others he printed like he was still in Infants'. That much I could see, but the words swam into each other a bit. Finally, we swapped papers.

"So you knew Warsaw," I said. I wouldn't have minded if he'd beaten me by one. Probably.

He squinted at me. "What d'ya mean?"

"You know Warsaw? The capital of Poland?"

"It was in the book."

"And that's the only way you knew it?" I thought maybe his dad had told him or something.

"What? Yeah." He looked puzzled.

When the other boys came back in, Ossie spotted the *Alpha* book and the encyclopaedia on the floor. He informed us that if you stood on your head, the blood from the rest of your body dripped downwards and fed your brain with genius-making vitamins. It made sense. Us girls were already smarter than the boys. Me, with hanging upside down on the swing, and Manuela with doing cartwheels and handstands at school. Even after you died, Ossie added, the pull of gravity made your blood travel towards the earth, so if you died when you were sitting down, your bum would go bright red. Mr. Isaac Newton from Kingston in Jamaica had discovered that, and it was a fact. Ossie was obviously talking nonsense this time – nothing moved when you died. You could see that on films.

Stevo tried the brain gymnastics a few times and toppled over. But he persevered until he could headstand for ages longer than Manuela and me. He was getting a bit too good at it in my opinion.

When he tipped back onto his feet, he said he'd learned something else –

from the encyclopaedia. That the River Vistula flowed all the way from Cracow to Warsaw right up to Danzig on the Baltic coast. I told him it was Wisła, Kraków, Warszawa, Gdańsk and Bałtyk.

He whistled. "Oooooh. Lah-di-dah. All right, ya win. Ya think yer such a bloody clever clogs, Mrs. Polish Queen."

Ossie and Manuela laughed like that was funny.

"Well, maybe I am," I said, pretending I didn't care. "Wisła, Kraków, Warszawa, Gdańsk and Bałtyk," I repeated on purpose, slowly and in my best Polish accent. Just so's Stevo would remember it, right until the flipping day he died.

CHAPTER SIX

DAY TWO: MORNING

Mum and I are dressed and waiting when Josie, the Macmillan nurse, arrives at nine o'clock. She's only been coming for a few days. Mum seems shy around her – Mum's done the best she can with her delinquent hair. I realise I forgot to cut it yesterday; Gorgonzola seemed more important at the time. For a moment, Josie stops to chat with Mum at the dining room table. It's covered with medical paraphernalia – more drugs with names I've never heard of like Omeprazole, catheter bags, large cardboard boxes which Mum says contain another version of Complan because Dad hates Complan. The way he's eating now it would take him four years to consume that lot. I pull up a chair, try to look as if I'm with it. I stare at what's on the table instead. Omeprazole. It could be Italian. I hear Manuela shouting *Torta di Mele Omeprazolay*.

Focus on now.

Josie is tall, about forty, a sturdy size 16 in what looks like an M&S trouser suit. She has sinewy, ringless hands that could just as easily strangle you as pump your heart back to action. She knows the way and Mum and I follow her as she breezes into his room with a cheery "Good morning, Witek. How are you today?" Her air of calm efficiency makes me jealous, irrational. Dad rallies at the sight of her, tries to raise himself higher on the pillows, and speaks to her as if she's a capable grown-up, old enough to deal with the realities of life. And death.

She says, "No, no, don't worry, lie back."

"Ah, Josie. You and I – we know how it is." Dad winks at her like he's flirting. I don't know why but I want to cry. Silly old fool.

"We do, Witek," she replies and pats his shoulder as if they are in this together, in cahoots, just the two of them.

Dad asks Mum and me to leave, says he wants to talk to Josie in private. I close the door behind me and consider eavesdropping then think better of it. We're in the kitchen when the door bell rings.

Mum says, "I'll go." She ushers two district nurses, a man and a woman, into the sitting room and offers tea while Josie finishes talking to Dad. I introduce myself, and the woman who's about my age, Sarah, walks round looking at the photographs in the room, as if she's visiting a friend's house. When Mum brings the cups in, Sarah asks her who's who in the pictures. The man, Tom, about thirty, sits on the edge of Dad's Lazyboy. I'd prefer him to be on the sofa. Josie comes out, has a brief chat with them both, then bids us goodbye, adding that Mum can call at any time. Mum and I hover while Sarah and Tom go into Dad's room. When they come out, Sarah says he needs Lactulose for his constipation; it's not just the lack of food that's preventing a bowel movement, she says, it's the combination of other drugs.

Ten minutes after they leave the priest turns up, "just for a brief visit". It's like Piccadilly station. I don't know him; he's newish, fresh from some Vatican- or mohair-beret-funded priest-making factory in Poland, no doubt; they roll them off conveyor belts there. His baby-like forehead gleams as if the Virgin Mary has given it a final burnish, ready for dispatch. I haven't been to Polish church, any church, in years. The priest, Father Moczek, stands waiting for me to make the first move.

"I don't think we've met before," he says pointedly. There's something gluttonous about the way his religion and his perfect diction spread through the room, like a B movie earth-devouring blob.

"I don't live in Manchester," I reply, stumbling over the grammar. In my head I go through the cases; it must decline like a masculine noun; *Manchest-er*, *Manchester-a*, *Manchester-owi*, *Manchester-em*, *Manchester-ze*. Stupid bloody language. I'm losing the plot – you don't decline proper nouns, of course you don't. I said it right.

Mum brings him tea and cake and he has it with Dad. From my bedroom, I hear the murmurs of their conversation, their little laughs, their silences.

When the priest leaves, I go to check on Dad. He's asleep again.

I wish people would stop coming. The moment to ask Dad seems as elusive as a will-o'-the-wisp, and as perilous.

THEN

Fortunately neither Granny nor Grandad entered the garage often, so the absence of the key wasn't noticed. By some miracle the fact that the padlock wasn't jammed shut also went undetected. I'd been there twice on my own since that first time, but it'd be pushing my luck to hold on to the key any longer. I had to return it to its rightful place.

I sat in their kitchen, getting some much needed peace and quiet from Janek and Iwonka, and wondered when on earth Granny would find something to do in her bedroom. Then she asked me whether I wanted to earn some wages. So, eager for the money – but only because I wanted her to turn her back on me and excavate the handbag – I foolishly said yes.

She opened the cutlery drawer and handed me a small knife. "Here – use this".

It wasn't looking good. She bent over to peer under the curtain hanging from some plastic wire which camouflaged the shelf beneath the worktop. She'd grown a new blue lump on the back of her left knee below her bloomers, I noticed. In front of me she dumped a gigantic brown bag full of bloody potatoes.

"Tonight we'll have *kluski*," she said, pretending to be nice. "I'll make enough for your mama for today and tomorrow. You'll like that?"

Well, yes – I liked *eating* them, but since when had I become the kitchen maid? That was grown-ups' work in my opinion. But I was so desperate to return the key, I stopped myself from pointing out the obvious. I'd do a couple of potatoes and then tell her I had to go home.

I must have sat there for months scraping at those flipping spuds, with that tiny blunt knife, trying to get rid of all the bobbly bits. Grandad came in from the shed, made a black Nescafé and puffed through two Woodbines on the trot, the second one lit from the first. He blew silent smoke rings as he observed my misery, not showing any inclination *what-so-ever* to save me. He said what a good girl I was to help. Each time I finished a potato and rinsed it in the pan of cold water Granny had oh-so-kindly provided for me, the darn thing still had gubbins on it. I told her I was sure I was doing it wrong in the hope she might at least tackle a couple herself to 'teach' me. It didn't work. She said she was too busy making the gloop for the cheesecake – I'd soon learn and become a master craftswoman. And after all, she said, she was already making butter, milking cows and peeling potatoes in Tarnopol when the First World War started which, she informed me, was when she was six. I bet she wasn't. All grown-ups, even Mrs. Deptford at school, said that kind of thing, just to make you do stuff. Grandad returned to the shed. I still hadn't reached the bottom of the bag when he came back four spuds later, had another coffee, two more cigarettes and read all the obituaries in the Polish Daily.

Potato Purgatory. That was where I was going when I died. I pictured myself on my lonesome cloud, a pan the size of a skip in front of me, the rain from black clouds pouring down my face. How many potatoes did I have to peel, scraping, scraping, scraping until St. Peter decided I'd done enough penance and let me in? And to think – I was in this position entirely because of Stevo.

My bum cheeks had grown calluses as big as half crowns by the time it was over, and I sprawled back in the chair, legs spread open. Oh, but it was good to be free of it. Blessed relief. Granny cut the spuds into quarters and put them on to boil.

"Come," she said. "Wages." She wiped her hands in quick flappy strokes on her apron and led me to the hall where she took her bunch of keys out from her skirt pocket, riffled through them and opened the door. While she unearthed the black handbag, I stood beside the sewing machine and quickly returned the key to the wooden box.

"You worked hard today," she said. "This time you can have a shilling." I wasn't going to share it with anyone – that was for sure.

I *had* worked hard, as hard as a slave. Looking after Stevo and keeping his secret safe was proving more difficult than I'd ever imagined. He'd better start being grateful.

*****

"Oz, over here!" Dermot shouted as the ball went flying into Mrs. Czaplińska's drive.

Ossie walked towards us, his expression grave. "He's gone," he said. "Left a note. And gone."

The rest of us had been playing rounders with the Barking girls and their stupid cousin from Alabama. Dexter – whatever his name was – whistled through his fingers like he thought he was *someone*. "Who's gawn? Y'all playing? Or what?"

Ossie gave him a scornful look then ignored him. Jerking his thumb over his shoulder, Ossie said, "My garden."

We took the command and trooped to the side of Ossie's garage where we sat on the old tyres to hear the rest of it.

"Gone where?" asked Manuela. "Where's the note?"

"I left it there," Ossie said.

"What did it say?"

"Nothing much. Gone home."

"Why?"

Ossie said, "How should I know?"

Manuela asked me if anything had happened, as if I might have something to do with it. So then I was annoyed with her and Stevo, after all I'd been through for him. Because not only had I raided the garage with Ossie, I'd gone back again on my own, *and* I'd also suffered that eternity of Potato Purgatory for him. Could my questioning have upset him? Maybe he thought I'd tell someone he was there. Perhaps I shouldn't have put him right on Polish towns and rivers? But you wouldn't go back to being beaten and starved just because of that, would you?

I found myself grabbing at Ossie's sleeve. "What did the note say? Exactly."

Ossie shook my hand off and looked up, moving his eyes from side to side. "It said…"

"Speed it up." If it was my fault, I wanted to know.

"Gone to see how my Mam is."

That didn't sound remotely right. "Can't be. Why would he do that? He hates her," I said.

"Don't shoot the messenger."

"What messenger?"

"I mean," Ossie put his hands on his hips and shoved his face right up close to mine, "don't get mad at me. I'm just telling you, right?"

Manuela pulled me back. "Leave it. Let's go and see."

At the other end of the avenue the Barking sisters and Dexter were playing piggy-in-the-middle with the rounders ball. Dermot yelled down that we'd finished for the day. The sisters didn't seem bothered, but Dexter yelled, "Sore losers."

No sooner had we entered Spooky than Dermot called out, "Where are you? *Torta di Mellay Jenno Vazay*. Stevo, you there?"

Ossie said, "Told you."

Dermot ran up the stairs two at a time to check. The rest of us went into the den and sat cross-legged in the painted circle with no Stevo.

"Perhaps it was too cold?" Gianni said.

Manuela dropped her elbows on her knees and supported her chin with her hands, like her head had grown too heavy to think about the reasons. "He had enough to eat, didn't he?"

"Food, games, blankets…" Gianni said. After his meanness about the damsons, you'd have thought he might want to get rid of Stevo, but he was as cheesed off as the rest of us. "Did anybody have a fight with him?" he asked. No-one owned up.

Dermot completed his investigation of the upstairs, returned to the den and slammed the door behind him. On the door handle the eye amulet and rosary beads that were supposed to protect us clinked against one another.

Dermot flopped onto his letter D, cracking his knuckles as he pulled on his fingers. "Got bored on his own all day. That's probably it, i'n't it?"

We couldn't think of a better explanation, and the rest of the gang carried on glumly mulling over what his dad would do to him, whether his mum would be kind to him, what he'd eat. But I couldn't sort out what I felt at all – just a jumble of emotions impossible to disentangle and put into categories. Was it me? My fault he had gone because I'd shown off about Polish words?

Eventually Gianni said, "Nothing we can do about it now. I'll get what for if I don't get home for tea. I'm off."

So we traipsed back heavy-hearted to our own houses, wondering if we'd ever see him again.

*****

For a few days misery reigned at Spooky. Maybe if he hadn't painted the circles and the hopscotch grid, we'd have perked up sooner, forgotten him, got on with the patterns of what we did there. But those circles served as a constant reminder, especially that stupid S. I got sick of it. Why had he gone? Why?

I found the tin of paint – he'd put it back in the same cupboard – and levered open the lid with the nail lifter edge of the hammer. With the glued-together rock-hard bristles of the paintbrush, I smacked a huge blob of lime on his S, then smeared it round and round until it was completely covered. Manuela watched me in silence. I put the lid back on the tin, whacked it down and felt instantly better.

"That's that, then," I said.

*****

I tried not to think what might be happening to Stevo. I should try to forget him.

At school the next day began relatively well. Ten out of ten for a spelling test, and I was the only one who got 'commemoration' right. For a moment, I also thought I might get star prize for my embroidered canvas because I created a brilliant new shape. Except Mrs.Wilkins told me not to count chickens. It was called feather stitch, she said, and someone had discovered it centuries before me. It seemed like the story of my life. I'd also invented the marvellous *kiełbasa* and raspberry jam sandwich only to discover at Polish Brownie camp that people had been eating them for years. Just not in our house.

Iwonka had been gripey in the morning and stayed home, so Mum said I had to walk back with Janek. The walking home I didn't mind – I'd meander down through Lindum Avenue with Manuela. Granny had given me thruppence the night before for emptying the grate, so we could drop into the Candy Box in Carlton Street. The rubbish bit was 'with Janek'.

Manuela and I hung around the front entrance till his class came out, and I gave him strict instructions to keep the length of two cars behind us at all times, and not get lost, and not dawdle. At the sweet shop, I told him to stay outside. He complained, of course. I gave Manuela a couple of chews and opened one to scoff myself.

Janek eyed me dolefully. "Aw, give us a—"

"No."

He whined, "I'll let you—"

"No. Them as ask, don't get," I said, and refreshed his memory about maintaining the distance as Manuela and I carried on down the road. Was it him who cleaned the grate? No, it was me. So my sweets. And it wasn't as if Granny never gave him any money. She did, except in his case it was always for absolutely nothing.

Manuela went into her house and I, with himself in tow, arrived at the back door two minutes later. Mum was in the kitchen. Within seconds – he'd barely removed his coat – he told her I'd ignored him, not looked after him, not given him a single sweet even though I had loads.

Mum told him to go get changed, and over his shoulder he tittle-tattled, "She's still got five in her pocket, Mama."

Mum opened her palm.

I dragged out my last chews and she snatched them from me and put them in the tea towel drawer.

I was beaten for now, but he wasn't going to get away with this.

In the sitting room I whispered to him, "Prepare to meet thy doom…" For a good hour I followed him round repeating "Ready yet? Prepare to meet thy doom…" He'd crack soon enough. He always did.

When Janek's best friend Tomek turned up, my moment arrived. The boys went behind our garage to fiddle with the rubbish bows and arrows they'd tried to make a couple of days earlier. I nipped round the other side to carry out my plan. Tomek would be my witness to events. He would in all honesty be able to say I didn't start it.

One more "Prepare to meet thy doom," and I got my wish.

Janek laid into me. First with his left – feeble – then with his right, which was a bit unexpected and made me bang my head against the garage wall. I grabbed hold of his hand and sank my teeth into it. As he screamed and rubbed at the marks my bite had left, I lunged and punched him one straight in the nose which, unfortunately for me, began to bleed, both nostrils streaming like two crimson liquorice strands. He howled. Next thing, Mum was outside, and Granny – who appeared from nowhere – and Ossie's mum who'd poked her head out of her kitchen window, and was shouting "Sweet Jesus! Whachoo doin', you noisy chil'ren?"

Mum took one look at Janek and hauled me by the shoulder of my jumper towards the house. Granny oy-ed and cuddled him to her, wiping at his nose with the hem of her apron. She asked Tomek what happened. I had no idea what he told her because by the time he'd stopped stuttering, the backs of my legs were being slapped in the kitchen.

"You'd better have an explanation ready for your father," Mum said.

*****

An hour later when Dad came home Mum was folding clothes in the kitchen, and Granny was with us three watching telly, sitting guard, ensuring Round Two didn't commence.

Groucho heard Dad's tyres turn into the drive and barked by the front door. My heart dropped to my stomach. The key turned slowly in the door, Groucho stopped his racket and made squealy noises instead. My heart by-passed the rest of my body and slid to my soles.

When Dad saw Janek's gargantuan hooter – at least plum size – the intake of breath he took almost whistled through his teeth. Janek sniffed. Granny stood quickly, said Grandad was waiting for his *kolacja* and disappeared. Dad invited us to join him at the table, and as we took our places, he asked Janek how it happened. Janek, for once in his whiney life, was mute.

Waiting for Janek and Mum to dob me in was excruciating. I knew they were going to do it because they continued staring, as if it was all my fault, and Mum kept raising her eyebrows and nodding at me, trying to force it out of me.

Eventually, I could stand it no longer. "It was me, Tatuś. I hit him, but he hit me first," hoping this would be taken into consideration.

"You did it?" Dad played a non-existent piano on the table with his right hand, starting with the pad of his smallest finger, the same scale repeatedly. His gaze switched to Janek. "I'm listening."

Janek was on the verge of blubbering. "I d-don't know. She was g-going on and on."

The position of Dad's hand changed. Same scale, but now the tips of his nails rapped out a rhythm like the William Tell tune on telly.

Mum muttered, "Anka, own up."

Janek, bleaty like a sheep, said in English, "Prepare to meet thy doom. She said prepare to meet thy doom."

My parents exchanged glances as Mum placed a serving dish of *kotlety* in front of Dad. He picked out one of the slightly burnt ones and transferred it to his plate. Underneath the *kotlet* he took lay a brown, crispy perfectly-formed, oval one that I immediately earmarked for me.

"If you own up that you're *entirely* to blame," Dad said, as he spooned three potatoes next to the *kotlet*, "you can choose your own punishment." I weighed up my options – it seemed like a good deal. I'd elect to stay in my bedroom, no great loss. A couple of hours with a *Chalet School* book would be quite pleasant.

For the moment it seemed more sensible to go along with it. "Fine then. All right." My voice did that stupid thing of its own accord, making me sound insolent when I didn't mean to be, when all that was intended was a clear statement of facts. "My fault. I provoked him."

Dad's chest rose and fell, and then, without a flicker of emotion, he said, "To your room. When I finish, I'll come upstairs. Decide how many straps you deserve." With that, he lifted the *kotlet*-laden fork to his mouth, nodded at Mum and started chewing.

What? *What?* My innards shrank into a walnut. *Straps?* Like the boys? And Stevo? What was Dad talking about? Whoever heard of girls getting the strap? He couldn't possibly mean it. I was his favourite girl. Boys and men weren't supposed to hit girls – that's what he always told Janek. And, after all, Dad didn't draw horses for Iwonka or Janek or show them his stamps – only me. And I was always chosen to go to the factory, so he must be saying it to scare me. Surely. I began to withdraw my confession. "But it wasn't my—"

"Upstairs," he said, tone even. His eyes bore into me. "No back chat."

As I pushed my chair from the table, Mum asked Iwonka how many potatoes she'd like as if absolutely nothing had happened, and would she prefer carrots, creamed beetroot or both. Did Mum not understand that Dad was about to beat me? Why didn't she do something, stop him? What was the matter with her? Was she going to let me down too?

I crawled up the stairs, Groucho following, wagging his tail, like he was on his way to a party. In my room I attempted to digest the last ten minutes. Whichever way you looked at it, Dad was a brute, monstrous just like Stevo's father.

So much for Polish honour. My dad, my Tatuś, was going to belt me, and there was nothing I could do about it. Unbelievable. I parked myself on the edge of the bed and, the more I thought about it and wound myself up at the injustice, the more I knew I'd beat Dad at his own game. I'd show him. I wouldn't cry – no matter what.

In the meantime, the thorny issue of how many straps were owing confused me. The possibilities whirled in my brain, like socks in a spin-dryer. I mean, one bloody nose was only worth one strap in my reckoning. Certainly not more. On the other hand, Dad might view it differently. Maybe he'd consider this a six of the best job, like boys who were caned in comics. But a cane wasn't the same as a belt…

I heard someone switch the telly on. Groucho, deserter and turncoat, skulked out from under the bed and trotted back down, leaving me alone. So much for him.

My head continued to whirr, trying to figure where Dad's logic might lead. Did 'Them as ask don't get' apply in this situation? If I suggested more than I deserved, maybe I'd get less. A nightmare worse than anything I'd ever had to work out in school. The threads of my own arguments twined around each other, and as pinpricks of moisture gathered in my eyebrows, another horrendous thought occurred to me. The aftermath. One way or another, one strap or six, my bum would hurt. Ossie had said his was on fire when he got the strap. What could I do to relieve the pain?

Downstairs, I heard Dad tell Janek off for speaking to Iwonka in English, Mum mentioned an electricity bill, the whistle of the kettle for tea, assorted murmurs and clatterings, the phone ringing and being ignored.

In the bathroom, I soaked the sponge in cold water, then hid it under the bed, ready for first aid when Dad left. I propped myself at the pillow-end of Iwonka's bunk, then at the feet. Was he coming or not?

After shifting to the middle, I leaned against the wall, drew my legs up and found raggedy splinters on my fingernails. I chewed them, one after the other, with the corners of my teeth. He was making me wait on purpose – that was his game. When every single nail had been bitten off, chewed up and spat out, I began on my cuticles.

Finally, I heard him limping on up the stairs. The door hinge creaked as he pushed it open. I'd show him. I couldn't even imagine Dad's face now – the only picture in my mind was of Bill Sykes in Oliver Twist, with his thick, black eyebrows and snarling mouth, smashing Nancy to death while his dog, Bullseye, scrabbled at the door.

Dad entered, looking exactly the same as he had at the table. He manoeuvred himself under the top bunk and sat next to me.

"How was it up here?" he asked. His face, the same features as always, had nothing else in it, like he wasn't even human. The belt, one-inch wide, black leather, was in his right hand. He folded it in two, and with his fist round the buckle, smacked his left hand with the other end. Smack. Pause. Smack.

"Horrible." My tongue seemed to have swollen.

"So, how many straps do you deserve?" Smack. Smack. Smack. They sounded like the slow, ominous clap of fake applause.

No more putting it off. "Three?" I squashed my hands together so he wouldn't see what had happened to my nails, all the while praying he hadn't been thinking of six.

"Is that enough?" he said. The belt came to a halt and his left hand grasped my knee. "Three?" A smile flickered across his mouth. I hated him. Hated him so much. Why was he smiling? He was a horrible, vile pig. My throat felt like a twisted wire. No! No crying. He would not, not, not have the pleasure.

"Stand up," he said. He'd made no further comment, so I prepared myself for three.

"Bend over," he said. I did as told, my bottom hanging over the edge of the bed, and he lifted my dress up. I squeezed my eyes shut, every sinew and muscle in my body tensed hard as a washboard. I would not scream. Then I heard him sigh, then the whoosh of the leather through the air, resulting in an almighty crack on my backside. The million volt sting shot through me. A tear that wanted to betray me as a coward dribbled out into the eiderdown. At least he couldn't see it.

I waited for Strap Number Two, my face scrunched in concentration, focusing with all my might not to have a full-on bawl-out. Because now the wait was worse. The next one would be even more excruciating. Groucho barked twice on the landing as if he'd finally woken up to what was going on here. But, still, like Bullseye, he wasn't there to defend me.

Why didn't Dad get it over with? He was taking his time, wanting me to suffer each whack individually. I could stand it no more. Not one second. I'd have to beg him to finish it.

Then, the whoosh of the belt, and silence at the end of it. Nothing. And Dad saying, "Will you ever hit Janek like that again?"

What happened? Had Dad missed my bum? Where had the second strap gone?

I knew the right answer. "No. I promise," I said, the words muffled by the plumpness of the eiderdown.

"Have you learned any lessons?" he went on.

"Yes, Tatuś."

Thankfully, he didn't ask me to elaborate, and it was a good job because I wasn't at all sure, apart from "don't wallop Janek so hard that he bleeds." My backside throbbed like crazy. I peeked out sideways at him. He was threading his belt back through the loops of his trousers.

"This time," he said, "one is enough. Get ready for bed. Stay in your room. No Hollywood musical." And with that, he left.

I slid off the bed, crawled under the lower bunk and pulled out the sponge. Most of the water had dripped out, but it was still cool as I plonked myself down and wriggled from side to side, easing the stinging along the length of the belt-shaped agony on my cheeks.

I spent the remainder of the evening listening to the thrum of stuff going on downstairs, the rumbles of my foodless belly complaining that it never received the earmarked *kotlet*, and reading my *Chalet School* book.

After Iwonka came upstairs and got into her pyjamas and bed, Janek paid us a visit. He stood at the door, staring. I glared back. "What do you want?" I growled.

"Did it hurt?" he asked. His face looked exactly the same as when he'd found a dead bird in the by the rose bushes.

"What do you think?" I bet he'd have been screaming his head off if he'd been the one to get it.

He began, "If you hadn't—"

"What? Tell-tale!"

He saw the sponge I'd forgotten to return to the bathroom.

"Nothing," he said.

I wouldn't speak to him for the rest of my life. Let him stew. One day I'd finally be rid of him.

CHAPTER SEVEN

DAY TWO: AFTERNOON

The phone rings. Iwonka asks who's been this morning and says she'll be over when the heating engineer's finished fixing her boiler. I can't wait for her to come. She finally arrives bearing a small, scruffy wheelchair that she got second-hand from the charity shop, and a device to put under Dad's pillows to make sitting up easier.

"How much?" I ask.

"Bobbins. Twelve quid," she says, while examining the inside of the fridge.

"Let's tell him three."

"He won't believe it. We'll tell him five. I'll get away with that. What's all this cheese for?" I sit at the kitchen table and admit I went overboard.

She says, "Over cheeseboard!"

I wince, half-laugh. "How much was that thingy? I'll pay for it."

"Don't be so daft. Eighteen from the mobility shop. I'll say that's from Oxfam too – six quid. Don't worry – I'll get rid of the box before I give it him." When did she become such an arbiter of what Dad wants to hear? I feel like hugging her. She comes and stands behind me, hooks her arm across my throat and pretends to choke me while she plants a resounding kiss on top of my head. I know she's somewhere in the same unstable, shifting place as me, must be. But she's airy-light by comparison, like a brightly coloured helium balloon. I think it's innocence. I want to catch her balloon ribbons and float back with her, twine the curls of her childhood ponytail through my fingers, make myself feel better.

She sits opposite and shares out the *Telegraph* between us. She reads, I do the sudoku. I'm tempted to riffle through the paper even though I know the finding of a child's remains from almost fifty years ago won't have made the nationals. Mum is watching telly in the sitting room. It's as if we're all in an airport lounge, waiting for something to happen, suitcases packed, killing time.

I have to ask her. "Is there anything you want to know…from Dad?"

"Eh?"

"I don't know how to put it. Any…unfinished business? Before he—"

She laughs. "What? Like where he's buried the Walewski family jewels?"

How can she joke about this? "Don't you ever wonder about anything?" I say.

She folds the paper and leans towards me over the table. "I don't have the foggiest what you're on about. What do you mean? What's wrong with you?"

"Evie, did you ever see *Shoah*?"

"What's that? A film?"

"Kind of."

"Why? Good, is it?"

She's still my baby sister, even in her fifties. If she doesn't know, I won't tell her.

"Never mind. Doesn't matter."

She's staring into me, so I lower my eyes back to the sudoku and pretend to fill in a square using the first number that comes to mind. I'll pay for that later.

She slides her slim hand across the table and stops my pen from moving. A blue plaster covers one of her fingernails. "Annie, he hasn't got long. Whatever you've got…left over, leave it," she says. "Just leave it."

Dad wakes at 2.42. Mum makes lunch suggestions; Dad says he doesn't want soup, nor porridge, nor Gorgonzola. No, he doesn't want any type of cracker. No, he doesn't feel like eating today. I'm grasping at straws. "Crème brûleé?"

His face lights up. "You have crème brûleé?"

A brownie point. "I have!"

Iwonka offers to feed him and he tells her to stop being a clucking chicken; he's perfectly capable of getting a spoon in his mouth. We sit on either side of the bed, Iwonka and me, trying hard to make conversation, both of us ignoring, trying to ignore, how long it takes him to scoop a trembling spoonful and guide it to his lips. After the fourth he puts the spoon down and says, "Music! Let's have some music. Iwonka, bring the CD player, child." When he accepts my offer to feed him the rest, my heart loosens, puffs up like a doughnut.

Iwonka brings old cassette tapes and CDs as well as the CD player. We listen to a compilation. Halina Kunicka sings an upbeat number about a brass band. He used to fancy the pants off her!

Iwonka asks me, "Do you remember the album cover?"

I do. Kunicka was a beauty, perfectly shaped eyebrows, gorgeous long eyelashes, black-brown eyes. Iwonka says to Dad, "She was your favourite, wasn't she?" His eyes are closed, but he raises his eyebrows and inclines his head slightly, a smile playing on his lips, like he's being enigmatic, wants to tease us.

I picture myself rising above and observing what's going on; Iwonka one side of the bed, head bobbing, me the other, tapping, Dad in the middle, the duvet moving from side to side where his feet are. We're all humming. I have X-ray vision; inside his torso, I see cancer cells with little tentacle-like legs jiving with each other.

Next it's Irena Santor. The CD player is on Iwonka's side. Irena sings 'Nobody can give us back these years'. Jeez. Switch it off: I glower at Iwonka. Dad's not bothered; he's still humming. It's me who is in this 'everything's symbolic' mode, not him. And he's apparently pain-free and happy now, so relaxed that I can't bear to spoil it. Or open my Pandora's box, but I have to. And soon.

THEN

The bell rang just as Part One of *The Beverley Hillbillies* finished and the adverts began. Since nobody seemed to be moving – Janek and Iwonka had taken root, sprawled out and merged with the carpet, and no sign of Mum – I went to answer it myself.

"He's back," Gianni said. "Can you bring some food?"

"Shush. Really? Honestly?" My heart leapt then sank as I remembered that I'd painted over the S.

"Dermot told me. Saw him earlier. We'll find out everything when we get there."

"Stay here."

Mum had been preparing *kolacja* earlier – she'd already laid the table without me – so she couldn't have gone far. I found her behind the closed door of the dining room, lounging on the sofa, legs up, with her latest book, *Angelique in Love*. A dog-eared Christmas postcard from Poland, a baby Jesus in a manger surrounded by sheep and cows, served as her bookmark. On the stereo, the Filipinki sang 'Batumi' and Mum was moving her foot in time with the tune. Good, it wouldn't be hard to get something.

In the kitchen, I quickly pocketed an orange, a square of cheddar cheese and a few biscuits. Why was I doing this though? I was half-mad at Stevo, but maybe also half-curious as to why he'd gone and come back. I hurried to the front door and handed the provisions to Gianni who was still waiting there. Groucho dashed through into the porch.

"Hang on," I said, and asked Mum whether I was allowed out.

Since she wasn't what you might call paying close attention she said, "Yes, all right," forgetting it was almost teatime.

Groucho decided to come out too. He followed us out of the gate, keeping closer to Gianni's leg than mine. I hadn't cuddled him much since he'd left me to my fate with Dad.

When we got to Spooky, Stevo was in the den, sitting on the window-seat staring at nothing on the wall.

I felt peculiar. "You're back then?" I shoved the food at him.

"Yeah. Ta."

Gianni said, "Good to see you. You okay?" First, he shook Stevo's hand, like they were grown-ups, then he put his arm round Stevo's shoulder and slapped him on the back. Why was he being nice to him? He'd been a pig to him about the damsons.

Gianni suggested a game of jacks and they sat on the floor to play, Gianni with his feet curled under and Stevo with his legs spread. Stevo scattered the jacks and threw the ball up in the air. I watched them until it was Stevo's turn to pick up three. The metal clinked as he scooped them into his hand. He wasn't remotely concerned that he'd hurt my feelings.

So what! I didn't care. I opened *Woman* magazine and flicked straight to the back for the problem page, doing my best to ignore them ignoring me. The first letter was from a lady who said she didn't like the 'lower side' of married life. Me neither, I thought – I hated it when Mum and Dad argued. Evelyn Home told the lady she should consider her husband's natural needs with more understanding.

Another problem came from a boy who'd never had a girlfriend because he had spots, and what should he do? Evelyn said that a special girl would not be concerned with his spots. She would see the person he was on the *inside*, but that he should wash his face at least three times a day with lemony water.

The last one was from a wife who said her husband was getting very close to her best friend who was very glamorous and looked like a model. The wife was worried he might like her friend more and run away with her. Evelyn Home said she should talk to her friend in 'gentle tones'.

When I'd read all Evelyn's advice, some of which I agreed with, there was nothing to do except stare through the window and wait until they'd finished. The garden had bits of lawn where only moss grew, all soft and lush. The rest of it was disappearing under wild flowers, weeds and brambles. I found nothing much to absorb me, just the same old greens and browns.

"So, how's your mum?" I asked eventually. I nearly added "the one who lies in bed all day", but I resisted the devil on my shoulder, whose one hand was in my mouth pinching and pulling my tongue out.

Stevo kept his eyes on the jacks. The boys were up to six apiece now.

"Same," he said. He wasn't really listening.

My hackles were rising. "Your dad?"

He looked up for that one. "Haven't seen him for ages."

I waited for him to carry on. Why wasn't he paying attention? Very rude, considering I'd brought him something to eat, put myself out, *yet again*. I said, "How long are you staying this time?"

Leaning back on his arm, Stevo shifted position and crossed his feet at the ankles. "Dunno," he said. "I'll see."

Charming. I really wanted to slap him now. "Hmph. Well, if you plan on leaving, tell me so I don't go to so much trouble."

Gianni's face questioned mine. "What's got your goat?"

I couldn't tell him. Time had changed properties – become longer, draggier when Stevo was gone. I'd enjoyed doing naughty things and missed organising who'd get what for him, how it could be accomplished, and the buzz of being like a spy. I even missed the stupid quizzes. As I went through all this in my mind, I realised with a shock that I'd missed Stevo too.

Gianni put the jacks in his pockets, and Stevo got up, ambled to the circles and stood on the blob I'd made. "Who did this?"

I didn't want to own up, but somebody else would tell him anyway. "Me," I said.

He scraped at the paint with his heel. "Ya did, did ya?" and bent down to scratch at it with nails he didn't have. "It won't come off."

"Probably not. It's paint, don't you know?" I'd put loads on. Tons.

Gianni brought one of the jacks back out of his pocket and used it to scour the paint without success. "We need a wallpaper scraper. That'd get it off."

Stevo looked at me. "I'll have to fix it. Won't I?"

"Do what you like," I said. Something told me he'd be off again soon, so what was the point of fixing it or, for that matter, us letting him back into the gang on a part-time basis. Either he was in, or out. And if he was in, he'd better start telling the truth. I knew I was getting muddled again, not knowing what I wanted at all. It was like everything about him, his mum, and his supposedly Polish dad, threw out little, hooky burrs that clung to my thoughts.

*****

When Gianni left for his music lesson, I recognised my opportunity to pick off the burrs. Stevo handed me a twig and one of the knives I'd borrowed from the garage.

"Go on then," he said. "Make a point at the end."

For a while we whittled in silence and then I plucked up the guts to ask him. I wanted to know if anything had happened to him. Dad's thrashing hadn't turned out half as bad as I'd expected, but I had enough imagination to know things could have been a lot worse.

"So. Why've you come back then? I mean, really?"

"Ya know how it is."

"I don't. That's why I'm asking. Did anything happen?"

He dislodged a ragged piece of bark, pulled a long sliver away with his teeth and spat it out.

"Uncle Tony's staying," he said, jaw sliding from side to side as if he were considering whether to bite off a chunk from inside his cheek. I knew this wasn't true because he'd said he had no family. No aunties – therefore, how could he have uncles? His explanation was inadequate. I was certain that English people, and especially people from Eccles, wouldn't have the random add-ons and spares we had in Polska Land. After all, Dermot didn't call Mrs. Brennan 'Auntie' and she lived two doors down from him. But maybe that was because Dermot was Irish.

"Who's Uncle Tony? Your mum's brother?" I asked.

"Nope."

"Your dad's brother?"

"Nope." That left me no wiser. I wanted to say, "Who the flipping heck is he then?", but I didn't. "Are you going to be here all the time he's staying?"

"Dunno. What's yer problem?"

I took deep breaths to stop myself from calling him a liar. I wanted to be friends. "I haven't got one," I said. "It's just that…"

"What?"

The itch was still itching, the devil still poking and I couldn't seem to let it drop. "Don't you like him. At all?"

"Bloody hell!" He hurled the knife and twig across the room. "Shurrup! I don't like any of them. All right? Happy now? Why don't ya clear off? Go on. Go back to yer Polish crowd and leave me alone." He had his back to me now.

"Fine. I will!" I was mad as a wasp in a bottle, both with him and myself. Me for phrasing the questions clumsily, him for being evasive, angry for nothing. Lying might be okay to your family, but as far as I was concerned a major crime in the gang. But what did that mean 'any of them'?

"Have a good time on your own!" I flounced out, ran all the way down Whalley Road, and by the time I reached Upper Chorlton Road, I realised I'd been an idiot. Now what was I going to do? I loved being at Spooky with the gang.

*****

The next day I hung about, sitting on Ossie's wall, waiting for something or someone to happen because I couldn't go back to Old Spooky on my own in case Stevo flew off the handle again. But when Manuela asked me to go with her, I swallowed my pride instantly. Unable to come yesterday, she'd got a couple of sandwiches for him, two candles and some matches. I didn't tell her much about the day before, just in case he'd scarpered again and someone blamed it on me.

The den was transformed when we got there. Stevo had painted over all the letters in the circle, between the letters too, creating one broad outline. The letters of our names were now made up of sticks, twigs and bits of rubbish he'd found in the garden. I guess the paint ran out. On mine and Manuela's places he'd even arranged a few wilting wild flowers. Not very

71

efficient or artistic, but he'd done his best. I understood the apology and accepted it. So much so that I immediately left Manuela to play with Stevo while I went back home to get the Morse Code book I'd wanted to give him before he disappeared off the face of the earth. I also went via Granny's garage from where – since I'd never reinserted the loop of the padlock – I nicked another rusting can of paint. White this time.

Stevo appeared pleased when I got back and handed the book and the paint to him. Yesterday seemed forgotten.

He opened the tin with the screwdriver. But I wasn't going to help him any more – he could paint the letters in on his own.

He began carefully fashioning Manuela's M.

I asked, "That means you're staying? Or messing about?"

Manuela lay on her tummy, propped by her elbows, supervising him. "Aw, don't be horrible, Ania," she said. "Look – he's doing it proper nice."

"What? I'll make it look good," Stevo said. They'd both misunderstood me.

"No. I mean are you going to be in the gang for always?" I asked.

He carried on with the right downward stroke of the M, going over it a second time to get the edges straight. Manuela beamed at him and started fiddling with her plait, pretending the tip was a paintbrush and doodling hearts with it on her hand.

"Got to go home sometimes. What d'ya think it's like being here all the time?"

I hadn't thought of that. It occurred to me it would be great to stay at Spooky occasionally, when home was a pain, and only when it was warm. And light. I didn't mind being alone, I told myself. But life without Mum's grub and Iwonka would soon pall, probably by the second day. Janek I could do without permanently, of course. When I imagined it further, thought of wandering from room to room on my own, bats smacking into my face or another bloody crow, and hearing scary noises, I knew I'd miss everything and everyone by midnight. Maybe I was asking too much of Stevo. But why would he want to go back to the home he'd described? His mum didn't even cook for him.

With Manuela there to dilute things, I had one more attempt. "When you first went back, was your mum nice to you?"

"Yeah, okay. She went on holiday."

Manuela swished her plait behind her back. "You've missed a bit, Stevo. Here." She pointed to something or other on her M. I wished she'd stop interrupting.

That was weird though. "Without you? Where?" I asked.

"She does that. Comes back." He was listening, but not. For some reason those lines had to be absolutely perfect. He went on. "Uncle Tony—" his voice was high, sarcastic, "—bought me some Blackpool rock—" He shivered and hiccupped as if he was trying to yank his words back in. "Look. I've finished now. I'll do the rest later. Manuela, I'll show ya the wheels in the garden. We can make them into summat. A cart or summat." He didn't ask me to come with, and he hadn't even started on my A.

*****

Janek kicked me sideways in the shin and told me to *shurrup* – he wanted to listen. We were lying on the carpet in front of the telly. The windows were wide open, and the breeze was making the net curtains sway. The clip-clop of a horse sounded from Upper Chorlton Road.

As the horse trotted past our gate, the man yelled, "Any old rag and bone?"

Mum was in the kitchen, so she didn't hear him, but she never wanted his brown or white stones for polishing the front steps anyhow. Our step was black.

"Any old iron?" the rag and bone man shouted again.

Janek grunted, banged his fist on the floor, slid nearer the telly and turned up the volume.

The news showed photos of two people called the Moors Murderers. The man's name was Ian Brady. He didn't look *that* scary – he could have been in a pop group or something. But the woman, Myra Hindley, was definitely evil with her beaky nose, bouffant, dyed-blond hair, and thick black eyebrows. When the newscaster said the judge had sentenced the murderers to life imprisonment, pictures of Lesley Ann Downey, who was the same age as me, and a boy called John Kilbride, who looked a bit like Dermot except chubbier, appeared on the screen. They both looked so happy in them.

"Now we don't have to be scared," Janek said, sighing as he rolled over to stand.

I wasn't scared anyway. Horrible things like that didn't happen in Old Trafford, Whalley Range or to Polish people. For a moment I worried a little about Stevo being all alone at Spooky. But those murderers had been locked up for ages already and would stay in prison forever now, so Stevo was safe.

That night I dreamed of running round in a maze, hiding from an invisible monster who was growling into my ear. I turned to shout, saw her – Myra Hindley – and woke with a jolt. Iwonka's gentle snores and snuffles kept me company while I tried to picture something nicer.

As I dozed off, there was a banging then Dad's bellow in Polish, "Wanda! Sweetheart! Open up. We're home. Get a move on – we're soaked." The sound of male voices, bantering, complaining, laughing, hovered by the front door, ready to spill into the house in the usual after-midnight fashion.

Mum swore a growled *Cholera!*, bumped around in her bedroom and plodded downstairs. After a moment, I heard them come in and leapt out of bed to see who it was. The upstairs was in darkness as I flopped over the banister, wishing I'd stopped to put on my slippers and dressing gown. The men shook out their dripping coats, hooked them on the coat rack on the wall and went to the breakfast room. Mr. Franek, Mr. Waldek, Mr. Edzio and Mr. Jurek who always came back to our house after Kombo's.

Dad said that sandwiches wouldn't come amiss. Then, "We need another small bottle of vodka to keep us going, don't we, boys? What do you say?" I stretched my neck further trying to earwig what they were chatting about, maybe some good gossip, but Mr. Franek droned on about poker, ten pounds, and Dad being a fool to bluff.

Mr. Jurek said, "See. Don't play so clever next time. You certainly got it in the arse from Kardasz, I'll say that."

Who? Had I heard right? I'd never come across that surname before I met Stevo. Could it be the same man? Had Dad played cards with Stevo's father? Surely not. Who could I ask? And how could I ask it?

Dad replied, "What's ten pounds? Never mind that. Boys! Here's a joke for you. From one of my customers. Where are those sandwiches?" I hadn't heard Mum's voice since she'd opened the door.

But this was more like it. I dismissed Kardasz and focused on the joke. My toes were now stuck to the lino, like a tongue on an iced Vimto Jubbly, but I was loath to miss anything.

"Go ahead," said Mr. Franek, then, "Na zdrowie." Glasses clinked.

"One moment. I'll be right back." I waited for Dad to do what he was doing, only to discover he was on his way upstairs. I scooted round the other side of the banister balcony, the spindles of which, happily for Janek, Iwonka and me, were boarded up and painted white – good for night-time snooping. I listened to his walk – step, drag, step, drag – as he climbed all fourteen stairs. He left the toilet door ajar while he had a pee.

Just as he pulled the loo chain, Janek, sleepy-eyed and disoriented, came out of his room. Even though I was speaking to him by then, I bared my teeth – he was bound to give me away, like always, but Dad told him to go back to bed, then returned downstairs.

In the breakfast room Dad began his tale. His voice changed into theatrical mode, all intonation and rhythm, intimate.

"A little old Jew walks into a train carriage in Kraków," he said. "It's already full of people and because there's a fishy smell coming from him, not a smell – a terrible, awful stink – a stink like you've never smelled before – a stink from hell – none of the passengers wants to shift down to let him in. But he doesn't give up, the little old Jew, he lifts his hat and says—" Dad adopted his Yiddish accent, the one he used when he talked about a supplier called Mr. Baumzweig. "'Excuse me, excuse me—'"

As I pictured Dad's expression and shoulder shrugs, the ribbon slid off my mangled ponytail and landed halfway down the stairs. I'd have to try and retrieve it later, the creaks would be heard downstairs.

Dad continued, "—and he squeezes between two *górale*, a fat one, a thin one, chomping into a *kiełbasa* apiece."

A *góral* – of course, what else? Jokes with Jews and highlanders were the best.

"So, the train rolls for fifteen minutes, and the little old Jew opens his briefcase and removes a paper package tied with string. The passengers smack their heads back against the seat, so disgusting is the stench. 'Oh my God!' they say, 'Moyshe! Throw that out the window or we'll throw you out.'"

Ha! A Moyshe this time, not an Itzek, or an Abraham.

"But the little old Jew ignores them. Slowly," Dad said, "he undoes the string and opens the package, and in the package – dozens of raw herring heads! He takes one and sucks, first the inside, then, he curls his tongue round an eye and sucks that out too.

"'Oy! *Cholera*! What are you doing?' the thin *góral* shouts, grimacing. But the little old Jew picks another fish-head up and carries on sucking. Then he says 'You don't know? You never heard? Oy…'"

Dad would be shaking his head and letting his lips droop at the edges. I knew the look, could even do it myself. Why couldn't I be at the table instead of hanging over the banister?

Dad carried on. "The little old Jew says, 'Fish-heads are brain-food. Eat fish-heads, improve business. Good business, more money. More money, any *shiksa* in Kraków.'

"The *górale* exchange glances. Any woman you want? Rich? From fish-heads? Something to consider.

"'How much for those fish-heads?' asks the fat *góral*.

"'Oy,' says the little old Jew. 'My fish-heads aren't for sale. I'm travelling to Warszawa to buy stock and my supplier is a clever man. I need my wits about me otherwise he might swindle me.'"

Mr. Franek chipped in with a "Must have been a cunning *Warszawiak*. *Zdrowie*!" and glasses clinked again.

Dad said, "The *górale* say 'We'll give you good money. More than fair.' The little old Jew displays a herring's eye between his teeth, bites and swallows. 'Well,' he says, heaving a great sigh. 'You look like honest men—' and he strokes his beard. 'These fish-heads,' he finally pronounces, 'I can give you… maybe … ten.'

"'Only ten? How much?'

"'For you, ten *złoty* each.'

"'You crazy, Moyshe?' says the fat *góral*.

"'Whether I'm *meshugener* or not is no concern of yours. You want the fish-heads?'

"They empty their pockets and jointly arrive at ninety-eight *złoty* which they offer to the Jew, who says the Talmud taught him to be reasonable, and since *górale* are decent people, he accepts. He counts ten heads and wishes them, '*Aby gezunt!*'"

I heard Mum say, "Would anybody like some tea? Or coffee?" and the back door opened and closed. I was shivering like washing in the wind now, and the goose bumps on every inch of my body were fat as hailstones.

Dad ignored Mum's question. "Now it's the *górale* eating heads," he said. "All the way to Warszawa they nibble, suck, lick, spit out bones while the Jew looks out the window, twiddling his *peyos*. When the train arrives, the passengers step into the bustling station, and right in front is a stall with a sign – two herrings for ten *złoty*.

"'Two herrings, head, body, tail for ten *złoty*! He charged us ten *złoty* per head,' shouts the fat *góral*. 'Come on. They run after the Jew. 'Hey, Moyshe. You thieving scoundrel!' he says when he catches up. 'Give the money back. On the stall we can buy a whole herring for five *złoty*.'

"And the little old Jew lifts his hat…" Dad paused, "…taps his forehead and says…" Dad paused again, "'…you see… I told you it was brain food! *Mazeltov*! The fish-heads are working already.'"

I squeezed myself into my arms, relishing the punch line. I'd worked out the maths. I loved Dad when he told jokes. He was so good at all the accents and gestures.

I stayed for a while longer, but the loud banter stopped when Mr. Jurek mentioned the Warsaw Uprising, so I skedaddled back to bed, leaving my ribbon on the stairs. Next it would be the entire flipping war and Churchill, Roosevelt or Stalin. And all those angry-old-man voices. When I climbed the ladder to my bunk, Iwonka was snoring watched by the cutesy kittens on the wallpaper she'd chosen with Mum when I wasn't there to veto it. I snuggled under the eiderdown, hands tucked into my armpits, feet up to my bum, and turned to the wall. The moon sent a thin beam from between the clouds, through the slit in the curtains, and over my head onto a lady cat in a mortar board. She was pointing at the outline of India on a globe. To see her better I turned and tugged back the curtain an inch. In the back garden, Groucho's black curly shape patrolled the perimeter, sniffing. He stopped at the swing and cocked his leg. Then I remembered what Mr. Franek had said – Dad had got it in the arse from Kardasz. How did Stevo's dad, if it was him, know Tatuś?

*****

I was still awake when the men left, and the silence that followed made me anxious. Mum said something, but I couldn't distinguish the words. Dad's retort, on the other hand, boomed through the ceiling and up the staircase. "It was a joke! Only a joke. *Cholera jasna!*"

I plunged my head under the pillow, not wanting to hear any more. Whatever was about to happen would make my muscles shrink and make a giant hole in the top of my stomach. The muffled argument finally stopped and I came up for air. Mum's shoes clicked off the lino, padded onto the hall and trudged up the stairs, stopping for a moment on step seven. When she came into my room, I pretended to be asleep. She quietly opened and closed a drawer then left.

My eiderdown wrapped tight around me, still feeling cold, I pictured Stevo in the pink bedspread at Spooky. Maybe this was the real reason he kept running away.

B. E. Andre

CHAPTER EIGHT

DAY TWO: EVENING

We've been listening to all those Polish singers for forty minutes or so when Janek arrives. He and Mum join us. Janek kisses Dad on the top of his wispy head, then blows a raspberry on it. "United won, old man."

Dad shifts a little and then scrunches his face. "In that case..." he pauses "...it must be time to celebrate." He lets out an almighty fart. We all dissolve into fits of giggles. Five adults doubled up over a fart – I'm so glad no-one else can see us.

Dad hasn't finished. "I might have another one. What was the score, child?"

Janek is still chortling, as if he's never heard a fart before. "One nil."

"I won't bother then."

"Quite right. You might follow through." Dad and Janek are laughing again and Mum clicks her tongue, then says, "They might grow up one day." Mum watches, her hands on her lap, and listens as if beatified while Janek gives Dad chapter and verse of the match. I'm sure he's beefing it up, making it more exciting than it was. I don't recognise any of the players' names now.

When they leave, Dad manages to take his medication and has another nap.

In the kitchen I listen to Mum talking on the phone to some family member in Poland who wants an update, when I hear Dad calling feebly. He rings the little crystal bell. As I go into his room I turn the dimmer switch to brighter.

He says, "Sit down. We have to talk." This could be the moment.

I sit.

"You know your instructions?" he says. Which ones? There've been thousands over the years. Elbows off the table, comb your hair, get into third gear, DON'T SLOUCH, turn the central heating down, take it back – it costs

78

too much, swallow the sprouts now, I said NOW.

I don't answer so he continues. "I've told Iwonka everything already. But you're the eldest so you should know too." I squeeze my neck and try to rub out something caught in my larynx but it refuses to budge; he's told Iwonka. I think back to yesterday when she said, "Leave it."

He's examining me. "About after."

"After?"

He's matter-of-fact. "After I'm dead." Oh. That after.

"Tatuś, I know your instructions. You told me when I was seventeen. Remember?"

"But do you remember?"

"Of course I do."

His little grunt accuses me of something and he adds, "Everything else you need is in the drawers in the desk. Ask your mother to come in now. I want to watch some television."

I call Mum, she hurries in, and we move to help him get into the rickety wheelchair and he raises his palm as if to stop the traffic. He tries on his own. The effort is too great, his shoulders sag, and he says, "All right." We heave him into it as gently as possible and Mum drives him to the sitting room where we lift him back out and install him on the Lazyboy.

I think I'll wait until she's washed him and they're both asleep before I open those drawers. What has Dad left for me there? I'm scared of what I'll find.

THEN

Manuela and I were lolling around on the window seat, flicking through magazines, choosing the model we most wanted to be. The boys were outside in the garden trying to fix a plank and two orange boxes to some old pram wheels to make a cart. Then it started raining so they came inside. They bambled about, sat on the floor, stood up, came and irritated us by nabbing the magazines and poking us.

Manuela lost her temper. "Find something of your own to do, you imbeciles!"

Stevo tweaked her ear. "Hark at 'er! Ooh! Lah-di-dah," and winked at Gianni. "Okay, we will. Right, lads. Competition time. Laccy willies."

That didn't sound very nice to me. Grimly fascinated, I wondered if they'd join them up with elastic bands.

"Line up then," said Stevo. "Ruler?"

Dermot, who stood by the fireplace crossing and uncrossing his legs, shuffling from one foot to the other, glanced at us girls just long enough to catch me watching him. He said, "There's one in the kitchen."

Stevo disappeared for a minute and returned triumphant, a stub of a pencil and old exercise book in one hand, ruler aloft in the other. "Here's what ya do…get yer dick out, pull it as far as it'll go and measure it. Then I write it down. And we see who's the winner."

I'd never looked at the boys' willies before – that's to say, I'd seen one – Janek's, but I'd never *examined* it. We'd only stopped taking baths together when I was eight. Dad had said it wasn't right, and Mum had said he was being ridiculous.

So willies could stretch, could they? But could they really get as long as a whole ruler?

Stevo opened the proceedings. When he unbuttoned his trousers, I watched for a moment then had to turn around. It didn't seem a very bad thing, but it might be one of those sins you ought to mention in confession, and I wasn't prepared to keep Granny and Mrs. Wróbelska waiting.

Manuela, who was still facing the boys, stood in front of me. Her lips pulled down at the edges like she was drinking cod-liver oil. Then she inserted her finger into her throat and stuck her tongue out.

Stevo said, "Two and a quarter. Go on, Oz."

"Me? No, Gianni next," Ossie said.

Gianni hesitated. "This wasn't my idea."

I felt a bit of a 'nana, standing with my back to them, so I returned to the window seat while they argued. Then Stevo said, "I get it. Manuela, don't look. Oz, get on with it."

After they all persuaded one another into stretching and being measured, Ossie put on an American accent, like Hughie Green from *Opportunity Knocks*, and said, "Well, there we are, ladies and jennel-men, in first place we have an outright winner. All the way from Manchester in the Yoonited Kingdom – put your hands together for…Dermot O'Donnell!"

Stevo added, "Or, as his friends like to call him – Wormy Dermy."

I nearly wet myself laughing. *Wormy!* Poor Dermot. I felt a bit sorry for him. It was really funny though.

When I turned round, Stevo grinned at me. He was such good fun. I hoped he'd stay forever.

*****

Two weeks later Stevo disappeared again. Although his note said he'd definitely be back, and soon, and not to make changes in the den, I had a bad feeling about that Uncle Tony. Stevo had shivered when he mentioned him. What *exactly* did that mean?

*****

Iwonka drew some lines with wax crayons on the front of the boiler. Then she squashed two bits of red and yellow on top of it and mushed them together. The boiler. The flipping boiling hot boiler. She performed this ground-breaking scientific experiment minutes before Dad was due home.

Granny hastily took over stirring the *bigos*, and Mum, who nearly had a fit, was still scrubbing the daubs, us standing behind her giving cleaning tips, when the front door opened.

In the morning Dad had said he'd pop into Kombo's on the way from work to lend somebody a book. He must have left the factory earlier than usual because us kids knew the instant he walked in that now was the time to scram upstairs. Only we weren't quick enough.

"Interesting scene," he said, taking his jacket off. "What's going on?" His voice was strangled, as if he had a gobstopper in his throat.

For a second Mum stiffened and stopped. "An accident."

"What's *that?*" He pointed at the molten orangey mush.

Mum continued scouring. "It's nothing. I'll soon have it done." She wasn't going to tell on Iwonka. We heaved a collective sigh of relief.

Dad stood behind me and Janek, bent in over our shoulders, inspecting it like he'd inspected those flipping purse frames.

"I see," he said in the gap between our faces, breathing out the Kombo's whiff with his words.

"We'll eat," he said.

I turned round and saw Granny dithering by the cooker. She wiped her hands on the embroidered tea towel from Zakopane and, light as spring air, said, "I brought you *bigos*, Witek. I hope you like it. So, good—" she handed the towel to Mum, "—time for me to go." As she walked past Dad, she smiled – but not for real – you could see her gold tooth when she meant it. Behind his back, when he went to sit down, she wagged her finger at us.

We joined Dad at the table. Iwonka's chair scraped the lino as she pushed it back too far and hit the sideboard, making Mum's collection of Krosno crystal jangle and teeter like a slow-motion disaster. But nothing toppled.

"Sit still!" Dad shouted. Mum, Iwonka, Janek and I were caught in a kind of circuit, all linked, a painful current zapping through us. Janek pulled his sleeve up over his hand and chewed at the already frayed edges. Dad took out his pipe and walnut-coloured leather pouch from the inner pocket of his jacket. His pinked-up left eye closed as he pulled a pinch of tobacco and dropped it into his pipe. Thin brown threads fell on the table. With the top of his thumb, he plugged the wad, but it spilt over the top, so he pulled it all out again.

Speech slurring, he said, "Time we had a talk." Dad and his flipping bloody talks. Now we knew we were in for a horrible time.

He closed his right eye and repeated the pipe process, this time satisfied. Part of me wanted to laugh – he looked like Popeye. But Iwonka, sitting next to him, had tears in her eyes – she knew she was in for it. I felt sorry for her because she wasn't as brave as me yet. She was only little.

When his pipe was stuffed, he lit a match and put it to the bowl, inhaling in quick drags. The last one seemed to go on for ever. The stinky smoke billowed out in individual grey clouds towards the ceiling while we sat motionless, nailed to our seats, watching them disperse.

On the wall opposite me, above Dad's head, next to the straw picture of the *Lazienki* Palace, was a black and white photo, now more black and yellow, really. It showed Mum, Dad and baby Janek. Mum looked so beautiful with her dark, curly hair and pretty smile, Dad was as handsome as James Dean, with a floppy quiff. Now his hair all went backwards, glued in place with Brylcreem. He was so different in that photo, sort of normal, like a happy person. Janek was the same old tub, though shorter and fatter, but in the photograph he was laughing. Now he only ever smiled for Granny.

"A talk," Dad paused, as if he couldn't find the right words, "about your cavalier attitude to your possessions and your mother." With his left hand he took another drag of his pipe and the fingers of his right hand, stained with black dye, beat painfully, slowly, like jungle drums warning of danger, into the table. Mum glared at us.

"Do you understand?" he said to Iwonka, who now looked like she was facing a firing squad.

"When I was your age," he continued, "I had nothing. No parents to look after me. No brothers or sisters. No toys."

Inside I thought, "Yes, yes, we know all this," but I resisted rolling my eyes – I'd only get a clip round the ear – and counted the wrinkles on my knuckles instead. Seven. Then I tried to imagine what my veins would look like with no skin on my hands. Blue or red? A hangnail on my thumb begged to be nibbled off, but I didn't dare.

Whenever Dad went to Kombo's, he'd come home like he'd been infected by deadly war-germs. He'd go there half-normal, almost like English people, and come out with this crippling disease called Memories which he'd then deliberately pass on to make us feel sick, dreading the rest of the evening. Would he start yelling at us, or Mum, or Granny? Maybe it would be Groucho. One of us was about to get it in the neck.

Dad said, "One day, I was looking out of the window. A child's head appeared through the manhole in the road. Then his arms. Two Nazis were smoking, laughing. Then one of them boots the boy in the face," Dad lowered his face to Janek's level. "Like a football."

Janek sniffed and started gnawing his other cuff. Under the table, I slid my foot next to his to give him a reminder with the toe of my shoe then put my hand on his thigh. He stopped chewing and clasped his hands in his lap.

Dad hadn't finished. "The boy begs him, *bitte, nein, bitte*. The Nazi swine kicks him again. The other one's laughing. Haha! Hilarious. A game. Understand?" Dad fixed each of us in turn with his bleary gaze, then turned round to slide open the panel of the sideboard from where he removed a bottle of whiskey.

Of course we understood, poor child, a terrible story, but what exactly did it have to do with us and the boiler?

Dad put down his pipe and with his head bowed spread his hands out on the tablecloth. I heard something like the squeal of a braking car in his voice. "They drag him out. Shoot him. Give me a glass," he said to Mum.

She handed him one immediately, "Maybe the children should have tea later, Witek?"

His fist made the condiments on the table jump. "You had nothing but mangoes and sunshine for five years, you people in Africa, in your refugee camps. What did you see while the rest of us battled on? No. We eat together." While Dad unscrewed the bottle, he continued, "I crawl on my stomach onto the balcony and see the boy lying in the street. It could have been me."

When Dad stopped to look at the light above, all the alcohol from Kombo's seemed to want to drip out of his blood-shot eyes. "I crawl to the railing and looked down. They were hanging from the balcony. I heard nothing. I knew he had told them."

What were hanging? Who were 'they'? I supposed Dad must have meant the black, red and white swastika flags. On films they always hung at the front of buildings. I knew they were a bad thing, of course, but I still drew them in secret because if you filled in the white bits with different coloured patterns, they made a really good design.

Dad filled half the tumbler with whiskey and wrapped both hands around it. He swigged it back in one. "The whole family hanging by their necks. Yankel too." The heavy base of the glass thudded back onto the table. Iwonka whimpered. After Dad pushed the glass away, his bottom teeth pulled his top lip down and, most bizarrely for him since he only ever went to church for weddings and christenings, he muttered a phrase I recognised from Polish mass – "through deed and failure to do". Three times he said the same words from Latin Mass, "mea culpa."

Mum cleared her throat and ladled tomato soup with rice into our bowls. "Witek," she said evenly, "go lie down on the sofa for a while. I'll bring you something when you've had a nap." She'd had the same voice when Iwonka was howling because she'd grazed her knee, and Mum had to put antiseptic on it. I braced myself for another fist in the table.

"You're right." As he left, wobbling slightly, he pulled his left trouser leg higher on his hip so that the cuff wouldn't catch in his shoe.

The rest of us finished both courses, mainly in silence, only daring to whisper amongst ourselves when his snores reached a safe crescendo. Mum said it would be better if we got ready for bed straight away and played quietly upstairs until it was time to go to sleep.

Dad was still on the sofa in the morning. Mum closed the door to the sitting room, and we tiptoed round getting ready for school. In the car, to cheer Iwonka and Janek up, I sang a song from Brownie camp – 'Grizzly Old

Bear Is Fast Asleep'. As I launched into the second verse, I changed the words to Grizzly Old Dad.

"Anka!" Mum shouted. "Don't you dare ever speak about your father like that. It's a miracle we have him. A miracle he survived."

CHAPTER NINE

DAY TWO: NIGHT

Mum and Dad are both asleep now; nothing but that gurgling in Dad's throat. The house is in darkness and I steal into his study. Look in the drawers, he said. I know I won't be able to do it straight away. Need to build up to it, be prepared.

I switch on the Anglepoise. It's aimed at the centre of the A3 blotting pad that Dad's had since I don't know when; it used to be in his office in the factory. The blotting paper is free from ink, just a couple of empty brownish circles, ghosts of tea mugs, that I expect drive him mad. I'm surprised he hasn't inserted a new sheet. I lean back in the chair and gaze at what's on his desk, run my finger along a scratch in the teak; he's tried to hide it with brown wax.

It doesn't feel like generic Dad stuff now; something's changed. Everything's a separate entity. A hand-crank pencil sharpener and a red sellotape dispenser hug the wall; the dispenser's tiny teeth face the front, and it's obvious the last strip was pulled off neatly, no curling edges. On the right of the pad are two flip-over telephone books, the crisp, new one on top of the ancient, dog-eared one. Next to these lie four packs of M&S Christmas cards – he hasn't got round to writing any – and a thick A5 size brown-paper-covered address book. I open it on the first page. I'm wobbling, as if I'm barefoot, like Larysa Latynina on an Olympic beam, unbalanced, hesitating, scared of the dismount.

He hasn't just covered the book any old how, it's a work of precision art. That's Dad for you. The edges of the paper are folded over with a razor crease, the corners glued in at forty-five degree angles. I take the twelve-inch metal ruler from the desk tidy and measure; not a millimetre out of place.

I flick through the address book; I can't see Mum's writing anywhere. Some people turn up several times as they move from place to place, country to country, their previous address eliminated by a thin, ruled, black cross; many only have one address, but they're still crossed out, a discreet AK and RIP or *Śp* in the corner. Warsaw mainly. Nearly all men.

Someone in Poland will be putting *requiescat in pace* by his name soon.

The faux-teak desk-tidy contains the usual: paper clips of all sizes, which I remove, examine then put back again, a metal sharpener, pens, pencils – all of them chiselled to a fine point, and in one compartment two of his old pipes with their mouthpieces downward. I pinch the bowl of the curve-shanked pear-wood one, pull it out and sniff inside to check whether he's still there. Why hasn't he thrown them away? He hasn't smoked for a good twenty years. I close my teeth round the bit and cup the bowl again. I'm going mad.

I open the wooden box. Inside, there are round- and flat-handled scalpels with different shaped blades, bits of thongy leather, scraps of nubuck, a four ounce bottle of Fiebings leather dye, green. I put the pipe in the box, pour some dye into the bottle cap, put that next to the pipe, bend over to try again. I breathe it all in. Where are you, Dad? Who are you, Dad?

As if he knows I'm here, Dad groans. I wait to see if he'll call for me, but he settles quickly. He had an increased dose of drugs. It might take him through the night.

There are no handles on the drawers, just a groove at the base. I pull and see a pile of papers, on top of which are three envelopes. They're addressed to each of us separately – me, Janek and Iwonka. I can't believe it; he's left a paper knife for our convenience. Oh, Dad.

I want to read theirs first, but my clammy hands open mine instead. I'm back somewhere in time, opening a present, wanting it to be something nice, knowing it'll be total crap.

There's not much to the letter at all. It's his list of things we have to do; who to inform about his death, which utilities should be put in Mum's name, share-holdings to be dealt with, odds and sods about bank accounts. Is that all? Where is his confession? I check through the other two drawers; nothing there except writing papers, envelopes, a cassette recorder and a camera.

Dad's calling. "Wanda, quick."

Mum and I collide in the hall in our rush to see what's the matter.

The desperation echoes through the house. "Wanda, please…" As we enter the stench knocks me back, Dad says, "Not you, Ania." I look through the crack of the door hinges. He whimpers. I see only Mum's back as she bends over him, then she moves to the left. He takes her hand and kisses it. "I'm sorry. Forgive me. I don't know how—" He sounds as if he's going to cry.

"It's nothing. Don't worry," she says.

I wait for her to come out because although it's obvious what's required, she may have another way of dealing with it. I knock on the door, Mum opens it slightly and whispers, "Get some kitchen roll, the grey wash bowl and the navy towel on the laundry rack. If the sponge isn't in the bowl, it's under the sink. Oh, and Ania, bring two plastic bags."

I watch through the crack, then don't. It's horrible. It's like I'm fourteen and I've walked in on them having sex. I shouldn't be here. How's it even biologically possible? He's eaten nothing in the past couple of days, so where's it come from? He's curled up foetus-like and Mum is wiping his backside. It's runny, messy shit. Cancer shit. Shit that's seeped through his pyjamas and onto the sheets. Into our life. I want to help her, but he wouldn't let me. There's no point in offering.

"Sorry," he repeats in a powder-thin voice I've never heard before.

She replies, "You're my husband." The granny-person who used to be my Mum pulls the brushed-cotton sheet from under her husband while he tries to lift himself and roll. Two skinny little people. While I – healthy and sturdy now – stand outside doing nothing. There's a plastic undersheet; this must have happened before.

Mum uses five anti-bacterial wipes to wash her hands, then sits at the side of the bed in that heave-inducing stink, and slowly runs her hand from his temple down his cheek, letting her palm rest on his jaw. Delicate as butterfly on a lavender plant.

Dad's things are askew in the study so I return to put them in their rightful place. Mum calls me back and I hear him say, "Don't let her do it, Wanda. She's not strong enough."

"She's fine now. Don't worry," she says.

I tap on the door and Mum hands me the plastic bags.

"Shall I change the duvet cover?" I ask.

"Not now. It's not dirty. Put these in the utility room, child. I'll deal with them." Child, *dziecko*, that's Dad's word, not hers. I realise what Dad means; not strong enough *mentally* to witness my future. That's why I'm not allowed in his room. Protection.

THEN

From the avenue Dermot called, "Stevo's back!"

I nearly fell off the top of the swing. I grabbed the sides of the frame and did a swift backwards flip. Pulling my skirt out of my knickers, I dashed round the back of Ossie's garage. Stevo was back!

"Good news, i'nt it?" Dermot said, beaming.

Yes, it most certainly was. As we tramped down the road, though, I wondered if he'd returned just because he'd fancied it or whether something nasty had happened at his house. Had that Uncle Tony been all right? Would Stevo be covered in bruises again?

He wasn't, or not that I could see. This time he'd brought two things with him – a brand new bike and a transistor. When I saw them, I thought he must have been stealing. The radio was his mum's I thought, but where would he have got a Raleigh from? I couldn't help being a little disappointed in Stevo. Somebody just like me had probably got this bike for their birthday and was now crying their eyes out because a thief had nabbed it.

Dermot hadn't worked it out and didn't seem bothered where the bike came from. He asked if he could have a go, and when Stevo said yes, rode it round and round the den being a right pain in the bum. Finally, when I'd had enough, I asked him to stop or take it outside.

"Can I?" Dermot asked Stevo.

"Round the back. Wormy – I'll kill ya if ya break it," he said.

Stevo switched on the transistor which crackled then found the the the Beatles singing 'Michelle'. I sang along with them in French. "Sun lay monkey von tray be en onsom, tray be en onsom." When I realised that the next English words were going to be – I love you – I quickly asked him how he'd come by a brand spanking new Raleigh. He didn't reply at first, so I pressed him. "Come on, own up. Where did you get it from?"

"Ya think I nicked it, don't ya?" He thrust his chin out with his nose in the air as though he had something to be proud of. "Well, I never."

"If you say so… Okay then. Go on, tell me."

"It was a present from…" he paused, "me Uncle Harry, if ya must know." I'd already heard about an Uncle Tony for whom there'd been no plausible explanation, since he was related to precisely nobody. Now there was an Uncle Harry too.

"Was it your birthday or something?"

"For nowt. Said I deserved it. Coz it'd be good for me to get outta the house. Said I could ride it as long as I wanted."

There was something about this I didn't understand. Was he going to go back now? Had his uncle just given him the bike that morning and he'd come straight here? Why was my brain so muddled? I half-believed him about the bike and yet I knew he was lying. But about what?

"Have ya got a bike?" he asked. We never came to Spooky on our bicycles. Dermot was the only one who didn't have a bike of his own. His had been handed down through his sisters and maybe a couple of cousins beforehand, and it didn't have a cross-bar like boys' bikes. He wasn't fussed.

"Yes," I replied.

"I'm gonna be here for a while now," Stevo said. "We could ride up to Alex Park tomorrow if ya want."

Tomorrow, Dermot, Gianni and I had to go on the Whit walks. Dermot, I knew, was looking forward to it as much as having his teeth drilled. He'd have to embarrass himself yet again in a 'girly skirt' as Ossie called it, and 'Irish kilt' as Dermot called it. Dermot said Mrs. Delaney at Irish Dancing insisted, so he had no choice. Anyway, a trip to Alexandra Park wasn't on the cards.

When Dermot brought the bike back in and laid it on the floor, Stevo sat next to it, twirling the spokes and making the front wheel go round, until he put his thumb against the tyre and stopped it. Then he turned it again. And stopped it. Even though we were in the den with him, he seemed sort of lonely. Dermot and I watched.

Eventually Stevo said, "I dunno why I said that. About me bike." He looked worried, almost shifty. I knew it. He'd stolen it, the dirty liar. He put one palm on top of the other, fingers facing the opposite wrist, and rubbed the balls of his hands back and forth. "It wasn't me Uncle Harry," he said.

"Who's Uncle Harry?" Dermot asked.

"Never mind," Stevo said. He stopped the rubbing, clasped his hands and, looking at me, said, "It was me dad."

"Your dad bought you the bike?"

He now sounded as if he might be telling the truth.

"Your dad?" I asked again. Why would somebody who hit their child with a poker buy them a bike? It didn't make sense.

"Yeah. For me birthday. He came round week before last."

"Oh, happy birthday. D'you get anything else?" Dermot said.

I stopped Dermot from further questions. "Came round? How do you mean?"

Stevo had already forgotten half of what he'd told us. 'Came round' implied his dad didn't live there, like his house was up the road or round the corner. But Stevo had said his dad lived with them and went away for work, I was sure of it.

Dermot, who ought to have been as curious as I was about Stevo's dad, stood abruptly. He said his mum would wallop him if he wasn't back in time to kneel in front of the kitchen chairs for Hail Mary.

Stevo said, "What d'ya mean – kneel in front of chairs? What for? Ya mean to pray or summat?"

Dermot coloured up into his freckles. "It's Irish, i'nt it? Everyone does it. All of May and October."

"It's not Irish, it's Catholic," I told him. Granny seemed to do nothing but pray in May. She used a huge safety pin to attach her rosary beads to the inside of her apron pocket so it wouldn't fall out when she white-washed the garden walls. She looked as if she was talking to herself the entire month, like a loony person. Except she didn't kneel in front of a kitchen chair. That *was* a weird Irish thing.

"Yer nuts, Wormy," said Stevo. "All of ya."

We'd moved on so far from the bike that I didn't know how to bring the conversation round again. I would, would, would get to the bottom of this one day.

*****

Iwonka must have fidgeted all night. She'd dislodged her rollers, so one side of her hair was bouncy, the other stringy and flat. Mine didn't look much better when I pulled out the obnoxious spiky pink curlers. Mum said it didn't matter. She took the long bits next to my ears, tied them up in an elastic band, then made a Swiss roll on top of my head. I looked a complete twit. I begged her to take it out, but she said she did not intend to spend all day dealing with me and my complaints.

When she got all our national costumes out, we discovered my velvet *Krakowski* waistcoat no longer fitted and half its sequins were dangling by the threads. Janek's hat had also shrunk, so Mum attached it with my hair grips, which served him right. Iwonka's headdress was crumpled and all the flowers in it looked like Groucho had been at them. We sat on the sofa and sulked.

*****

At the church, just about everyone from Polska school was there. We lined up according to our regional costumes, and the teachers put us into groups round the older girls holding the ribboned cushions. Would I still have to flipping do this when I was sixteen? Even if my legs were that fat?

We spread out from the cushion – Iwonka holding the ribbon next to mine so I could look after her if she got tired – and started the procession past the onlookers on Moss Lane. There were hundreds of people on the pavements when we reached the junction with Oxford Road. The Italian contingent passed with a brass band coming up after them. I expected to see Gianni somewhere, but there were just too many people to make him out. Dermot, I knew, would be coming into town from another direction with everyone from St. Alphonsus.

The brass band stopped, let us in, and, as we turned left onto Oxford Road I saw him – Stevo – right at the front of the crowd, leaning on his bike.

I remembered what Mum had done to my hair and quickly turned my face and my stupid Swiss roll in the other direction, praying he hadn't spotted me. What was he doing here, so far from home?

*****

I was thwacking a tennis ball against the wall by the kitchen window when Granny stopped at our gate to tell me off. I couldn't see the problem. Mr. and Mrs. Nasmith from Ghana had gone out, so there was nobody to complain about the ricochets against the side of their house. I changed the subject. "Shopping, Babcia?"

"Only Brooks's Bar for potatoes. Do you want to come?"

I thought about it for a second – after all, she might buy me something – then said no. With her out I could get some provisions for Stevo.

When she'd gone, I went back indoors, took the one thing worth having at our house – a packet of custard creams – grabbed my satchel and nipped out via Ossie's. I stood behind the mass of raspberry bushes that separated Number 76's back garden from Granny and Grandad's early crops and

90

watched Grandad through the shed window. He was absorbed, fiddling with a plug, peering inside, jabbing it with an awl. He'd be at it for ages, so I grabbed my chance and sneaked in the back door.

The kitchen, which contained a cooker, a sink, a two-person table, a fridge and a small recessed pantry, yielded a few dead-fly biscuits and a jar of Granny's home-made jam. Apart from that there was nothing but useless stuff like flour, sugar, rice, a few sprouting potatoes and some stale bread. Poor Grandad. She'd make him eat that later because of "in Siberia when we were starving… in Pahlavi when your mama had dysentery… in Bombay when we clung to the sides of the ship to Mombasa… in Kampala at the refugee camp…" And all that usual endless Granny blah-blah. The only other things there were the massive sweet jars crammed with last year's raspberries and three tons of sugar on top that Granny would eventually strain through a muslin cloth into clean vodka or *spiritus* bottles.

Unlike the bedroom, always locked because of Granny's top-secret black handbag, the sitting room contained poorer pickings for thieving lodgers and was generally open. I filched two apples from the fruit bowl and nabbed three packets of Golden Wonder salt and vinegar crisps from the sideboard drawer.

The first section of the sideboard had a shelf at the top and beneath it, the bottles. On the left, alcohol. On the right, soft drinks, but the stock was low, just some orange squash and fizzed-out ginger ale. No Vimto or decanted raspberry juice. I rooted some more and found a bottle of the raspberry behind the Chartreuse, Tia Maria and Benedictine collections. She'd put it in the wrong place. I was done. Time to go.

*****

The gang were assembled when I arrived and, since everybody apart from Dermot had brought something, we had the makings of a small feast. Manuela turned up wearing new earrings – small, dangly roses – that she flaunted to all and sundry.

"Sophisticated, aren't they?" she said, flipping them with her thumb in front of Stevo's face.

He pulled his chin back out of the way. "They're all right."

Manuela tossed her plait over her shoulder, and sniffed. "Is that all?"

"Ya look nice, like a model," he said.

What was she on about? Since when were boys interested in earrings? Why didn't she ask me instead?

I opened the bottle of raspberry juice and took a swig. It wasn't the same as usual. At first I thought it might be off, like the sprouting spuds, but the taste improved.

"Here, try this." I passed it to Stevo.

He took a mouthful and squirmed, flushing the thick, sweet liquid round his mouth. After he gulped it back, he screwed up his eyes and smiled. "Not bad after it goes down."

Gianni had a sip. "This is alcohol."

I said, "It's raspberry juice. From Granny's."

Ossie was next. "It *is* alcohol."

"Can't be." I didn't believe them. How had Granny made it into alcohol? I knew for a fact that alcohol was vile because Janek and I had tried Dad's whiskey once, sort of sour and tongue-burning, nothing like this juice which, apart from the first swig, was *delizioso*.

We all drank it apart from Manuela who baulked at the smell. Instead she set about the custard creams, nibbling away the top layer, then scraping off the filling with her teeth, like she always did.

The Monopoly board was set up in the middle of the circle, and in between munching our way through crisps, dead-fly biscuits and cake, we passed the bottle round until it was almost empty. The flavour just got better and better. And the more I drank, the more irritated I became with Manuela's endless gnawing at the biscuits, and fiddling with her earrings every time she spoke to Stevo. Nor was my mood improved by the fact I'd only bought the Old Kent Road and Whitechapel Road and seemed to spend most of the time in jail, not even collecting the rents. At least it was Gianni not Manuela who won.

When I stood up, my head span and I began to gag.

Dermot yelled, "Oh no—"

Manuela pulled her legs in. "Get out of the way! Get over there."

But I was bent over double, unable to move. After three heaving retches the puke gushed out of me, splattering over the board. Everyone jumped back, screeching and yukking, like they'd never seen someone be sick before. I tried to hold the rest in, but my stomach felt like a burbling geyser. I spewed again and slumped back down on the floor. They stayed as far away from me as possible, all but Stevo, who put his arm around me.

"Ania? Finished?" he asked. I thought I was going to die, not just from being ill, but also the shame. Why did it have to be him of all people who came to my rescue?

Ossie moved forward, pinching his nose. With his other hand, he made a circle of his finger and thumb and put it to his eye, like he was Mr. Isaac Newton or Einstein or someone. He began to list the former contents of my stomach. "Hmm. Cake, chocolate, carrots—"

Stevo told him to shut up and gave my shoulder a gentle squeeze. "Ya'll be okay. Sit there for the mo." Then, with his fingers barely skimming the edges, he folded the board and put it and everything on it – the metal tokens, the money, the Community Chest and Chance cards, the title deeds and all my slimy, stinky, mainly maroon vomit into the paper carrier bag Gianni had brought his food in. Then he scraped up the remaining dribbles with a couple of magazine pages and deposited those into the bag as well. Finally, he flung the whole soggy mess out of the window. Nobody uttered a word while he worked.

I wanted to go home and Stevo offered to walk me back to the end of the secret passage. But Ossie, who'd been useless so far, insisted on taking me instead. He said Stevo had done his bit.

Once we were out of the house, Ossie said, "You okay now?"

"My head's going round."

"I told you it was alcohol. Just like you not to listen."

We walked on. After a while, I said, "Nice of Stevo to clear up, though, wasn't it?"

He shrugged. "If you say so."

*****

When I got back home, Mum didn't notice I was looking a bit green because she was reading *Angelique in Revolt*.

I mumbled, "I'm going upstairs," and managed to sneak past without her looking at me. I drank a gallon of water in the bathroom and washed my hands and face. Then I curled up on my bunk, head still aching, praying for it to end. After about two hours, when the worst of it had stopped, Mum called me downstairs. I had to haul myself to the kitchen.

She was making up one of the regular parcels to send to Polska. The kitchen table was littered with bags of tea and sugar, jars of Nescafe, a stack of folded crimplenes – navy, black and maroon – and boxes and bottles of assorted medicines. She said, "I had some biscuits in that cupboard. Where are they?"

Since when did people in Polska need custard creams? It wasn't worth lying, so I admitted I'd eaten them all, which was why I was feeling a bit sick and needed to lie down. Mum just tsked, shook her head and continued crossing out items on her list.

"Why do you always have to do this?" I asked.

"They don't have these things," she said simply.

"Tea? They don't have *tea*? Or *sugar*?" Was there a famine or something? Polska sounded more primitive than Africa. And the stack of fabrics suggested they didn't have any proper clothes either. Or shops. I imagined a country where people all looked grey, miserable, and thin. If Dad ever made us go there – God forbid – what would we eat? Suppose they had nothing but Christmas carp? I'd starve.

The picture of carp made me want to retch again. "Who's this all for?"

"Your Babcia and Dziadzio, and Tatuś's brothers and their families. And the medicines…" She paused and lifted her shoulders a fraction, "for whoever needs them."

"Is it really horrible there?"

Mum made no reply at first, then said, "Ania, Ania, Ania. So many questions. It's communism. Be glad you live here." My stomach hadn't stopped churning and I thought Mum might suddenly turn into Granny or (worse still) Dad and start with "During the war" and that horrible balcony story, so I excused myself and went back upstairs to lie on my bed and wait for the nausea to pass. As I shifted around trying to find a comfortable position, I replayed what had happened at Spooky and went all hot thinking about how Stevo had looked after me. He'd been kind. Really kind. Why, oh, why couldn't I think of a way to persuade Mum into the earrings?

*****

Two days later, Ossie rapped the coded knock on the wall between my bedroom and his. As we leaned out of our windows, he suggested a trip to Old Spooky in the middle of the night. I felt so disgraced by the puking, such a wimp, that I wanted to improve Stevo's opinion of me. So I agreed.

That evening, soup of the day was gherkin, and the main course consisted of *kotlety*, creamed beetroot and potatoes with dill. None of it required major chewing and creamed beetroot wasn't much of a vegetable, nor was it green, so that was okay, and neither Iwonka, Janek nor I moaned about it. As a reward for good behaviour, Mum said we'd be English today and have a third course – tinned fruit cocktail and evaporated Carnation milk. We scoffed two cans between us, relishing every mouthful, especially the neon-pink cherries. Wouldn't it be great to be English all the time?

At bedtime, I took myself off without having to be reminded or nagged. But first I had a quick root in the kitchen. The result of that latest parcel being dispatched to Warsaw was that there was more or less nothing left to pilfer. All I could muster were two part-shrivelled apples. I also decided to borrow the carriage clock from the dining room. Iwonka was already out for the count when I climbed on the top bunk, fully clothed, and snuggled under the eiderdown with my torch and *Chalet School* book. I hid the clock under my pillow. Now I just had to wait. Mum and Dad's footsteps eventually sounded on the stairs. I heard movements in the bathroom, then their bedroom, and the click of their door shutting. Good.

The clock said 11.30. As I waited and waited, the butterflies in my stomach changed into scrabbling ants. Why had I accepted such a stupid dare? Ossie, I knew, wouldn't be scared at all – he was the king of daft capers, like when he shinned to the top of the pear tree and got stuck until Mr. MacDonald borrowed Grandad's ladder to rescue him.

In my *Chalet School* book, Jo was trapped in a blizzard, bravely leading the younger girls to shelter. Why couldn't I be more like her? And hadn't Dad said he'd wandered round Warsaw in the night, drawing maps, when he was a scout in the Grey Ranks? I had to shape up.

At 12.30 exactly a rap on the pane told me Ossie was ready. I climbed down from the bunk and leaned out the window, hoping he'd tell me he'd changed his mind. No such luck. He tapped me with the stick and whispered,

"Five minutes. At the tree. Easier by the back."

There were snores coming from Mum and Dad's room. A glow came through the window in the upstairs hall from the lamppost outside. That was all the light I had to guide me as I felt along the banister and, tip-toeing on the outer edge of the stairs, made my way down, carrying my wrinkly-apple-filled shoes.

When Groucho barked as I reached out to open the door, I almost leapt out of my skin. I waited for a few moments to see if he'd woken up Mum or Dad. Nothing. I unlocked the door, gripped the handle, turned it slowly. Groucho moved to make a break for it. I shoved him back with my foot and closed the door. On the step I put my shoes on. The moon and night were clear, yet I couldn't see Ossie by the tree. Where was he? Had he been kidding me? Had I gone to all this trouble for nothing? The ghost-like 'woo-woo' from behind the tree startled me. I went over to him. "Pack it in," I hissed.

"Scared already?" He winked and prodded me in the stomach. "Let's go. I dare ya t'step over dis line," he said in Bugs Bunny's voice.

We went round the back of his garage and into Knutsford Avenue. No lights shone in the houses and the only sign of life was the Barking sisters' tabby cat, which skipped onto the ground from Granny's gate post then hopped onto Mr. MacDonald's car bonnet. No sound, either, apart from the patter of our own shoes as we darted across Upper Chorlton Road. A few cars were parked next to the pavement. Was somebody hiding behind one? My eyes darted everywhere, heart hammering.

At the secret passage to Spooky, Ossie turned round, peering out to check nobody had seen us. There was no moonlight down here – the Territorial Army wall was as overgrown with trees and bushes as the other side – and I couldn't see my hand in front of my face. Ossie clicked on his torch and directed it into the darkness.

"Watch it to your right. Holly." What possessed me to go along with this hare-brained scheme? And I just knew my skirt would be torn on the brambles. How to explain that? Ossie shifted the holly branches to the side. I shot out my arm to protect my face from their backlash, blinked then tripped. Great. Flipping nettles. I gritted my teeth against the pain.

"You all right?" he said. "Thought you'd catch 'em."

I'd never listen to him about anything ever again. Ever. By the time we got out of the undergrowth at the other end, my face, hands and legs were stinging like billy-o. It was one thing getting through there in the daytime and something entirely different by night. All right for him – he'd got long trousers.

We entered Old Spooky by the broken window in the basement, me glaring at Ossie's back as we clambered over the cupboards and made our way up the flights of stairs to get to Stevo's night-time hidey-hole. My face was now burning and itching like I was wearing a horsehair balaclava.

We couldn't tell if Stevo was there or not. His bedding was piled high. Ossie kicked gingerly at the edges.

"Wake up," he said. Nothing moved under the pink bedspread. "Come on, Stevo, wake up." Something scraped in the corridor and Ossie spun round, the torchlight aimed at the door. Stevo sauntered in, face in the beam.

"Bloody hell! I nearly cacked meself when I heard someone coming up the stairs! I climbed on the roof. What the hell're ya doing?"

I let my breath go and heard the relief in Ossie's voice. "Thought you'd like some visitors," he said.

"Yer bonkers, you are. What time is it? Here – shine the torch in that corner." Stevo followed the beam and found the matches. He struck one and lit a candle that had nearly burnt down to the end. I gave him the apples and Ossie took a KitKat out of his pocket then switched the torch off. We sat on the floor.

"Whose idea was this?" asked Stevo.

Ossie grinned and straightened up.

The candle flickered in the middle of us, spreading a ghoulish glow, making the boys look like something out of *Armchair Theatre*. Stevo shook his head. "I can't believe ya roped Ania in, Oz. How'd he get ya to come?"

"What's that supposed to mean?"

He shrugged. "Manuela wouldn't have…"

Why did he say that? Did he mean, "At least you're not a girly drip like Manuela?" That's what I hoped he meant. It made me go all peculiar inside – sort of mushy.

He leaned towards me and pointed. "What's that on yer nose?"

My bubble burst. As if most of my face wasn't burning already, I felt the rest of it colour, past through my eyebrows, right into my stupid cowlicks. Even my hair follicles were pinging. "Nothing. I'll be okay. I fell over."

A picture of Manuela saying "Sophisticated, aren't they?" popped into my head. I chased it out.

We stayed only long enough to tell him how we got there, to catch up on news and share Ossie's KitKat. I could hardly bear to think of going through those bushes again. But I knew I had to do it because "Manuela wouldn't have…"

*****

Ossie was even more cocky now that we'd done it and were on our way back in the passage. At the road-end of the hollies, brambles and nettles, he spoke at full volume. "You know, I didn't think you'd—"

"Who goes there?" bellowed a male voice from way beyond the Territorial Army wall.

Ossie muttered, "*Psha kreff!*" With his black pupils popping against the whites of his eyes, he slapped one hand on my mouth and pretended to zip his lips with the other.

"Who is that?" came the voice again. "Speak up!"

I tried not to move, breathe, blink or choke on the smell and taste of garlic and tomatoes on Ossie's hand. Finally, he muttered something I didn't catch, and when I didn't react, he pinched me and almost bit into my ear. "Shoes off. Run for it." The man's boots clacked as he marched towards the Spooky-end of the drill ground. Ossie whisper-shouted "Geronimo-oh" and, shoes in hands, we legged it across the road, past his house, through his back gate, up behind his garage where, *in my flipping socks,* I squelched into something slimy and squishy.

"Ossie, shine the torch on my foot," I said. The beam hit the brownish mess. Marvellous. One of Groucho's poos.

"A most un-foyt-unate occurrence," Ossie said, imitating Bugs Bunny again. "You really are in de shit now." He doubled up in glee.

"Very funny. Wetting myself laughing." I bid him goodnight, and once I'd tiptoed across the garden to avoid any other mounds that might be lurking, I removed my socks and hid them under all the other smelly rubbish in the dustbin. This really was the last time I was going to listen to Ossie. Ever.

Groucho was already whining on the other side of the kitchen door, so I quickly got inside to stroke him quiet, then crept back upstairs, this time straddling the stairs with my cold, bare feet to avoid the annoying creaky bits.

Once comfortably back in bed, I thought perhaps the adventure had been worth it after all, especially if it had impressed Stevo. I half-wished I could tell Dad how brave I'd been, how me and Ossie had negotiated that tunnel of darkness and managed to evade the enemy, just like Dad used to do.

CHAPTER TEN

DAY THREE: MORNING

It's 8.20 when Dad says he needs a doctor. I phone the surgery, explain Dad's in a lot of pain and the receptionist informs me Dr. Buckingham will call in the afternoon. I tell her Dad's been seeing Dr. Gupta, and wouldn't it be better if he came round instead since he knows all the background. She says Dr. Gupta's on holiday and won't be back for another week. Fucking brilliant.

I grind Paracetamol and Ibuprofen with the pestle and mortar, unsure what effects the concoction might have; slow-release painkillers are useless. All the other tablets seem to control nothing. I've no idea what I'm doing but it's better than witnessing Dad's agony, listening to his groaning, watching his moist, closed eyes clog at the corners with yoghurt-like sleep-dust. I add water, make a paste, then transfer it to a ramekin and show it to Mum.

We try to lift him to give him a drink; his yelp is as meagre as a kitten's.

He says, "When's he coming?"

What should I tell him? He'll be mad as hell to have somebody new. All the time he was in hospital he complained it was one face after another, never the same one but always asking the same questions. Nurses, consultants – even the porters who rattled his bed over every single bump on the corridors, the lifts, the ambulance. All to get him from one hospital to the next, just so he could have another round of useless tests in whichever department the latest face had sent them to. Why couldn't they have done the obvious tests earlier, the ones that might have given him a chance?

That's why he insisted on coming home, Iwonka told me. "Get me out of here," he'd said. "I can't stand hospitals. I've spent too long in them."

I'd make a crap nurse. I'd better tell him now so he's prepared. "Tatuś, Dr. Gupta's on holiday. Somebody else is coming. He'll be here this afternoon."

Dad breathes an almost imperceptible sigh and says, "Thank you." I feel lost when Mum's and my eyes lock. He's giving up; he's never done that before.

"Medicine," Mum says.

I squeeze his arm a little. "I've mushed the pills and I'll put them on your tongue. Okay?" His eyelids flicker but he doesn't answer. "Tatuś, okay? With a spoon, okay?" He nods. I put the spoon in his mouth, try to smear the paste onto his tongue and he starts gagging. I quickly withdraw it. Shit. Now what? "Tatuś, I'll do it with my finger, okay?" I scoop it onto my finger, open his mouth wider with my other hand and lodge the paste between his lower dental plate and his cheek. Dear God, these bloody dentures. I'll speak to Mum about them, get her to remove them. "Try to keep your head straight. I'll pour some water in, you try to swallow." He nods again, not that you can call it a nod, it's hardly there. The drips trickle towards the paste which absorbs some of them. "Swallow." I realise I've never looked into Dad's mouth before. When did I last look into an adult's mouth? Never. You don't unless you're a doctor, dentist, nurse. I remember my children teething, the smell of Bonjela.

Dad tries, but he's struggling. We do this three more times and he murmurs, "Enough." Mum asks him if he wants anything else, can she bring him anything, does he want her to stay, to go, does he want anybody else to come?

"Sleep."

In the kitchen, I ask her to persuade him to take out the sodding dentures. Mum says she'll try. Why's it become such an issue? I ask. What's the big deal? They must taste of congealing residue, acrid plaque. When did she last clean them properly?

"I clean them every night... after I've done everything else," she replies, the bones under her ears suddenly jutting out in her downy skin.

My teeth fell out once, in a dream. Just before chemo that was. I spat them out one by one until there was nothing left, just gummy-pink helplessness. No blood or discomfort. One minute they were there, next they weren't; and when I explored my mouth, it was like a newborn baby's, no gaps. Weird. I won't mention his dentures again.

It's clear she's upset, so I give her a hug and say, "Let's do your hair, hm? How about a Judi Dench?"

Mum looks horrified. "Oh no, not that short. She's much younger than I am."

"No, she isn't."

"Yes, she is. Of course, she is."

"Mama! She isn't!" Well, not in years anyway; she didn't have to live with Dad.

"Trust me." I find Dad's scissors – the only ones in the house that are ever sharp – and wet her hair. It doesn't take much, just my hands under the tap and a ruffle through the thin, silvery feathers. After I've done the back, I snip round her ears. Old ears, but pretty. Aren't ears and noses supposed to keep growing throughout your life? Mum's must have stopped when she was sixteen. A heart-shaped liver spot the size of a Smartie stains the skin at the end of her eyebrow. She sits in silence, lets me concentrate. I move to the front and tackle her fringe; the plan is to cut slightly on the diagonal, sort of raffish, yet urchinesque, disguising the faint threads of her scars. The snippets fall on her black, stretch-polyester trousers. I realise I haven't seen her wearing a skirt in years, not even for weddings and christenings; this has been her uniform since the nineties. We are face to face as I check her fringe is even, scan every blemish, scar and wrinkle. I see goat's hairs on her chin. I'll do those later. Our eyes lock. Her hand grips my wrist as if for dear life, as if I'm already halfway over the cliff.

"Mama – what's the matter?"

"Thank you," she whispers.

"It's only a haircut…"

"No. I mean – thank you."

My pupils are clamped in place by her gaze. "You're welcome." I kiss her forehead. Silly old bat.

When Iwonka turns up, Dad's still snoozing. She admires my Toni and Guy efforts, twirling Mum round and chucking her under the chin. "You look great!"

Mum self-consciously smooths her fingers down the back of her neck, then wanders to the conservatory and switches on the telly. Iwonka and I are at the kitchen table. Mum sits, then gets up again and does something in the utility room. Goes back to the telly. Five minutes later she's up again doing something in the bathroom. Comes back, sits, gets up again and goes to the garage. Comes back.

In English, Iwonka asks her, "Are you feeling okay?"

Mum shakes her head; it's not a 'no' shake, more like what dogs do when they come out of the sea. In Polish she says, "I'm fine." Then she puts her coat on over her those polyester trousers and polo neck jumper. Psiuńka's looking up at her, wagging her tail so fast she's creating a breeze. Mum says, "I'm going into the garden."

Outside, there's a thin layer of snow on the ground; the sky sags low and heavy, and although the clock shows 12.39, it's like dusk.

Iwonka says to Mum, "If that's what you want." She widens her eyes at me, compresses her lips.

According to Iwonka, Dr. Buckingham is Iranian. Dad's been seen by her before and he doesn't like her much. She speaks with a foreign accent apparently – that's a laugh, coming from Dad – and mumbles. She doesn't look him in the eye either. So there's Dr. Gupta who sounds so posh he probably went to Harrow – unavailable. And Dr. Buckingham who speaks pidgin English – on her way. Great.

We discuss the night's events and when Mum hasn't returned after ten minutes, Iwonka goes to the window. "Come and look."

Mum, wearing her yellow-and-green-spotted gardening gloves, is kneeling by a plant pot, a half-full bag of compost spilling on the flagstones next to her. Psiuńka sits to attention waiting for Mum to do something with the trowel that's parked vertically in the soil. It must be minus two out there. She didn't even put a hat on.

Iwonka sighs. "Oh God, let's get her in."

I watch through the glass as she helps Mum to her feet; she's chattering, smiling, curling Mum's arm round her elbow as she walks her to the back door, patting the polka-dot gloves.

"… so you peel the potatoes, I'll grate them and Ania can do the onions…" Iwonka's saying as they enter through the utility room. She slides the coat off Mum's shoulders, hangs it up, then gives her a warming hug. She hands her the peeler and puts the potatoes in front of her. Iwonka's decided on potato *placki*, just like Granny used to make.

THEN

In the morning I didn't go to the bathroom before I came down for *śniadanie*, so had no idea what I looked like. The minute she saw me, Mum got herself into a lather.

"What on earth—? When did you get that rash? Was it there yesterday?" She ran a finger along the red-raw nettle bumps I'd scratched until I fell asleep and inspected my hands too, first palms up, then palms down. "Lift your pyjama top."

I showed her my tummy where, of course, there was nothing. Then she bent to examine my legs. She patted at my calves.

"Groucho!" she called and, to my surprise, ferreted in his coat. As she parted and re-parted his matted locks, she said, "No. Nothing here…No." Finally, "What did you eat yesterday apart from *kolacja*?"

"Nothing." There was only the KitKat finger at Spooky and that didn't count.

A deep furrow developed between her eyes, and she looked from me to Groucho, to the food cupboard, and back at me again. "Fruit cocktail. All it can be…" Parents say the strangest things so I didn't take it to heart, not immediately. Not until I realised my English-tinned-fruit-cocktail-for-pudding days were over before they'd even begun. Gone for ever. The midnight caper hadn't been such a good idea after all.

*****

Now I knew that if I ever wanted to use the short cut when it was dark, I'd have to persuade Mum to let me have long trousers. My below-the-waist wardrobe had nothing but skirts and an old pair of gingham shorts.

B. E. Andre

She was kneeling in the front garden planting out annuals. I crouched next to her and offered to help, working myself up to the request.

"You'll get dirty, Ania."

"No, I won't. I can do it."

She passed me the trowel, sat back on her haunches and watched me while I dug a hole and inserted the Busy Lizzie, patting it in well, like she did. In fact, exactly like she did. I had to broach the subject soon, get an okay, otherwise she'd be back with her nose in *The Temptation of Angelique* and her bosoms, and I wouldn't get a look in.

"Can I have some trousers?"

"Little girls don't need trousers." She took the trowel off me, jammed it in upright, and dolloped another two handfuls of compost onto my perfectly planted flower.

I said, "Manuela has trousers. Yellow ones."

"EM-manuela is Greek." What kind of a reply was that supposed to be? And why was she using Manuela's full name? We never called her that.

"But, Mama, at *kolonia* all the girls have trousers. Everybody. Except me."

"Do they?" I had her attention – the *kolonia* idea was a stroke of genius.

"Of course. Everybody. It's miles easier to do things in trousers."

"What things?" She was twisting a fork in the soil, and when I tried to help her again, she pushed my hand away. I could hardly tell her that night-time forays would be a great deal more comfortable, or climbing trees, or sliding down the banister in Spooky.

"Rounders," I said. "Running... And look at this, Mama..." I showed her my knees which had gone all knobbly from kneeling on the path. "And I could have short socks, so they won't flap. And the swing..."

"Do you have to hang upside down? Isn't it about time you stopped?"

Stop hanging upside down on the swing? She couldn't possibly be my real mother.

"It's gymnastics, Mama...I could get gold in the Olympics. Like Larysa Latynina?"

She paused, examining my face like I was somebody who'd just plonked down next to her on the number 81 bus. "Ania...I don't think so...I could ask Tatuś about piano lessons. Latynina is Russian. It's different there."

Oh no, not piano lessons, anything but piano lessons. "And?"

She bashed the trowel around the last flower, picked up the flower pots and stood up abruptly. "Ania, do you ever stop? Yes. Fine. I'll get you trousers this weekend."

"From Marks and Spencer's?"

"Yes. If you want."

I knew I could do it! She was striding off to put the tools away, so I ran with her before my chance disappeared. Ever since Stevo had said Manuela looked like a model in those rose earrings, and I'd had my jumbled feeling, I'd

102

been hankering after a pair even more than usual. I knew Manuela had her ears pierced at the jeweller's opposite Marks and Sparks. Maybe Mum had forgotten the last time I'd asked her. It had to be worth a shot. "Mama, can I have my ears pierced?"

Mum sighed and tried to swat me away. "Ania, please, go and find something to do. Be a good girl."

"Please?" I knew not to mention Manuela because Mum would only say "She's Greek" again. Why was everybody else – English, Greek, Italian, Irish, Cypriot – normal except us? And I was sure girls at Polska school wore earrings but no-one came to mind.

Mum stopped in her tracks and looked down at me. "Enough. You can have them done when you leave school."

Not the result I wanted, but with just fourth form left, I could probably wait that long if I absolutely had to. I'd turn up at grammar school looking as if I was *someone*. "So – next year in the summer holidays? That's a promise?" I said, hoping to make her swear on it, sign a contract there and then.

"Next year? What are you talking about? When you leave school. When you're eighteen."

Eighteen? How could she do this to me? Eight years to wait while Manuela went round in her psychedelic dresses and yellow trousers, swishing her plait and her Mary Quant earrings at the boys. It was so unfair.

And Stevo liked earrings.

*****

Stevo stayed for all of half-term and a bit more. As the days wore on, I forgave Manuela her fabulous gear and her groovy mum who bought her all those things, although I still wanted to take a pair of gardening shears to that plait when she swished it at the boys. I even managed to stop asking Stevo about his family – it didn't seem quite so important now.

The best afternoon was when we got our bikes out. In the morning, Ossie challenged everyone to bring some money so we could visit the chip shop on Ayres Road. Neither Dermot nor Stevo would be able to magic any up, so I ran an errand for Granny, another for Grandad. And, when we pooled my wages with what I'd borrowed from Mum's purse, what Manuela borrowed from her Dad's bedroom tray, what Gianni borrowed from the tea caddy labelled GAS, and what Ossie borrowed from I don't know where, we had enough to feed the lot of us.

The sun was warm, the air balmy, and a hint of breeze cooled us as we raced up and down the back alleys of the terraced houses on Powell Street and Carlton Street, bumping along the grids, egging each other to ride no-handed or feet on handlebars. As we circled St. Alphonsus church for the umpteenth time, a fat lady wearing a straw hat and carrying a bird cage containing a budgie, shot out of the presbytery and hollered "Hooligans!" in an Irish accent, then "Dermot O'Donnell! Is that you, you eejit? I'll be speaking to your Mammy, see if I don't. She'll send you to the Brothers, she will." She wagged her finger so hard I thought it might fly off her hand. Dermot hightailed out of there as if the devil himself was riding pillion, and the rest of us pedalled like the clappers and followed him round the corner. Only when we got to the chippy did he put his brakes on. Ossie sent Dermot in to get four portions to share, while we stood outside laughing our heads off at the fat lady's daisy-covered bonnet and wondering why she'd come out with a budgie.

We took the newspaper-wrapped chips to the playground in the park, dropped our bikes, and sat on the base of the roundabout to eat. Manuela had turned up wearing sunglasses, those yellow trousers, and a sleeveless orangey top cut in at the shoulders. She was leaning against the centre post of the roundabout, face lifted to sun, looking rather too glamorous for my liking, not at all sweaty either. I, on the other hand, was in the obnoxious navy crimplene trousers Mum had bought me because they'd be practical. No ironing, she'd said. But even crimplene didn't seem to matter that day.

Then, while he was unwrapping his chips, Stevo announced, "I'm gonna see me mum today. Not sure when I'll be back. Might stay for a while. See how it goes."

My insides seemed to empty.

"Why? Why now?" I asked, and instantly regretted it because my voice had decided to go whiney.

Ossie's eyes were drilling into me. "We not good enough for you, Ania?"

"What? No. Course you are." Of course, they were. They always had been. My gang. Somehow though, ever since Stevo arrived, we'd had so much more fun. While he was around, every day had more purpose. I wanted to ask when Stevo was going to come back, but Ossie was in a strop about it, so I didn't.

Manuela lifted her sun specs from her face till they were perched above her eyebrows and said, "You'll be okay?"

"Yeah, should be all right."

"We'll miss you."

And I realised that was what it was, the jumbled feeling I kept having.

*****

I thought about him non-stop when he was gone and half-hatched a rather splendid plan for his return. I'd get him and Manuela to come on a joint venture to Harrington's. Gianni had to be kept in the dark because he'd try to talk us out of it. So would Dermot probably – he'd never steal from a shop. I told Ossie though and he wanted to come along, but his school was too far away.

Stevo was, by his own account, already a dab hand at stealing from shops, but I'd never done it. It was quite easy at home and Granny's. I'd felt as smart as the Artful Dodger sometimes.

Each night, while Stevo was away, before reading my book, I imagined how we could do it, picturing the layout of the shop, working out the timings and the sequence of events.

At home time, rain or shine, everyone barged into Harrington's through the entrance on the corner. Chattering nineteen to the dozen, nudging and shoving, gripping pennies, thrupenny bits and sixpences, we occupied every inch of the floor space. Most mums stood outside and chatted.

On the left, stored behind glass sliding doors, was a tiered display. The upper shelves contained expensive toys and games – race tracks, train sets, Monopoly and Cluedo, posh Sindy dolls, and common-as-muck Tressies whose hair grew if you pressed their belly button. On the middle shelves were lighters, pipe cleaners, weird pipe tools that opened up like penknives, pipes in all shapes and sizes, and even a Sherlock Homes calabash I'd once fancied buying for Dad for Christmas, except it was too dear.

Directly to the right were the comic stands I made a beeline for on Tuesdays and Thursdays if I'd wheedled sufficient funds from Granny. *Bunty*, *June and Schoolfriend* and *Judy* mainly, but sometimes I stooped to the *Topper* or *Beezer* and pretend I'd bought them for Janek.

Beyond the stands, behind a thick wooden counter, towered the hawk-eyed Mrs. Carol Harrington or, as we called her, Carol the Big Fat Blubber Barrel, usually shortened to Carol the Barrel. Her face didn't spill over as much as the rest of her, and though most of her teeth were even, one of them hung over her bottom lip giving her the look of an angry dog even when she smiled, which wasn't often. I'd heard one of the mums say Mr. Harrington was a sailor and only came back to do his business in Old Trafford when he wasn't doing his business in Newcastle or Valetta, which, according to the *Alpha Book of Facts for Girls*, was the capital of Malta.

The other counter, running the length of the remaining wall, contained the delicious posh chocolates and sweets. One of Carol the Barrel's four gloomy teenage children was usually responsible for that side of the shop.

In between the two long counters stood the ice-cream and lolly freezer, and next to it a little corner stand on four levels with boxes of sherbet fountains, penny chews, black jacks, gobstoppers, mojos, anything for a penny. All at below-waist nicking height.

This, I reckoned, was the best place to start.

I knew I'd end up doing a longer stint at the altar rail, holding up the queue like Mrs. Wróbelska, but I didn't give a hoot. My normal sins were dead boring anyway – I didn't listen to my parents, hit Janek and Iwonka, didn't say my prayers, blah-blah. The priest might, in fact, be grateful for a bit of variety. All in all, a few Hail Marys and an Our Father were worth it, and if I reeled them off in a minute, nobody would suspect I was one of those deviant mortal sinners Granny went on about. And since Mr. Harrington was doing business all over the world, he must be very rich, so we'd merely be redistributing his wealth. Like Robin Hood.

Just in case, once again, I did what the priest told us before confession – thoroughly canvassed my conscience – and, taking all pros and cons into account, it was a smashing idea. I thought of Dad stealing notices the Nazis put up in Warsaw – what might happen to us wouldn't be anywhere near as bad as what could have happened to him, would it?

When Stevo returned, I put my suggestions forward. He was up for it instantly. But other than him, I needed Manuela as an accomplice. Suppose she was a drip about it?

*****

It took me all of dinner time to appeal to Manuela's better nature and persuade her. My guaranteed totally foolproof scheme finally swayed her. She was in.

After I'd got Manuela's promise and gone through the details with her, I spent all afternoon scared stiff and excited at the same time. As agreed, Stevo was already outside the gates at Seymour Park when school ended. When Manuela and I came out of the front entrance, we walked past Stevo and went across to Dad's van to ask Mum if I could go home with Manuela. Iwonka and Janek were already in the back petting Groucho, and Mum said yes – as long as I didn't dawdle – and drove away.

"We're doing it?" Stevo asked, as he joined us on the other side of the road.

"Definitely," I said.

Manuela turned to Stevo. "Don't look at me in there. Coz if anything happens I'll pretend I've never seen you in my life."

*****

The shop was teeming with children, sweltering and edgy, same as us. Since dinner time the classrooms had felt like chicken coops inside tropical greenhouses.

I scanned the comics first, also keeping an eye on Carol the Barrel. We'd decided that if I bought something first, legally, she'd be less likely to watch me. I picked out a *Bunty* and went to the counter, where I paid for it with money Grandad had given me for getting his Woodbines. My fingertips itched as I imagined a cartoon skunk's whiff-bubble behind me with the words "Keep your eyes on this one." I wove between the other children and up behind Manuela, who was standing in the crush in front of the freezer and little counter.

Stevo, meanwhile, edged towards her from the other side.

While the kids at the front were being served, Manuela whipped her hands between them to the lower shelves and passed the goods backwards to me on her right, and Stevo on her left. Foolproof. If anybody noticed anything, she could say she was waiting to pay, and if someone frisked her, she'd have nothing on her.

It worked like a dream. About six times. That is, until a fire engine drove past and half the kids in the shop swarmed to the door to see what the kerfuffle was about. One of the rabble infants knocked into my arm, and I dropped the three sherbet fountains I was about to lodge in my blazer. Stevo groaned.

I glanced at the long counter to check Carol the Barrel's whereabouts. She was there, hands buried in the spare tyres of her lime-green nylon sweater, jaw clenched so tight that her clip-ons were trembling. Glowering. Straight at me and Stevo.

"Oi, you! You with the ponytail!" she screeched, her massive beehive wobbling. "I know what you're up to!"

I nearly peed myself. Pictures zapped through my head, just like on *Z Cars*. A white-wigged lawyer. A jury foreman shouting "Guilty!" A van with black windows. Strangeways. A cell. A warden saying "You have a visitor." Dad breathing in the smoke of his pipe, his fingers rapping out the William Tell song on the table...

I snatched the sherbet fountains and legged it, cramming myself through the kids by the door, totally forgetting Carol the Barrel had seen Stevo too.

"Hang on, wait for me," he called, "I'm comin'." I didn't care if he was coming or not.

Carol the Barrel wasted no time. Thundering after us, she squawked, "Get back. Right now! You hear? I'll give you what for..."

We could still hear her when we bolted into the first alley on the left, onto the junction and sprinted right. We just needed to make it to a wall. Behind it, we'd find sanctuary in one of the backyards of the terraced houses.

As we dashed and darted from one side to the other, my hands were all stupid, useless, wet and shaking, heart exploding in my chest. Stevo frantically tried all the handles of the alley gates. First one – locked. Second one – locked. We were going to get caught. How long would I have to go to prison for? Now I'd never flipping well get my ears pierced.

"That one," Stevo said, "the green one. Quick."

Just when I thought we were done for and we heard a rasping "Don't think I won't find you!" from the junction, I tried the green gate, my lucky colour. Thank you, God! It opened. We bundled in and Stevo shut it behind us.

Her high heels clipped up the cobbles, nearer and nearer. "Where are you, you buggers?"

I wiped the drips of sweat from my chin. I couldn't stop panting. My lungs were going to burst. Stevo put his hand over my mouth to muffle the racket, but it only made me worse. I pushed him away, curled my fingers into a loose fist and took steady breaths through it, trying to keep my mouth in the shape

107

of a whistle. Breathe in. Out. In.

We heard the clunking and clatter of wood on brick, and the tinny sound of latches. She was checking all the gates on the other side. She'd be here any second.

"Stop it," Stevo whispered and squeezed his neck, like a hangman's noose. "Ya'll get us caught." Easy for him to say. In comparison to me, he was a picture of cool. Clearly, he was used to it. Well, that's what he'd said, done it loads of times before. We crouched behind a dustbin that smelt of ancient dog pee, pinched our noses and waited for the inevitable. My knees were now reduced to rice-pudding and I was dying to go to the loo. No sooner did I lean against him to stay upright than I remembered.

Blimey! Manuela!

"I'm not giving up. I know you're here, you little blighters," bellowed Carol the Barrel, still banging on gates. She was getting closer.

I nearly fainted when a black cat skipped on top of the backyard wall and, smug as you please, started meowing in our direction. I glared at it with my fiercest stare and Stevo flicked his finger at it, but the flipping thing refused to budge. The game was up.

Carol the Barrel clomped her way to the other side of our gate, now mumbling "Bloody kids, sodding shop, I could've been a beautician if I hadn't married Cyril…" She puffed and panted a bit. Then, to my ever-lasting relief, her voice grew soft, sweet, purry, "Elvis. Aw, Elvis, treasure. What you doing here, puss? Come here." The cat gave us a look that seemed to say "Eh, small fry" and jumped off the wall. Stevo grinned and gave the thumbs up sign.

Carol the Barrel stood a mere three feet away from us on the other side of the wall. "Aw, chuckie, chuckie. Give Mummy a kiss. Mmm. Mummy's best boy, better than that good-for-nothing, no-good layabout. Mmm. You're not like him, are you, puss? You'll always be my boy, won't you, Elvis?"

Stevo and I both had our hands across our mouths, dying to laugh now. Elvis!

She mmmed a while longer, said "Mummy's Strudel Woodel" a few times, and finally we heard, "Oh, I give up. Sod 'em. Let's go home for a cuppa, eh?" When the clip of her shoes retreated towards the shop, Stevo opened the gate a smidgen to see if the coast was entirely clear.

"She's nearly at the corner – hang on – yeah, she's gone. Better wait a bit. Maybe she's trying to trick us." I couldn't hold out though – I was about to disgrace myself, and I'd never be able to look Stevo in the face again if that happened.

"Turn round," I said.

"What?"

"Turn round or get out and wait for me."

"We've gotta go. What's up?"

108

I was squirming but he wouldn't budge if I didn't tell him. "I need to wee."

"Well, hurry up then." With Stevo now in the alley, I pulled down my navy blue knickers and began to empty my bladder. He said, "Flippin' 'eck! Come on, will ya?"

I'd never weed so much in my life.

We ran to the end of the alley, in the opposite direction to the shop, and came out at the bottom of Reynolds Road. As we crossed King's Road, we examined the contents of our pockets. Not bad, not bad at all.

Stevo put his hand on my shoulder. "Quite a team, eh?"

But the whole team wasn't there. I was now feeling the weight of blame for my not-so-perfect, foolproof plan.

"Do you think they caught Manuela?" I asked.

He put his hands in his pockets and shrugged, as if he didn't care. I tried to feel bad about that.

*****

Stevo sat on the far end of the wall outside the Barking girls' house while I rang Manuela's doorbell. Mrs. Karageorgis came to the porch. She must have been to the hairdresser's because her hair didn't have the usual silver stripe down the middle, and it was back-combed, froo-frooed and lacquered.

"Ania! You come for Manuela? She came house crying. What is matter? You know?"

I said no, and she asked me whether I was sure, and I said yes. She called Manuela down and motioned me to the front room, then she disappeared into the kitchen. I sat on the white, plastic-covered sofa, surrounded by ceiling-high potted plants, twiddling my thumbs and wondering if we'd ever have a posh corner bar like the Karageorgises. It was so pretty. Hundreds of minute mirror tiles and a canopy with coloured bottles hanging upside down on ropes. I knew exactly what Mum would say if I asked if we could have one – "They're Greek."

Three ceramic eyes, like the one Manuela had brought to the den to protect us from evil, stared at me from the wall. They seemed to know what I'd been up to. When Manuela came in and saw me, she looked fine, radiant even. In fact, she was grinning.

"What happened?" I said. "Why were you crying? Did she catch you?"

"No, I just got scared on the way home, like when you wake up in the night and think everybody's dead, and you don't want to go and look, and then you wake up again and they aren't. What about you?"

I told her how we'd avoided capture while she listened, eyes wide and blinking, and occasionally removed her thumb from her mouth to say "Wow!" I even owned up about almost wetting my pants in front of Stevo.

She jumped to her feet. "Hang on. Back in a tic." A few moments later she returned with a bulging, frill-edged, pink dolly bag and handed it to me.

"Have a dekko."

I peered inside.

"After Carol the Barrel ran out after you two, I copped a load more. I've still got some under my pillow."

An excellent day's work, all things considered, and I didn't have a shred of guilt. Only now I'd have to do my comic shopping at the other end of Ayres Road.

Stevo and I went to the back of Ossie's garage, sat on the tyres and redistributed the spoils. Most of it he took back to Spooky, but I kept a few mojos for me and Iwonka.

When I got home, I told Mum I needed a new, more grown-up hairstyle. Carol the Barrel's "Oi you! You with the ponytail!" was still ringing in my ears. To my surprise Mum let me get it cut next day. But with my hair loose around my face, the two cowlicks on either side of my fringe spiralled even more.

Soon after, Mrs. Karageorgis decided Manuela should have her hair cut too. A sharp, trendy bob. She looked better than Sandie Shaw on *Top of the Pops*. Earrings, yellow trousers, groovy hair... Would it *ever* be my turn?

CHAPTER ELEVEN

DAY THREE: AFTERNOON

Dad's awake when the doorbell rings at three-fifteen. He's managed two mouthfuls of porridge and has taken a bite of a TUC cracker with Brie.

Dr. Buckingham seems pleasant, likeable, in her early thirties; she wears a taupe scarf, similar to a hijab, over her head. She doesn't so much mumble as Dad said, she's merely shy, hesitant. Iwonka takes charge, briefs the doctor on the latest. I'm aware of extra odours in the house-blend. Our onions and oil, and something sweet and musky which Dr. Buckingham has brought in with her. I wish we could open the windows, just for while, but it's brass-monkeys outside. Dad greets her as if she's an old friend – or perhaps an old friend's daughter – when she sits beside him, no sign of animosity.

Mum waits in the corridor. Dr. Buckingham and Dad are alone together for ten minutes. She comes out, pushes the door to. Mum calls Iwonka and me.

Dr. Buckingham says, "I think Mr. Walewski is anaemic. He may need a blood transfusion."

"Can you do it here?" Mum asks.

For a second Dr. Buckingham looks at Mum as if she's asked her to build a nuclear reactor on a bread board. Then says, "He has to be in hospital," her voice soothing as balsam.

"Have you told him yet?"

"Not exactly."

"Will you tell him?" Mum's eyes are lowered, darting from one side of the corridor to the other as if cockroaches are scrittering around her feet.

Iwonka puts her hands over her cheeks, spreads her fingers and drags them slowly down to under her chin. "I will." She breathes way into her stomach and sculpts a smile onto her face. I follow her in. She tucks the sheet where it's come away from under the mattress and says, "Tatuś, Dr. Buckingham

111

thinks you need to go back in hospital."

"No." His reply is so swift, robust, that you'd think there's nothing wrong with him.

"If you had a transfusion, you'd feel better."

"No."

So that's that then.

"Ask her back in, child," he says. "Wait. My glasses." I put his specs on for him. After Iwonka explains the situation to her, Dr. Buckingham stands on the right of Dad's bed, her hand resting on his upper arm and says, "Mr. Walewski, you understand what this means…if you don't have a transfusion?"

He rewards her with a faint, rueful laugh. "I been here before." Eyes fixed on Mum's face, "This is my choice."

There's an elephant in the room the size of K2; there's no space left. We can't move. By the time I've played his words several times through my head, English grammar gone to pot, they sound like the script for a Russian meerkat advert. Mum's sniff catches in her throat and becomes a strangled hiccup.

Iwonka is first to regain her composure. "If you are sure," she says to him in English.

"Absolutely certain."

We leave Mum and Dad alone. In the dining room, Dr. Buckingham prescribes something stronger at last, Oramorph, and suggests we get Josie, the Macmillan nurse, and the district nurses back. It's their field from now on.

I know that means soon.

THEN

It was spitting, so rather than play hide-and-seek outdoors in Spooky's jungles, we did it inside. In the den, Gianni started counting to a hundred at the top of his voice, and we scattered over the house. He reached sixty, when something thudded and a scream echoed all the way to the rafters.

Manuela shrieked, "Help! Somebody help!" It sounded as if she was in the room above the kitchen. I ran down from the attic and when I got there she was sobbing and trying to keep her balance. Her foot had gone though the floorboards and her leg was trapped up to the knee. Gianni was patting her on the arm, Ossie stood beside them, unusually pathetic, staring and sniffing, and Dermot seemed to have glued his back to the wall by the door. If Stevo had been there, he wouldn't have been so gormless.

"I can't move," Manuela wailed.

I lay on the floor next to her and squinted down the side of her leg. Blood was seeping from a deep gash through her white socks, and drifts of a mushroomy, soily smell, dank and rotting, wafted around my face.

"I can't get out," she moaned, wincing. "Pull the wood back someone."

Gianni heaved at it, and Manuela did her best to wriggle, but it was impossible.

"Take your shoe off," Ossie said.

"How am I supposed to do that, you idiot?"

Ossie flinched. Silent tears dribbled from the crease by Manuela's nose to the edge of her mouth. She licked them away and bit on her lip.

I squeezed my hand down the side to undo her buckle so she could slide her foot out, but I couldn't reach it either. My fingers came up patterned with blood, red lines around my cuticles. What could we do?

"We need a…the spade," I said.

Dermot still hadn't moved. "We're gonna to dig her out? From floorboards?"

"Don't be so daft. For a lever – to jemmy the floor. Get it, will you?"

He was gone ages. When he returned, Ossie woke up from his semi-catatonic state and took control of the spade. Considering it wasn't big and the handle quite thin, it stood up well to his attempts to prise the boards apart. Another small piece of wood broke off, giving me just enough space to reach her ankle and undo her buckle. Manuela inched her foot out. I pulled out her mangled shoe and put it back on for her while she rolled down her shredded sock and examined her wound. It was about two inches long and still oozing.

When she tried to stand up, she squealed again. "My ankle…I think it's broken."

Ossie bent over to inspect, skimmed it with his thumb, and pronounced it swollen.

She whined, "Get me to my house, please."

Gianni and Ossie lifted her between them. She put her arms around their shoulders, and the boys supported her around the waist and guided her out of there. Dermot, who'd finally unglued himself from the wall, and I followed. I hoped Manuela wouldn't end up with a limp as bad as Dad's.

The rain was still mizzling, the clouds low, when we emerged onto Whalley Road. Manuela was barely hobbling, her face the same colour as the sky. All the pink had drained from her lips. On the way, we invented a story to tell Mrs. Karageorgis. A story with no mention of Spooky. We had to have our facts straight.

By the time we arrived at her door, we were drenched to the skin, hair dripping. Mrs. Karageorgis had a Greek fit when she saw Manuela's leg and deformed ankle, but she thanked us for being good friends and bringing Manuela home. She told us to wait, helped Manuela inside, then came out with a piece of baklava for each of us.

Gianni and Dermot went in their direction, and Ossie and I in ours.

"We'd better stay out of that room," Ossie said. He took his lucky rabbit's foot out of his pocket and gave it a rub. "There's something wrong in there.

113

Like the devil."

I'd sensed it too.

*****

Three more flipping weeks before Polska school finished for the holidays. I lay on my bunk, staring at the ceiling, taunted by the sun's rays coming through the net curtains. Here was a perfectly gorgeous Saturday about to be ruined, squandered on the likes of Bolesław Twistedmouth, Thingy the Elbow, What's-his-name the Tanglefoot. And as with every other week in that school year, I wasn't in the mood for one more second of another King Oojamaflip the Deformed-Something-Else. Especially since everyone else would be having a great time at Spooky, even Manuela – who hadn't broken her leg, just twisted her ankle. I threw my clothes on and took up the issue with Mum over *śniadanie*, wildly hoping against all previous experience that I'd get out of it for once.

"Mama, my English friends have Saturdays off, so why can't we?"

Mum ignored me as she put toast on the table. Janek piped up in his usual style with "Yeah," as if his opinion about anything mattered.

Had she heard me? "Mama?"

"Sit and eat, Ania. There's no time for that now."

I smeared the toast with prune jam, put it to my mouth and then dropped it back on the plate, aware that without renewed effort on my part, I'd end up having to get into the van in thirty minutes. My insides felt baggy, hopeless. How was I going to sit through those lessons yet again and not go going stark, raving mad? It was worse than prison. Strangeways suddenly seemed appealing. Language first, and Geography, Dancing, History. And then, to cap it all, Polish Religion as well. Five days of arithmetic and fun Progress Papers ruined every week by an eternal four-hour Saturday morning. And another eight years before I could leave home. It didn't bear thinking about.

To make matters worse, as soon as Iwonka joined us and Dad shuffled in, he was on at me, same as usual. He'd gone to Kombo's straight from work the night before, so I at least escaped him asking whether I'd finished my homework. Which I hadn't.

"Ania, comb your hair," he said. I'd done it already, but no matter how much I tried to flatten them, get my fringe to stick to my forehead, the cowlicks pinged back in obnoxious spirals. I ran to the bathroom, stayed for a minute, and came back again having done precisely nothing except stare at my face in the mirror.

"What were you complaining about?" Dad asked, examining my forehead as I sat down. I hadn't intended to conduct this particular debate with him. Mum, yes. Him, no. I stifled a gulp and took a tiny bite of toast, hoping he'd drop it.

"You had something to say?" he insisted.

"I don't see why we have to go to Polska school. My English friends have Saturdays off and—" I was in my stride now, "It's not fair you make us slave six days a week. We aren't robots, you know."

Mum was about to put Dad's tea glass on the table, but she stopped half way, as still as a photo. Janek tugged at a thread in his pyjama sleeve, then scratched the tablecloth, and Iwonka found something fascinating on her lap. Dad seemed to be listening, so I continued my roll.

"And if that's not enough, we have to go to church on Sunday too. English children don't have to do that either." Ploughing on, now convinced I was getting through to him, I added, "And besides, it's not as if we'll ever live in Polska, is it, so what's the point?" I folded my arms. I'd finished.

His nostrils flared. "I beg your pardon?" Why was he begging my pardon? Wasn't he paying attention after all? I'd been clear enough.

"I said—"

"I heard!"

I jumped so high in my seat that my knees walloped the underside of the table. Out the corner of my eye, I saw Janek's fist fly to his mouth then back to the table.

Dad spread his hand across his forehead, closed his eyes, and pressed his little finger and thumb into his temples. His pores had disappeared, clogged with grease. "And I don't want to hear you say it ever again!" Then he yanked the cord of his dressing gown, knotting it tight around his waist. "Learn this now, child. You *will* go to Polish school. And you *will* be proud—" Mum put the glass in his hand, "—of your legacy." He took a mouthful of tea, swished it round his mouth and added the lemon slice to the glass.

Iwonka, who hadn't made a sound so far, mumbled, "What's legacy?"

"It's when someone dies and you get something," Janek whispered. How the heck did he know that? It wasn't your usual every day kind of Polish word. Mum eased onto the chair next to Janek. With sharp, small movements, she buttered toast, smeared the jam, cut the toast, passed the slices round, all the while glancing at Dad as he drank the tea. What was going on? She never did any of that usually, just dumped everything on the table for us to sort out ourselves. Janek had taken one bite of his toast and now appeared to be waiting for it to melt in his mouth.

"Witek, do you want Alka Seltzer?" Mum asked.

"Maybe later."

I thought it was over when he stood up. But it wasn't. He leaned forward over me. "Don't you ever forget how your forefathers suffered for you." He wagged his finger in front of my nose.

"One day you'll be grateful they had the courage to make it possible for you to carry on."

Make what possible for me exactly? Doing stuff I didn't want to do? Flipping What's-His-Name Tanglefoot? Carry on where? They needn't have

115

bothered. How was it my fault they suffered? I wasn't even born.

Dad hiccupped, swallowed something and rubbed his stomach. He looked like wallpaper paste. He sat back down again. "Tell them, Wanda."

"Tell them what?"

"Why we…Polska…free…"

Mum hesitated, then she cleared her throat. "They're children. Why do they need to know? Go back to bed for a while. Hm?"

This was not my idea of a pleasant start to the day.

"You think I want to be here?" he continued, looking at me with his Adam's apple bobbing.

Oh God, would it never end? I hoped he wouldn't start remembering dead Jewish people hanging from balconies. Why hadn't I kept my trap shut? Even Polska school was better than this.

"Stray dogs, that's what we are. You too. We take scraps from whoever feeds us." What was his problem? Our house was okay, and the fridge was never empty, if you counted the stuff that sometimes went green and hairy. And Dad had a factory, for goodness sake! How – when – had Janek and Iwonka and me suddenly become stray dogs?

Dad began, "If Churchill…"

Mum broke in. "Witek!" Her tone softer, she said, "Go back to sleep, dear. Churchill can wait."

I also thought he could wait. The mere idea of him – spongy jowls, like a big, blubbery slug with toad's eyes, chomping on his cigar, smirking – was enough to make me queasy too. Whenever he came on telly in *All Our Yesterdays,* Dad huffed and talked to himself about thirty shekels, a girl called Yalta, and Judas – except it wasn't Jesus' Judas, it was another one – and we'd skedaddle upstairs until a better programme came on and Dad had calmed down.

Dad wiped at the white dots of spit-cheese at the corners of his lips. "If it wasn't for Churchill, I'd be a lawyer. Yes, university and the law."

Mum rolled her eyes and sighed. "Witek…"

He was looking at me again. "You know that?"

I shook my head. I didn't even know they had universities in Polska. Weren't there just farms, piles of rubble and kings with stupid names? He must have got it wrong. I pretended I was a statue, so he'd finally shut up.

"Look at these. Look at them." He opened his dye-stained palms in front of my face, as if I'd never seen them before. "This is not my choice."

How had a teeny observation on the injustice of Polska school degenerated into this? A minute of silence followed. None of us so much as blinked.

He said, "I'm going back to bed. Wanda, tea and a fried egg when you get back. I have to go to work."

As he headed for the stairs, I licked at the prune jam and, under my breath, I said, "I hate being Polish."

Dad whipped round and bellowed, "What did you say? Put down that toast! Wanda, take the toast from her. Take the toast from her. In the corner. Kneel!"

Huge mistake. Mum groaned. I scrambled off the chair and was already on my knees, spine rigid, before he was back in the kitchen.

"You," he said, pointing at Janek and Iwonka, "get dressed. And you, Anka, stay there. And don't slouch!" I suppose because it was *śniadanie* Dad forgot the bag of dried peas for under my knees.

As Janek walked past, he mouthed "stupid" at me. I couldn't do anything about it then. I'd clobber him later on the way to school.

*****

In July Stevo returned looking surprisingly clean and shiny. He didn't have any bruises that I could see either.

He decided he'd stay at Spooky for the rest of summer. All he said was, "I'm not goin' back if he's there."

I sympathised. Since the last rant, I'd avoided Dad and kept my head down as much as possible.

Nobody else pressed Stevo to know who the 'he' was and I didn't ask either. It could have been one of his uncles, his dad – anyone. But feeding and keeping Stevo in water and juice would now be a problem. Ossie couldn't help – he was flying to Jamaica with his dad. Nobody believed him though because he'd said that the year before and the one before that. But this year, Ossie said, it was definite because his cousin was running the 100 metres in the Commonwealth Games, and he and his dad were going to support him. So that was Ossie out. Manuela's family were driving to somewhere peculiar called Torky as soon as school ended. And I, of course, had to go to flipping Brownie camp, *kolonia*, which meant more non-stop Polski everything.

Gianni and Dermot were, thank goodness, going nowhere. The trouble was, Dermot could never be relied on to bring anything – not because he didn't want to – there was never any spare food in their house, apart from cabbage and potatoes. While we were mulling it over, I had a brilliant idea. I'd get out of *kolonia*. Simple.

If I could be sick and miss the coach on Saturday, then I was sure Mum, who'd already had her annual M&S navy-knickers-buying frenzy, wouldn't want to drive me there a week late.

This seed was sown on the Sunday before I was due to leave. I faked a stomach ache which continued, when I remembered, when Mum was watching me, until Tuesday. She called the surgery and asked Dr. MacArlon to visit. He arrived an hour later. I got down off my bunk and onto Iwonka's, and lay trying to look like the patients in *Emergency Ward 10*, while he examined my abdomen.

"Does that hurt?" His fingers rummaged below my ribs. "What about

117

that?"

I winced.

He removed a stethoscope from his bag and placed the end of it on my chest. "Breathe in." His eyes looked up at his caterpillar eyebrows as he listened. "And out." With his other hand, he took my wrist and pressed it. "In and out. And again…"

I coughed twice to help him with a diagnosis.

Stroked his orange beard, he said, "Hm. I can find nothing significantly wrong with her." He paused a moment, smiling at Mum. "Do you by any chance have any specific plans this week?"

Here I was – at death's door – and he was discussing plans. What kind of doctor was he?

She said, "No – but Ania is going to Brownie camp on Saturday."

"For how long?"

"Three weeks."

"Three weeks, hm? And… has she been before?" By this time he had taken out his prescription pad and was scribbling something in hieroglyphs.

"Yes, twice."

He signed what might have been his name with a final flourish and ripped off the sheet. "Did she enjoy it?"

Why was he asking these silly questions? And why didn't he ask me instead of Mum? After all, I was lying right in front of him, at death's door.

"Yes, you enjoyed it, didn't you, Ania?" She stroked my hand. "But she pined for her sister a little."

True enough – I'd longed for Iwonka, I don't know why. The big girls in Penrhos had been bossy with me, and I suppose I preferred it the other way round.

Doctor MacArlon continued. "I'm almost certain she'll be fine by Saturday, Mrs. Walewska. Please don't worry. Give her two spoons every four hours." He handed the prescription to Mum, lingering a second when her hand reached out for it. Then, pausing between each sentence, he added, "Make sure she stays in bed and has as little to eat as possible. A few spoonfuls of porridge. Made with water. That should soon get her back on her feet."

As little to eat as possible? Flavourless, watery porridge to boot?

I could hear the pair of them muttering as Mum showed him to the front door, then she chortled and he called from the bottom of the stairs, "Bye, Ania. Enjoy yourself at camp."

Tuesday, it was only Tuesday. I still had time to think up something better.

On Wednesday morning I announced my miraculous return to health.

During my two-day recovery I managed to get oranges and cheese to Stevo, saw the gang, then I had a relapse on Friday. Now desperate, I retook to lying on Iwonka's bunk and upped the agony in order to have my temperature taken. I'd planned this meticulously, having taken the toothbrush

118

cup from the bathroom and filled it with warm water. Mum inserted the thermometer in my mouth and said she'd be back in a minute. Meanwhile, I took it out, put it in the mug for a few seconds, then slipped it under my tongue. When Mum came back, she pulled the thermometer out of my mouth – the news was not good.

She eyed me, pursing her lips. With a voice like sliced lemons she said, "I'm sorry to tell you, Ania – you're probably dying. I'll phone the undertaker."

I thought my fever might move her to feel sorry for me, but no.

Then she said, "You *are* going to *kolonia* and that, my dear child, is the end of it. Cup?" She extended her hand, palm up.

How had she worked it out? I slumped back on my pillow. No other brilliant plans left, and Stevo had no option but to go back to his Mum's and whichever *he* he'd referred to. A *he* that might hit him, or whack him with the poker again.

I had to try one more time. "Under the bed. Do I have to? Can't I stay home this year?"

"Why do you want to stay here?" she asked. "What's the matter? Anything wrong?" For a moment, she rested her hand on my brow and stroked my temple with her thumb. "Is there something you want to tell me?"

I had nothing to tell her. The gang had made a pact – no talking to anyone, especially parents. The boys would have to see to it on their own. Maybe Stevo would be okay. But worry was not the only emotion I found myself experiencing. It wasn't just Iwonka I would miss. Three weeks was such a long time.

In the evening, I hung out of the bedroom window and told Ossie to convey the sorry state of affairs to the rest of the gang. Manuela would be justifiably miffed with me. I imagined her accusations. "You said you'd swing it. You said your mum'd believe you. You said you were good at acting." I gave him a note to pass on to her in which I apologised and asked if she'd write to me at camp. I didn't know the address except for Kolonia, Penrhos, North Wales.

*****

Next day, despite my best efforts, I found myself standing outside the coach heading for Penrhos. We'd screeched up at Kombo's, late as usual. Mum had realised we didn't have any sparkling white face flannels, so we had a stop-off at the chemist's to buy a couple. There were only two spaces left. Janek, the lucky beggar, happened to walk on before me so got a better seat towards the back. And as if He hadn't done enough already, God heaped another misfortune on me. I had to sit next to flipping Krysia Nowicka. Who spent the first part of the journey going on about the millions of badges and grades she'd attained for piano, tap, ballet, swimming and herding yaks on the

Ukrainian steppe. And who then threw up into a paper bag half a mile beyond Altrincham.

I looked over the top of my seat to see if I could squeeze in on the back row.

It wasn't just the usual crowd from Polska school and Polski church. There were also children I'd never seen before – from the Polski Circle in Cheetham Hill, I presumed. Not a single inch left for me to squash myself into. Lumbered.

After her initial bout of selfish vomiting, Krysia Nowicka repeated the process near Colwyn Bay, and again at the turn off for Caernarfon. And by the time we drove past the chip shop in Pwllheli, I was nauseous myself. I asked to swap seats. But Druhna Nowak, camp commandant, said I had to stay put and be stoical, like a good Brownie ought to be.

When the coach turned right into Penrhos territory and the shop, volley ball pitch, playground, white barracks and dinky church rolled by, little ripples of guilt washed over me. Almost in spite of myself, I was looking forward to it after all. And since Ossie wasn't going to Jamaica for another week, he, Gianni and Dermot would manage between them.

We arrived to a welcome from half a dozen old Polish folk, permanent residents of Penrhos, and our guide and scout supervisors. When the coach came to a halt, the Penrhos residents clapped like we were film stars getting out of limousines on Oscar night. Maybe they only saw children in summer.

We spilt out, identified our luggage and the supervisors helped us carry everything indoors. I hauled the suitcase onto my allotted bed – nowhere near Krysia Nowicka, thank goodness – and thought my luck might be improving. I had the same bed as last year, not too far from the loos if I needed to go at night.

Next we had juice and biscuits in the dining room, then unpacked. Mum had surpassed herself – I counted twenty-one pairs of new navy Marks and Spark's knickers.

After I finished making my bed, I sat on the mattress and looked around me. I knew both the girls on my right and left from Polska school, but opposite was a girl with short sandy hair, aged about seven. I hadn't seen her before. She sat huddled up as if she was going to disappear into herself. She was rubbing her hand over and over a seahorse-shaped birthmark on her collar bone. Her face was oddly familiar.

One of the guides, Druhna Renia, stopped beside her and said, "Shall I help you?" When the girl gave a shy nod, Druhna made her bed, patted and smoothed out the ridges, and told her not to be worried because camp was super. The girl's bedding, a gorgeous purple and white checked counterpane, made mine look like army-issue mud-coloured rags. Why Mum saddled me with ugly blankets (that everybody saw), yet thought new pants and shiny flannels (that nobody saw) were vital, was a mystery.

Now that her bed was ready, the girl sat on top of it cross-legged, and acknowledged me with a smile I also half-recognised. In my mind I went through people on the telly to figure out who it was. Who had that up-tilted nose? Those green eyes?

"I'm Ewa," she said, in a purr-growl of an accent.

"I'm Ania." Was it someone at Seymour Park? "Where are you from?"

"Cheetham Hill now, but we used to live in Rochdale."

No. I didn't know anybody from either of those places, although I'd always wanted to go to Rochdale with Dad to see one of his customers there. It sounded so exotic.

"That's my big sister." She pointed beyond the half-wall that separated the sleeping quarters into an L-shape. "Kinga's with her friends," she added, weaving her fingers through her fringe, eyes averted, like she was speaking to a grown-up. I turned to look who she meant.

"Which one?" I asked.

"The one with the pigtails and earrings."

Earrings indeed. I loathed her already. Kinga was one of the group attracting attention, laughing, bouncing on their mattresses. Three weeks. I was stuck here for three weeks. I opened the tuck box Mum had provided and offered Ewa and the girls on either side of me a Penguin.

Next day, scouts, guides, brownies and cubs trooped to church in the morning – much nicer than in Manchester because here the priest didn't go on and on and on and on and on, and I also didn't have Granny trilling in my ears. After *obiad* Druhna Nowak assigned us to our leaders and put us in our sixes. In the afternoon, we sortied single file from the village, along the Abersoch Road and down to the Wild Beach where we spent the afternoon swimming and climbing boulders. A boy called Stasio let me play with him in the rock pools and told me the names of the crabs and shells.

In the evening after *kolacja* we had our first *kominek*. We sang songs, danced the 'Green Waltz' and during '*Mam Chusteczkę Haftowaną*' a tiny cub wearing shorts that drooped almost to his ankles picked me. But he only gave me the kerchief, and shuffled off, eyes fixed on the floor, without giving me the usual kiss. When it was my turn to choose someone, I passed the kerchief onto Stasio and gave him the kiss, too. But just because I had to. He tried to kiss me back! Since when had *that* become part of the dance. Boys! Honestly! At least Stevo wasn't such a pain.

B. E. Andre

CHAPTER TWELVE

DAY THREE: EARLY EVENING

I return from the chemist and pull up behind Janek's jeep. There's already an inch of snow on the ground. If it falls for much longer, the medical team won't be able to get down the lane. I let myself in and there's music coming from Dad's room. Janek's soft baritone, louder than Iwonka's voice, cranks along to the track that's playing, a jolly tune about the black market in Poland, how the Nazis entered the train carriages and confiscated the pork, black pudding and bacon the Poles hid under their coats, under the seats. "…if you trade, you survive, it's war now, to hell with the Germans," the woman sings.

I've not thought about 'it' for a few hours, and now it's back – what Dad had to hide. Did he do it? What did he trade Yankel and his family for? I picture the nooses choking the last breath out of them, their convulsing bodies, a huge swatiska flag fluttering above. I can't bear it.

I think I could forgive him though. Could I? If I only knew there was a reason.

I wish I could rewind time, take it back to the day I saw *Shoah* and understood. Pretend I never saw the bloody film at all. I think my head is going to explode with it all.

As I drop the paper bag off in the dining room, the song ends. I hear Janek say, "Come on, wife! You can do better than that, Marie!" and another track starts. I go to the kitchen. Mum's at the table, her reading glasses on the end of her nose, playing patience with the pristine canasta cards instead of her usual tatty ones.

"Aren't they sticking to the plastic?" I ask. "Do you want me to get you the baize?" She waves me away. I watch over her shoulder but I can already see it's not going to work out; the aces are trapped. I don't tell her.

I go to Dad's bedroom. His eyes are closed, but his head is moving from side to side. The tune finishes. Iwonka opens the suspension of morphine

122

sulphate, says she's phoned Josie and the nurses to come early tomorrow, then dribbles two spoonfuls into Dad's mouth. He coughs, swallows.

In my absence, the duvet cover's been changed; it's one of those gaudy, God-awful floral ones, huge lilies and roses, that Mum insists on because they're 'cheerful.' Actually, Dad does look better with that peachy colour around him. The grey and black stripe made his face ashen.

Three more IKEA folding chairs have arrived from the garage guest stack.

A porcelain cup and saucer is balanced on Marie's knees, a fruit tea, I expect. We'll be doing take-outs soon.

Marie sits sideways to Janek, leaning back in her seat, her stockinged feet on his lap. Janek's rubbing the top of her foot absent-mindedly. "I think you've got a bunion coming, old woman," he says.

"I think you've got a slapped face coming, old man," she replies.

The room looks like an old-fashioned train carriage with a bed in the middle. "The train arriving at platform 5 is the 20.13 to The End, stopping at the church, the crematorium, purgatory. All aboard. Mind the gap."

My thoughts return to the film. Why did I have to watch it from beginning to end? Where does it come from, this irresistible compulsion to devour pain? I see the track leading to Treblinka, exhausted, terrified faces in the air holes of the cattle trucks. Make it go away, God, please.

Dad has a choice about the crematorium; they didn't.

I reach across him for Iwonka to give me the CD case. It has a monochrome cover that looks like a still from a movie; the album's called *Prohibited Songs*.

Mum comes in and sits next to me. We chat between tracks, and the rest of them listen and hum to each new song. Mum mentions Christmas, and Janek makes her swear we won't be having bloody carp. She promises her Polish version of gefilte fish instead. Why are they discussing Christmas when it's obvious we won't be celebrating one this year?

He seems to be asleep now. We exchange glances. Marie whispers, "Shall we go?"

Dad opens his left eye, the right side of his face bunched up like Popeye. He murmurs, "Thank you for coming. Come back tomorrow. I haven't finished yet..."

Marie mouths, "What?" at me. I shrug. I've no idea what he means either.

THEN

The next day *kolonia* proper was to begin. It was a bit like going back to school but better because we didn't have to sit at a desk all day. Mornings would be spent on survival skills, tying knots, constructing wigwam frames with string and branches, building a fire, using a compass and map, recognising plants, trees and birds and all that nature malarkey.

On Monday, we had a *śniadanie* of cornflakes served in tin plates and I was looking forward to lessons until the ritual humiliation of 'letters from your loving parents' began. Krysia Nowicka, of course, got her first letter that very morning – her mum must have posted it before we'd even left. Typical. Ewa had a letter by the end of the week, and I was thoroughly despondent when the next week came and I still had nothing. Maybe Mum didn't know mothers were supposed to stop reading *Angelique* books and send a reply. I'd written three to her (because Druhna Nowak forced us) – boring admittedly, since by the third one I struggled to make the same things exciting. Not unlike my pre-planned scripts for confession.

So I waited and waited. And waited. Meanwhile, Krysia flipping Nowicka got a new letter every day. Not to mention the parcel that arrived for her at the end of the week. Mum and Dad didn't love me at all.

*****

Janek received a letter on Monday of week two. He ripped it open there and then in the dining hall. As soon as Druh Dybek dismissed us to prepare for morning activities, I snatched it out of Janek's hand for inspection and to see if he'd got any spends. It was from Granny, of course. It said:

My darling Prince,

I hope you are enjoying kolonia. Dziadzio sends his best wishes. The raspberries are ripening.

I send you fond kisses,

Babcia.

My jealousy evaporated in an instant. No ten shilling note.

To my surprise, I had two deliveries the next day. The first said:

My dear Ania,

I hope you are enjoying kolonia. Dziadzio says he misses you. The raspberries are ripening.

I send you fond kisses,

Babcia.

Only '*my dear Ania*', no mention of princesses, and Grandad was obviously having to get on his bike and fetch his own flipping Woodbines. No ten bob note either.

The second, in an envelope addressed to Ania Walewska, Kolonia, Penrhos, North Wales, was on posh pink paper with a chain of daisies round all four edges. Manuela!

Dear Ania,

Are you having a nice time? We did not go to Torkee because my dad had business things to do in the club. So we stayed home. We have been to Spooky nearly every day. But there is some bad news. Wormy is missing. Gianni called for him to play and his mum said he was not aloud to call any more. Stevo put a tire on the tree in the corner and it is just like a swing. Gianni says hello and Stevo says bring him a stick of Welsh Rock please. A stripy one.

Love,
Manuela.
PS. Mum bought me some patent leather shoes like Twiggy's. Those ones in Womans Own.

To which Gianni and Stevo had added their signatures, Gianni's neat, Stevo's scrawly. Under Stevo's name there were two crosses. *Two* crosses. How would I manage to get him some rock? Perhaps Druhna would take us on a trip to Pwllheli?

But what did Manuela mean by "Wormy is missing"? Why wasn't he coming to play? Was he ill or grounded or what? I wondered what had happened.

The two crosses made me warm and fluttery inside, so I could ignore the bits about her shoes. Then the heat rose to my shoulders, arms and neck. I remembered how I'd given the kerchief and kiss to Stasio that time, and how I'd picked him for the dances. For some reason a scene on the telly popped into my brain. An old woman in a plastic rain cap was jabbing her finger at a younger blonde lady, and hollering, "You're an unfaithful strumpet, that's what you are, Bridie Beecham!" I wasn't sure what a strumpet was, but now I thought I might be one.

*****

Two days later, Druhna Nowak gave me the lead role in a sketch for the showcase parents' *kominek* on the last Sunday of camp. Druhna said the part required someone who could learn a lot of lines and enunciate clearly. Thanks to the billions of Dad ear-flicks at meal times – No English at the table! – I could get my teeth and tongue round all the *sz, cz, trz* and *szcz* words.

The action, she said, took place in a train compartment travelling to Kraków. Zbyszek Dąb and Władek Kaczyński would play two highlanders and I was the Varsovian who came in with a bag of fish. Hang about, I thought, I know this story. What a gift! Other roles were a ticket collector – Krysia Nowicka unfortunately – and a stall-holder, Kinga, Ewa's sister. Druhna Nowak handed us a copy each of the three-page typewritten script and ordered us to start learning the dialogue during free time that evening.

At the first rehearsal, we just read through it, making sure everyone knew the actions and could read the Polish words. I tried to imitate the voice of Jarema Stępowski, who I'd heard on Dad's records, but the more I practised, the more I realised my performance left a lot to be desired, and a Warsaw accent was beyond me. I was going to look a fool.

Several rehearsals later, now totally down in the dumps, I had a flash of inspiration, realised there was a way to pull it off. I made a suggestion. "Can I be a Jew instead, please?"

Druhna Nowak looked at me like I'd made a bad smell. "What?"

"I want to be a Jew. I can do Jews. I'm good at them. Honest. Instead of—

"

"You're a *Warszawiak*. That's the end of it."

"The trouble is…I can't say it like that. That is…I…but…if I could just be a *Warszawiak* Jew, I'd—"

"You are *not* being a Jew. Where do you get these crazy ideas from? Follow the script. Speak Polish like I do." She had no imagination, didn't understand that we'd have a hit if she let me do it my way. Her own accent, Polishy-Ukranian just like Granny's, with hard l sounds, poked out like fingers through a holey sheet.

I imagined the way Dad told Jewish jokes with the shoulder hunching, facial expressions, twiddling of the sideburns and best of all, the intonation – I could be so dramatic, so convincing. "You don't understand," I pleaded. "I'd do some really good actions. It would make it—" I slowed down to improve the sales pitch, "— much funnier."

"No. That's my final word," she said. I had to leave it. There was no shifting her. For now.

On Friday evening, Druhna told me Mum had phoned, she was arriving tomorrow, and I shouldn't stay with the other children at *obiad* time.

I was lying on my bed, proper cheesed off, when Mum turned up with Iwonka and Groucho around noon. She gave me a kiss and said we were going to the Old People's restaurant.

She tried to hug me. "Something wrong? Don't you want to come?"

I didn't mention she still hadn't written a single word to me. I explained my problem with the sketch – the accent was impossible to mimic. I wasn't Ossie who could take off Granny, his mum, Bugs Bunny and anyone he wanted. I kept the marvellous Jewish idea to myself. Mum bubbled and popped with "Oh, don't be silly. You'll be a wonderful *Warszawiak*." She didn't get it either. I was about to show myself up. In front of everyone. The sketch was such a monumental yawn that nobody, but nobody, would laugh, and she – along with half of Manchester – would be there to witness my mortification.

We went to fetch Janek from the boy's quarters – he, of course, went loopy when he saw Mum, hugging and kissing and being a general drip.

First, we had *obiad* at the same table as two old ladies who kept wittering on that Iwonka had the face of an angel. And after, Mum drove us to the sandy beach at the Warren where Janek and Iwonka built sandcastles, and Groucho ran in and out of the sea like a lunatic let out of an asylum. Meanwhile, I slouched on the blanket, unable to think about anything but the sketch. Mum kept telling to smile, "*Uśmiechnij się!*" If I heard it once, I heard it a thousand flipping times.

By the time Mum dropped Janek and me off back at our barrack, anxiety filled my insides from top to toe.

*****

126

On Sunday, as with every other day, we raised the Polish flag after *śniadanie*, and then marched in file in silence to the church. I paid no attention to anything, preoccupied as I was with imminent disgrace. Jesus was a Jew, wasn't he? Why couldn't I be one too? What was the big deal?

The coach carrying the parents rolled up when we'd finished *obiad*, and once they'd visited the toilets after the long journey, they congregated on the grassy area outside our barrack where the *kominek* was to take place. Songs, short sketches and dances followed. I was picked for absolutely nothing, thank goodness. After an hour and a half, Druhna Nowak beckoned me and the rest of the cast to get ready, picking out a few more Cubs and Brownies to fill up the carriage. I'd given up the whole thing as lost. Tears pricked behind my eyelids.

Zbyszek and Władek donned their over-sized highlander hats, I put on trousers, a flat cap and a man's jacket and grabbed the duffel bag containing the invisible herring. We were ready. Eight chairs stood in the centre of our stage, four on each side facing each other.

Druhna Nowak ushered the other kids into their seats in the carriage and addressed the audience, "Ladies and gentlemen. Now, for the last sketch of the *kominek*, imagine, if you please, a train compartment." A murmur of giggles rippled as Zbyszek and Władek walked in, swinging their elbows and poking their mountain sticks into the grass, beaming at everyone. The scene was set.

I squashed into my seat opposite the highlanders and began a useless attempt at Varsovian. Gradually, by itself, my voice became all Jewish. "Oy veh, oy veh," it said. "Let me sit, my poor back... You should have a back as bad as mine..." My shoulders began to hunch forwards. My chin grew a foot-long beard and my hands were stroking it down to a point. "Oy veh ist mir. I'm so hungry my kiszki are skveeking. Oy... gevalt."

And then, when the moment came to explain why I was eating herring heads, my voice and tongue hammed it up for all it was worth, just like Dad, lingering over loud slurps, sucking out the fish brains. A few people laughed. Quietly. I saw Stasio observing me, his face twisted into a question mark.

A voice hissed in my ear. "You stop that now! Or you'll be back to Manchester, in disgrace, straight after *kominek*." Druhna Nowak then strode to the other side of the arena where I saw her, glaring and clutching her whistle. I spat out one more fish bone and one more sentence in Jewish mode, just because I could, knowing full well I'd gone too far already. With teeth clenched, I adopted a slow monotone. The punch line, of course, disappeared down the deep, dark, slimed-up well of Varsovian awfulness. Only when I finished did I remember that Mum was somewhere in the audience at the back of me. A few people clapped their applause. The actors returned to their places on the grass.

Mum said nothing about my performance before she, Iwonka and

Groucho left to go back to Manchester. She kissed and hugged Janek and me, told us to be good – me especially – and said goodbye. We waved them off as they drove down the lane, the van shrinking until it disappeared over the white line of the Penrhos boundary gate.

That wasn't the end of it. Once back in the barrack after the parents had gone, Druhna Nowak gave me another lecture, including numbers four and six of the Brownie Law – a Brownie is mindful of her responsibilities and always tries to be better – adding that I wouldn't be made up to a guide until I learned to obey instructions. Et-cet-era, et-cet-era.

Was *kolonia* never going to end? If I could only be at home, I'd even tell Manuela her shoes were gorgeous. I ached for my friends at Spooky. Something exciting was bound to be happening there.

*****

In the middle of the week that followed, I received my first letter ever from Dad. It was addressed to *Zuszka* Ania Walewska, giving me my full Brownie title. I realised he'd composed it at the factory because it came in a logo-ed Whitcher envelope. This was such an extraordinary and scary happening that I waited to read it in private.

During Quiet Time when we weren't allowed to speak and had to lie on our beds being bored stiff, I took the envelope out of my pocket and used my penknife to open it.

My dear child,

Kolonia is nearly over and we look forward to having you at home. Mama said you made a bad decision at the kominek and had to suffer the consequences. It is important you learn two things. Sometimes you must fight for what you believe in even though everybody else disagrees with you. This can be the mark of a strong character. Most times, however, you must obey orders even if they do not suit you. When you get home, we can talk about this. Remember to be a good Brownie. I send you kisses,

Tatuś.

I hated Mum. I just knew, knew, knew she'd tell him. And what was he talking about anyway? How were you supposed to know when to fight and when to give in? You couldn't toss a coin. I hoped he'd forget by the time I got home. And anyway, why was he allowed to be a Jew in our kitchen when I wasn't? I couldn't bear the idea of looking forward to seeing the gang so much and having it ruined by one of those 'Dad conversations' the minute I set foot in the house.

*****

The ceremony to distribute skills badges and silver stars took place on Friday. After three stars, there was a promotion to scouting with a silvery-black cross that had a fleur-de-lys on it and bore the inscription '*Czuwaj*'. Be prepared. I'd already been to *kolonia* twice before and was due my third star. I longed for that cross. Just one more year to wait before camping in tents.

That evening, before the dancing and singing started, Druhna Nowak called us to order and praised us for being good children (she didn't look at me, I noticed) and for trying so hard. Druh Dybek – in charge of boys – said we'd worked with "diligence and courage, a credit to the Polish nation." They began the roll call. Brownies and Cubs lined up on opposite sides of the hall. Druh Dybek awarded the boys first. Then Druhna Nowak did the same for the girls.

I switched off, knowing I'd be among the last, what with my surname beginning with W. I was thinking how to apply the things I'd learned at *kolonia* back at Spooky. The new knots would come in handy for tying those orange boxes properly onto Stevo's cart. While all the other girls received their stars, I carried on dreaming. Perhaps we could make a hammock at Spooky. I woke up with a start when Druhna Nowak loomed into the picture. She congratulated me when she gave me my star, adding she forgave me for "that other unfortunate matter". She wanted to me to come to *kolonia* next year.

Then it was the turn of those being promoted. There weren't so many of those.

Druhna Nowak stood in front of Ewa's sister. "Brownie Kinga Kardasz. Step forward. What is your full name?"

Had I heard right? Kardasz? No – surely not. That was Stevo's surname.

The answer came. "Kinga Barbara Kardasz."

But Stevo told us he had no brothers or sisters. He was an only child.

Druhna Nowak said, "Brownie Kinga Kardasz, do you wish to become a guide?"

Kinga straightened her shoulders and looked as if she was pulling in her podgy stomach. "I do."

Druhna invited Kinga to kneel. She placed the sword on her left shoulder then transferred it to the right. "Arise, Guide Kinga Kardasz."

I looked from Ewa to Kinga and back again. They looked nothing like each other. This was really weird. Ewa and I hadn't exchanged surnames on the first day. And here they were – Ewa and Kinga *Kardasz*. At last I knew who Ewa resembled. Not an actress off *Coronation Street* or someone from Seymour Park – she was a younger, girly version of Stevo. But why would Stevo run away from his sisters?

In my head I reran the conversations I'd had with him. The unanswered questions about his various uncles, the absence of aunts and grannies. Then there was the mum he wanted to see, but who went on holidays without him and was too lazy to go shopping. And the Polish dad who beat him with a poker but didn't live with them. I didn't get it. In addition, Ewa came from Cheetham Hill and I knew Stevo lived somewhere in Whalley Range or Moss Side at the farthest. He couldn't have found his way to Spooky all the way from Cheetham Hill. I'd been to the Polish Circle with Dad once and it was miles away, further than the factory.

That night after we'd lowered the Polish flag on the mast outside the barrack and were getting ready for bed, I asked Ewa whether she had a brother.

"No," she said. "Just Kinga."

"What about a cousin?" I asked.

"Only in Poland. Why?"

"Nobody here? In England? Are you *absolutely* sure?"

"Yes." She sounded a bit cross. I think she just wanted to get to sleep. "'Course I'm sure. Ask Kinga."

Druhna Renia shouted, "Into bed," then "Lights out," and I was left to ponder what all this could possibly mean. Kardasz seemed an unusual name to me. Polska Land in Manchester was full of people with names ending in -*ski* or -*wicz*. Why would Stevo lie about his name? Where had he got it from? I'd stopped asking questions when he'd looked after me after I puked at Spooky that time. But now I knew I had to find out the truth.

*****

I got on the coach early to make sure of a seat nowhere near the puking Krysia Nowicka. Throughout the return trip, all I could think of was how much I wanted to see Mum and be with Iwonka and Groucho. And cheese on toast, like a normal Saturday. Lots of cheese on toast. Above all, no porridge.

I'd expected to be picked up by Mum and go straight home. No such luck. We got off the coach outside Kombo's on Shrewsbury Street, and Dad was waiting for us. He asked Janek whether he'd enjoyed himself and patted him on the head. Janek burbled how he'd learned to build a forest shelter and a campfire and how to follow a secret trail someone had laid. Dad smiled and gave him the three-fingered scout salute. "*Czuwaj!* You, my son, will make a first rate scout."

As for me, not so much as a "Welcome home." Dad launched straight in. Had I received his letter and had I understood it? I said yes – I couldn't be bothered with a lecture or any Dad explanations. Would I like to discuss it further? No. Had I learned from it? Yes. Would I ever be so thoughtless again? No. Never.

All I wanted was to get home. And afterwards, the gang.

He took our cases, put them in the boot of his car, and said he needed to discuss an important matter with someone inside – it would only take a few minutes. We traipsed behind him down the sauerkrauty corridor, past the empty family restaurant, and waved at Mr. Kucyk who was in his kiosk on the left. Then we went into the grotty bar. Smoke hovered in a mustard-coloured cloud near ceiling. The bar contained a dozen or so square tables. Some men sat chatting, others arguing about God knows what, dropping their ash as they jerked their cigarettes to make a point. There were several, more scruffy than the rest, who sat alone, concentrating on the *bigos* on their plate and mopping up the juices with thick slabs of rye bread. They always seemed to be here, like someone had misplaced them, or maybe displaced them out of their houses and put them in Kombo's for the rest of their lives, waiting for something to happen to get them out.

Nothing but flipping men. I was the only girl. Even the waitress had disappeared. To make it worse, my favourite bar tender, Mr. Skowroński, wasn't around either.

"You can sit here," Dad said as he installed us at an empty table and put glasses and bottles of orange juice in front of us. For himself, he'd bought a lemon tea, then went to talk to his friends. Two small bottles of vodka stood on their table, one empty, the other half full. Dad greeted the men and one of them poured him a shot. Which he declined. A minute later, I saw him drink it.

We twiddled our thumbs for half an hour. Then Mr. Kucyk ambled in from the kiosk. As always, he was wearing a dark grey woollen blazer with a waistcoat underneath, sharply pressed trousers, black lace-up shoes that glinted, and a dicky bow. Today's had a navy and white diamond pattern. He reminded me of a button-nosed, bald penguin. Even his ears were shiny. He placed his order and leaned against the bar, facing the room. When the men at the tables noticed him there, they nodded. He raised his badger eyebrows and inclined his plump head.

With his one arm across his waist, he lifted the little finger of the other to his mouth. The ruby and gold signet ring gleamed as he tapped his lip with his nail, his eyes moving back and forth between Dad, and me and Janek. He looked sad. I smiled at him to make him feel better. When his drink was ready, he hesitated then approached Dad's table.

Bowing from his shoulders, Mr. Kucyk said, "Good day, gentlemen. Good day, Pan Witek," he said and extended his hand. Dad shook it with both of his, drank another shot, and asked how business in the kiosk was going.

Mr. Kucyk's tone was like warmed honey. "Very well. Very well. Thank you. It must be time for you to visit my humble establishment, surely. I've missed your custom. And how is Pani Wanda? I'm sure there's something for her too." Mum's *Angelique* books came to mind. I hadn't seen her read anything Polish for ages. Mr. Kucyk lowered his voice and gave a faint cough. "May I ask a small favour, Pan Witek?"

Dad shifted his chair back a fraction. "Of course," he said, without a trace of hesitation. "How can I help?"

Mr. Kucyk bent towards him, put one palm on top of the other, squeezed and smiled. The other men at the table stopped talking.

"I need some help in the kiosk," he said.

"Yes?" Dad was frowning.

"Yes."

"What can I do for you? What do you need? Money? Stock? What's the problem?"

Mr. Kucyk chortled. "No, Pan Witek. That's not what I mean at all."

I was teetering like a skittle on my seat, trying to find out what was going on. I turned my face to Janek. Out of the corner of my eye, I saw Mr. Kucyk looking in our direction. Janek had been sitting in the same face-in-hands position for a good ten minutes. I pretended not to be listening by pulling my Brownie scarf in and out of my toggle.

Mr. Kucyk said, "I see your children aren't busy. May I borrow them to help me unpack a few boxes?"

"Ah, I see." Dad barely glanced at us as he threw back another shot. A large third bottle had appeared from somewhere. I glared at Dad. I wanted Mum, Iwonka, Groucho and cheese on toast.

"Of course," Dad said, "by all means. Take them. There is no need to hurry back," and pulled the bottle towards him.

CHAPTER THIRTEEN

DAY THREE: EVENING

I'm sweating. I check the thermostat; Mum's put it up to twenty-three. It's impossible to breathe in this house and the heat makes the musky sourness more potent, transporting it through the hall, into the bathroom, into the kitchen. A few open windows for half an hour would help. It's not going to happen.

At 8.37 Dad wakes, rings the crystal bell.

"Drive me to the sitting room for the news," he says. Mum and I lift and help him into the wheelchair, arrange the piss bag, and as he tries to straighten up, the side panel of the wheelchair detaches itself, clunks to the floor along with the two screws that are supposed to hold it in place. Great.

"Where can I find a screwdriver?" I ask.

He raises his hand and says, "It's a short journey. Don't bother." So I don't; I'll do it when he's on the Lazyboy. With the panel missing, the chair's unbalanced and I push down harder on the left side, so it doesn't topple. The wheel prangs against the skirting board, Dad makes a 'tsss' sound through his dentures. I feel even more clumsy than those hospital porters he complained about. When we lower him onto the Lazyboy, he's calmer; the Oramorph's brought an improvement, a respite. Mum says she needs to do some ironing, which may be true, but I know she's bored witless by the same-old, same-old of Dad's masochistic evening viewing.

I switch the telly to TVN24 news channel on the satellite. Why he wants to watch it is beyond me; all he ever does is rail at the hick, redneck or religious politicians who, he says, embarrass his country from here to New Zealand. "The shame of it. Look at how he's dressed for parliament, Ania. Do you see? Where's his tie?" Nothing could interest me less, but I sit with him anyway, trying to follow what they're talking about so I have something intelligent to say on the subject if the need arises. There's rolling news tape at the bottom of the screen; a car crash near Bielsko-Biała killing six people, an MP in Rzeszów caught insider-dealing, a man arrested in a village near Opole on suspicion of murdering his seven year-old stepson, whose decomposing body was discovered on the bank of the Oder.

A child just like Stevo. That sets me to thinking about Ossie. The whole thing was his idea. He should make the call to the police. So okay, I wasn't a mere bystander, I was a participant, but whichever way you look at it, it's more Ossie's responsibility than anyone else's. He made us do it.

The phone rings on the occasional table next to Dad. He clicks the green button and motions me to turn the telly volume down. He's speaking in English, saying he's feeling better today, and yes, if you drop by between Christmas and the New Year that will be very nice. Thank you. No, of course not, that's how it is when you have a business. He even manages a laugh about Man City. He says goodbye, clicks off and is still chortling when I ask who that was.

"You don't know him, child. The man who owns the hardware store on Anstey Road." He laughs again; a complete stranger has lightened his day. Mention of hardware reminds me of the missing panel and I fetch a screwdriver to repair the chair. The screws won't screw in so I botch it with string. My clove hitch knot looks scrappy. I make another attempt with a pile hitch, add a transom, and the panel seems secure.

What titbit can I give him now? "How about some Dolcelatte?"

He thinks about it and says yes.

It's 9.36 when Dad's had enough of people talking rubbish and asks to go back to bed. I make sure to steer with care. After Mum's done her usual routine around him, I ask if I can get him anything else. He instructs me to sit. I sit.

"Ania, you know where I want to go, don't you? Move closer," he says. What a peculiar question. I'm assuming it's heaven, if that's what he means. Where is this leading?

"I think so..."

He reaches for his glasses, puts them on. His tone is didactic. "It doesn't have to be immediately. And don't spend lots of money. Or go to the consulate for anything official. They will rob you."

"I don't understand."

"If you tell the consulate, all that paperwork, you'll have to pay. Put me in a Tesco bag, in the hold luggage, not the cabin luggage because they go through that, ashes don't weigh much, and buy an urn in Warsaw. Cheaper there." His expression is matter-of-fact, verging on smug; he's worked it all out, how to buck the system. "Half at Powązki cemetery, the other half with my parents." I'm trying not to laugh; it's nerves, that's all. It's the way he's saying it, as if I'll be dolloping bits of him into various receptacles with Mum's orange Lakeland measuring scoops. Practical. One for me, one for you, one for the pot. A leg here, a shoulder there. Add a slice of lemon. I try to strangle my sob, make it seem like I'm clearing my throat.

I've always known he wants to be scattered at Powązki. I was going to leave that part to Janek or Iwonka, but he's never mentioned the rest about distributing him hither and yon. Anyway, three of us can't do it together at the same time. Iwonka will take charge.

He taps my knee. "Ania, are you listening? Where precisely, child?"

Lord in heaven. He's told me so many times and now I can't bloody remember. Because, of course, I've only ever half-listened. "Where your comrades are, the scouts. The Grey Ranks, I mean," I say, hoping that's enough. I wish Mum would come in and relieve me, or help me out.

Dad's doesn't let up. "And where's that?" Before I can fake an answer, he says, "Bring me *Hej, Chłopcy* by Zygmunt Głuszek from the bookshelves. Bottom left." I find the book in no time and return with it. He pulls out several folded sheets of paper and hands one to me. I open it. It's an A4-sized map of the cemetery, drawn by himself, I assume. A red X marks the spot.

Dad takes the plan from my hand and smooths it out on the duvet. He shows me which entrance to take, tells me which monuments I'll walk past, the who's who of famous dead Poles, and that I should wear thermal socks and gloves because it'll be cold until March, at least. I haven't got long then.

"Is there a Jewish cemetery in Warsaw?" I ask.

"Hm? Yes, of course. It's right next to Powązki on Okopowa Street. Why?"

"How long has it been there?" If all of Warsaw was reduced to rubble, how did the cemeteries survive? This must be a new one built since the war.

"I don't know. Early 19th century I imagine."

"Have you ever been there?"

"Once or twice. When I've visited my comrades."

I try to compose the script, the open-ended questions, find the words to ask if he visited someone specific at Okopowa Street, someone he knew.

He folds the paper up and gives it back to me. "Let me finish, child. I'm tired." He says he mentioned all the details to Iwonka and Janek a few months ago, but we all have busy lives, so whoever's available should *załatwić tą sprawę*, arrange this matter. That's how he puts it.

"Child, one other thing. When I'm gone, buy your mother some flowers. Lilies. They look like... I don't know. No petals. Tell her I'm sorry."

Lilies with no petals? I ask, "Sorry for what?"

"She will understand."

It's time for his medication again. I give him two large spoonfuls which should see him through for four hours at least. Tonight's not the night for further questions.

B. E. Andre

THEN

Mr. Kucyk strolled to our table. "Come, children. Time for work." We followed in his flower-scented wake, as his short steps clicked towards the door, and once again he inclined his head to those he passed on the way out. In the corridor he said, "Now, that's better, isn't it?" I was still thinking about the cheese on toast and Iwonka, but the kiosk was an acceptable alternative, given our other riveting options. And lily of the valley was a vast improvement on the blanket of tobacco smoke.

The kiosk had floor-to-ceiling shelving and was the same size as our sitting room, except square instead of rectangular. On the shelves was all the paraphernalia you had to have to be really Polish – newspapers, novels, text books, rosary beads, crucifixes, Christmas, Easter and birthday cards from Poland, carved boxes and wall plates, records from Poland, costume dolls from Kraków, the Highlands and everywhere else, pictures of the crowned White Eagle and photos of the usual uniformed old men with moustaches.

At the rear stood Mr. Kucyk's counter which had drawers beneath it, and by the door, there was a small table with two stools. He invited Janek and me to sit on them. He gave us a pencil each and a sheet of paper. Then he went behind his counter, pulled out one of the drawers and brought out several large envelopes.

"I have a very important job for you," he said, all the while slicking the non-existent hair on the back of his head. I wondered what had happened to the box opening he wanted us to do.

"Janek, somebody ordered these stamps and he said he's coming to get them tomorrow." From one of the envelopes he withdrew a sheet of mushrooms and another of butterflies. "I need to remember what they look like so I can order them again if necessary. Can you draw them for me, please? Do you children fancy a *krówka?*" We accepted his offer of fudge.

"I have an important job for you too, Ania," he said, as his eyes scanned the walls. "Do you write neatly?" I could – if I took ages, but I didn't tell him that. I just said yes.

"Be so kind as to make three columns, my dear. In the first one, please put the number of stamps. In the second, write whether they are flowers, butterflies, trees, or insects – whatever you see. In the third column how many *złoty* or *groszy* they cost. I need this information for my catalogue. Another *krówka?*" I really, really, really would have preferred cheese on toast, but both Janek and me accepted again. Mr. Kucyk gave Janek six pencil crayons to complete his task. From the inside pocket of his jacket, he removed a gold fountain pen which he handed to me by the tips of his fingers. "Never mind the pencil, my dear. This, I believe, is the equipment a beautiful princess such as yourself should use." Nobody had ever called me a beautiful princess before. I would make my columns perfect.

We set to our missions while Mr. Kucyk nestled behind his counter, reading an enormous book with ballet dancers dressed as swans on the cover. He hummed a tune I knew from the film *Fantasia*. When I started humming along with him, he asked me if I'd ever had ballet lessons. The horror – I could think of nothing worse – well, maybe piano. And violin. And had anyone told me he'd been the choreographer of the Warsaw ballet at the *Teatr Wielki* before the war? They hadn't, I said.

"What was it like?" I imagined this *Teatr Wielki* to be the same size as Kombo's, with a stage of Kombo's proportions too.

Mr. Kucyk stared at the ceiling as if he could see through it all the way to the stars. "Magnificent, my dear, magnificent." He sighed then looked at me. "Until they bombed it. One wall left standing...Ah, but it was a long time ago. One mustn't always look back...I worked for your Tatuś a long time ago too. Did you know that, my dear? He was exceedingly generous, you know. He helped me set up my small enterprise here." I wondered what he meant by that. Maybe he'd asked Dad to unpack boxes as well.

Because Mr. Kucyk had been so kind about the pen and looked so sad about the theatre, I blurted, "It's always been my dearest wish, ever since I was little, to be a ballerina."

He smiled. "Everything is possible, my dear. We shall see to it."

I hadn't considered the consequences – me and my big mouth. He threw me a benign smile and carried on flicking through the book. Every now and again, he looked at his watch, left us in the kiosk for a minute or so, then came back. After one of his exits, he brought us a packet of chocolate *katarzynki* too.

I'd catalogued the contents of three envelopes now – we'd been there some time – and Mr. Kucyk had disappeared again. My bladder was bursting. I put the lid on the pen so the nib wouldn't dry up, walked down the corridor towards the bar and turned to go to the ladies. The public telephone was on the left. In it, his back to me, Mr. Kucyk stood talking to someone. The ruby in his signet ring darted from side to side like a confused ladybird as he rubbed his hand across the nape of his neck.

"Yes. Perhaps you should," he said. "Mm hm. Yes. I'm so sorry I had to phone you." A pause. "In the bar...Mm hm... I can't say...possibly four bottles... No. Between them... Mm hm." Pause. "In my room. No. Only *krówki* and *katarzynki* I'm afraid." I wondered why he'd said that. There was a lot of other stuff in his room too. I didn't hear any more because I couldn't last out any longer and dashed to the toilet. When I wandered back into his kiosk, he was already there, singing behind the counter again, but now pat-patting the top of it.

Janek must have drawn ten mushrooms. They were all right, but I could have done it better. My columns looked as immaculate as Dad's in his customer book at the factory.

Mr. Kucyk inserted several papers in his crocodile-skin briefcase, slid the catch in and unhooked his gold-handled, gold-tipped walking stick from the edge of his counter. He pulled a volume off the shelf, flipped a couple of pages, then glanced at his watch. He was standing next to us, adjusting his dicky bow when Mum appeared from nowhere.

She was panting. "Thank you so—"

He interrupted before she was half in. "Pani Walewska – how delightful to see you!" He lifted her hand and skimmed it with his lips. "I am so glad you've come in for your book at last. *Lalka*, isn't it? Bolesław Prus is an excellent novelist. Possibly our greatest, I always think. Don't you?" He bowed as he handed the book to her.

At first Mum hesitated as if she thought this Bolesław Prus person was a rubbish writer. Mr. Kucyk folded Mum's hands round the book and kept his eyes trained on her face.

"And how fortuitous that you should come for it now when Ania and Janek, such delightful children, are here assisting me in compiling my catalogues. Leave everything on the table, please," he said, smiling at me and ruffling Janek's hair. I thanked him for loaning me his gold pen and the *krówki* and *katarzynki*. Mum bustled us out of the door where we waited. As Mr. Kucyk turned to lock it, he said, "Would it be a frightful inconvenience to give me a lift to Chorlton, please? Normally I walk, good exercise—" he patted his little paunch, "but I fear I may be a little late for my engagement today." Mum said, "Of course." And thank you. Then "of course" again. We trundled down the corridor, Mum first, him, then me and Janek.

"Pani Wanda, Ania mentioned she would be interested in having ballet lessons."

Oh no! Why on earth had I said that? I'd turn into Krysia flipping Nowicka. The prospect was revolting.

He went on, "I'm afraid I no longer give private tuition myself. I do, however, know of an excellent teacher, if you are interested."

Mum jerked her head round. Her voice rose an octave. "Ania said she'd like ballet lessons?" She looked past the side of Mr. Kucyk, and when she saw my horrified face, she said, "Thank you so much. It's very kind of you. I'm afraid Ania's ambition outstrips her ability. She has two left feet. Poor child." I could have kissed her.

Janek and I clambered into the rear of the van.

Mr. Kucyk cleared his throat, then straightened his jacket before he parked himself on the edge of the seat. "Do give Pan Witek my very best regards, won't you?"

Janek asked, "What about Tatuś?"

Mum said thank you to Mr. Kucyk then looked in the rear view mirror at us. "Tatuś – oh, he's... He's still busy. Somebody will bring—he will come home later."

Now I understood. We'd have the war and all those *mea culpas* again when he got back.

*****

At home, Granny and Iwonka were waiting. Granny greeted us with hugs and kisses then scuttled off to feed Grandad. Iwonka clung to me, her face snuffling in my chest. I felt her hands clasp together behind my back and squeeze with all her might. Then Mum made us cheese on toast with Kraft slices, and she even put bacon on top. Oh, the bliss, the joy. No more *kolonia* food.

When we finished eating Iwonka asked me to play with her. I hadn't thought about it before – she must have been dead bored with just Mum, Dad and Groucho for three weeks.

I shelved my plans to visit Spooky or at least question Manuela in the afternoon. Dermot's whereabouts were still a mystery. And there was still that whole matter of Ewa and Kinga.

Janek mooched around telling Mum about his badges, and Iwonka and I went upstairs to the landing. She wanted to play with her cooker, pots and pans and plastic dinner service. I didn't like those games any more, but she asked so nicely I caved in. She said she'd be Mum and I'd be Dad. I wasn't keen on the idea. So then she said she'd be *a* mum, and I could be *a* dad, and Groucho could be our little girl. That sounded better. She chopped, stirred, dished out, and Groucho and I ate the pretend scrambled eggs, jelly and cup of tea.

Afterwards we snuggled on the sofa and I pushed my nose into her hair. I'd forgotten she smelt as good as the inside of an eiderdown on an icy winter's night. Nobody had given me a proper cuddle in three weeks. The Iwonka-shaped hole inside of me had filled up again.

We were twined around one another, Groucho included, watching the telly when Dad came home. He shoved his head round the door and told Janek to turn down the volume. Neither of his legs were working properly.

Dad started talking to Mum in the kitchen, his words slurred and loud, so after about three minutes Janek turned the knob back to the right so we didn't have to listen. When the programme finished, I wanted something to drink. I stood by the sitting room door wondering whether it was safe to go in or not. Dad's voice was quieter now. He was talking about that story again, the one with those poor people hanging from balconies. It sounded as if Mum wasn't there anymore.

Then, in a gentle voice, I heard her say, "Please. Stop torturing yourself. It wasn't your fault. You know…he forgave you a long time ago."

Dad said nothing for a while. There were no movements from the kitchen, just the buzz of the telly behind me.

Mum continued, "You remember what you told me? Do you? What you promised me? When Ania was born? You said you drink to forget. But it's

139

not true. When you drink, you remember. Please stop, Witek. Please." A space. It seemed like it was full of something scary about to happen. I held my breath. But nothing did.

Mum said, "Enough of this. I want them to be glad they're home after *kolonia*. Please – go to bed."

Silence.

I heard him scrape his chair back. I pushed the door to within an inch of closing so he wouldn't come in, and peeked through the gap. He hobbled past, lurching from wall to wall, muttering, "Enough of this."

*****

On Sunday morning, as I lay in bed trying to think of a sparkling, new, never-used-before excuse to skip Polski church, there was a tap on my window. I opened it and leaned out to find Ossie, also still in his pyjamas. Above us clouds spread across the sky like pulled white candy floss. In the distance though, over the other back gardens, there was hardly any blue left. I hoped it wasn't going to rain today of all days.

"Hurray. You're back," he cheered. "How was it?"

I said, "Never mind me. How was Kingston? Was it good?" I imagined Jamaica resembled the background of that naked lady picture Manuela brought to Spooky. Pineapples and lush palm trees. Except with brown people. In clothes. "Did your cousin win?"

Ossie's face dropped. "No, we didn't go. Again. My dad's an idiot."

Apparently, what Mr. MacDonald said way back in May was *maybe* they'd go to Jamaica, pretty much like he said, "Cold today, Mr. Witek. Nah. *Maybe* warmer tomorrow" to my Dad whenever they met. Ossie had misunderstood. I told him you shouldn't believe your parents about anything – easier that way. We commiserated with each other briefly about our hopeless dads, then I remembered what Manuela had written in her letter.

"What happened to Dermot? Where is he?" I asked.

It was quite a story. Ossie said Gianni had gone to Dermot's house. His mum said Dermot wasn't coming out for the 'foreseeable future'. Gianni wasn't to call again.

Later in the week, Gianni buttonholed Bernie, one of Dermot's sisters. She said her mum sent Dermot away in disgrace because Mrs. Riordan had seen Dermot stealing in Macwood's grocery and hardware shop. Mrs. Riordan, it seemed, was the lady with the budgie and hat covered in fake daisies who'd chased us out of St. Alphonsus. She'd said nothing to Mr. Macwood because he was a proddy dog, but she'd dragged Dermot by the ear all the way to his house to tell Mrs. O'Donnell. According to Bernie, Mrs. O'Donnell ranted and raved like a demented banshee on the door step, and yelled "Jesus, Mary and Joseph" at least a hundred times. Mrs. O'Donnell then called Dermot a "thievin' little bollix" and a "stupid feckin' eejit" and slapped him on the back of the head in full view of the entire street. And afterwards, when Mr. O'Donnell got back from work, he gave Dermot a thrashing.

Even worse, said Bernie, was that since they didn't have a phone at home, her mum had used Macwood's public one to call family in Ireland. She'd had to whisper everything in code in earshot of Mrs. Macwood who always stood nearby eavesdropping. And that made Mrs. O'Donnell madder. She'd come home and given Dermot another couple of thwacks with the oven glove.

Mrs. O'Donnell then sent Dermot off with his eldest sister, Mary Frances, to their grandparents in Limerick, Bernie said. Where, God willing, he would learn the error of his "thievin' tinker ways." And if he didn't learn there, he would have to go and stay with some brothers in a place called Seminary.

I hadn't said a word while Ossie was talking. It made no sense. Dermot didn't deserve it. Whenever I'd been at St. Alphonsus, I saw Mrs. O'Donnell smiling when he took communion. He was first, ahead of the other altar boys. *And* he went to confession every Sunday and did all that kneeling of front of chairs stuff in May and October.

What made him suddenly steal from a shop? Was it because he always brought the least to Spooky for Stevo? Perhaps he felt left out.

"Blimey. Poor Dermot. Did she say when he'll be back?" I asked.

"He'll have to come back for school, won't he?" said Ossie. "And you'll never guess what…"

"What?"

"Bernie said Dermot's got to go to church every day. Morning, night and dinnertime."

Flipping heck. Mass three times a day. The very thought made me shiver. How would he stand it? Poor, poor Dermot. For once, I was glad to be Polish. Mum and Dad couldn't get rid of me like that. Polska was too far away, I hoped.

Ossie said Stevo had given him a weird message to pass on, then wrinkled his nose. "I don't get it. He said, 'Tell her she owes me some Welsh Rock.'"

*****

Neither Ossie nor I could avoid praying though. I went to Polski church with Mum, Granny, Iwonka and Janek. Ossie went with his family to the Pentecostal one at Brooks's Bar where at least the hymns didn't send you to sleep in an instant.

After mass – during which all I could think of was the rock I hadn't managed to get for Stevo – Dad returned from the factory. Mum had roasted two chickens because Granny and Grandad were eating with us. Fine by me. That meant we had a couple of legs going spare. Handy. I hoped they would make up for the rock – I had to bring him a present of *some* kind.

When *obiad* was over, Dad drove off, Grandad shuffled away, and Mum went to Auntie Teresa's for a chat. Granny was supposed to be baby-sitting, but I guess she was tired because she started snoring on the sofa. I watched and waited. She was in one of her Sunday-best suits, a petrol-blue crimplene, with a frilly, pale lemon blouse underneath. No Monday to Saturday headscarf. Her knees were apart, her head on the backrest, and her mouth gaped, a dribble of saliva escaping into her chin crease. Every now and again she raised her eyebrows above her glasses as if dreaming of something shocking. Yes, she was out cold.

Janek, who'd been lying on the carpet, scratching peeling paint off the skirting board, got up and whispered he'd be at Tomek's if she woke up.

So that left me and Iwonka, and she was busy trying to make Groucho respectable with a hairbrush. A lost cause.

The coast was clear. I went to the kitchen, opened the fridge, removed the chicken legs and wrapped them in aluminium foil. If Mum asked where they'd gone, I'd tell her I'd put the plate on the table to eat one, just one, but Groucho had hopped on the chair and scoffed the other.

I'd never taken anything this tasty before. It ought to work. As good a way as any to butter up Stevo and stop a to-do. He'd slammed the draughts when I asked if his mum spent the day in bed, and hurled the knife across the den at the mention of Uncle Tony. How would he react if I started that up again?

After he put his arm around me when I'd thrown up from the juice and our Harrington's adventure, I'd stopped caring, more or less. But Ewa had been adamant she had no brothers or cousins and she, as far as I could see, had no reason to lie. Why did they look so similar? The questions mounted up and itched. There must be a way to phrase them.

But before I escaped to Spooky, I had to do something else.

I checked my face in the bathroom mirror. Perhaps hairspray would control the cowlicks? I went to Mum and Dad's bedroom and sat at the dressing table. Earrings might help. I tried on all of Mum's clip-ons, but I just looked flipping stupid because they were so big. That wasn't going to work. I flattened my fringe to left, sprayed. Hopeless. I pressed to the right, gave it another coat. No improvement. What else could I do?

Mum kept her lipsticks in an ornamental bowl in front of the mirror. I removed the tops and compared colours. The *Rouge Allure* made me look as if someone had smacked me in the mouth, so I wiped it off and settled for a thin layer of pinkish *Sugar Shine*. I rubbed a dab into my cheeks too. There. Put that in your Twiggy shoes and smoke it, Manuela!

Next there were three half-full bottles on the corner of the dressing table. Lenthéric *Tweed Mist*, Worth *Je Reviens* and Carven *He Loves Me*. They'd been there for at least four years and still had almost the same amount in them. Mum hadn't cottoned on that food had been vanishing since April, so she'd not notice if I borrowed a few drops. The first perfume smelt of wet sheep, so I blended the other two and patted behind my earlobes and at the bottom of my neck, exactly like Mum when she went to dances, except more. It should do the trick.

I peeked into the sitting room. I didn't want to leave Iwonka on her lonesome with Granny, still snoring loud as a buffalo. But Iwonka seemed happy enough, now tying bows in the ribbons she'd put on Groucho's ears. I said I was going out and instructed her not to wake Granny. On any account.

*****

Ossie and I called for Gianni and Manuela on the way. She sniffed and threw me a funny look before giving me a gigantic hug. So I gave her one back. I did miss her at Penrhos. She wasn't wearing her new shoes and she'd been kind to write that letter. We took the longer route to Spooky, and because we discussed poor old Dermot as we walked, I didn't get round to mentioning the details of what I'd found out at *kolonia*.

Inside, at the bottom of the banister, Gianni called, "*Torta di Mellay Jenno Vazay,*" until Stevo bounded down the stairs.

"He-e-e-y, Ania!" Stevo eyed my silver parcel first, then looked at my face. "Ya look nice. Different. What've ya done?"

I didn't get a chance to reply. The tops of my ears were feeling sunburnt.

"What've ya got? Where's me rock?"

I hadn't bought him any because they didn't sell it at the shop in Penrhos. Gianni, Manuela and Ossie gave him their bits and pieces.

I said, "Sorry, no rock. Chicken."

"Bad news for Wormy, eh? Give it 'ere then." He almost snatched it out of my hand. "Owt else?"

I fished in the pockets of my anorak and found a white paper bag with cherry drops inside. They must have been there since the end of term. I handed them to him.

We stayed for a couple of hours and played in the garden. When Gianni said he had to return home, Manuela and Ossie said they were going too. I said I'd stay. Manuela gave me a funny look, so I whispered I had to talk to Stevo about something important that happened at *kolonia*. I promised to tell her later. She looked at me sideways but seemed to accept my explanation.

Stevo and I went inside and sat on the window seat. It took a while before he said anything.

"I wanna ask ya summat."

"What?"

"D'ya think I'm thick?"

"What?"

"Well, do ya?"

Not thick exactly. But sometimes when we talked, he didn't have the foggiest idea about stuff the rest of us took for granted. But then, we already knew he didn't go to school much. And anyway, he'd learned loads of new things from the *Alpha Books of Facts for Girls* and the encyclopaedia. No, he wasn't thick-thick, not like Pamela Blackburn at school.

He leaned back against the window frame. "I'm not thick. Not daft ya know."

What was all this about? "Never said you were."

"Not gonna stay in Manchester, ya know. When I grow up I'll live in London or summat. Or America. Don't you wanna go somewhere else?" Then, he leapt up and said, "I'll prove it." I listened as he ran up the stairs. A minute or so later he returned, looking chuffed with himself and holding the *Alpha* book.

"Test me," he said.

"On what?"

"Anything ya want. Open the book." I did as he asked, picking topics at random. We went through languages spoken in various countries, the currencies there, rivers and capital cities. Some fun things like weights and measures – furlongs and chains for length, rods, poles, perches and roods for area, fathoms and knots for the sea. Then a few science facts like who invented the Bunsen burner, cement, rubber, telegraph, television. Stevo's face lit up with every answer he got right. Eventually he took the book from me, flicked through it, and passed it back open at the page headed The Basic Laws of Chemistry and Physics.

"This is the good bit," he said.

I didn't think so. I'd had the book for years and the one thing of any interest in the science section was the Periodic Table. As for the rest, I couldn't understand what it was for or what it meant. We never learned anything that hard at school.

"Which one?" I asked.

"Avogadro's."

I tried to find it on the page.

"Go on then. Hurry up," he said.

He took a deep breath and quoted, "Avogadro's Law says that equal volumes of all gases under the same conditions of temperature and pressure contain the same number of molecules."

Gibberish to me.

He went on. "Boyle's Law states that the volume of a given quantity of any gas varies inversely as the pressure acting upon it, provided that the temperature remains unchanged."

I corrected him. "Provided that the temperature of the gas remains unchanged."

He didn't understand a single word of it either, I was sure.

After twenty minutes of him getting most of the answers right, I realised he was far cleverer than I'd given him credit for. And he was in such a bouncy mood, pleased he'd learned so much, that I broached the subject.

"Stevo… You know when I was at camp…"

"Was it good?"

"It was okay… Well, there were two girls with the same name as you…"

He pulled his chin in and squinted at me. "What? *Stevo?*"

"No. Not that." I wanted to laugh, but stopped myself. "I mean, your surname. Kardasz? That's what you said – Kardasz?" I thought it better to wait for him to speak in case he got riled and ripped up my book.

He gazed through the window, quiet and still. His hands clenched and he caught the left side of his bottom lip with his teeth. A fly settled on the ball of his thumb and we both watched it as it crawled down to his knuckle onto his middle finger. It rested there and rubbed its fore legs as if knitting without any wool. The right wing had a piece missing at the tip. I could hear Stevo's breath. The fly froze for a few seconds. Then the legs moved up and wiped its eyes.

Stevo's fist sprang open with such force that I flinched.

"So?"

"So. Nothing. Their names were Ewa and Kinga."

His face was expressionless. "Never heard of 'em."

So that was that.

CHAPTER FOURTEEN

DAY THREE: NIGHT

I look in on Mum. The lamp on the wall above her head is directed away from her. She's in bed propped by pillows reading *The Consolations of Philosophy* by Alain de Botton. I can't imagine she'll find solace there. On the bedside table, I see the Bible, *The Shadow of the Wind*, the BMA A–Z Family Medical, and *Herodotus – the histories*. What? What the hell… It's a far cry.

Her eyelids tremble and her head lolls forward. She's going to drop the book. I move to slide it from her hands so she won't wake when it falls.

She opens her eyes, stretches them wide. "Hm? Does he want something?" she asks, her voice thick with the first taste of sleep.

"No. Is it good?" I ask, flicking through the consolations. Good luck to her.

She gives me a rueful smile. "No idea. I've been reading the same page for a month. Are you going to bed now?"

"In a while. Is the computer working?"

"I think so. I can't remember the last time he used it. Don't stay up long."

"I won't. Password?"

"Comet," Mum says and turns her lamp off.

I go to the sitting room, pull the laptop from under the occasional table, sit on the Lazyboy and adjust its angle. My legs rise and my back slides down.

The laptop takes ages to power up. Outside, the security light switches on. Psiuńka wanders into the room, sniffs the French windows, gives a low growl, then settles in front of them as if to protect us from the lurking threat.

I type in the password, which takes me straight to a Polish page without asking, then Google, and Okopowa Street, Warszawa. It's the official website of the Jewish cemetery. Dad's right. Early nineteenth century. 1806 to be precise.

I should know more of the great and good listed, but I don't. Rebe this,

Rebe that. There must be hundreds of rabbis there. I think of *Fiddler on the Roof* – "If you please, Rebe Tevye, Pardon me, Rebe Tevye…" but that was the Pale of Settlement. And the pogroms. And the Russians. This is Warsaw. My eyes skim the other names on the left of the page.

Janusz Korczak – what's he doing here? He didn't die in Warsaw, that's a fact. I read it's not his grave, just a monument. He's carrying one child, holding the hand of another, and more orphans are trailing behind him. I know where they're going. Treblinka. His real name's Henryk Goldszmit.

I scroll to Adam Czerniaków. I've heard of him. He was in charge of the Warsaw ghetto and committed suicide when the worst began.

Oh, my God. Ludwig Zamenhof. *The* Ludwig Zamenhof! What the hell are you doing here? Why did I assume you were German? Born in Białystock. I see my sixteen-year-old self hunched over the yellow and blue *Learn Esperanto* book, stupidly convinced an invented common language can stop war. Ha. So easy. Two cases, nominative and accusative. What a sensible man you were, Ludwig, a genius if I may say so. And the first grammar of Yiddish … Well, I never.

This is ridiculous. What the hell's the matter with me? I feel trapped in a slow-turning centrifuge, spinning, spinning, buried under millions of people by its relentless force.

I click onto the photograph of Ludwig's grave. The design is a pentagram. Why not the Star of David? Maybe it's something to do with the Pentateuch. There's so much I don't have a clue about. Ludwig Zamenhof was Jewish…

I continue to go through the black and white gallery of headstones and tombs. Around me nothing but the sound of clicks and the blackness of night.

What am I looking for? I know the destiny of most of them, where they're buried. But what about those in Warsaw? What happened to them? The ones who died before it began in earnest. The ones lynched with ropes tied to balconies. Yankel.

I close the website. It can't tell me anything.

I open my *Eco Crafting Monthly* account. The usual stuff and an email from a woman who has made a garden canopy out of *Highland Spring* water bottles. We might be able to use it, run a whole feature on recycled plastics. Another from someone who puts all her kitchen waste through a Thermomix before throwing it on the compost heap. I reply suggesting she writes to *Gardener's World* magazine.

I know I'm procrastinating. I must do it – google Oswald MacDonald. I type his name. Pages and pages of entries.

THEN

One day towards the end of August, I saw Dad hunched forward on the sofa, arms folded, staring at his legs, his right ankle balanced on his left knee. Hairy white flesh peeked out between his trouser leg and sock. Since the telly was off, I knew something must have happened. Probably better to keep out of his way. Time to go upstairs. He tapped the space by his side. "Come here, child." I didn't want to sit next to him, but not having the wit to find a quick excuse, I perched myself on the edge a foot away. I put my hands in my lap, tried to look invisible, for once hoping that Mum, who was clattering in the kitchen, would find me a job to do.

"Nearer," he said, as he put his arm around me and drew me closer. He pulled my head right under his armpit and held me at the waist. My face was trapped against his jumper where I smelt traces of Dad sweat and Omo. A cuddle when we watched the telly together was fine, but this was something else. What was going on? My unease grew as the minutes rolled by, with the heartbeats that thrummed in my ear, with every breath he inhaled then let go. I felt desperate to wrench myself away.

After we'd sat there for an age, Dad gazing at the window, me counting the hairs on the exposed strip of his leg, something astonishing happened. He sobbed. A heaving gulp of a sob from the depth of his stomach. I started. And when I sneaked a peek to find out what was happening, I saw the rims of his eyes had reddened. Not red like when he'd been at Kombo's though – they were brimming with tears.

He looked down at me and a single drop escaped. He caught it by the cuff of his jumper and wiped it against the stubble on his chin. I wanted to ask him what was the matter, but my throat was scratchy like someone had strangled the words out of it. He stared and stared as if he was trying to see into my brain.

Finally, he kissed the top of my head. "A great man died today."

I'd never witnessed Dad crying before. Mums cried non-stop. At night after arguments, during the day if there was sad bit in a book or on telly. Or when they listened to records by Jim Reeves and Vikki Carr. Dads didn't. It was an unspoken law of nature. Dads were brave.

I wanted to say the right thing, something meaningful to make him feel better, a grown-up comment. Instead I blurted, "Was he your friend?"

Dad stroked my cowlicks. "Mm. Like a father."

I relaxed a little to see his eyes clearing, and shifted on my bottom so he'd loosen his grip.

"Who? Do I know him?"

Was it one of the men from Kombo's who came round for midnight sandwiches? Could any of them be like a father? They were much older, but no-one seemed old enough to be his dad. And I'd never heard him treat any of them differently – they were just friends.

"It was in the war, child. During the Uprising."

I don't think Dad meant to do it so hard, but as he curled my hair round his finger, it felt like he was twisting it right out of my head. I did my best not

148

to wince, praying he wouldn't go off on one of his war rants and scalp me by accident. I pictured myself hairless and it wasn't pretty.

Dad continued. "He came to Manchester after. To visit his boys from the Grey Ranks."

I waited for more while Dad twiddled on, tighter and tighter, my impending baldness approaching with alarming speed.

"Who was he then?"

He sighed, wiped his eyes again, then let go of my hair and allowed me look up at his face.

"His name was Generał Bór-Komorowski."

I knew the Grey Ranks were scouts, but the ones in Manchester only had scout leaders, like Druh Dybek from *kolonia*. Where did generals feature? Something was telling me it was more sensible not to ask, not now anyway.

Fortunately Mum called me to lay the table, so Dad unwound his arm from my neck and released me. Mum shouted up the stairs for Janek and Iwonka to come down. When she produced the serving dishes, I almost cried myself. Now of all times she chose to give us Brussels sprouts, and Dad was in such a peculiar mood that I had no choice but to swallow them. I didn't fancy one of those spectacular, finger-drumming rows. Nor kneeling on the bag of dried peas.

We ate *kolacja* in total silence – even Janek and Iwonka sensed something unusual. Just the chinking of spoons during soup, the odd ignored slurp, the scraping of knives and forks during the main course, and Mum's tap on Iwonka's hand when she started sucking her knuckles. We scarpered from the table as soon as possible. Dad had said nothing throughout. The silence was scarier than his tellings-off.

*****

Some days later, Auntie Teresa arrived at dinner time, done up to the nines, in a dark grey woollen skirt, a navy jacket and a little black velvet hat perched on her dyed auburn hair. Her long nails were lush-red as always. On any other day she started on the rude jokes about priests as soon as she walked in. Now she appeared subdued.

Mum made her a cup of tea and pushed a slice of poppy-seed cake at her.

Auntie Teresa slid the plate back towards Mum. "Thank you, no. No appetite." She unzipped the side pocket on her handbag and drew out a packet of Embassy cigarettes. She inserted one in her cigarette holder, pulled a lighter out of its pink suede pouch and lit up.

"What time are you meeting?" Mum asked.

Auntie Teresa sucked in a long breath. "Two o'clock. We should be in London by eight at the latest. Is Witek on his way home yet?" Her index finger and thumb pinched the tip of the holder while the rest of her hand spread out like a wing in flight.

"I don't know. How many are going?" Mum said.

"Maybe forty."

I pulled up a chair. It sounded as if Dad was going too. Hurray – how marvellous. Several advantages in one. Fewer flicks round the ear for speaking English, far less green stuff to force down my throat, no *kolacja* arguments.

When the phone rang and Mum went to answer it, I asked Auntie Teresa why they were going to London. She said it was to attend the funeral of that general I'd lost half my hair for.

I'd imagined something more exciting. "Oh, is that all? Why's everybody so sad? Was he like a father to you? That's what Tatuś said. That he was like a father…to the Grey Ranks. Were you in the Grey Ranks?"

"No. Not me. In liaison, dear." She tapped the ash off her cigarette, balanced it on the rim of the ash tray and sat sideways in her chair, crossing one leg over the other. The silver trim on her black court shoe caught the light as she jigged her foot from side to side. Mum returned.

Auntie Teresa asked, "Was that him? Where is he?"

"He'll be here soon." Before Auntie came Mum had been sticking the Green Shield Stamps in the book. She was saving them to buy a mixer. She resumed licking the sheets.

Auntie Teresa leaned back over the table and put her manicured hand on my forearm. "Sorry. What did you want, dear? Ah, yes. The General. An extraordinary leader – Bór-Komorowski."

It wasn't making much sense to me. Why was a dead Polish general going to be buried in London? Why wasn't he in the army in Polska? I remembered the time Dad had droned on and on about us being stray dogs, blah-blah, that time I didn't want to go to Polska school, and wondered if the general was a stray dog too. But that didn't ring right either. He was obviously someone very important, whereas we were normal. Well – as normal as anybody else in Polski Manchester.

Auntie Teresa drank the remains of her tea. "Is there time for another, Wanda?" Then to me she said, "Do you know why your Tatuś limps, dear?" I told her he was wounded in the war by something called shrapnel.

"That's right, dear. When he was in hospital, Bór-Komorowski came to visit him."

Auntie Teresa held my gaze as if to check I was paying attention, so I tried not to fidget. A desperate need to look elsewhere was getting the better of me.

She persisted, "Are you listening, dear?"

I nodded.

"Your Tatuś introduced himself with his codename. The General kissed him on the forehead." She paused, her voice faltering. "I'll tell you what he said. 'May God reward you, Comet, my son. The homeland will remember.

Thank you.'" Auntie Teresa removed the butt from her cigarette holder and put in a fresh one. Her hands were shaking. Her words sounded funny to me, like a speech from an old-fashioned film. Only in Polish.

Remember what? Why would this general say "Thank you" – what had my dad done for him?

The question that came out of my mouth though was: "Why was he extraordinary?" London was a long way to travel just for a funeral, it seemed to me, and Auntie Teresa had said forty people were going.

"Bór was the commander of the Underground Army, our commander, dear. Mine too. He gave the order for the Warsaw Uprising. And over here, he was Prime Minister of the Government in Exile."

I half-knew something about this from Dad's tirades. Now it made even less sense. I said, "He couldn't have been that marvellous, could he? I thought the Warsaw Uprising failed."

"Anka!" Mum's rebuke stung like a slap.

Auntie Teresa pulled in nearer the table, put her elbows on it, cupped her face in her hands. Her eyelid was twitching, making her eyelashes tremble like a moth on a light bulb. "No, Ania, dear. We most certainly did *not* fail. It was an enormous victory…but not a successful one."

How could you have an unsuccessful victory? Bonkers. I mean, if I got five out of ten for my Progress Papers at school, would I shout from the rooftops about that? I wouldn't think myself successful in the least. I'd be at the bottom of the pile with the dummies, like Pamela Blackburn.

It was all so flipping complicated and I didn't get it. And why, since there was a Polish government in Polska already, was there a Polish one in England too? As well as a British one. What was the point of it?

Sometimes, now for instance, I *did* want to understand things better – not KingTanglefoot, What's-His-Face Crookedelbow and that other ancient malarkey, just the war stuff. But it seemed so huge – all those Polish people who'd travelled half way round the world just to end up in Old Trafford. Why hadn't they gone to a hot country with palm trees like Jamaica? But then why had Mr. MacDonald come to England? And Mr. and Mrs. Karageorgis.

The trouble was, I suspected that if I did ask another question, hours-worth of blah-blah would follow. Too high a price to pay. While I sat there ruminating over this, Auntie Teresa told Mum she'd give herself a stomach ache from the glue in the stamps. She went to the sink, moistened a dish cloth and gave it to Mum to rub over the Green Shield sheets. Then she opened her handbag, retrieved her compact, clicked the lid open and dabbed a lacy hankie into the corners of her eyes and underneath, where her mascara had run.

Dad came home soon afterwards. He went upstairs to change from his work clothes. He emerged in a suit, a crisp, white shirt, a black tie and black shoes, and said, "I'll be gone for a while. Be good for Mama." Then, wagging his finger at Janek, added, "Speak Polish in the house. Otherwise…"

On his way out, Dad pecked Iwonka, checked himself in the hall mirror and adjusted his lapel, where he'd pinned a gold badge with white and red enamelling – a P with its tail spread into an anchor-shaped W. I knew what it stood for – *Polska Walcząca*, Poland in Battle – the insignia of the Underground Army.

*****

We knew Dad was back even before he walked in because Groucho was at the front door, sniffing, yapping and shaking his tail. Iwonka and I sat at the kitchen table, her by the window, me at the end, sticking chopped up bits of cardboard onto a washing powder carton. We were creating a mosaic jewellery box for Granny's birthday. Mum was with us playing patience. *Pick of the Pops* was on the radio. It had been such a nice, peaceful weekend (even the warbling at mass hadn't ruined it) that I half-hoped a few more important old people would kick the bucket in London. Once every two months, say. Except then I realised they might be grannies and grandads.

The front door opened. Dad ignored Groucho, strode into the kitchen, then didn't say hello to any of us either. He was already steaming and grumbling. "Not one Member of Parliament …" Mum whipped her cards into a pile, hid her *Forever Amber* book under her cardie, switched the radio off and put the kettle on to boil. She returned to the table. My skin began to prickle.

Dad sat next to Iwonka, kissed the top of her head and loosened his tie. He hadn't even noticed that I'd tied her hair in bunches.

"Not one MP…" he said again, this time louder, whamming his fist on the kitchen table. Iwonka jumped in her chair and our mosaic bits went flying as if a small grenade had exploded. I didn't try to retrieve them.

"Can you believe it, Wanda? The Commander of the Uprising, the Prime Minister of the Government in Exile! It's a scandal, an insult. *Kurwa mać!*" He was clenching his teeth and drops of spit sprayed from his mouth. The last time I'd heard him say that bad K word was when he'd gone berserk at the man with the numbers tattoo at the factory.

"Witek – children! Nobody? How do you know? There were hundreds of people there."

I swear I could have throttled her. If she'd kept quiet, he might have stopped. But no – he carried on.

Another almighty thwack shook the table and the mosaics bounced again. Iwonka was still, probably expecting it this time.

"How do I know? It went round in seconds. Delegates from everywhere. Each community." Now he stabbed his finger into the table as he listed the towns. "Manchester, Bradford, Huddersfield, Glasgow, Leeds, Birmingham." And then he lifted his hand and poked the finger in Mum's direction.

"Nobody from the government!"

Janek, who'd had the good sense to remain in the sitting room so far, came in at that moment to ask for a drink. Mum made a tumbler of orange squash, thrust it at him and shooed him back out. I was squinting sideways when I saw her tuck *Forever Amber* behind the stuff in the bread bin and slide Groucho's food bowl under the cooker with her foot. She poured Dad some tea.

As she put the glass in front of him, Dad was shaking his head at no-one in particular, staring at his wedding ring. He made a grunty noise through his nose.

"Fmm. If not for the Polish 303 squadron, there'd be no *zasrane* Houses of Parliament. No London either. Nothing but ash like Warszawa."

Iwonka's eyes popped at me when he said the rude word.

Dad grunted again and looked at Mum. "I'm tired of it. You know? There's no end to it. Ignored in 1939. Betrayed at Yalta. Denied our rightful place at the V.E. celebrations. Now this. They have no—" Dad was moving his lips as if something peppery had lodged under his tongue, "—honour."

Mum had taken to tugging at her ear lobe. "Let's stop this, shall we? Why get upset? There's nothing you can do." She opened a drawer and took out a fresh tablecloth. "Are you hungry? Ania, Iwonka, tidy the table. Put those pieces inside the box. Then go and play."

We brushed the mosaics scraps into our palms and dropped them in. Dad let Iwonka clamber out over his knees, and she and I joined Janek, who was lying on the carpet in front of the telly, supported by his elbows. Relieved to have escaped, we splayed out next to him. Iwonka made herself comfortable by resting her leg on top of mine but I didn't mind.

Dad still hadn't finished. I heard him say, "And I'll tell you something else. The British fixed Sikorski's plane. They wanted him out of the way."

That must have been the last straw for Mum because she half-shouted. "Witek! Stop that now." Her voice became softer again. "Listen...drink your tea. Watch television. It'll do you good."

None of us budged as he entered the room, his presence sucking up the air behind us. He sat on the sofa and punched into a cushion twice. Janek's right elbow crept towards my left one, touched it and stayed there. I felt Iwonka's foot twitch. After a few minutes, we heard Dad's snore. Our eyes remained fixed on the telly, our bodies like stone on the carpet.

*****

Dad woke up in a slightly better mood, but not much. Just before bedtime, he said I wasn't going to school tomorrow because I'd be accompanying him to mass in the morning. My stomach glued up instantly. What had I done to deserve it? Church two days on the trot? Nothing. I hadn't been naughty or cheeky, hadn't uttered one single word when he'd been raving, and I'd tidied up like Mum had asked.

Dad said I had to get dressed in my grey *zuch* uniform because even if the British government had no respect for Generał Bór-Komorowski, we Walewskis would show we knew how to honour war heroes, the men to whom we owed our freedom. Let them put *that* in the *Times*.

"What about Janek and Iwonka?" I protested.

"You're the eldest, which makes you the family delegate. They're going to school." I had school too, and it was the first day of term. And since when had they stopped being Walewskis? Why was it always me who got lumbered? Did I ask to be born first?

*****

On Monday, Mum woke me at half past six and hung my newly ironed uniform on the rung of my bunk ladder. I heaved myself out of bed and dragged the flipping thing on, knowing full well I'd be the only child made to dress up, probably the only child there. Other Polish parents wouldn't make their kids go. My dad had a screw loose. Fifty screws loose.

I looked at Iwonka, lucky beggar, still sleeping, snug as a bug, with her face turned to the wall, then went to the bathroom.

When I came downstairs, he was already there. He smelt of Old Spice and was wearing the same clothes he'd worn when he'd left for the funeral. The only addition was an armband and a tiny bit of bloody loo-paper stuck to his jaw. He told me to hurry and eat, so I gobbled down a dish of cornflakes. Then he sent me back upstairs to change my socks for shinier, whiter ones. And to comb my hair. Again.

Outside in the drive, Dad installed himself in the delivery van, switched on the ignition and began to reverse. I stood inside the porch, all togged up, as he drove straight out without so much as a glance in my direction. What joy! He'd forgotten me. My stomach emptied of the glued-up feeling. Hurray! I stayed for a moment, hardly daring to believe my luck, then turned to go in.

"Anka! What are you doing?" he shouted. He was unlocking the door of the Corsair which had been parked up in front of the van. "Get in."

He'd only driven as far the pavement outside our house, the privet had blocked my view. I shambled round the flower bed to the passenger door of the car, slumped in the seat and asked why we weren't going in the van.

He said, "*Nie wypada*," and began to reverse again. Why not? I didn't see why it wasn't fitting. The general wouldn't know which car we came in, would he? What did it matter? He was dead as a doornail. Dead as dead can be.

Dad drove in silence while I slouched next to him. At the junction with Princess Road, he ordered me to stop sulking and sit up straight – I was disgracing my uniform.

We arrived at Polski church at seven-fifteen. Dad adjusted the rear-view mirror so that it reflected his face, and he tightened his tie. Then he licked his finger, and I watched him carefully peel off the scrap of blood-soaked tissue.

In the forecourt people were milling about, murmuring to each other, all dressed in dark colours, some with armbands like Dad's. The uniformed standard bearers of the various organisations, including that of my *zuchy* troop, Gdynia, stood by the gates in solemn 'at ease'.

Auntie Teresa approached us. She was wearing a different hat now, a black velvet beret with three purple feathers on the side.

"You've brought the younger generation, I see. Excellent. So it should be. Good morning, dear. A little early for you, perhaps." That came nowhere near it. She opened her handbag, took out her cigarette holder and began fishing for her Embassy packet.

Dad raised his eyebrows. "Now?"

She said, "No, you're right. I'm sorry," and dropped the cigarette holder back in.

Dad went to talk to the Gdynia scouts and left me and Auntie Teresa together. People wearing the PW in their lapels came up to talk to her, each one making a comment about my being there. I did my best to smile at them and be polite. I thought my face might crack. Why did he make me come? I bet Iwonka and Janek were still in bed.

Then, as if an order had been given, everyone moved towards the entrance and lined up along the steps.

As we passed through the two soot-blackened columns to the entrance door on the right – me in front, Dad behind – I felt his knuckles dig into the bottom of my spine and run up the vertebrae all the way to my neck. He pulled my hand out of my pocket and slapped it flat against my thigh. In my ear, in a clipped growl, he said, "Don't slouch! *Szacunek!*"

Why did I have to show respect to someone I didn't even know?

The church was full, even the balcony seats. I stood next to Dad, arms rigid by my sides in case he suddenly decided to give me a flick round the ear in public. The tallest altar server came in first, carrying the Eucharistic Cross in front of him. The smaller boys followed, then the priest in his black garb. Behind him came the standard bearers, who processed beyond the communion rails, lined up at the far ends of both sides of the sanctuary, and stood at attention.

I switched off as soon as it got boring. Which was, as usual, immediately. Whenever the scouts lowered the Gdynia ensign, I made my eyes spin like a kaleidoscope and pretended the green and gold sections were the blades of a toy seaside windmill. I got quite dizzy.

At the end of mass, after 'O Lord! Who through so many centuries surrounded Poland with the brilliance of power and glory' the organist struck up another droney tune that made my ears want to make a dash for it.

The old lady next to me in the pew smelt of mothballs and Granny on Sundays. She began to sniff and make burbling noises. From her pocket she pulled a tissue and blew a pint of snot in it. Who could blame her? The organ sounded so croaky I felt like crying too.

On the way home, Dad said the dirge was by Polska's greatest composer, Fryderyk Chopin. I hoped this Chopin person had written something more cheerful as well, more on the lines of the Beatles or Lulu. No wonder Poland wasn't in the Eurovision Song Contest. It wasn't just because countries behind the Iron Curtain weren't allowed, like Mum said.

A few days later, the pretty Hawaiian girl who'd hung above the sofa disappeared off the face of the earth. She was replaced by a large, framed, black-and-white photo of a bald-headed, weasely, gaunt man with a triangular moustache that spread from his nostrils to the outer edges of his mouth. His hooded eyes sagged, and he looked like misery itself in his uniform. The thought of him spying on us, all disapproving, while we played or watched telly made me shudder.

Our sitting room, our place of refuge, would never be the same again.

CHAPTER FIFTEEN

DAY FOUR: EARLY MORNING

I wake. Dad's saying "Wanda." I hear Mum go into their bedroom. My watch says 5.16. The laptop is still on my knees, gone black in hibernation. I close it and return it to its place under the table. I'm at the door when Mum comes out of their bedroom and says, "Can you give him some more medicine? Why aren't you in your pyjamas?"

I wonder why she can't do it herself. Dad's face is contorted as I enter. He attempts to decontort it when he sees me, but it doesn't work.

"One spoon," he says. "That's enough."

"In one go?"

"No."

I oblige. I tug his lower lip and trickle it below the plastic of his false teeth. "Anything else?"

"No. Go back to bed, child."

"In a minute. I'll stay until it kicks in. Say if you want more."

Dad's eyelids drop. I sit on the chair next to him. Sitting is good. Sometimes it's enough. It's what he did for me, unflinching. Didn't bat an eyelid when I turned up with my mouth, eyebrows and eyeliner tattooed in. It doesn't look so bad now, faint, almost invisible. Why did I do it? Fury, I guess.

I count. I've had an extra thirteen years.

I picture me in my old bathroom. I'm looking in the mirror. Nothing but a few wispy patches left. I insert a new blade into the razor and smear my head with gel. I work from the crown downwards.

One stripe. I rinse the blade.

Two stripes. I rinse the blade.

Three stripes, four, five.

The black-rimmed dead-fish eyes staring at me belong to someone else. I put my hands to my ears and silently re-enact Munch's Scream. I scream at John for having the affair, scream at him for leaving us and for telling Sam and Rachel he will always love them. Scream at the fucking cancer cells.

The magnifying mirror is in my hands travelling round every blemish and scar left behind. Do I even want another chance?

It was Dad who opened the door when I arrived. Funny – he said nothing about the tattoos, accepted it all, the shaved head, the turban, the angry, spiky auburn wig I wore at breakfast next morning. No more "Ania, go comb your hair." Mum scuttled round me, wringing her hands, driving me crazy. Dad just stayed, waited, reacted when called upon.

My watch says 5.53. Dad's mucus is gurgling now; he's asleep. Iwonka will be here in three hours. I place a cushion on the floor and lie down next to the bed, next to Psiuńka. And stay.

THEN

The other new photo, a smaller colour one, arrived soon afterwards. I came in from hanging upside down on the swing, and there it lay, next to a copy of the *Dziennik Polski* on top of the fridge. I heard Dad talking to someone on the phone in the sitting room, so he must have brought it home with him from work. It hadn't been there earlier.

I examined it while Mum was slicing cucumbers for *mizeria* salad.

In the background I saw serious-faced guides and scouts wearing berets with *fleur de lys* brooches pinned to them. In the foreground, four people – Dad, Auntie Teresa, Mrs. Kurka from Polska school, and a dark-haired man I thought I recognised. They were dressed in black or navy and were walking side by side, spread across the breadth of a path. They wore white and red armbands on their right sleeves. Between them, in front of their bodies, they carried a long banner inscribed with words written in gold. In the middle of the banner, the ladies held a wreath shaped into a P with the W anchor. The inscription said, "For our beloved Bór from the *Armia Krajowa*, Manchester."

I couldn't remember seeing that dark-haired man at Kombo's, the factory or church. Or anywhere specific. I could only picture him at a steering wheel.

He was taller than Dad, with a chin like the pointy bit of a trowel. Quite handsome really. I picked up the photo by its edges because Dad would go bananas if I left finger-marks on it, and showed it to Mum.

"Who's that man?"

Mum stopped chopping, glanced at the photo, then turned away and flung the knife and cutting board into the sink where they landed with a clatter, shattering a plate. She swore as she wiped and rewiped her hands on her apron.

"Mama?"

Her voice was brittle. "Him? You don't know him. His name's Sławek Kardasz."

First there was Stevo. Then Ewa and Kinga. And now a Sławek. I'd already heard that a Kardasz had beaten my dad at cards that night he told the herring joke. Was this man Stevo's dad or Ewa and Kinga's dad? But if it was Stevo's father, what was my dad doing with *him*? Someone who beat his children and burnt them with pokers? And this man was a member of the Polish Underground Army, just like Dad. Whenever Dad talked about the Resistance in the rare moments that he wasn't ranting, he always made everyone sound so honourable, courageous. Everybody standing together against the enemy, never giving in.

So it just couldn't have been Stevo's dad.

If I asked Mum about anything to do with Stevo, I might give the game away. We'd promised him – and ourselves – on that first day that we'd not tell our parents he half-lived at Spooky, and now I couldn't figure a way of getting any further information without tripping myself up. I had to choose my words carefully. And why had Mum suddenly gone all snarky and peculiar? I had to approach it the other way round.

"Mama," I began, "When I was at *kolonia* there were two girls called Ewa and Kinga Kardasz…"

Mum was bent over the sink, fishing out the broken bits of plate. "What?"

"Are they related?"

"Ania, I'm busy."

"Does that man have children?"

She made a 'tsss' sound and when she removed her cupped hand containing the fragments, I saw she'd cut herself. She dumped the shards into the bin and wrapped a tea towel around her hand.

"What is it, Ania? What do you want?"

"I'm asking a question. Can't I ask questions any more? Is it against the law?" I didn't mean it to sound cheeky, it just came out that way.

Mum stared at me for a moment in silence, then said, "I haven't seen him for years." She mumbled a swear word and added, "Probably. I have to make *kolacja*. Go and find something to do." She waved me away, opened a cupboard, took out the first aid box and stuck a plaster on her thumb.

I heard Dad saying goodbye to the person on the phone and I quickly put the photo on top of the fridge.

Dad was back in the kitchen. "Is there time to wash?"

"Ten minutes," Mum said.

Dad picked up the photo and the newspaper and went to the dining room. I followed him as far as the door. I saw him fold the *Dziennik* and insert it at a flyleaf in one of his Polish books. Then he put the photo into one of his albums, but not in the neat front sections he collated by subject. He slipped it in the back among the out-of-focus uncategorisables, the ones he didn't have a place for, or maybe the ones he didn't want anyone else to see.

*****

159

I didn't know how to use the new information. How could I ask without getting it in the neck from Stevo? I liked him even more than Ossie, Gianni and Dermot now, and they'd been my best boy friends for ages. I'd even had to hug Dermot when he returned from Ireland because it was true what Bernie had said – he did have to go to mass three times a day.

If I could work my way towards my questions while the rest of the gang were there, those specifically aimed at Stevo might go unnoticed.

One day after school, when we were lounging on the steps at the back of Old Spooky trying to think of what to do next, I brought up the subject of how annoying and weird parents could be.

Everybody contributed on that one, especially Ossie. He said his mum made tea out of something from the garden, added it to fried pepper and oil, put this soup in a washing up bowl, then had a wee on top of it. She put her feet inside this brew – her feet! – and sat in the armchair soaking them for hours. Ossie was doubled up, laughing. "Me restin' me chilblains!" Manuela and I yeughed and pretended to be sick. I steered the conversation onto the things parents talked about. Did any of their parents go on about the war like mine did?

Ossie said his dad had been in the army, and he flew off the handle about it because Jamaicans were treated differently to white people. When Mr. MacDonald first came to Manchester, he wanted to rent a room, but when he knocked on the door, people opened it then shut it in his face. "No coloureds," they said. But it was okay in the end because his dad got a job at Carborundum.

Dermot's jaw dropped. It had happened to his dad too.

"Your dad works at Carborundum?" Ossie asked.

"No. I mean about getting a room."

"Give over! Your dad's white!"

"Not 'No coloureds' – 'No Irish'. Mam said there were signs in the windows saying 'No niggers, no dogs, no Irish'."

I didn't need to learn about any of that now, and anyway, the conversation was moving in the wrong direction.

"What about the war?" I asked.

"My dad wa'n't in the war," said Dermot. According to Dermot's mum, the Teashop, who was the Irish Prime Minister like Churchill in England, said Ireland shouldn't be friends with England because the British government had invaded Ireland loads of times. The English had stolen land and then the Irish people had no potatoes to eat, and that's why everybody left for other places like America. The English, Mrs. O'Donnell said, were as bad as the Germans.

"Really?" Manuela asked, face crumpled like a paper bag.

"Really." Dermot stuck his chin out.

Then it was Gianni's turn. He said his step-dad, who was also Polish, sometimes told stories of when he'd been a pilot in the *303 Kościuszko* (except Gianni pronounced it "Kosh-chooz-kow") Fighter Squadron in the Royal Air Force. But mainly his step-dad described his airplane. It was called Hurricane. And that was why he was good at fixing cars and the machines at the printers.

Gianni turned to Manuela. "You?"

Manuela didn't have much of a clue about anything, not even that there'd been a war. She said Mr. Karageorgis didn't go on about the Germans. Sometimes lost his temper with Turks, sometimes with the British. But usually not at the same time.

Stevo was leaning back on the steps, hands behind his head, face to the sky, listening. His eyes were closed.

"What about you, Stevo?" Ossie asked, straight out with it, as if he'd forgotten everything we'd learned of his home life. I recognised he'd done half my job for me. Good old Oz. I held my breath.

Stevo gave a grunt the size of a pea. "Yeah. He said he was in the war." He hadn't moved a muscle apart from a tiny flicker in his eyelids. "Showed me a medal once…I bet the bastard nicked it."

The sky seemed to drop to our shoulders, and everyone fell silent.

Eventually Ossie said, "Anyway, I've got to go home for my tea now. I'm starving," and everybody else said they had to go home too.

My plan hadn't worked. And I had no intention of asking Stevo outright now.

But I had someone else apart from Mum and Stevo – Granny and Grandad. Because if Mum knew Kardasz, they'd be bound to know him too.

*****

When I walked into the kitchen, Grandad was sitting, socks off, paring his corns with a razor blade. A stained tea towel lay beneath his feet. The *Dziennik Polski* was open on the table next to him. He was wearing his beret, overalls and an over-the-head canvassy apron covered in brownish, oily smears.

A faint smell of something vinegary and beetrooty came from the cooker. A pan with the lid half-off was the cause. I looked inside – *barszcz*, with black bits. I replaced the lid properly, wondering if Granny had learned to cook flies "in Siberia when we chopped wood for twenty hours a day " blah-blah.

I sat on the chair and looked at the newspaper. There it was – unbelievable – the exact same photograph that Dad had brought home, him and the other Underground Army members. It covered half the page. I moved closer and tried to read upside down. On the other page was a smaller copy of the picture that now spied on us in the sitting room, and the headline "Memorial Masses Held in Great Britain." I couldn't read much of that article – I wasn't as good at reading upside-down in Polish as I was in English – but I managed to pick out names of lots of English towns.

Eventually, Grandad pulled his socks and shoes back on. He wiped his glasses free of the usual sawdust and said, "Babcia's not in." I'd already fathomed that out for myself. I watched as he threw the dead skin in the bin and washed his hands.

When he rejoined me at the table, he rummaged between his teeth and his cheek. "Do you want something, Ania?"

"Not really. I just fancied coming to see you." I waited a moment or two. "Tatuś went to that funeral, you know. There he is." I put my finger on Dad's face.

"I know." Grandad flipped the page, took a sip of his Nescafe and continued reading.

"Why didn't you go?"

Dziadzio shrugged. "I served under General Anders in the 2nd Polish Corps. In Italy."

"I thought you were in Africa."

"No. Your babcia and mama were in Africa. You've heard of the Battle of Monte Cassino? That's where I was. Not in the Underground Army."

Oh. I remembered. I'd heard of Monte Cassino because of the song about the red poppies that sprouted from all the Polish blood that had been spilt. The guides and scouts sometimes sang it at the special occasion *kominki* in the theatre hall at Kombo's. I bet the Chopin man wrote that one too.

My brain felt as if it had broken to bits – why were we talking about this? I was here with a purpose.

Grandad stood up and took a bag of sugar out of the cupboard. While he poured some into the bowl, I flipped the newspaper back to the previous page. He sat down and added two more spoonfuls to his coffee.

I knelt up on the chair and leant over the table. "The other man. Who is he?"

"Why do you want to know?"

"It's just… There's Pani Kurka," I pointed to each of them in turn, "Ciocia Teresa and Tatuś. I wondered who—"

"That," Grandad said, without taking his eyes off the picture, "is Kardasz. A very unpleasant fellow." His cheek changed shape where he'd poked his tongue into it and short grey bristles stood out like on a baby hedgehog. He turned the page again.

I wasn't sure what to say next. I hadn't worked it out beyond this point, and I wasn't expecting the brick-wall tone in Grandad's voice which usually meant he'd said as much as he was going to say.

At that moment, Granny bustled through the back door. Grandad said "Mnh" to her, then bent over to retie his shoelaces. He stood and straightened his beret. "I'm going to the shed."

Yet again I turned the page back to where those two photos were. Granny filled the kettle with water, unpacked her shopping and slumped down sideways in Grandad's chair. She lifted her skirt a little and rubbed her knees.

It had to be worth one more go. "Why is that man an unpleasant fellow? That's what Dziadzio said."

Granny's eyes skimmed the photo, then she slammed the paper shut and unknotted her kerchief. What was going on?

She clamped her teeth so tight I could hardly understand her, like she was speaking Lithuanian or something.

"We don't talk about him, but I'll tell you this...your father entrusted him with the entire payroll for the factory and that man gambled it away, every last shilling, penny— Agh, never mind."

I thought she was going to choke herself as she retied the knot. I waited.

"Your Dziadzio got a loan to help. And then we had to... No. I'll say no more. And don't tell your mama I told you." Her index finger was up vertical in front of my nose. It smelt of peardrops.

So that was why Mum had thrown the knife and board in the sink. I felt strangely elated, as if I'd got another piece of a jigsaw right. Until I realised that I hadn't at all. What about Ewa, Kinga and Stevo?

"Babcia, you know that man... Does he have any—?"

Her finger was between my eyes again. I was squinting at wrinkles.

"What did I say?"

"What do you mean 'what did you say'?"

"I'll say no more."

I weighed it up. If I continued, she might go berserk and I'd be in for it. But if – the image of all the sixpences and shillings popped in to my head – if I shut up, I might get her to pay a visit to the black handbag. As usual, the handbag won.

*****

Our new teacher, Mrs. Moscrop, looked like Aunt Clara from *Bewitched*, except she was vile, horrid, disgusting. She had a complexion like a grey Victoria sponge and bloodhound-jowls. Her hair, parted on the right, lay flat against her head and resembled the used-up Brillo pads Mum put under the sink 'in case of emergency'. Aunt Clara stammered a bit, but Mrs. Moscrop spat coffee-breath drops right in your face. And she had spider-leg hairs growing in the ridgey bit under her nose. Nine – Manuela and I counted them.

On our first day back, she informed us of her plan. "I expect you all to put your backbone in and—" she banged the blackboard with the board rubber, "—worrrk, worrrk, worrrk. No shirrrking!" The dust went flying. It wasn't just Aunt Clara, she reminded me of. It was someone else off the telly, but I couldn't think who.

This class would be the best ever at Seymour Park! Better than any other school in England! She beat her chest. Everyone would pass their eleven-plus.

"The front page story in the *Manchester Evening News*!" she said, changing her posture with every sentence, from hands on hips to arms folded across her chest. Each time she moved another flake of dandruff dropped onto her shoulders.

Manuela and I glanced at each other. I knew what she was thinking. Mrs. Moscrop was raving mad, a proper nutcase. She must have escaped from a lunatic asylum or something. We had some real dummies in our year – Pamela Blackburn would never pass it.

Soon afterwards Mrs. Moscrop gave me a letter for Mum. She didn't reveal its contents. And, unfortunately for me, it contained what I'd half-suspected way back at Easter.

Mum opened the letter, sighed, and told me what Mrs. Moscrop had said. I needed to go to the optician. I was squinting at the blackboard and often copying things down incorrectly, she said. Furthermore, I was an intelligent girl whose chances of passing the exam may be thwarted if this matter wasn't dealt with promptly.

Not glasses! Was it not enough I had a pancake-face, two stupid cowlicks that made me look a right dork, and never got good parts in the plays at Polska school because I wasn't blond, dark or pretty? Oh yes, I could be a tatty old Varsovian at *kolonia*, but when had I been a queen, princess or the loveliest flower in the field? Why did God want to punish me like this? Why did He hate me so much? What had I done to *Him*? And there, on a daily basis, to make things worse, was Manuela in her earrings, yellow or lilac or lime-green trousers, and her Sandie Shaw haircut. You didn't see any of the models in *Woman's Own* wearing specs. I was doomed. I'd never have a proper boyfriend and nobody would want to marry me. Not even Ossie or Stevo. And I'd have to live with Dad for the *rest of my life*. It wasn't fair. It just flipping well wasn't fair.

I sat in silence thinking it through, wondering what I could do to change my miserable destiny.

Mum folded the letter, returned it to the envelope and put it in the letter rack. She'd phone the optician as soon as she had a moment, she said.

*****

Next morning, Mum called us to come *at once*, and ordered us to sit, shut up and eat *śniadanie*. Wherever she moved, whatever she did, she made a racket, clattering around, slamming the front door after she'd picked up the milk bottles, banging things on the table, on the cooker. Something must have happened.

Upstairs, Dad was humming. Then, as he walked downstairs, in English he sang, "*Vokking beck tu heppiness, oopah, o yeah, yeah,*" He sounded much better when he sang Polish songs.

"Good morning, my beloved family! Iwonka, come here, child," he boomed. Iwonka pulled out her chair and squished herself between me and the wall to get to Dad.

"And how is my favourite youngest daughter in the whole world?" he asked.

Iwonka said, "Very well, thank you," and waited, as did Janek and me, to find out the reason for this miraculous turn of events.

Dad beamed at us. "Today's a special day."

Mum muttered under her breath.

Dad said, "Iwonka, choose a pocket." She looked at him, her expression blank.

He smiled at her and planted a kiss on the tip of her nose. "Pick one of my pockets. Go on."

She chose his left trouser pocket.

"Put your hand in and see what you find. Don't show anyone else. And don't look at it yourself." He ruffled her ponytail. Iwonka found something, and when she removed her hand, eyes wide and expectant, she kept it clenched.

"Now sit down. Janek, my favourite only son! You too."

Janek picked his right jacket pocket and did the same. Dad resumed *Vokking Beck tu Heppiness* and Mum's face developed two big furrows between her eyebrows. Her mouth was a thin line, and the ridges from her chin down to her neck were standing out like corrugated cardboard.

She sat in Dad's place. "Do you have to?"

Dad ignored her. "Ania, my favourite eldest daughter! Which one for you?" I went for the inside breast pocket. Something like a paper cigarette with a raised ridge in the centre grazed my fingers. Intrigued, I rubbed at it and tried to guess.

"Yes. Yes. That's enough," said Dad and pulled my hand out with the cigarette in it. "No peeking."

He turned to Mum. "Wandzia – my favourite, one and only wife. You too." He lifted her hand, but she snatched it away.

Mum said, "Stop. It won't work."

He bent over her to give her a kiss. "I'm sure I can tempt you, my darling."

She moved her face so that his mouth landed in her hair. Something very peculiar was going on, I knew, because Dad never, ever said those things to Mum except when he'd been drinking, and this was *śniadanie*.

Mum was ruining the fun – why couldn't she do as he asked? How often was Dad in a good mood like this? And when was the last time a Polish Helen Shapiro appeared at *śniadanie*? Would it kill Mum to be nice for once, for heaven's sake? Honestly, what a misery.

She tsked and sighed. "Never again. You better understand that. We can't afford it."

"Yes, yes. As you wish. It was Franek's name day. Now choose one." Her mouth was straight as a ruler when she inserted her hand into his right trouser pocket.

Dad said, "Ready everyone? One, two, three – open!" We looked at what we had in our hands. Iwonka uncrumpled, Janek unfolded and I took off the elastic band and unrolled. All of us had paper money. Loads of it.

"Save it, spend it, do what you like! *Oopah o yeah, yeah.*"

I was too busy to notice how Mum's stash was presented because I was eyeing how much Janek and Iwonka got, checking on whether the notes were green, pinkish-brown, blue or brownish-black.

Mum put her notes in one of the brown envelopes in the letter rack and didn't say thank you or anything nice, just "This is the last time. The last. You obviously learned nothing when *he* lost the lot."

In the evening Mum and Dad didn't talk to each other at all. Actually, it was Mum who didn't speak to Dad, except for things like "*kolacja* is ready" and "pass the butter."

When Mum wasn't looking, I counted her share in the envelope. She got the most, then me, then Janek, then Iwonka. I wondered how Dad had done the magic trick to get it so fair. How did he know which pockets we'd choose? I put Mum's money back and spotted Mrs. Moscrop's letter. Then it came to me. What a brilliant idea! I folded the letter lengthways twice and hid it deep under the wad of brown envelopes in the letter rack.

Next day Mum was a right old meany. She made us open Post Office accounts because we had to 'consider the future'. My future looked better already though. I might have a *handsome* boyfriend one day, not just Ossie and Stevo. No specs.

*****

A few days later, Granny took me with her to Chorlton and while we there she bought me a box of notelets, felt tips, a red exercise book, and a new biro at Quarmby's. They were free and for nothing – I didn't ask for them or anything – just because Granny wanted to be kind. So when she said we'd stop by Mrs. Jeleńska's to exchange Living Rosary holy cards, I thought I shouldn't make a fuss, even though Mrs. Jeleńska was the last person on earth I wanted to visit because she was dead scary.

Mrs. Jeleńska often talked to herself, shouting and waving her arms about. When the weather was sunny, she looked more or less okay. But if it rained, her jet-black permed hair frizzed out, and her eyebrows, one thick, one thin, disappeared and gave her two panda eyes. And she had a brown wart at the side of her mouth which sometimes sprouted silvery hairs. One Sunday they'd vanish. Then they'd reappear next week.

Once, when Ossie, Manuela and I were waiting for the bus to Chorlton library, we saw Mrs. Jeleńska having one of her sensational rows with herself across the road. The old Jamaican lady from number eighty took her by the arm, whispered into her ear and guided her by the elbow back to her house. The lady opened the gate and watched. We heard her call, "Off you go, love. That's right, have a cuppa tea with Jesus."

Ossie creased up. "Cuppa tea with Jesus. Ha-ha! Who ya looking for? Little me?" he said, pretending to be a chimp from the Brooke Bond Tea advert.

The Jamaican lady heard and threw him a fierce look. "Oswald MacDonald! I'll see you in church!"

Manuela couldn't stop cackling because she'd called him Oswald.

But nothing horrible would happen now. I had Granny with me.

Granny put her hand on my shoulder as we reached the gate. If Mrs. Jeleńska offered a cup of tea, I could open my felt tips and draw, she said.

The house stood well back from the road and the garden was almost as overgrown as Old Spooky's. It was impossible to see into it because rhododendrons, lilacs, laburnums grew through the privet. The branches of the trees that dropped pink May blossoms formed a tunnel to the house. My hand itched to grab hold of Granny's as she strode up the path ahead of me and rang the doorbell.

There was a clunking noise as someone unbolted two locks. Mrs. Jeleńska, whose eyebrows were even for once, opened the door a fraction, saw it was us, and said, "May Jesus Christ be praised." Glancing up with every movement, she unhooked three chains to let us in.

The hall looked worse than Granny and Grandad's garage. I sneezed. We manoeuvred past the floor-to-ceiling piles of books, newspapers, magazines, and bundled up reams of paper with Polski-style loopy handwriting on them. A peculiar smell, like cat wee and boiling cherries, rose off the carpet.

Mrs. Jeleńska led us to the sitting room. "Please, please, sit down both. I must find my prayer book," she said, waddling off.

The fusty sitting room reminded me of *The Munsters* house, except smaller. Grey nets hung at the windows, half-hidden by maroon velvet curtains with cobwebs trailing from them. Dust covered almost everything, even the lacy, embroidered antimacassars on the armchairs and the visible bits of the yellowing doilies under the ornaments and plant pots. Only the leaves of the plants were shiny, as if she'd just carted them in from a florist's shop. Granny and I jigged between more heaps of books, trying to find floor to put our feet on, and sat down.

Mrs. Jeleńska returned almost immediately. I didn't get my felt tips out because she hadn't brought any tea or cake. They spent a while talking about Mysteries and the Living Rosary. Not too long, thank goodness. Then there was a bit more about Mary, the Mother of God, a bit more about the Ten Commandments, and a lot more about that godless heathen Mrs.Wróbelska, whose knees – according to Granny – were too crepey for the short dresses she wore. Brazen, Granny decided. Mum would have gone mad if she heard her talking like that! When Granny finally finished complaining about having to wait at the confessional rail, she lifted herself off the sofa with a groan.

"But we must go. The Devil dictates when you are in a hurry." She pulled her skirt down then her stockings up.

We managed to get out of the room without tripping on anything.

In the hall, suddenly all holy again, Granny said, "Praised be Jesus Christ. I will see you on the fourth pew."

Mrs. Jeleńska opened the door to let us out. "Forever and ever. Amen." The door closed, I heard her say "May God go with you" and she began to slide back the bolts.

I hadn't noticed it on the way in, but coming out I spotted Mrs. Jeleńska's apple tree, laden with red fruit, ten times better than the brownish-green ones in Grandad's little orchard in the back garden. Right next to the neighbour's wall.

I had one of my marvellous ideas.

CHAPTER SIXTEEN

DAY FOUR: MORNING

I feel a gentle prod.

"What are you doing here?" Mum whispers.

I open my eyes. "Time is it?"

"Quarter to nine. Iwonka will be here soon. And the nurses."

I sit up, pausing to straighten the crick in my neck, and take a look at Dad. Should we wake him for his medication? Mum asks if I want a cup of tea.

"No, I need a shower." I feel sticky, want a good scrub, as if the smell in Dad's room has permeated every part of me. I need to feel and look good today, groomed and alert; like the way I used to prepare for exams to stop the panic. Revision, deodorant, a tidy pencil case. No snags in my tights.

In the shower, I push their old people's chair tight up against the tiles. There's a bit of mildew on the shower mat which I scrub to no avail.

The hot water sprays my face.

I recall when I saw Ossie being interviewed on the TV about the oil spill, waves crashing against the rocks behind him, the camera lens misty from the rain. Must have been the late 90s. I didn't recognise him at first, but that was partly because he'd lost his Mancunian accent, just a trace remaining, and because he was so good-looking he made Denzel Washington seem like Shrek.

I'm applying mascara, still thinking of Ossie when Iwonka arrives.

"You ready? Come to the kitchen. I've brought you some home-made croissants."

"You've made actual croissants? Yourself? Why don't you do what normal people do? Buy them."

"I couldn't sleep. The Babcia legacy." She has the tell-tale bags under her eyes.

Outside there's three inches of snow and the sky is grey. All the lights are

169

on in the house.

"How was he?" Iwonka says, as I sit opposite her at the table. She's already put out knives and plates and made me tea, exactly the right colour, in my favourite china mug. There are three more plates apart from mine and hers.

"Who's this for?"

"Janek and Marie. They'll be here in a minute. He's got an appointment in the city centre then he's coming back here."

"Mum?"

Iwonka lowers her voice. "Sitting with Dad. I hope she puts that bloody rosary away when he wakes up. How was he?"

"Not too bad. Did I tell you we've got to take him to Poland in a Tesco's bag?"

Iwonka laughs. "Yeah, he said that to me too. Loony." She sighs. "We'll have to do it though. Not the Tesco's bag, obviously. We'll go together, yeah?" She takes a bite of croissant and chews.

"He showed me a map," I say.

She grins and parks a bit of croissant inside her cheek. "Me too. What's he like! Talk about dotting your I's and crossing your T's! What's the betting he'll book the flights for us from the other side. Janek's had the same instructions, too."

"Oh God, Evie, how can we – *you* – joke?"

She shakes her head. "Don't beat yourself up. It's Dad. He's a realist. In the genes."

"What about all his books? Not exactly the kind of stuff they'd want at St. Bernadette's Hospice, is it? Three thousand four hundred and twenty-five volumes of Polish history? Half of them about the Grey Ranks. And all the Cold War and Solidarity books. Most of them in Polish anyway. Who's interested in that now? It's done."

Iwonka blows out hard as if she's trying to extinguish one of those reigniting candles. "No. Can't throw them out. It's his treasure."

"His treasure. Mum's junk. And all the poetry books, documents and ephemera..."

"Don't call it that, Ania." Her tone is quiet.

"What's wrong with ephemera?"

"Ephemera makes it...trivial. He's kept some of those things for almost seventy years. That's not trivial, is it?"

"Sorry. I didn't mean it that way. I just meant it's not...well, what can we do with it?"

"We'll think of something," she says and opens today's *Telegraph* at the letters page. Her fingers drum a little tune on the table.

I realise I'd better start throwing my own garbage out now. So Sam and Rachel don't find out about the me they don't already know, and the grandfather they thought they knew. I have hazy recollections of letters I wrote to Dad and didn't send, yet couldn't throw out. It may not be the kids who find them: they'll get a house clearance firm, and one day someone will pay ten pence for a tatty copy of *Zen and the Art of Motorcycle Maintenance* and find my questions, my accusations.

Iwonka licks her thumb and dabs at the crumbs on her plate. She doesn't write letters. She writes recipes and lists with sub-categories like Kids, Husband, Mum and Dad, Dogs, House, Car, Work.

"Have you ever thought about the crap you'll leave behind?" I ask.

She doesn't look up. "I don't have crap, thank you very much, you cheeky sod. I have *objets d'art.*"

"Yeah, no you don't. You have crap."

She lifts her eyes. They're twinkling. A smile flickers around her lips. I love you, Evie. Thank you, Mum. Thank you, Dad. Thank you for doing this thing right for us.

"Careful," she warns, smile spreading wider. "Sudoku?"

As usual she pulls out the puzzles page and hands it to me. I start with the hardest, can't fill in a single number, then go back to the easy one. It seems the current pattern. I can't settle to it because I'm back to thinking about all those entries under Ossie's name. And there's the other thing. Shall I ask her?

"You know when we were little and Dad talked about the war..."

"Mm?"

"Do you ever remember him mentioning a Yankel?"

Iwonka's face is blank. "Who?"

"Yankel?"

I sense Mum standing behind me, waiting to interrupt. I turn round. Dad wants some tea, she says.

Iwonka rises to fill the kettle. "What did you say?" Water gushes out of the tap and spills down the side. "*Psia krew!*" She puts the kettle on the draining board and wipes down the sink, as if it isn't clean enough already. "Oh, yeah. No. Jankiel? There was that one from *Pan Tadeusz.* Jankiel, the tavern keeper. He played the zither or something. Him? You didn't do that for A-level, did you?"

I groan. "*Z Ogniem I Mieczem.* With Fire and Sword. I wanted to blow my brains out."

Iwonka laughs. "You still got it though."

"B," I say. I think back to when my results came through. How dissatisfied I was I hadn't worked harder. How scared that Dad would be disappointed. And then the celebration at Polish school when... "Do you remember Krysia Nowicka? She got an 'A' with some kind of special recommendation."

"Course I remember Krysia. Bright girl," Iwonka says, beaming. "She was great. In Seattle now. Stayed in Manchester for uni though. She used to come and help me with Latin O-level. "

"She did?"

"You'd gone by then."

I'm suddenly aware that so much has passed me by and Iwonka's obviously forgotten Dad's Yankel. Maybe she was too young to understand any of it.

"Evie, do you remember Ossie from next door?"

"What's got into you?" she asks. "Why wouldn't I? We lived next to them for God knows how many years! Melinda was with me at St.Mark's for sixth form, though they'd moved by then. Stockport or somewhere. What's with all this ancient history? Are you all right?"

It's 9.48. Janek and Marie arrive. Janek gives me a pretend flick on the nose, pats me on the bum and informs me I need to lose some weight. I flick him back and tell him I know a good plastic surgeon who could sort out his gargantuan hooter.

Marie stands shaking her head and grinning. "Children! Behave."

THEN

We walked from Mrs. Jeleńska's back to Granny's house. In her kitchen, Granny gave me a glass of juice and a sandwich. She told me to be quiet for a moment and write a story. She took her everyday rosary from the pouch in the cutlery drawer and, twisting the beads one by one, silently mouthed several Hail Marys. Then she stood in front of the mirror above the sink and tied a piece of white thread around a pea-sized skin-bobble that had grown on the side of her chin.

"What's that for?" I asked.

"If I put a new piece of cotton on every day, this will fall off," She said, pointing at the bump. No way was I going out anywhere with her with *that* on her face!

When she finished poking it, I asked what all those books were for. They weren't paperbacks with pictures on the front covers like Mum's *Angelique* books. They were more like Dad's books in the bookcase in the dining room. And why was the house such a flipping mess? What were all those stacks of paper with writing on them? Why didn't they throw them out?

The bundles, Granny said, were Mr. Jeleński's history of the Polish-Ukrainian War that he'd been working on for twenty years. As for the rest, Mrs. Jeleńska never cleaned, wiped or hoovered because she was a countess, or as Granny referred to her, "a *hrabina*." And countesses weren't born to housework.

Granny was fibbing. Even putting all other peculiarities aside, how could Mrs. Jeleńska – short, dumpy, with blobs of food congealed on her blouse – be a *hrabina*? Was there ever a less countessy countess?

"Babcia – you're not telling me—"

"Things aren't always what they seem. We were all beautiful once. You'll find that out one day," she said. Since her voice didn't have the "in Siberia when red beetles fell on our heads from the ceiling" blah-blah tone, I listened.

Granny continued. Mrs. Jeleńska's lack of housewifely pride – not that Granny had much to be proud of either – was because she'd been brought up in a huge white manor on a vast estate. Inside, the walls were covered with paintings of Mrs. Jeleńska's ancestors and deer antlers. Granny said she'd heard that the gardens were modelled on those at Versailles, which I knew from the *Alpha Book of Facts for Girls* was near Paris. The road to the manor house was bordered by rows of silver birches which was why it was called *Srebrzysty Gaj*, Silver Grove. This manor, which also had forests full of deer and bison, a lake with swans, and storks that nested on roof tops, was near Białystok about forty miles from where Granny and Grandad lived. Granny made it sound like a fairy tale.

Mrs. Jeleńska, Granny said, was looked after from morning till night by maids and butlers who did everything for her. She went to balls in sequinned and beaded dresses, and took long journeys to exciting places, travelling in first class compartments. She'd been to Switzerland, Italy, some place called Odessa, and France, where she'd even met the King of England, except he wasn't the king at that time because he married the woman he loved, Granny said, and nobody liked her.

"Babcia...stop it."

"Stop what?" She was teasing me, I could tell.

"A real king?"

She pushed the scarf back to her hairline and nodded, her eyes blinking wide behind her glasses. "Oh yes. Queen Elizabeth's uncle." This was so much better than her other stories. I sat on the edge of the chair, elbows on the table, my chin in my hands. Could it actually be true that I, Ania Walewska, knew someone who knew the King of England? I wanted to believe it. Wait till I told Manuela!

"What happened next?" I asked. Perhaps Mr. Jeleński was, in fact, a prince, and Mrs. Jeleńska met him at a ball where they'd fallen in love and got married. Manuela would like that bit.

Granny sighed as if she'd suddenly grown tired.

She said it was February and the snow was deep when the Russians came to the manor, in the middle of the night – same as for Granny and Grandad. Mrs. Jeleńska was twenty-three then. The soldiers told her family to pack what they could carry and stand outside in the blizzard, but Mrs. Jeleńska hid in a wardrobe in the servants' quarters.

My fingers were tingling, thinking how clever of Mrs. Jeleńska to hide. I remembered when Ossie and I escaped from the Territorial Army man, and how Stevo and I crouched in the backyard when Mrs. Harrington was banging on all the gates. How scary it was, but thrilling too.

But a servant told the soldiers Mrs. Jeleńska was missing from the group. Three soldiers stayed outside and pointed their bayonets at Mrs. Jeleńska's parents and brothers, while the other five searched until they found her. They were furious she'd caused them so much trouble.

"What did they do?" I asked.

Granny paused and removed her glasses. With her fingertips she pressed into her eyelids and rubbed outwards until she looked Chinese. Her fingers stopped at her temples, and she pushed in as if trying to plug her brain.

"You must never talk about this. Not even with your mama." Why was she whispering? We were alone in the kitchen. Nobody could hear anyway. Grandad was in the shed.

"I promise."

"They were animals those Russians, not men. They took off their coats…and their belts. They punished her. All of them." Granny hesitated. "I'll say no more."

But after a few seconds, she did. Granny said they hurt Mrs. Jeleńska so badly that she couldn't walk and they made her brothers carry her to the sled. Mrs. Jeleńska didn't speak for over two years. She stayed curled up during the journey, and when they got to Siberia she was mute.

"A tragedy," Granny said. "We were all beautiful. Once."

I stared at Granny's powdery glasses, her wrinkles and the threads dangling from her skin-bobble. It was hard to imagine.

*****

It wasn't as if I forgot the entire story the minute I left, but Mrs. Jeleńska had been punished a long time ago. And I'd managed to get over Dad giving me the belt, hadn't I? And that was only a few months back. *And* I'd been prepared for six straps, and Mrs. Jeleńska only got five, even if they did hurt more than mine. What was the fuss? She should have been strong like me. I'd even gone to school the next day and everything.

Anyway, none of that changed the fact that her apple tree was better than Grandad's.

I had a good wheeze in mind, so I proposed it to the gang when Gianni wasn't there. I knew he'd find reasons why we shouldn't go ahead.

The other boys had to do most of the work because Mrs. Jeleńska knew my face. Ossie and Stevo could climb over the neighbour's wall straight into the crown of the tree, Dermot would sneak in via the gate and crawl through the bushes. If the boys stayed on this side of the garden, Mrs. Jeleńska wouldn't be able to see them from the bay windows either. Meanwhile, Manuela and I'd keep guard at the gate and sound the alert if anyone opened the front door.

At least, that was the plan. Until scaredy-cat Manuela said no. She said the idea of Carol the Barrel had been bad enough, and she wasn't going to go through that again. I might have known. I expect she didn't want to get her earrings dirty.

So it ended up being the four of us. The boys followed the strategy to the letter. From my vantage point I saw Ossie and Stevo dropping apples to Dermot who'd stretched the bottom of his jumper out to catch them.

The door opened and Mrs. Jeleńska came out in her coat and hat pulling her tartan shopping trolley behind her. I squealed and bobbed to the pavement. The boys must have turned green like the leaves because Mrs. Jeleńska strode straight down the path without seeing them. But she sure as heck saw me when she opened the gate.

"*Dzieńdobry.* What are you doing there?"

"Hello." I raised my face and attempted a charming smile. "Fixing my buckle," I answered, inching up from my haunches, trying not to stare at her wonky eyebrows.

Someone grunted "*Psha kreff*" and yelped by the apple tree.

"What's—" she whipped round towards the noise. "—that? You! Boy!"

I heard several shushes, a loud whisper of "She's got Ania", then a few small thuds. She began to head towards them, stopped, and came back at me, still frozen to the spot, mouth agape.

"What do you know about this?"

"I—"

"Speak!"

"Nothing. I—"

She never gave me a chance to answer. She picked up a thorny dead branch and whacked me with it across my arm. The sting was excruciating.

"You find this amusing?" She hit me again. I looked up and down Upper Chorlton Road to see if there was anyone who might help me. Not even a single soul at the bus stop.

"It's acceptable, is it, to steal my property?" I was going to protest that I hadn't done anything when she yanked me by the shoulder, and began to push me towards Granny's house. I glanced at the wall in the neighbour's drive. There was no-one there. The boys had skedaddled, leaving me to her. How could they?

Next, there was a thump into my kidneys and I lurched forward along the pavement. I heard the wheels of the shopping trolley squeaking behind me.

"Move!" she said.

She slammed Granny's gate open, shoved me up the two steps into the porch and rang the bell. She moved back onto the path, still with a hold on me. The nails of her thumb and finger were pinching into my underarm like crab claws. I had to squash my teeth together to stop myself from crying.

The scratches looked really bad – blobs of blood had appeared and they were dripping. Where the heck was Granny? Why didn't she answer? What on earth was she doing in there?

When Granny finally opened the door, Mrs. Jeleńska thrust me forward.

"Take her," she said.

Granny saw my arm. "What happened?"

"I taught her a lesson."

Granny wiped her hands on her apron, lifted my arm and took a closer look at the scratches.

"Ania, what happened?"

"She hit me," I mumbled to my shoes, avoiding her gaze so there'd be no further questions.

Granny's nostrils grew as big as a warthog's and her eyes looked as if they were about to pop out of her head. Her chins sank into her neck. She was looking at her over the top of her glasses.

Mrs. Jeleńska's stood her ground, an expression of victory on her face.

Granny's words came out one by one. "You did this? *You* did this to her?" She sounded like Groucho when the postman dropped letters into the porch.

Mrs. Jeleńska moved the trolley from her side to the front. "She was stealing."

I wasn't, so I attempted to argue my case. "I was just outside—"

One moment it was quiet, next an almighty screech that must have scared people in Brooks's Bar. Granny shouted, "You *wariatka*! You crazy woman, you hurt an innocent child? How would you like it, you lunatic?" Then she took a wide swing with her right arm and slapped Mrs. Jeleńska across the face. "How dare you!"

Mrs. Jeleńska walloped her straight back, her cheek now blazing with the red imprint of four chunky fingers.

Grandad appeared in the hall, a half-smoked Woodbine dangling from his lips.

"Enough!" he said, grabbing Granny's wrist from the back as she was about land another whopper on Mrs. Jeleńska.

He pulled his beret down forward, and squinting at us through the rising smoke of his cigarette, said, "You and you, in." At first, I thought Granny was going to punch him one too, but she composed herself, put her hand on the back of my neck, scooped me towards her. We stepped back to the doorway.

Grandad's voice was tender and kind when he spoke to Mrs. Jeleńska. "Home?"

She pointed a hooky, knobbly finger at me. "That child should be thrashed. She—"

"I'll deal with it." He turned her round. "I'll come by tonight."

Grandad lifted her arm and, with a gentle tuck, wrapped it around his elbow. He escorted her to the gate, stopping for moment to split off one of the few remaining roses. When Mrs. Jeleńska accepted it, Granny grunted, pulled me inside and closed the door.

I expect Grandad went down the side of the house to his shed because he didn't come back indoors after that.

Inside the kitchen, in silence, Granny washed my arm, dried it with the tea

176

towel that Grandad always used to slicing his corns and smeared Savlon into the bloody bits. She applied three plasters.

"What did you do?" she said, now opening the cupboard.

Normally I knew not to tell when I'd be the worse off for it, but Granny had been such a heroine that I thought it was safe to admit the truth, the part about the boys included. I mean, they were only apples, and Mrs. Jeleńska had enough to stock a greengrocer's.

Granny turned to face me. "So it was your idea?" Her voice was like a chicken squawking. "*Psia krew*! After what I told you?"

She whisked me off the chair and thwacked me with a wooden spoon on the back of my calves. I hadn't cried so far, but this was more than I could take.

Granny didn't soften. She told me to stay there and cry as much as I liked. I could howl for the next four hours as far as she was concerned. Ten years if I wanted.

*****

Half an hour later, when I'd stopped bawling and Granny had calmed down and was making *kluski*, the door bell rang.

She mumbled, "*Psia krew*. If that *wariatka* is back..." and bashed the same wooden spoon she'd used on me into the mixing bowl sending a cloud of flour into the air. Her hands on her hips, she took a deep breath, lifted her chin and stood there a moment as if she was preparing to jump out of an airplane.

"Stay," she said and marched off to open the door.

"Vot you vont?" I heard her say, now switched from Polish to English.

Then, to my horror, Stevo's voice. "Is Ania here, please?"

My eyes, I knew, must be fat red slits and my nose the size of a belisha beacon. He couldn't see me in this state. Please send him away. I saw him trying to bend round her and peep into the house, so I tried to blend into the wall.

"Is she okay?" he asked.

Granny adopted her best English accent. "You come in."

It felt peculiar to have one of my friends at Granny's, like a proper guest. The rest of the gang never got beyond standing in front of the back door when I was getting instructions for an errand or persuading Granny into a small donation.

Stevo said thank you, polite as you please, and followed her, poking his head round her sides, grinning at me from her left, then from her right, pushing his bottom lip out pretending to look sad.

"Sit you," she said to him indicating Grandad's chair. "You friend Ania?"

Stevo nodded.

"But I think you not good boy. Vot you name? Ver you live?" Oh no, how

177

could she do this to me? I felt myself colouring up even more, hot, bothered, wondering what she planned. Was she going to see his parents or something? She was examining his general state of grubbiness, the grime beneath his fingernails, the muddy marks around his neck. He resembled one of those kids on *All Our Yesterdays*.

He replied, "Steven," and then, all grown-up, extended his dirty hand as if he expected her to shake it. Which she didn't.

Granny moved to the sink, poured water and a blob of washing up liquid over the dishcloth and put it in his palm. "Vash youself. Tell me truth. You take apple Mrs. Jeleńska?"

This was just too much. I squirmed at her English and remembered the time we'd gone to buy me a new school blouse. She'd asked the assistant to bring her "a white shit, size ten years." Now the same desire for the ground to crack open and swallow me was spreading through my bones. I was crumbling into little pieces inside. Why couldn't he have stayed at Spooky?

"You take apple Mrs. Jeleńska?" she repeated, eyes narrowing.

Stevo shifted on the seat and rubbed his nose. "It wasn't Ania's fault. We were all in on it."

Granny looked puzzled, as if she hadn't understood. In Polish, I asked her to stop this interrogation. I'd owned up, hadn't I? Why wasn't that enough? Hadn't I already paid for my sins?

She tapped Stevo on his hand. "You very naughty boy. Bad girl. I very angry. You never do again. Mrs. Jeleńska not happy person. All brothers died in Siberia."

Granny hadn't mentioned it earlier. That was sad. Why hadn't she told me before I'd had my marvellous idea? But on the other hand, why should we be kind to Mrs. Jeleńska when Granny wasn't?

In Polish I said, "I'm sorry about her family, but you said she's a lunatic."

Granny did one of her bone-cracking wrist-squeezes on me, right in front of Stevo. "Never say that again."

I asked her why she'd slapped her if she wasn't crazy.

Stevo sat in silence, bemused, not understanding a word, looking from me to her as we swapped sentences in Polish.

Granny said, "Because you're my granddaughter. I love you. That's the end of it. I'll say no more."

Then, her gold tooth gleaming, she smiled at Stevo. "Is finish. You drink raspberry juice?"

Stevo grinned. "Raspberry – I've never had that before." He winked at me. "Ania said you make *delicious* raspberry juice."

"I bring you." She went to the sitting room to get a bottle, and while she was gone, Stevo said he thought her weird, but nice. I stopped being so embarrassed. And I realised he was the only one who'd had the guts to come round and ask whether I was alive or dead. That meant something, didn't it?

Like he must really care? As if I was important to him?

Granny came back, buttered a piece of her home-made brioche and gave it to him to eat with his juice. When he announced he was leaving, she said, "You remember. Be good boy. No steal from Mrs. Jeleńska. She nice lady."

*****

A few days after the apple incident Stevo and I were waiting for Ossie to show up at Spooky. We were trying to learn semaphore from the *Alpha Book of Facts for Girls*, and since we had no flags, we made them out of twigs and pages from *Woman's Own*. He got fed up when we reached the letter F which was the same sign for six.

"Shall we do summat else now?"

"Like what?"

He considered it. Then, out of nowhere, he said, "D'ya wanna snog?"

I nearly fainted. I didn't know where to put myself. He was crazy. It made me squirm just to watch Simon Templar snogging on the telly. And sometimes, if Mum or Dad were there, I had to stroke Groucho or pretend to be rubbing out a stain on the armchair. I kind of knew I might *have* to do proper kissing *one day* when I had a proper boyfriend. But *he* was going to be handsome and wear a signet ring and everything.

"What for?"

Stevo said, "Why not? Don't ya like me?" My toes froze into hook shapes and I prayed for Ossie to arrive so the conversation would be over.

"Course I do, but…no thanks," I said, hoping that was the end of that and I hadn't hurt his feelings.

"I bet ya'd kiss Gianni or Ossie if they asked. And Wormy."

"I bet I wouldn't."

"Bet ya would."

"Wouldn't."

"Would. Promise not to tell anyone." He wasn't going to let this slide, I could see. He'd go on and on and on until I'd have to smack him one, like Janek.

"You ever kissed a boy?"

My heart began to race. There was Stasio at *kolonia*, but he didn't count. I resisted an urge to flatten my cowlicks. My tonsils seemed to inflate, like when we'd first walked into Harrington's, and later when Carol the Barrel was bashing the gates.

He said, "I've never kissed a girl before either."

"And you've never thrown yourself in a chip pan. Doesn't mean you have to do it."

"Aw, come on. Dare ya."

There it was. I should have been expecting it. That word 'dare' was a small explosion in my ears.

179

"Okay. But I'm telling you—"

His grin spread across his face as if he'd known all along I'd cave in. "Stand up, go on."

As I got to my feet, sure I was a complete 'nana, he reached out to help me. I did my best to change my prunish expression. I had to remember I liked him on his inside because he was kind, even though he was a liar. Just not so much his outside. And it was somebody's inside that counted. That's what Evelyn Home had said on *Woman* problem page to the boy with the spots. And I wasn't going to marry Stevo or anything. But even if I did, I'd buy him soap on a rope for his birthday, so he'd be normal and clean by then.

He said, "Ready?"

I nodded.

"Give us yer other hand. Put yer head this way, and I'll go the other way." He must have lied when he said he'd never kissed a girl. He knew everything you had to do. "Now?" He placed his scratchy lips on mine. Where they stayed, not moving. It was nothing spectacular, and I hardly noticed he was a bit whiffy.

He detached himself from me. "What d'ya think?"

"Don't know. Not great, is it?"

"Maybe we did it wrong."

"Doesn't matter. You said one snog."

He held onto my hands. "Let's try again. Got a better idea."

"I have to go." I lied and wriggled out of his grasp. Where was Ossie?

"Go home in a minute," he said, taking hold of my wrists again.

"All right. Do it. Then I'm going."

Stevo shifted closer, his eyes fixed on my chin. When his lips landed, they were hard. He pressed and rubbed from side to side. No, no change. Why did Simon Templar always have to do it with every lady he met?

And then Stevo did something different. His mouth covered my bottom lip as if he was going to bite me, except he didn't. At first it stayed there, and I stood still as still can be. I felt his tongue lick me on the inside. It was kind of nice. Interesting. I wondered how it would feel if he did that on my top lip too. So I tried it on him. Instead of being rigid, his lip tasted the same as lumpy bits in strawberry jam. It was *super* nice.

"*Torta di Mellay Jenno Vazay,*" came Ossie's yell.

We broke away. I thrust two semaphore twigs into Stevo's hand, picked up the others and dashed to the other side of the den.

Ossie trundled in, whistling and carrying a paper bag. "I brought da loot," he said, in his mum's accent. "Me trifle peckish."

Stevo wasn't bothered. He grinned at me, then pulled kissing faces behind Ossie's back. I thought I'd die. Just die. I couldn't look at Ossie because he'd suss it somehow. After five minutes I said I had to go.

As I pelted out and down the path, I imagined Stevo telling Ossie and those two laughing their heads off together.

I ran into our house, panting. Mum put knives and forks in my hands as soon as I walked in.

"Where have you been? Janek said you weren't in the avenue."

My face was boiling hot, and I was taking long breaths to stop the thudding in my head. I took my time arranging the cutlery. "Nowhere."

Mum must know too. Surely I looked different to the person who'd left two hours ago.

"Nowhere where?"

"Nowhere at Babcia's."

"Hm." Mum paused. She was standing right next me, so I kept my face averted. "Don't forget the salt and pepper."

Apparently 'this girl snogged Stevo Kardasz' wasn't branded on my forehead in giant capitals because no-one mentioned it over *kolacja*, not even Dad. And apart from being told off for collecting the tomatoes on the side of my plate, nothing else happened. Except for one thing.

Something else had disappeared from our sitting room. I walked in ready to watch telly, and there the print of Notre Dame Cathedral wasn't. Gone. I'd spent hours gazing at it, imagining myself strolling in the sunshine by the river walls, looking at the cheerful paintings in the artist's case, being ooh-la-la and hon-hi-hon French.

Now another black frame was in its place. Behind the glass was a typewritten letter in Polish. I stood on the sofa and read:

Dear Colleague,

From the depths of my heart, I ask you to accept my sincerest thanks for your condolences and for the words of sympathy from the committee of the Underground Army in Manchester in these my difficult times.

Your warm words moved me greatly as did the beautiful Poland in Battle wreath you laid on my husband's grave. My husband always enjoyed coming to Manchester to see the members of the circle who worked so selflessly. I hope, that is to say, I believe you will continue to honour his memory by being as united through shared battles as you always have been, and that you will continue working tirelessly for the ideals my husband strove towards throughout his life.

With fond regards,

Irena Komorowska.

I suppose it was nice of Mrs. Komorowska to send that letter, but I so wished she hadn't. Our sitting room was looking more and more like Manchester museum, except it was Polish. I half-expected the telly to vanish and a glass box of dinosaur Polish bison bones to appear as an exhibit. That was all we needed.

That night in bed I tried to perfect the kissing technique on the back of my hand. I put my thumb up against my forefinger and licked them, closed my eyes and attached my lips to Stevo's pretend mouth. Not the same, but it had potential. It was probably something you had to learn to do, like cricket. I decided I'd give it another go if he asked. If he hadn't told Ossie.

CHAPTER SEVENTEEN

DAY FOUR: LATE MORNING, EARLY AFTERNOON

Dad says he'd like us to sit with him and listen to some more music, preferably songs from scouting, the *Armia Krajowa* and the Polish Legions. It's like he's stuck in a time warp that doesn't even belong to him. Why the Legions? They were around during the First World War and the twenties, weren't they? The Polish-Bolshevik War and the Miracle on the Vistula in 1920 and all that stuff? Still, we do whatever Dad wants now.

Janek roots out the appropriate CDs. I hold Dad forward while Iwonka plumps up the pillows now slipping down his sit-up contraption.

I haven't spent so much time in Dad's company since those two weeks following my chemo when he and Mum put everything on hold for my sake. She'd lowered her voice when a friend phoned to invite them for canasta. "No. I'm sorry. We can't make it for a while. Ania's here," as if I couldn't manage without them for a few hours. Afterwards, life went on, trundling or careering. Mum and Dad here, me there with Sam and Rachel. Lonely every weekend after I'd dropped them off at John's, containing the pain and anger when Rachel said Daddy's new wife was really nice because she let them eat Angel Delight and drink Coca Cola. Angel Delight... I'd tell someone else, "Don't blame yourself."

I ought to have had the courage to ask Dad as soon as I saw the *Shoah* documentary and made the connections. Maybe Iwonka is right – I should leave it. I must let it go. That knowledge doesn't change the person I am, not really. But why does it make me feel I lived a lie?

We sit in our allotted chairs, the music begins. I glance at Marie, wondering how she's coped for 25 years being part of this family, never complaining about the quaint rituals, carp and *bigos*, or sudden changes mid-conversation into Polish. She's heard these songs often enough to know the words. Like me singing Eurovision Song Contest songs when I was little, not having a clue what they meant. Mum thinks Marie is one of God's blessings.

First the old staples: '*Serce w Plecaku*', Heart in a Rucksack, '*Przybyli Ułani Pod Okienko*', The Ulans Came to the Window. Janek's grinning, putting on a baritone show for the lower notes, tensing his face towards his chest, having a bit of a Bryn Terfel moment. He's taken his shoes off and his feet rest on the bed, his hands together on his paunch, thumbs dancing to the tune of the march.

Mum pops her head round the door and asks if we all want tea. Daft question.

Now it's '*Pierwsza Kadrowa*', First Cadre; Dad opens his eyes, winks at Janek, and joins in twice for the chorus, *Oj da Oj da dana*. He attempts it again after the third verse when the soldiers vow to reach Warsaw no matter what, but his strength is waning. If Rachel and Sam were here, they'd probably glow with affection, with those "What can you do? He's Polish…" expressions on their faces, similar to the "What can you do? We're lumbered with her" look they give me. I try to recall if I ever did that. Probably, at their age.

Mum returns. She's used the posh set, not the mugs, as if this is an occasion. She passes the cups and saucers round then leaves.

A plaintive accordion introduces '*Dziś do Ciebie przyjść nie mogę*', I Cannot Come To You Today. Dad loves this. Janek doesn't sing the words now. He's humming. The partisan says goodbye to his beloved, telling her he may never return. If he's not back by spring, his friend will have buried him and his bones will be overgrown with moss. By the end of the song, Dad's breathing is even.

Iwonka reduces the volume and we sit together not speaking as the CD plays on quietly. My mind wanders to Katy Carr's version of '*Dziś do Ciebie*'. What drives a young woman to live in the 1940s and devote her musical career to visiting decrepit Polish fogeys round the world? One minute Buffalo, the next Oslo or New Zealand? Artistic temperament, I expect. Or else she's barking mad.

It's 12.29. Marie slips her shoes on, Janek his, saying he'll probably come back this evening. Iwonka's going to prepare dinner for the family.

Dad sleeps.

It's 2.27. I'm alone with Dad, reading my Kindle. Mum's ironing in the kitchen. He clears his gurgly throat so I put a tissue to his lips, let him spit out the phlegm.

Then he speaks. "*Keine Messe—*" and his throat clogs up again. He tries to cough, so I lift his head a little.

More spittle, then pausing between words, "*Keine Messe wird man singen Keine Kadish wird man sagen*," he licks his mouth, "*nichts gesagt und nichts gesungen wird an meinen Sterbetagen.*"

Why's he speaking German? I pour a few drops of water on another tissue and moisten his mouth. What does he mean? No mass will be sung, no kaddish said, nothing sung or spoken on the day of my death. I sit down again. "What's that, Tatuś?"

He inhales. "Heine, I believe."

"Heine? Where did you get that from?"

His hand is seeking mine on the top of the duvet so I move it nearer, let him find it.

"I went to school, child," he says with a tsk, giving my hand two pats. Is there a hidden meaning there? Is it about the year I wagged it every Wednesday? He opens his eyes, moves his head to the left to look at me. Now I'm sixteen again.

"You like German poetry?" I say.

"It came back in a dream."

"Bit miserable, isn't it?"

Dad emits a little grunt. "It's German," he says, by way of explanation. "It may have escaped you... they aren't known for their good cheer."

I feel I'm getting nearer though. "You hated them."

Dad's chin retracts. "Whatever gave you that idea? Pass me my glasses."

"But you said—" I can't carry on, I'm stumped. All those war rants, Dad. Remember? They were a slight indication, I'd say.

He pushes his glasses up his nose. "Not *Germans*. Nazis." I can't make out if the look of disgust is for them or me because I ought to know what he thinks.

"You can't blame a whole nation for the crimes of a few," he says.

"Few? What? How can you say that?"

I'm thinking of the Nuremburg rallies, the Nazi eagle above the swastika, an audience of hundreds of thousands gazing in admiration while Hitler yells in German, from hands on hips to arms folded, beating his chest to ram home his point.

"The trouble with you, child, is that you would like everything to be black or white. Life's not simple. How old are you?"

The doorbell rings. Mum's talking to someone. I was getting somewhere with Dad, getting nearer.

"Please, come in," she says. I recognise the priest's voice. Who asked him? Mum brings him into Dad's room and I wonder how long I have to stay to appear polite.

Getting to my feet, I ask, "Would you like something to drink? Tea?"

"I wouldn't want to put you to any trouble... One sugar."

I escape to the kitchen, take my time, return with tea, and realise he's going to be there for a while. He's put the paraphernalia for Holy Communion on the bedside table.

"My bones will be overgrown with moss." The words of the song have become earworms, nagging, haunting. And there's nothing I can do for Dad while the priest is here.

Back on the Lazyboy I open the laptop. It takes forever to boot up. I type Comet, find Google, and search for Dr. Oswald MacDonald, marine biologist.

THEN

Soon after the kiss, I borrowed nine cigarettes from Grandad. He'd dropped the packet on the way to the shed. So there it was, part-hidden by the browning leaves of the strawberry plants, just begging me to pick it up.

I showed them to Ossie behind his garage.

"Wow! This is gonna be good!" he said. He didn't mention anything about the snogging, so I assumed Stevo kept his word. Ossie said he'd call on Dermot and Manuela and get them to go to Spooky if they were allowed out.

"What about Gianni?" I asked.

"Gianni? Ciggies?" Ossie had a point.

I said, "He can watch, can't he? Anyhow, tell him we'll be there if he wants to come."

I flopped down, my back against the garage wall, while Ossie went to pass the message. This would be the first time I'd seen Stevo since that day. The others had been there to take food, of course, but I'd found excuses. What would it be like? I pictured Stevo pulling those daft faces at me again. Would Manuela clock on? I might turn bright purple. Perhaps I didn't want him to kiss me again after all? Except I did. I really did.

Ossie interrupted my musings. "They're coming. Let's go."

We walked down Upper Chorlton Road and I was fine. As we turned into Sylvan Avenue all my body parts – legs, arms, head – seemed disjointed, as if my bones had lost the glue that kept them in place. And yet somehow it reminded me of the day before birthdays. I'd been the same at home too. I couldn't stand, sit or do anything without having to do something else the next instant. My heart was racing.

Stevo acted perfectly normal when we got there. But he was less talkative than usual. He and Ossie went outside and kicked a ball around, Ossie darting here and there, showing off, transferring the ball from his knee to his shoulder, while Stevo shuffled, giving the odd half-hearted pass. Why was he so miserable? Was he mad at me or something?

I was still watching them from the bay seat when the others arrived in the den. Dermot rapped on the window. When the two of them came in, Ossie said, "Tell them what you've brought, go on. Circle everyone. Hand them here."

We took our places on the letters. I gave the Woodbines to Ossie and he lined up the cigarettes in front of him.

"Enough for a pow wow. Stevo, get the matches," he said.

Stevo didn't answer, just stood and went to find them.

"Don't be daft," Gianni said. "That's pipes."

Ossie mimicked that Dexter boy. "That's in the Ye-oonited States. This is Old Trafford. One each." He rolled them across to us, though Gianni sent his back as predicted.

While we waited for Stevo to return, Ossie kept us entertained. He put his cigarette between his lips, letting it dangle, squinting his eyes and impersonating Daffy Duck. "Tho, ya wanna thmoke a thigarette? Thertainly do. Got thumthing to thay, thucker?"

Stevo walked into the den, examining the contents of the matchbox.

"There's only three left. The candle kept blowing out last night. It's prob—" He stopped.

"What's up?" Dermot asked.

Stevo shook his head, and waved the question away, as if he was trying to swat a fly. Ossie struck a match and moved from person to person until the five Woodbines were lit. Manuela coughed before we even started.

"Pretend it's a straw," Dermot said, "See?" He leaned back on his arm with his legs stretched out in front of him and blew a straight grey line towards the ceiling. I never realised he was an expert.

Ossie let out a long whistle of appreciation. "First one to blow out's a sissy. Come on. All together. One, two, three." We drew the smoke into our mouths, sat there faces reddening, cheeks widening, eyes bulging, until Manuela cracked and coughed, and Dermot, and me.

Then Stevo dropped his bombshell.

"I'm goin' back. For good."

Ossie spluttered, and we gaped at Stevo, all cigarettes except Dermot's forgotten. Mine tasted horrible anyway. I stubbed it into the floor, suddenly feeling sick.

Manuela said, "What do you mean?"

He said he'd been visiting home for a while "to check things out" and see his mum. It ought to be all right because she wanted him with her now, really wanted him. It was different now. And it was freezing cold at Spooky at night, what with the draught under the door.

Gianni said, "Aren't you scared he'll hit you?"

"He's not there no more," Stevo muttered. His mum had promised it would be just her and Stevo. But who was 'he'? Was it his dad or that Uncle Tony? I couldn't remember whether the others knew about Uncle Tony and the other man Stevo had mentioned. Which one had his mum gone on holiday with?

I wanted to understand, not because his lies or half-truths mattered now – I needed to be certain nothing horrible would happen. "Who's not there?"

Stevo cast me a filthy glance, as if I'd betrayed him in front of everyone.

"Why're ya so interested?"

I flinched at the tone of his voice and stared at my knees. My eyes were gritty, as if someone had thrown sand in them.

187

Manuela sprang to my defence. "Whoaa. That's nasty. She was only asking, weren't you, Ania?" She slid her arm round my shoulder, put her face up close to mine and made me look up.

Stevo lowered his head. "Sorry. I didn't mean it. I don't wanna talk about it. Just tellin' ya so ya know."

Dermot, who'd continued to puff at his Woodbine, was now spitting, blowing raspberry noises as if something was stuck to his tongue. He threw the butt towards his shoe and stamped it out. "How can you be sure he'll stay away?"

Stevo shrugged. "I can't. But it's changed. Mum's sort of... Dunno. It'll be okay. And if it isn't..." He didn't sound at all convinced to me.

"You can always come back here," Manuela said. "We'll still look after you."

"Yeah."

"Yeah."

He left that day.

*****

At first, I missed Stevo like crazy. I forgave him for being mean because it wasn't his fault, was it? Each night I practised kissing my hand, hopeful that one day he'd come back and we could try it again. For a while he appeared in my dreams. Once he picked me up from outside Polska school in a red sports car with no roof on. I waved like the Queen to Krysia Nowicka, and we drove from a mountain ridge down a narrow, bendy road all the way to the turquoisy ocean. My sunglasses were on top of my head, my gold earrings were glinting in the sun, and my cowlicks had disappeared. I had eyeliner too. Such a lovely dream. I woke up so happy that I managed to do what I was told and be pleasant to Janek throughout the day.

But with Stevo gone, gang visits to Old Spooky fizzled out. Autumn crept upon us, getting chillier, the nights darker, days shorter. And generally during the week, apart from a brief game of rounders and kicking up the piles of fallen leaves, we stayed home in the evenings.

Weekends weren't much livelier because mornings meant Polska school until one o'clock, of course. Then Mum stopped off at the Polski deli on the way back and queued for hours to get the Walewski share of the weekly delivery of *kiełbasa* and ham. By the time we'd eaten our cheese on toast or sandwiches, it was already four o'clock, so Janek and I just nipped to Grandad's to watch the wrestling.

Spooky adventures fizzled out, treadmill life in Polska Land resumed, and the only thing to look forward to was my birthday. I'd already told Mum and Granny what I'd like for my present. I'd seen it in a shop window on Alexandra Road. It was very, very expensive.

But now when Mum remembered to come into our bedroom and tell

Iwonka and me to say our prayers, I prayed for real, eyes closed, hands together and everything. Please God, make Mum forget about the glasses. Please God, make 'Them as ask, don't get' not be true. Please God, can I have an Olympia Splendid portable typewriter? And I included *Our Father*, *Hail Mary* and also *Aniele Boży Stróżu Mój* because if anyone was likely to swing it, it would be my guardian angel. Best to cover all available bases. That's what I thought.

*****

On my birthday morning there was precisely nothing for me by the side of our bunk bed. Just my slippers and yesterday's clothes. Nor in the kitchen. Not even a card or anything.

Mum kissed me and said Happy Birthday in English and then *Sto Lat*, and told me my official birthday had to start after school when Dad got home. Was that good or bad – that Dad had to be there? Probably good...but maybe not.

I asked Janek if he knew what my present was. He giggled and said he was sworn to secrecy. Maybe Mum had bought me something rubbishy. Or worse – nothing at all. *What-so-ever*. It hadn't even occurred to me before. I wasn't *that* naughty, surely... But maybe I was.

At school I mulled and fretted all day, break times too, and when lessons were over, I arrived at the conclusion that mine were the horriblest parents in the whole wide world, they hadn't bought me anything, and I wouldn't speak to them for the rest of my life. Which would serve them right. And then I'd go to live in London, and if they wanted to come to my wedding, I wouldn't let them. And they wouldn't be allowed to fly to Hollywood for the Oscars either. And when they were old and doddery and had no teeth I wouldn't even phone or send a postcard from my mansion in America. *Koniec*. The end.

I came out of school and Mum, Janek and Iwonka were in the van outside the school gates. I stomped over and jerked the door open.

"Home for present time," Mum said, pretending there was something to look forward to. "Tatuś is waiting for us."

*****

We took off our coats and Dad called everyone to the dining room. I went in last. The table was covered in green baize as if for bridge or poker. On top was an off-white carrying case.

"Well, come on," Dad said, drawing on his pipe. "Open it."

Hands shaking, I slowly unzipped it and lifted the cover. There it was. Lovely creamy yellow with maroon keys. The most gorgeous thing I'd ever seen. Now I wouldn't have to beg Grandad to use his big black Smith Corona, or wait till Mrs. Markham went to scoff her dinner at the factory. Now I'd write more letters to *June and Schoolfriend* and *Bunty* and earn some real wages for letter of the week. Did I really want to be a film star when I could be a newspaper man instead, and type my story and then run to the telephone booths under clocks that showed the time in every city in the world, like on films. And if I was in Peking, I could ride in rickshaws... Or, even better, if I was a newspaper woman in India, I'd probably have to ride on real elephants!

Mum presented me with another gift of a ream of typing paper in a box, and Janek and Iwonka gave me white correction tabs. They sat back watching while I tested my talents using two and a half fingers – q, a and z with my little finger.

The quick brown fox jumped over the lazy dog.

"Try to do it more quickly, like Dorothy." Dad said it to me but he was smiling at Mum. Mrs. Markham typed like the clappers, so it was obvious I'd never be as good as her. Dad was asking too much in my opinion, as per usual.

The qick bnwoen fox jumpd ovr the lazy dog.

After a few more attempts, I was getting the hang of it better, and when Dad wanted a go, I thought it was the least I could do to let him, seeing as he'd bought it for me and everything.

He typed a few random letters in quick succession and stopped. "Excellent. No jamming. Light touch." He pulled the lid away and pronounced the ribbon spools perfect, and as he began to turn it upside down, my heart skipped a beat because I thought he might bend the keys. He peered at a little brassy plaque attached to the bottom.

"Hm. Wilhelmshaven. *Olympia Werke AG,*" he said. "Hm. Long serial number...another fine example of German engineering. Efficient machinery for every purpose..." He'd said that before, that thing about Efficient Machinery For Every Purpose, when he praised the Singer sewing machines at the factory. Except those ones came from a place called Karlsruhe. The only thing that broke on them were the needles. The machines could last a lifetime, according to Dad. You could sew six million purses and they'd still never stop working until somebody took an axe to them.

I'd thought my typewriter might be Greek, not German, because last year when Manuela couldn't come out to play for two weeks it was because her Auntie Olympia and cousin Yannis from Cyprus were visiting.

Dad turned it back over and let out a little sigh. "Our side, the Allies, bombed Wilhelmshaven. All the factories and warehouses. The shipyards. It was almost as bad as Warszawa. Rubble."

Oh no. Please, not the war. Not on my birthday. Please don't ruin it.

Dad must have seen my expression even though I'd tried not to let it show, but he wasn't angry this time. He pretended to adjust his imaginary cufflinks, straightened up and put his fingers on the keys. I watched the words come out, letter by letter in English.

t-o–m-y–f-a-v-o-u-r-i-t-e–e-l-d-e-s-t–d-a-u-g-h-t-e-r–m-a-y–a-l-l–y-o-u-r–
w-i-s-h-e-s–c-o-m-e–t-r-u-e

"So you like it?" he said.

"Thank you," I replied, hugging him round his neck. "It's the best present I've ever had."

*****

The news report began at the normal time but kept going on. On the screen it was rainy, foggy, dark, and the picture had no black or white, just blurs of grey. Lots of men wearing helmets with lamps were removing slurry with diggers, spades, even their hands.

Janek asked whether everybody in the school had died, but I didn't know. The newscaster said over a hundred children were in the building when the slag heap slid down the hill. The community in Aberfan was distraught and they would work through the night to search for survivors. More silent images followed.

Upstairs on the landing Mum and Dad were talking, normally at first, then Mum's voice went quieter and a bit whiny. I couldn't hear the words.

Dad shouted, "I'm there seven days a week. I need to relax."

"Relax at home – with us," Mum replied.

"At home? What more do you want? Three people were off sick today. There are orders to get out. And an hour and a half wasted on fixing the framing press. That idiot has been told a thousand times how to work it." I knew he must mean that poor man with the numbers on his arm. Would Dad give him the sack now?

Next to me Janek put his fingers in his ears and curled into a ball.

"Witek—" Mum started.

"I'm going," Dad shouted, limping noisily down the stairs. He stopped to do something in the hall, and the front door slammed.

Mum swore, "*Choleraaaaaaaa,*" like she was trying to make it echo through the tunnels of a cave. Then there was a rapping on the landing window.

From the bathroom Iwonka called, "Mama, I'm cold!"

"Witek! Witek!" Mum shouted as Dad's car screeched out of the drive. I heard her footsteps dashing about upstairs from room to room.

Janek took his fingers out of his ears. "Do you think they will get a *divorce thing?*"

The divorce thing had been on telly earlier in the week in *Coronation Street*. It didn't look too good. I shook my head. "I don't think so…I don't know."

On the screen a line of men in a long human chain were quickly passing buckets full of mud, and mums and grannies in wellingtons waited, silently crying, while other men carried stretchers away.

Suddenly a massive thud, smashing glass, Mum's scream – all at the same time. Next, Mum shouting that we should run and get Granny. I pushed

Janek into the porch, with no coat even though it was pouring, and told him to go and get Babcia. Then I ran up to see what had happened. Mum was in the spare bedroom slumped on the floor, blood spilling from her face and hands. I ought to do something, but what? The window at the end of the room was smashed, just a few red-edged jags remaining on the bottom.

Mum moaned. "A towel. Quick. Get a towel."

I ran to the bathroom where Iwonka was still in the water, hair shampooed up and frothy on the top of her head. I grabbed the pink one and darted back to Mum.

Iwonka was shouting, "What's wrong? What's happened?"

I told her to wait for me, I'd help her in a minute.

As I gave Mum the towel, she mumbled, "Is Babcia co——?"

"Janek's gone to get her."

I tried to stop the tears from falling and help Mum wipe the blood off her face. She nudged me away with a gentle push, I lost my footing in the pool of yellowy liquid on the lino and keeled over.

She stopped swabbing herself and moved forward, as if to help me, but instead she slid sideways and lay on the floor. "Did you hurt yourself, love?" she murmured.

"No, Mama…" I had, but only a little.

"Don't – I'm all right," she said. Her voice was getting further and further away. "Get Iwonka out of the bath. Rinse her hair."

"But Ma—"

"Please be a good girl and do as I…" She closed her eyes.

"Mama! Mama! Please don't die," I begged her.

Her hand was on the floor and she tried to lift her fingers. "See to Iwonka. I promise I won't die. Not now, not ever. I'm resting. Go on, be a good girl."

I did what Mum said and left her there. She whimpered all the time I was in the bathroom with Iwonka. Iwonka kept asking me what had happened and I reassured her that Mum would be okay. She'd cut herself a bit.

Soon after, Janek returned with Granny, who shrieked, "Wanda? Wandzia?"

I left Iwonka for a moment and leaned over the banister to tell Granny to hurry. She ran up the stairs and into the spare room, then kept saying "*O mój Boże, moje dziecko*", oh my God, my child, again and again. Mum stopped moaning. Granny dashed back down.

Granny's voice echoed through the house. "Yes. Yes. Ambulance. My daughter. You come now. She fall in window." She almost yelled our address. "Come quick. She no awake. Please. Everywhere blood."

Iwonka asked if she could get out of the bath now and I said not yet.

The whole evening sped up, like in a film. The ambulance men arrived and came upstairs. Granny kept reminding me to look after Iwonka and Janek each time I tried to come out to see what they were doing to Mum. Except I didn't know where Janek was. Next she was shouting at Janek to go away. And then Mum and Granny and the ambulance men disappeared. The front door slammed and it was quiet.

In that time I'd rubbed Iwonka's hair dry with a towel, combed it, helped her into her pyjamas and told her a very long bed time story about the cats on the wallpaper. Eventually she'd fallen asleep.

I went downstairs where I found Mrs. Piotrek from Ashley Avenue in the kitchen. She'd arrived from nowhere and installed herself, still in her over-perfumed coat, in Dad's chair. She'd helped herself to a cup of our tea and our cake. Mum's latest *Angelique* book lay open in front of her. I wanted to snatch it and return it to Mum's armchair, but I didn't dare.

What was she doing here?

"When's Mama coming back?" I asked.

Mrs. Piotrek shifted our *sernik* in her mouth and licked the corner of her skinny, mean lips with her slithery tongue. She was cleaning her nails with the prongs of one of our forks and pretending not to be looking at the pile of bills and other papers on the table.

"When the doctors bandage her up."

"What about Tatuś?"

"Your father's been informed. He's gone to the hospital. He'll be back later too."

I didn't want to stay in the same room as her, nor did I want to watch the telly, especially if there were more sad pictures from that Aberfan place and bodies on stretchers. The ambulance men hadn't used a stretcher for Mum, they'd sort of lifted her between them, and half-carried half-helped her to the ambulance.

I said, "Thank you" to Mrs. Piotrek but only because I knew Mum and Dad would be mad at me if I didn't.

Everything in the spare room had been left as it was. Blood on the chest of drawers, the lino, seeped into towels, even on the wall where there was a frog-shaped blood blot. And it was freezing in there. I closed the door.

Where was Janek? I hadn't seen him for ages. I went to his room. The bedside lamp was on and he was still in the clothes he'd worn to Granny's, in bed with his face to the wall, crying.

Now, seeing him all bundled, I felt as if I'd been fighting against someone who'd been strangling me for hours, not letting me move. They'd set me free at last. I needed to get rid of what had built up inside me. Yet I knew I should comfort Janek first. I was the eldest. My job.

"Janek..."

He didn't turn round. "What do *you* want?" he said, trailing a sob.

I sat on the side of his bed and asked, "Can I get in?"

"What for?"

"I don't know."

"Are you going to be horrible?"

"No. I promise."

He waited an instant. "Okay, but don't be horrible." He shifted nearer the wall. I snuggled in after him, into his wet jumper, and let the tears I'd held back earlier soak his shoulder even more while he sobbed into the pillow. After some minutes, Janek's gulps subsided and he was still, his breathing even. To the wall he said, "Ania…"

"Yes…"

"Mum will be all right, won't she?"

I didn't know the answer, but I knew my job. "Yes, it's just a few cuts. I think so."

"Maybe we should tidy up in there? So it's gone when she gets back."

I hadn't even thought of it. Somehow, when I'd shut the door, I'd imagined everything would be normal in the morning because Mum promised she would never die. The blood would vanish, I'd find Mum in her armchair, flicking through *Angelique In Turmoil*.

Janek turned round, his nose half an inch from mine, and swallowed. "Will you help me? I can't do it on my own."

"Put your pyjamas on first."

We used all five towels, the pink ones and the brown stripy ones, to clear up Mum's blood. Lots of the little drops had dried and I had to scrub them with a wet face flannel. The frog refused to budge, although I tried and tried until I rubbed a hole in the wallpaper where its legs had been. I'd better leave it. Janek, who was shivering all the time, mopped up the bigger splodges on the floor.

"What's this yellow water?" he said.

"Don't know. What is it?"

He bent right over it and sniffed. "I think it's wee. Groucho?" He took another towel from the drawer, and dropped it on top. "Maybe the ambulance men frightened him?"

That puddle was there when I found Mum. I bet it was Dad's shouting that had frightened him. And Dad's fault all of this had happened.

We were discussing where to put the sodden towels when we heard Mrs. Piotrek's spikey voice at the bottom step. "What are you children doing up there?"

I didn't want her to come upstairs and poke about in our house then tell everyone at Polski church or Polski deli like she always did.

"Getting ready for bed," I lied.

Janek inserted the plug and turned on both bath taps. We dumped the towels in and waited for the water to rise above their level. The water spread pink and pinker into red as we mushed the towels back and forth to get the dark stains off. When no more would come out, I pulled the plug.

We hauled the first towel out. Both of us bent over the bath. Janek gripped one end of the towel, me the other, and we twisted it round and round until we'd squeezed out as much water as possible. It was hard to do the big ones. Janek's face creased up with the effort.

Even when we finished, the towels were still pinky. Janek arranged three of them on the side of the bath and I hung the other two on the towel rail where to our dismay they continued to drip. I fetched two dry ones from the chest of drawers and placed them on the spreading pools.

Janek sat on his haunches with his back against the wall and sort of hiccupped. The whites of his eyes were almost the same colour as the water in the bath, his face grey. His lips were trembling. He looked like a baby deer. "Can we go to sleep now?" he said.

I sat beside him and put my arm around his shoulders. For the first time, I realised that my skirt was covered in blood too. I'd try to wash it tomorrow.

"Yeah. We'd better be in bed when Dad gets home," I said.

Janek went back to his room.

I put on my pyjamas in the dark so that Iwonka wouldn't wake up and crept up the ladder to the bunk. I longed for someone from my own family, Granny or Grandad, to be in the house. When would they come back? Mum promised me she wouldn't die. I'd definitely heard her say that. Yes, I definitely did. And Mum kept her promises. Well, nearly always. I prayed to God and made a deal with Him. If He made sure Mum was okay, I would never nag her about earrings ever again. Or anything. And I really would try to be good. From now on and forever and ever. Amen.

I hadn't been there long when Janek shuffled in and climbed up the first two rungs.

Words trembling, he whispered, "Will they get a divorce thing when Mum comes back?"

I had no answer. Polish people didn't do the divorce thing as far as I knew. Part of me wished they did. Was that why Stevo's mum and dad didn't live together all the time?

"I don't want to talk about it," I said.

Janek waited a moment. "Do you want to sleep in my bed tonight?"

Yesterday I wouldn't have agreed to share a bed with Janek, not in ten million years. But now it didn't seem so awful.

"Yeah, I'll come."

He'd changed somehow.

CHAPTER EIGHTEEN

DAY FOUR: AFTERNOON, EVENING

It's 12.25 and Mum's flagging.

A Polish jungle drum must be sending messages from Manchester to Warsaw, Warsaw back to London, London to Johannesburg, Toronto and Sydney. It kicked off at eight this morning with Australia. She's been on the phone since, thanking people for their concern, their good wishes, and offers of help. They've spread out quite a distance, their friends, our family. Do they know these are the last moments? Probably not. Dad took the call from Sydney himself. It didn't last long.

Now Mum rests her elbows on the table, chin cupped in her hands, and stares blankly at the fridge. "I've cooked for him for nearly sixty years. Every day. What will I do now?" She's turning into Dad's twin, her clothes hanging off her. "I'll make something simple tonight."

"I'll cook. Don't worry," Iwonka says, back from medication duty in Dad's room. "It's only us. I'll knock up some pasta. You want carbonara?"

At 1.23 Josie drops by on an unscheduled visit, her expression neither too solemn nor too cheerful. If she's an example of all Macmillan nurses, they're a resilient bunch. To go from person to dying person and not let it get to you must require inner steel and sainthood. I'd be useless.

Mum tells her Dad's still not eating.

Josie gives her a smile of reassurance. "Probably kinder not to force him now, not if he doesn't feel like it."

And I suppose she's right – what's the point of nutrition at this stage? None, except to appease hunger, or a thrill for the taste buds if they're still working. That's so very intermittent with him now. You can't get much stronger than Gorgonzola.

After a few minutes spent with Dad, Mum, Iwonka and Josie, my phone pings in my pocket.

I go to the dining room and read the message. It's Sam; he hopes I'm okay, asks how Dziadzio is and tells me to give his love to everybody.

I try not to overstate my reply, relieved he and Rachel managed to visit Dad before this rapid deterioration.

I text: He's as comfortable as we can make him under the circs. Babcia is coping. Ciocia Iwonka is here with us most of the time. Wujek Janek pops in every day." Send.

Sam responds straight away: he can get on the train immediately if I want, he's worried about me too, his boss won't mind. We should be a family now.

I text: Not necessary. It's too distressing. We are a family. Don't be silly. Send.

He replies he's an adult and should he get in touch with Rachel?

I admit to some of the truth: Better if you don't. Honestly. Dziadzio wouldn't want you to see him like this. GTG. Speak later. Send.

By the time we've swapped all these texts, back and forth, back and forth, I realise how much easier a conversation would have been, like in the olden days twenty years ago when human beings used voices to communicate. But maybe he's somewhere he can't talk.

The reality contains more layers: there's too much on my mind and no brain-space to accommodate the kids. I'd rather not be forced to take their feelings into consideration or make compromises. And Rachel, knowing Rachel, would act as if Dad dying is her own personal drama, another reason for her silly friends to send Facebook hugs. It only ever rains on Rachel's parade, nobody else's. She'll grow out of it, I hope. The last time I looked at her Facebook status – one I didn't bother to *like* – she was whining about her ruined Michael Kors sandals. This, apparently, counts as news meriting twenty-six comments, condolences of the "Poor you. (((Rachel))) :'(:'(" variety. The four inch heel got caught in a grid, it seems. I despair; the sooner she stops working for Monsoon the better. I'll start dropping hints about Voluntary Service Overseas when life returns to normal.

No. Rachel, much as I love her, can stay where she is for now.

When Josie leaves, Iwonka and I sit with Dad, reminiscing about childhood holidays in Scotland. Mainly, he just listens. Really it's just more idle chatter, during which my thoughts catapult from Yankel, to Dad, to Stevo. Even my own voice becomes background noise, fading in, fading out as I wonder if I'll ever learn the truth. Time is moving on. Always people here. Or Dad asleep. I need to know.

At 3.47 Pan Dybek turns up. His daughter's waiting outside in her car. I've not seen him since the late seventies when he was still Druh Dybek, running *kolonia*. He refuses to come in, asks me to establish if it's all right – maybe Witek isn't up to it – and lingers in the porch.

I check with Dad who says he'd very much like to see him. Pan Dybek opens the front door, waves at his daughter and points at his watch. Then he puts one finger up. She drives away.

I usher him into Dad's room where Dad greets him with *"Czuwaj"* – be prepared. Scouts in short trousers forever, it seems; Pan Dybek must be well into his eighties too. As I leave to let them talk, Mum comes in.

Time has taken on a curious dimension. Sometimes it whizzes, then an hour feels like a day. Plodding, dragging, wading through mud. Biding. I'd like to go out for a walk, a wander down to Tesco's would do. But I can't even open the laptop without feeling anti-social. At least the Kindle feels less obtrusive.

I join Iwonka in the kitchen. She stands by the cooker, chopping pancetta. "That was nice."

"What?"

"Remembering Loch Doon. That giant mushroom we found..." She giggles. "Janek still loathes them. He says it's unnatural to eat anything related to athlete's foot. It drives Marie mad."

The back door opens. "Talk of the devil..." she says, as Janek shivers then takes his coat off.

He gives me a peck. "Double, double toil and trouble? What're you gossiping about?" He plants a kiss on the back of Iwonka's head, and nudges her out of the way to lift the lids off the pans.

She slaps his wrist and tells him to sit down. "The caravan actually. Good times."

We hear irregular chortles from the far end of the house.

Janek draws the other chair closer and sits sideways across both of them. "He-he. Yeah, good times." Leaning back, he sings, *"Scotland the Brave... Hark when night is falling, hear those mosquitoes calling..."* and breaks off with a wistful sigh. "Bloody mozzies. They *were* good times, weren't they? He stopped thinking about business there. And no Kombo's. Who's with him?"

"Pan Dybek," Iwonka says.

Janek drops his clasped hands from his belly and straightens his back. A grin lightens his face. "Dybcio's here?"

That's something else I haven't heard in years. The pet name the cubs and scouts had for him.

Janek stands. "Ladies, you're on your own. Man talk."

A moment later, Mum shuffles in, sits beside me. I notice her nails; they're uneven, split, with traces of black – compost, I think. Her skin is soft, translucent and mottled with liver spots. I'm suddenly aware those hands cradled my head when I was a baby; they held my face, wiped my bottom, spent nights patting my back to chase out the colic. I need to remember those hands forever. Give her strength, keep her well.

"Mum, can I give you a manicure?"

She looks into my eyes, perplexed. "Why?" Stretching her arm out, she attempts to focus on her hand. I pick out some glasses from the glasses basket in which there are approximately a dozen pairs, hers and Dad's tangled around each other.

She chooses a pair at random, puts them on, brings her hand closer to her face and says, "Oh. If you like…I used to have such nice hands before the accident and old age…"

Iwonka is silent, lost in her own thoughts of cooking, or maybe Scotland.

I pour some Fairy Liquid and warm water into a bowl, place it on the table, and sit opposite Mum. She's gazing at the clock on the wall. I take her hands and put them in the water.

When I lift her left hand out, she gives me a pained smile, as if she's indulging me. "I'm a bit of a mess, aren't I?" she says, a quiver in her voice. "Am I a burden?"

I feel my soul melt. I smile at her and shake my head. With a towel I pat her hand dry, lift it to my lips and kiss the liver spots and faint scars on the skin beneath her knuckles.

If I speak, I'll cry.

No, Mum. You're not.

THEN

We didn't go to Polish school in the morning. Dad went to work at eight as soon as Granny turned up. She said that Mum was definitely not going to die, definitely not, but she did have to stay in hospital for a while.

She bundled up the sodden towels to take to the washing machine in the cellar. From that moment on Janek grew an invisible safety pin between him and Granny because wherever she was, so was he. He was as stuck to Granny as her rosary beads in May. Iwonka spent all day asking for hugs, stroking her teddy and sucking her knuckle. We did nothing much except wander from room to room and watch wrestling with Grandad who didn't even shout at Mick McManus when he bounced on Jackie Pallo's head.

On Sunday, Granny made us go to church, of course, but we had to catch the 53 instead of going in the van. Without Mum we became those people who stood by the bus stop in the rain hoping a good Polish Christian might offer a lift. There weren't any that day. We got soaked.

Everything was wrong. Dad hardly said a word, which should have been great, but wasn't. Granny came by the following morning to chivvy us every thirty seconds, make us eat all our *śniadanie* even if we didn't want to and march us to school. Then she prepared different *kolacje* to the ones Mum made with loads more green stuff and put chopped-up radishes in the salad. And she scrubbed my neck far harder than Mum ever did. Mum hadn't done that since I was nine, anyway. She only helped me wash my hair now. When, oh, when would Mum be back?

I supposed Granny was doing her best, but without Mum our family wasn't our family. It was like burglars had broken in on a snowy night and stolen the fireplace.

On the last evening of Granny being commandant in charge, she told us Mum would be home the next day.

She said, "Don't be upset when you see her. The bandages will come off soon and the scars will heal. But the main thing is," she paused, "your mama won't be able to do anything for a few weeks. So you must be good. If she asks you to help her," she pointed her finger at us in turn, "you do it straight away." She stepped back, put her hands on her hips and looked into my eyes. "No arguments and no fighting."

The next day we walked from school together – Granny, Iwonka, Janek and me. Manuela came with us. She'd been my very best friend in the whole world for four days. When I needed to go and sit on my own in the gap between the Infants and Juniors buildings at break, she sat beside me instead of playing American skipping with the other girls. I decided to let her be my chief bridesmaid when I got married.

We arrived home to find Grandad there, which was strange because he never visited in the week, only on Sundays and special occasions. The house smelt of polish and everywhere gleamed. The cushions on the sofa were plumped up. The pile of clothes in the ironing basket had disappeared. The cooker looked as if it had been delivered that morning. It almost wasn't our house.

Granny told Iwonka and me to get changed into Sunday dresses. As soon as we came downstairs, Granny undid Iwonka's ponytail, then pulled it back up again, slid grips in to stop the curly bits escaping from the sides and tied a fresh bow. Then Granny did that other annoying thing of hers and licked her hand and patted my fringe flat. Never mind, it was nearly over. Mum was coming home.

We were in the sitting room when we heard Dad's car pull in.

Janek jumped up, pulled back the net curtains and squealed. "She's here!"

We dashed outside with Granny and Grandad following behind us.

Janek yelled, "Mama! I missed you."

Dad was opening the car door for Mum. She tried to swing her legs round, but she couldn't do it. Both her arms were in slings, bandages from her fingertips to her shoulders. She looked like she'd been in a fire or a war or something. Dad bent over, lifted her under her knees and swivelled her sideways. Using her feet as levers, Mum slid her bottom to the edge of the seat and stood up. Even though she was smiling, her expression seemed kind of shy, as if she'd never met us before. Her face was bruised and a bit swollen and she had three cuts sewn up with dark thread, one in her left eyebrow, one on her temple above it, and another to the right of her nose. Under her eyes the skin had turned purplish-blue and her lips looked like every last drop of blood had drained out of them.

My throat seemed to swell. She didn't look so very different though, did she? Still our Mum. Still our pretty Mum. "The scars will heal," that's what Granny said.

Iwonka ran to Mum and hugged her but Mum couldn't do anything except kiss her on the top of her head. Next, from nowhere, Groucho bounded up to greet her too, but Dad half-kicked him away.

Dad mumbled, "No more dogs."

My heart chilled and I gasped.

He looked at me. "*Koniec*. The end. He's going," he said, almost under his breath.

I couldn't believe it. He was the meanest, the nastiest dad on earth. That divorce thing sprang to my mind. We'd be happier without him. Just like Stevo was when his dad wasn't there. I gritted my teeth, then unclenched my fists and gave Mum a kiss.

Iwonka or Janek hadn't heard. I decided to say nothing. While Mum was bandaged up, it was my job to look after them. Brownie Law Number Four – a Brownie is mindful of her responsibilities. I'd simply have to be cleverer than Dad. If the worst came to the worst, we would kidnap Groucho from our own house and keep him at Spooky. He'd be okay there, safe, what with Dermot's rosary beads and everything. And Manuela's Greek blue eye.

*****

All evening I kept thinking about it. We'd come and visit Groucho every day, just like Stevo, and the gang would bring food and water, and play with him. And sometimes we'd treat him to chocolate buttons to make him feel better. Then I realised that if we left Groucho there on his own, tied by his lead to a door knob, he'd bark his stupid head off and somebody would come and steal him.

My brilliant plan was rubbish. I had to think of another one. I hunched up on the edge of the sofa and thought and thought. Nothing. We had Mum back, but what was the point of life without Groucho?

Dad came in and switched the telly to another channel. As he sat on the armchair he said nobody was going to Polska school tomorrow. He had things to do at work and no time to take or pick us up. Janek grinned. But he didn't know what was going to happen, did he? Who cared about not going to Polska school now?

"Here," Dad said. He was looking at me and patting the arm of the chair. I walked over. He beckoned me to put my face nearer his. I knew I had to do it.

"Ania, child," he said really quietly. "Groucho can stay. I didn't mean it. Do you want to come to the factory with me tomorrow? Beat Pan Edzio and Pan Widzowski?"

On my outside I was still grumpy, but my insides were shouting Yipee!

*****

Since I now had more jobs to do, Mum woke me early. Today she asked me to change her slings because they were looking grubby. For *śniadanie* I made her two boiled eggs and tea which I poured from cup to cup until it cooled so that her special straw wouldn't melt. Next I fed her, and she didn't seem to mind that the eggs were a bit snotty. When she finished all of that, she asked for a Kensitas. I held it, she smoked it, taking little puffs all the way to the end. It wasn't so bad, being responsible.

At the factory, I visited Mr. Edzio and Mr. Widzowski in packing and dispatch, had a root in the stock room (a purse for Manuela was the result), and helped the gluing ladies for a while.

Finally at two o'clock as I began hallucinating that my stomach was talking to me, Dad announced he was ready to go. "Dom Kombatanta for five minutes, then home."

When we pulled up outside Kombo's, I saw Granny – the traitor – and Mrs. Jeleńska huddled together in the queue for the new Polski shop, chatting like they were best friends and hadn't walloped each other a few weeks ago. I prayed Dad would be quick. I hadn't eaten a crumb since *śniadanie* and the prospect of waiting in the bar or Mr. Kucyk's room for hours on end was less than appealing.

Luckily, Mr. Skowroński, my favourite bartender, was in so I went to chat to him on my usual bar stool. Dad left me and joined his friends.

Mr. Skowroński pulled the pencil out from behind his ear and asked for my order. He leaned across the bar. "We have some delicious *pierogi ruskie* if Madame would care for them?" He knew how much I liked cheese. I turned round and looked at Dad. There was a bottle of *Wyborowa* on the table. We could be here for hours. I shrugged.

Mr Skowroński smiled. "Wait a minute."

When he came back, he said, "*Sprawa załatwiona.*" The matter has been dealt with. I watched, fascinated, as he wrote down "*pierogi ruskie,* children's portion" using just his thumb and third finger to hold the pencil. He'd blown the other three fingers off all by himself, but that wasn't to do with any war things. One day, long before the war even started, he was working in his laboratory in Lwów when the experiment he was doing exploded taking his fingers with it. All the people from the *fakultet* (whatever that was) had rushed in to help, but it was too late. As the professor, he said, he had to teach his students they had "a duty to expand the field of human knowledge." So he picked up his fingers and using a special chemistry machine a bit like a mincer he had ground them up, and that was how he invented ketchup. He also invented Coca Cola, but he'd only used chemicals, rotten mushrooms and sugar for that. He'd told me those stories when I was six, and when I asked Mum about them, she said all of it *was* true apart from the ketchup and Coca

Cola bits. I supposed that was probably why Mr. Skowroński enjoyed being a bartender in England, so he could mix drinks, like in a laboratory.

Now he put the order on a spike in the dumb waiter, set it rolling down to the kitchen, and then explained how pulleys worked. By the time my *pierogi* came back up, he'd also taught me about weights and levers and how to lift a heavy rock if ever I need to. I think he was trying to take my mind off how hungry I was. He seemed to know everything in the world.

I was just nibbling round the boring pastry edge of my first *pierog*, getting ready for the good bit in the middle, when someone came and stood next to me.

"Józek, give me a beer," the voice said.

I looked up. It was the man on the photograph with Dad. Sławek Kardasz. Mr. Skowroński pulled him a pint and handed the glass to him.

Mr. Kardasz walked to Dad's table and shook hands with Dad's friends first. Then he extended his hand towards Dad who so far had not taken his eyes off the centre of the table. Dad did nothing for a moment.

Finally he said, "Sławek," and gave a slight nod. Then he accepted the handshake, but didn't move his hand up and down like he usually did, just sort of touched him and let go. Dad stood up. "Gentlemen, I have to go now. My wife is waiting for me." He called over. "Anka, the car. Home." It was the 'do it now. I mean NOW!' tone.

I quickly said thank you and goodbye to Mr. Skowroński, crammed two whole *pierogi* into my cheeks and jumped off the bar stool.

I was still chewing pastry when we turned into our drive. Dad hadn't uttered a single word.

*****

December arrived and Polska school was buzzing. The month began, same as usual, with Kombo's and *Święty Mikołaj* number one, who wasn't really St. Nicholas, even though Janek and Iwonka believed it, like they believed *Święty Mikołaj* number two brought presents at Christmas. Number One was just an old man with specs and a wooden crook who wore a dress and had a bishop's hat on his head. In real life he was the headmistress's husband. Another secret I didn't tell Janek and Iwonka.

A big celebration was coming up.

Back in September my new teacher, Mrs. Borecka, had told us about it in our second history lesson.

She coughed first, then scraped her bottom lip with her teeth. With her hands held together in front of her chest, she announced, "This year Poland celebrates a thousand years of Christianity. In 966 King Mieszko I, the first ruler of the Polish state, was baptised. My dears, we will have a magnificent event at Belle Vue to commemorate the occasion. Thousands of people will come. And everybody—" her smile started small then spread wide in a beam from one side of the classroom to the other, "—will have a chance to participate in the show."

My heart clunked to my shoes.

Not again. I just knew I'd end up having to play a holy cauliflower or something. I couldn't be doing with any of it. And guess who'd be the Virgin Mary or the most beautiful angel in heaven?

I sneaked a look behind me at Krysia Nowicka. Yes, there she was, the sun shining on her hair like a halo, doing her best "Pick me! Pick me!" face at Mrs. Borecka.

I turned back, unzipped my pencil case and took out a biro. One day I'd be a great actress like Julie Andrews and show them I really could act. I dug the point into the wooden desk lid and made a blue hole. And sing and dance (if I wanted to). Another blue hole. And do accents. They didn't need any old Varsovians in Hollywood. One more blue hole. Anyway, it would serve them right.

"Ania! What are you doing?" Mrs. Borecka snapped.

The biro clattered to the floor. "Sorry."

Two weeks later I learned Iwonka and me would be angels too. In fact, there were no absolutely rubbish vegetable or smelly sheep parts at all.

Mum tried to foist matching pink on Iwonka and me.

"You'll look so lovely together," she said.

Pink! No. No way would I agree to pink.

"She can have pink. I'll have lilac."

Mum shrugged. "Well…"

"Or I'm not doing it!"

Maybe Mum remembered that time I came to church in one short sock, one long sock and mismatched shoes. It was one thing being shown up in Polski church, a whole other story in front of thousands. I'd played a clever hand.

"All right."

Hurray! So Mrs. Dudek sewed them for us, floor-length bell-sleeved robes edged at the cuffs, hems and necklines with gold trimming. They were quite nice really.

On the Sunday of the show, I woke early to the faint hum of music. I slid my feet into cold slippers and padded downstairs. Mum was in the dining room with the light off and I couldn't see her face properly. She was in her dressing gown, a travel rug wrapped around her legs, staring into the drizzle through the gap in the net curtains. Jim Reeves sang 'Now and then there's a fool such as I'.

They must have had a row again.

Without saying anything I sat next to her, and she sighed and unwound the rug, placing it half on her knees and half on mine. Jim stopped being foolish, and now Pat Boone was crossing the 'Moon River'. There'd be nothing cheerful dropping on the turntable, I could tell.

"Are you excited?" she asked.

"A bit."

"I'm…I don't feel well, love," she said. "I'll ask Pani Nowicka if she'll take you."

Krysia, two days on the trot – it didn't bear thinking about. But Mum's voice was so tiny and crackly, like she had a nail file in her throat, that I didn't want to upset her further.

"You'll come though, won't you?"

"For the performance, yes."

Dad dressed and left for the factory without drinking his lemon tea, and we didn't even have to go to church, so that was good.

Early in the afternoon, Mrs. Nowicka arrived in her Morris Minor to pick up Iwonka, Janek and me. (Janek didn't have to be an angel. He was going to wear national costume.)

Krysia sat in the front seat with her entire head covered in scraps of tightly rolled-up cotton nappy. I tried not to laugh. Ossie's sister, Melinda, sometimes wore her hair parted into squares with little plaits, but she didn't look anywhere near as ridiculous as Krysia.

Mrs. Nowicka started the engine and proceeded to witter all the way to Brooks's Bar about how King Mieszko belonged to the Piast dynasty. I sank down the back seat in case people thought Krysia and me were related. Then Mrs. Nowicka continued about how he'd married Dobrawa, and that was when Latin came to Poland, and Christianity meant that Polska could belong to Europe properly, et-cet-era, et-flipping-cet-era. All of which I knew because we'd done it a hundred times at Polska school. The journey felt as long as the one to Penrhos.

Finally we arrived in Belle Vue. At the King's Hall the dressing rooms were already crammed and noisy with mums and teachers issuing instructions while the children shivered, goose-pimply in vests and knickers, jostling in queues for help with costumes. Iwonka was quickly scooped up by her teacher. Janek went off to find his class.

I had to wait for Mrs. Nowicka. She clucked, cooed and fretted around Krysia, pinning, tucking the robe, and undoing the bits of rag from her hair. Then she spent ages making sure that Krysia's halo was parallel to her head. She even made her rehearse by putting her hands together like she was praying.

"Now look to God," Mrs. Nowicka said. Krysia stared upwards.

Mrs. Nowicka nodded. "And at the audience." Krysia stared ahead.

Mrs. Nowicka pulled down one of Krysia's ringlets and let it bounce back up. "Good. Now smile."

I shuffled from foot to foot like piffy on a rock bun.

When it came to my turn, she attached my wings so loosely that I knew

they'd fall off. I asked her to fix them tighter. She told me not to complain. Didn't I know she had twenty more angels to sort out?

Mrs. Borecka ushered our class to the curtains on the edge of the stage. Everyone was whispering and bubbling. When the grown-up choirs began the hymns, we walked out in file, hands together. All the way to the platform I had to be a robot, back straight, head rigid, tiny steps, trying to stop those flipping wings sliding down my back. I stood on the podium step one higher than Krysia and resisted the urge to accidentally knock her stupid halo flying.

The multi-coloured stage lights panned the rows of angels on the other semi-circle of the podium. The angels were all a bit of a blur. But was that Ewa from *kolonia*? I squinted, my eyes following the lights, and thought I saw Kinga too. What were *they* doing here?

Three hours later, after hymns, mass, hymns, some singing and dancing in national costume, more hymns, lots of long speeches about who-knows-what, it was over, thank goodness. We changed back into normal clothes.

Mrs. Nowicka funnelled us to the stage door exit where our mums were supposed to collect us. I wasn't entirely convinced Mum would be there, but she was, with Granny. It was Sunday so Granny looked quite posh in her fur coat even though the grey bits in her hair were growing out.

They hugged, patted and kissed Iwonka and me, and to Iwonka's squealing delight, Granny said she was prettier than angels in heaven. I didn't even mind that Granny forgot to mention me because it was true. And, I didn't care what anybody else said, Iwonka was much more beautiful than Krysia Nowicka.

When we entered the parking area, I saw Ewa and Kinga again. They stood chatting with a group of people beneath a lamp post by the bushes.

Ewa was holding hands with the man on the photo of the general's funeral, the same man who'd been in Kombo's when Mr. Skowroński gave me *pierogi*.

It *was* him. Definitely.

So that confirmed it.

Sławek Kardasz was Ewa and Kinga's dad. Not Stevo's.

Most of the people moved off. A lady with dark curly hair, probably their mum, put her arm around Ewa's shoulder and guided her towards the back door of their car. Mr. Kardasz smacked the roof of the car twice and got into the driver's seat.

As the car drove past us, Ewa knocked on the window and waved at me.

I hadn't thought about Stevo properly-properly for weeks. Now I felt like kissing my hand again.

*****

Mrs. Moscrop wrote another letter to Mum saying I needed glasses. Mum had forgotten the previous ones, both the one in September that I'd hidden, and the other one at half-term. Mum couldn't take me then because her arms were still in slings and she wasn't driving. She took me to the optician's for an eye test. He said I was definitely short-sighted and asked me to pick some frames. They were all horrible, I said. So Mum chose a pair, and he said they'd be ready in two weeks.

That was the end of it then. Manuela probably wouldn't want to be my best friend anymore. She'd be Sandie Shaw, and I'd be Queen of the Dorks. In a fortnight, my life would be over.

*****

The week before Christmas I asked Janek if he wanted to come Christmas shopping. School had finished so we could go during the day and take our time.

"Why?" he asked suspiciously.

"We need to buy presents. Go halves?"

"You mean it, don't you?" he said. "You won't go off and leave me?"

How could he think of such a thing? Was I such a bad person that he thought every gesture had a hidden motive? I hadn't been mean to him at all since Mum's accident. At least, I didn't think I had.

"I won't leave you, okay? How much have you got?"

Janek emptied his piggy bank. I'd stopped buying comics and reduced my sweet intake at the beginning of November, so I wasn't stony broke either. We totted up our joint savings and reckoned we had enough to deal with Mum, Dad, Granny and Grandad and we'd still have enough left to get a special present for Iwonka.

When we said where we were going Mum instructed me to look after Janek and said we had to be home in two hours.

We set off for Brooks's Bar, blowing our breath out in steamy clouds into the cold. Janek asked if we could take the bus even though it was only one stop. He liked jumping on and off it. Because I wanted to prove to him that I could be nice sometimes, if I wanted to, I said okay.

The two women and one man standing in a queue weren't facing the road to check if the bus was coming. They were ogling something behind them in the garden park area next to King's Road. As Janek and I came nearer, we saw what they were gawping at.

Mrs. Jeleńska, dressed in her baronial fur coat and a Cossack hat, her lipstick smeared around her mouth, sat alone in the middle one of the three benches. She was peeling a tangerine, sitting next to someone who wasn't there. She bit into a segment, took a swing at the someone and shouted, "Get away!" in Polish.

Janek sidled up and half-linked my arm. She'd ranted at him once for sitting on the kerb in Knutsford Avenue and dropping bits of twig into the drains, like she didn't understand he was a boy. I led him to the end of the queue praying Mrs. Jeleńska wouldn't notice us.

In front of me the woman in the purple coat moved closer to the man and said, "Polish," then jerked her head towards Mrs. Jeleńska.

He turned round. "Bloody foreigners. We should send 'em all back. Too many by far."

"True," the woman said, "them and the Krauts – they're all the same."

My fingers snapped into my palm. What did she mean? Since when were the Germans the same as the Poles? White breath jetted out of my nostrils. Her words rankled like a ripped-off scab. So much that I had to bite my lip to stop myself from screaming. I remembered what Dermot's mum had told him. "No niggers. No dogs. No Irish."

But I wasn't upset or ashamed. No, this was another feeling altogether, one I hadn't experienced before. I clenched my fists tighter, rolling a film of options in my head. I felt the blood jam my temples.

Janek was gripping my elbow now. I grabbed his hand and whispered, "Don't be scared. Just come with me." He snatched his hand away.

"Come *on*," I said through gritted teeth. The apple scrumping was still as vivid in my memory as if it were yesterday, but there was no way these English people were going to be allowed to say that about Poles. No way.

This wasn't the moment for explanations, so I took hold of Janek's wrist. "You're coming with me. That's that."

Mrs. Jeleńska was now on her second tangerine, repeating "It's mine. Mine," and slapping the bench backrest. My heart thumped as we walked towards her. She might whack me again, and there was no Granny to defend me. Janek slipped on the icy pavement almost pulling me down with him. We regained our balance. That was all I needed with those people watching us. Their eyes were on the back of my head, I knew it. So what? *So what?*

I pretended I was in my uniform and remembered the second law of the code. "A Brownie is brave." My own voice was echoing in my ears, except it wasn't me now, more like a grown-up me.

"*Zuszka* Ania Walewska – don't slouch! You are not a drip!" it barked. My wobbly ankles told me something else.

Now we were in front of Mrs. Jeleńska.

"Pani Jeleńska?" I said.

She gazed through my anorak.

I dared put my face nearer hers. "Pani Jeleńska?" At this range I saw the lipstick had seeped into the creases above her mouth, sort of like a picture of radio waves.

She replied in Polish in the same tone she'd used with the invisible tangerine thief. "You? What do you want? Get away!"

I flinched and tried to recall what the Jamaican lady did that time when she'd called Ossie "Oswald". What had she said to her?

Slowly I lowered my bottom onto the bench, keeping my toes in a sprint position. The grown-up me voice repeated, "Ania Walewska – you are not a drip!"

Janek hadn't joined me. He stood behind.

My throat filled up with phlegm, and I was shaking as I said, "Pani Jeleńska, it's time to go home now." In the corner of my eye, those three English heads had melded into one gigantic one. Would she hit me again? Here, in full view of everyone?

"*Srebrzysty Gaj?*" she said and a smile spread the radio waves wider. Her eyes sparkled as if she was about to unwrap a birthday present, like she was six and I was her mum.

What was she talking about? "I'm sorry. I don't understand." Then I remembered that was the name of her family's manor in Polska. Silver Grove.

I said, "No. Home on Upper Chorlton Road," and inched my hand onto her furry coat on her leg.

Then something changed in her eyes. They turned groggy as if she'd just woken up. She wiped them. "A house. Yes. On Upper Chorlton Road." She swallowed. "Yes. Where is it?"

Janek tapped me on the shoulder. I had to ignore him.

I said, "I can take you there, if you like."

His second tap was more of a poke. I turned round and glared at him.

Mrs. Jeleńska pushed her Cossack hat up higher on her forehead, taking two fat streaks of black eyebrow with it. "Manchester," she mumbled.

When I stood up, she dragged her tartan shopping trolley towards her. "We're going now, aren't we?" she said.

I glanced over my shoulder and made sure Janek knew what I expected of him. "Yes, we're going." I put the two tangerine skins in my pocket.

The bus hadn't come yet and those people were still gawping at us. I guided her straight at them and their disapproving English faces.

Suddenly, my mouth seemed to detach itself from the rest of my body and became like a separate person with a will of its own.

"This lady, *if you must know*, is a royal countess. Countess Jeleńska, *thank you very much*," it proclaimed as we strode past.

The man snorted then laughed. "'Course she is, love. Whatever you say."

I snapped round again. "And my dad is a *war hero*! He killed *millions* of Krauts. And if it wasn't for my Dad, there'd be no flipping Houses of Parliament!"

The man said something, but I didn't hear him. I turned on my heel and caught up with Janek. I kept my eyes fixed arrow-straight ahead of me. *Ania Walewska – you are not a drip. Don't slouch.* I felt my shoulders pull back, my chin lift up, just like when Druhna Nowak called 'Attention' ready for marching.

As we strode off, the back of my neck felt as if six little screwdrivers were twisting into it. The bus we'd been waiting for drove past us and, moments after, the screwdrivers fell away.

Janek hung back a foot or so on my left, and I was by Mrs. Jeleńska's side, praying she wouldn't start up again. But she didn't say another word until we reached her gate. I opened it for her.

She said, "Yes. This where I live now," and sighed.

"Yes. Here."

It probably wasn't too late to go to Brooks's Bar now, but I asked Janek if he wouldn't mind going tomorrow and he said that was okay by him. We went round the back to get into our house. I found Mum in the hall on the way to the kitchen. "Back already?" she said.

I put my arms around her waist, hugged her as hard as I could and burst into tears on her chest. At last the gristly knots in my bones came undone.

CHAPTER NINETEEN

DAY FIVE: MORNING

It's 9.10 when Mum says, "Would you go and buy a few *ciasteczka* later today? There's nothing left in the freezer."

I do my best to hide my euphoria. "Sure. What kind? Brioche, doughnuts, Danish?"

"You decide."

Dad's had a relatively peaceful night. Mum and I took turns to be with him. The extra morphine I gave him seemed to stave off the worst of the pain, and Janek and Dybcio must have worn him out yesterday. So far as I know he only woke once.

In the evening, while Iwonka was with Dad, I could have opened the laptop, looked for Ossie, but Mum's "Am I a burden?" rang in my ears. I watched four recorded episodes of *Corrie* with her. She kept dozing off, waking, realising that she'd missed ten minutes, then rewinding it to catch up.

It's snowed some more during the night, a good three inches. Only one phone call this morning.

Mum sits on the sofa, flicking through her recordings.

I have to remind her. "Dad's bag needs to be changed." I'm still not allowed.

"I've already done it."

My heart drops as a line of text on the screen shows eight collapsed episodes of *The Bold and the Beautiful*. I may have to watch some of those with her.

Mum says, "Pan Śliwka will be here at half past ten if the Northwich Road is clear. Perhaps it's better if you go shopping now." Śliwka? I've never heard of him.

I look out of the window again, hoping the gritters have made the roads negotiable.

211

I leave, dressed as if for the Himalayas. At last. Fresh, cold, cancer-free air.

At Tesco's the shopping takes moments. I steer to the farthest corner of the car park and switch off the ignition. With the windows open, the seat pushed to its limit, the back rest almost flat, I lie down, pulling my scarf over my chin. Even Altrincham can smell fantastic on the right day. I set my phone alarm for twenty minutes, inhale deeply then shut my eyes, prepared to drift. Around and behind me, people transfer their bags from trolleys into boots, slam doors, drive in, out; mundane noises, now soporific, like water trickling in a pebbly brook. And no sourness anywhere.

When I return, Pan Śliwka is already with Dad. I hang my gear on the coat rack, then pop in to say hello. Pan Śliwka stands, walks round the bed and embraces me as if we're old friends.

"You've hardly changed." He beams.

From when? I'm sure I've never seen him before.

He looks at me sideways. "You don't remember me, do you?"

With a blush developing, I begin, "No, I do. I'm not entirely—"

"Hyde Park? 1981?"

Ah. The Solidarity demo?

"I brought your record player to – where was it – Balham?"

"Camden," Dad says.

I remember now. Not him, just the stereo, the records and the demonstration.

"Yes, of course. Thank you by the way."

Whoever he is to Dad, he looks younger than most of Mum and Dad's friends. His shock of dark hair contains few grey strands, reminding me of an ageing gypsy.

I say I'll come back in a minute with tea.

Mum is ironing one of Dad's shirts. I keep silent about that. Behind her on the sofa lie another three, washed, dried, folded. The iron travels in and out, in and out, several times, between the same two buttons that will never be used again.

"Should I remember Pan Śliwka?" I take the doughnuts out of the bag, arrange them on a plate and switch the kettle on.

All Mum can manage is, "Hm?"

"Pan Śliwka? Should I know him? Was he in the *Armia Krajowa*? Someone from *Kombatantów*?"

She arranges the shirt on a hanger then attaches it to the top of the door frame. "No. Tadek was a baby in the war. An orphan. And he never went to *Kombatantów* because he didn't need it." She puts another shirt on the board.

I wait for more. "Did you say he came here from Northwich?"

"He moved there in…1965…66…"

"So who is he?"

"In which way 'Who is he?'? A friend." A note of irritation has crept into her voice.

Is it some big secret or is Mum just preoccupied? This is hard work. "*How do you know him?*"

"Oh, I see. That's what you're getting at." She sighs. "Tatuś took him under his wing for a while. Tadek had nobody in England. Anywhere. He was in the Shah of Persia's orphanage…" Pausing, Mum stands the iron upright and looks through the French window. "No, wait…that was Marek." She closes her eyes tight as if something's hurting her. "No. Tadek was in the Maharaja's orphanage in Balachadi. Anyway, Witek gave him his first job. That's all."

"An Indian one?" I say, at the same instant realising how stupid that sounds.

"Mm." She's going to burn through those cuffs in a minute. I hope Iwonka turns up soon.

"Maharaja?" I repeat.

"Ania, I'm sorry. I can't think now. If you want to know, read the book. It's called…" Again she hesitates, pinching the bridge of her nose. "…*Stolen Childhood*. It's there somewhere."

I arrange the cups and doughnuts on the tray.

From Dad's room comes nothing but silence as I walk down the corridor. I expected chatter. I enter.

Pan Śliwka lifts a finger to his lips and shakes his head. "He's asleep," he whispers. He takes the cup from me and refuses the doughnut. "You don't really remember me, do you?"

I own up. It seems simpler now and the sincerity of his smile puts me at ease. He hunches forward in my direction and – returning to the only time I ever met him – says, "He was so proud of you. Especially when he saw your photograph in the *Dziennik Polski*."

What does he mean? There must be more spectacular achievements in my life.

1981. It was winter. I remember there was a phone call, a crazy, agitated discussion about the Solidarity march that was going to culminate in Hyde Park, Dad saying he couldn't go, that I had to be his delegate since I lived in London, and an instruction to create a banner. He even told me what to write. Then a short conversation with Mum. She kept her voice down, saying Dad had a kind of breakdown when Jaruzelski imposed Martial Law on Poland. Dad was watching the news non-stop. He'd shouted and raved at the TV when the footage showed tanks rolling down Polish streets, a reminder of what happened in 1939. At night he switched the radio on for constant updates wherever he could find them. He was in a bad way, Mum said.

I'd planned to attend, bannerless, on hearing about it, so he needn't have worried about that. His Walewski delegate intended to show her support.

Pan Śliwka observes Dad whose gurgle is growing louder. "Yes. He was

213

very proud." He turns to me again. "More than thirty years ago. *Jak czas leci.*" Time flies.

My going on a demonstration made Dad that proud? I hardly did anything; I ripped a white sheet in half, stitched the two pieces together, painted the slogan then sewed the edges onto garden canes bought in the hardware store on Camden High Street. My English flatmates were more fired up about the banner than I was; one of them promised to hold the other end for me. I didn't want Dad to have a heart attack, and my refusal, I thought, could tip him over the edge. But if a banner was a necessity, I'd have preferred the *Solidarność* logo.

The next time he called, I was able to say: "Yes, Tatuś, it's exactly as you want. It says 'Remember Yalta 1945: Do not forsake us now'." It was such a small thing to do for him, looking back.

Pan Śliwka grips both knees as if getting ready to stand. "That was in December too. It was a sad Christmas that year."

He clears his throat then places a hand on top of the duvet. "Well, my friend, brother, I must be going."

On his way out, he gives Mum a hug and whispers something in her ear.

She replies, "Thank you. I will."

As I open the door to let him out, he says, "Wandzia has my number. I'm in Witek's address book when…"

I nod to spare him the words.

THEN

Next morning, Janek and I went shopping again. I considered going down Knutsford Avenue and then up King's Road to bypass the bus stop on Upper Chorlton Road. But even if we avoided the bus stop, we might not sneak past Mrs. Jeleńska if she was on the bench because the garden-park was a little triangle where the roads joined into one.

We risked the normal route and no-one was there.

For Iwonka we bought some psychedelic hair slides, elastic hair bobbles and a *Bunty* annual (my idea). Janek said she probably wouldn't understand it yet, but I explained my reasons to him. The annual was a very good present because I could look at it first and then help her with reading it afterwards. He saw my point.

Dad got Old Spice aftershave, Mum Yardley's body lotion and bath salts, Granny another apron same as last year and the year before, and Grandad three packets of Woodbines. Grandad's present was a bit rubbish because we didn't know what to buy him, but if we put the packets in a bigger box and wrapped it in shiny paper perhaps he might not notice. That was an excellent plan. Janek and I agreed on absolutely everything. We didn't have enough money left to buy a present for each other, but it didn't seem to matter.

When we got back home, no sooner had we taken the carrier bags to his room than Mum called up the stairs.

"Ania, put your anorak on."

I left Janek and bent over the banister. "Why?"

"You're coming with me."

"Where?"

"The optician."

The flipping things were ready.

*****

The optician adjusted them on my ears and made me read the letters on the white poster on the wall. Blimey! A miracle!

Then he handed me the mirror to see 'how attractive' I looked.

I'd never be able to face anybody ever again. Seymour Park was going to be a nightmare. Polska school worse. I'd never have a grown-up boyfriend with a signet ring. And nobody would ever want to kiss me again. Not even Stevo.

*****

"Time to decorate the tree. *Święty Mikołaj* is coming!" Dad announced. Iwonka's face flashed like a diamond at the prospect of Father Christmas.

Dad had dragged the tree in earlier and jiggled it in the base until the trunk was absolutely straight. Now he disappeared into the cellar and returned carrying two cardboard boxes.

He fished out the string of fairy lights. Sitting cross-legged on the sitting room floor, the three of us listened while he crooned away, pretending to be Bing Crosby. I began to sing along with him. "*I'm drimmink of a Vite Christmas, chest like de ones ayoost to know…*" He winked at me. I loved it when he was Helen Shapiro or 'Bink'. Perhaps it would be fun tonight after all? It was only us lot and so specs didn't matter *really*. I put an arm around Iwonka who was wiggling her loose front tooth and rocking from bum cheek to bum cheek to the rhythm. Janek bottom-shuffled towards me and slid his arm round my neck. Together we swayed from side to side like three monkeys on a branch.

Dad was checking the connections. "*Ver de treetops glisten ant children listen to hear sleigh bells in de snow…*" He screwed four new bulbs into the fairy lights because they were broken, same as every year.

Then he informed us that we'd be entertaining guests at *wigilia*.

A groan barged from my stomach through my mouth and landed, welcome as a cow pat, on the carpet.

His head jerked up. "You have something to say?"

My brain crammed up with memories of other Christmas Eves…

No, Dad, please, no. Let's be happy for once. Don't ruin it. Can't it be just us? With you being Bink or Danny Kaye?

Why did we have to have this endless stream of guests eating our bigos and compote, planting slurpy, garlicky kisses and being nosy about lessons? That's the only thing grown-ups ever asked us about – boring school. I'd imagined we'd get away with it this year since nothing was said earlier.

"Sorry," I said, trying to act normal. "Who's coming?"

"Państwo Młotek and Pan Apanowicz," he said.

I suppressed another rumbling groan. More people I'd never heard of. What did they have to do with us?

Dad's eyes narrowed to a slit, more than enough to make plain what he thought of me. Janek's arm flopped down my back and he dropped his hands in front of his stomach. I felt myself shrivelling.

Dad said, "Will you *ever* develop compassion? The Młoteks' sons died in Katyń. And Pan Apanowicz left his wife and children in Warszawa."

Suddenly I wanted to scream. In my head I shouted, "Well, all right, that was really sad! As sad as Granny and Kasia and Mrs. Jeleńska! As sad as all the saddest Polish stories in the whole sad continent of Europe on the whole sad planet Earth in the whole sad Universe in all of sad Infinity. BUT IT WAS NOT MY FAULT!"

Mr. and Mrs. Młotek could come if they had no-one else. But *only* if they didn't talk about dead people like every Christmas.

I knew what was going to happen. Later in the evening when everybody left, Dad would bring up that poor Yankel again and he'd start on the *mea culpas*. I didn't want to have to think about it. Why couldn't I fall asleep and dream about nice things, happy things, like walking down Carnaby Street in yellow trousers or driving with Stevo in the sunshine with the breeze in my hair?

English children didn't have to listen to these war stories, did they? They had crackers and turkey and party hats and sixpences and thrupenny bits in puddings and games and a jolly Father Christmas who yo-ho-hoed in his red outfit and everybody laughing and telling jokes. It wasn't *fair*.

And as for Mr. Apanowicz, well, he should have made sure he brought his family from Polska so they could flipping well have *wigilia* at *his* house. A much better idea. Why were we getting lumbered with him whoever he was?

I tried to move my jaw because I was getting a pain in the bone in front of my ear.

Iwonka piped up. "Will they bring presents?"

Dad said, "We don't invite guests to get something from them, do we, treasure?"

Janek passed Dad a new green bulb from the box. "Didn't he love his children?"

"Who?" Dad said.

"Pan Owicz," Janek replied.

"Pan *Apa*nowicz, son." Dad shook his head like he did when Dennis Law missed a goal on the telly, and heaved a breath. "He *had* to leave them or he would be in prison now." He paused, then looked up at my face. "He was in the AK."

What was Dad saying exactly? It felt like a barbed, coded message about himself, but not for Janek and Iwonka, just for me. Why would Dad have been put in prison by Polish people in Polska? Did people in the Underground Army do bad things too? So that must mean…that Dad did something bad. And maybe Dad would have left me if I'd been born then. Perhaps he only wanted Janek and Iwonka?

"*Why* did he *have to* leave them?" I asked.

Dad shook his head and glanced at Iwonka and Janek who were fiddling with the one of the Christmas decorations.

To me he quietly said, "Because he would have been tortured by the Communists if he had stayed. Just as I would have been, Ania…if I hadn't escaped. That would have been the fate of everybody in the *Armia Krajowa*. Pan Edzio, Pan Franek too. Ania…try to be a good girl this evening… Let's have a Happy Christmas, shall we?"

I thought back to the general's funeral and photo in the *Dziennik Polski*. That must mean that Auntie Teresa, Mrs. Kurka and Mr. Kardasz would have been tortured too.

The lights were now glowing in full multi-coloured working order.

Dad shifted position, put his weight on his good leg and levered himself up. "Now it's *wigilia!*" He attached the end of the wire to the top of the tree and looped it through the branches.

"When they arrive," he said, "take their coats. Be polite. Don't slouch. Speak when spoken to. Oh, and Anka, put your glasses on." With his foot he nudged the box of decorations towards me and Janek and then swung Iwonka up onto his shoulders.

"Come on, favourite youngest daughter. Time for another song."

As they jigged out the door, him singing "*Dzhyn-gyel bells, Dzhyn-gyel bells, Dzhyn-gyel ol de vey…*," I watched Iwonka bouncing gleefully on the back of his neck, her ponytail curl bobbing up and down.

I couldn't remember what being six felt like any more.

*****

After Dad went out Mum said we couldn't have the telly on because today there should be carols, so the same LP of the Mazowsze choir had been playing for ages. Now they sang '*Dzisiaj w Betlejem*' for the umpteenth time. I chose not to labour the point of unwelcome visitors with Mum. I half-suspected she wanted just our family too.

The sitting room was dark apart from the glow of the reds, greens and blues coming from the tree, and the air smelt of pine now the lights had warmed up the needles. Under the branches the presents Janek and I bought lay glinting in shiny wrapping paper. They looked a bit lonely with only

Groucho for company.

Dressed in our Sunday clothes, Iwonka and I lolled in silence on the sofa. I was on my back counting the bumps on the coving and trying to ignore the General staring down at me. Janek lay across Mum's armchair dangling his legs over the side and chewing his sleeve. As well as fretting about my dorky specs and if I'd laid the festive table properly, I worried about what these people were like and would I manage to behave how Dad wanted me to. Gloomily I awaited his return.

It was half past five. *Wigilia* should have started at the sighting of the first star, but the sky was glittering with hundreds of them now. Granny and Grandad turned up first, Granny carrying the cakes still in baking tins. Then Dad came back with the Młoteks and Mr. Apanowicz. I stood to attention and took the coats as instructed. And even though they were heavy and smelt of dried rain and tobacco, I did my best to hang them properly on the hooks.

Mr. and Mrs. Młotek were new to me, I don't know where Dad found them. They were about the same age as Granny and Grandad, only kind of posher because Granny's nails were never painted and she only wore her wedding ring. But Mrs. Młotek had nice nails and wore lots of rings with stones.

Mr. Apanowicz's pear-shaped face was familiar. It didn't take me long to figure out I'd seen him at Polski church sitting in the balcony, up at the back, facing the crucifix, the only person in the pew.

The guests complimented me on the way I'd laid the table, and Dad asked whether I'd remembered to put the bunch of manger straw underneath the tablecloth. Which of course I had. I'd also remembered to lay an extra place for another guest or Jesus if he decided to pop in. And Iwonka had fanned out the holy wafers from Granny's sister in Wrocław and put them inside one of Granny-from-Polska's cotton crocheted doilies.

We stood behind our chairs and Dad said that as the eldest child I should say grace. I put on my best accent so as not to disappoint him and remembered all the words from *kolonia* correctly. Then we did the excruciatingly awful wafer-sharing and kissing with these complete strangers. Mr. and Mrs. Młotek said the usual Polish Christmas stuff, "I wish you health, happiness, good fortune and top marks at school." I knew it. Flipping school. But I said *dziękuję* and kept on smiling. Twenty-seven kisses by the end of all that malarkey, what with both cheeks and one extra.

Finally we sat down. On one side, I had Janek. On the other, Mr. Apanowicz, who was still as a rock, his chunky, pink fingers holding the empty plate like he was scared someone might take it away from him.

Dad poured the wine into everyone's glasses and raised the first toast to those present.

We began on the twelve *wigilia* dishes. Starters of different salads, stuffed eggs in mayonnaise and cream, marinated herrings with onions.

The second toast honoured the cooks. Next was beetroot soup with Polskie ravioli.

The third toast was to wives and mothers. Three types of *pierogi*. (Which was good because some of them had cheese.)

The fourth toast to absent family and friends. Time for Fishmas.

When Mum brought in the carp, Dad squeezed between our seats and the wall to get to the stereo. He took the needle off the record and returned to his place.

Now he asked everyone to stand before the next course. He paused and watched the three of us until we stopped fidgeting.

Holding the stem of the glass, he slowly said, "Our beloved family who perished in the war. We will never forget... The homeland will remember."

Dad was looking at Mrs. Młotek who sniffed while her husband squeezed her wrist. Then all the grown-ups put their glasses to their lips.

Janek, Iwonka and me sipped our ginger ale. Silence reigned for what seemed like ages. Across the table I noticed Mrs. Młotek staring at Janek as if she'd never seen a boy before. Her gaze examined his face. Mrs. Młotek swallowed, smiled, and patted herself twice, palm open, on her collar bone. She pointed her glass first at Janek, then me and Iwonka. "Children, *Wesołych Świąt!*" Merry Christmas. In unison we muttered *Wesołych Świąt* back.

Mum sliced the carp. She only gave us the teensiest bit, so that was kind of her. And when Janek whispered if I could eat his for him, I nodded and let him slide it on my plate while no-one was looking. It was like a replacement Christmas present for him even though it nearly killed me not to gag.

Several varieties of fish followed, more random toasts, then fruit compote, Granny's cakes, and tea and coffee.

Now at last Dad said, "Iwonka, have you been a good girl all year? Shall we see if *Święty Mikołaj* has left you some presents?"

In the sitting room mine and Janek's little gifts had vanished under the bigger packages. Dad said Janek could distribute the presents this year. He started with the biggest present there.

He read the tag. "For Ania..." then he stopped because it was curly Polskie writing.

Dad continued for him. "A most lovely girl. With our very best wishes, Lusia and Kuba Młotek and Mirek Apanowicz."

I felt a hot patch rush from my heart up to my ears. The present was huge and had a peculiar shape. I waited until Janek gave all the presents out and touched it through the wrapping paper to see if it was hard or soft. My cheeks scalded so much that my glasses were steaming up. Why did they get me a present? They weren't my family or anything.

I opened the other presents first because, I don't know why, I was sort of scared to open the big one. I got a collection of books – *Lorna Doone*, *What Katy did Next*, *Black Beauty*, *Robinson Crusoe*, *The Secret Garden*. Not one single

Chalet School book which was what I really wanted, but never mind, and notelets, an autograph book, a pencil case set that had a protractor, and a pair of pyjamas with daisies on them.

Janek opened his present from Mr. and Mrs. Młotek – it was a complete cowboy dressing-up set, with a sherriff's hat, waistcoat, badge, pistols and everything. Iwonka got a doll that cried.

Now, I put my finger under the sellotape of the mystery package. Someone was watching me, I could feel it. I pulled the paper apart carefully. The present had grey and white furry feet...grey furry legs...a grey and white body...teeth...Bugs Bunny. The biggest and best Bugs Bunny I'd ever seen. It must have been so expensive. And it was gorgeous apart from one little thing. I didn't play with toys like this any more. Keeping my eyes on his teeth, I circled my finger and thumb round the bottom of his ear and pulled up gently until it flopped out of my hand.

I did it again. And again. I told myself: "Stop chewing your lip or you'll make a hole in it and you won't be able to eat gherkins for weeks."

Now it was dawning on me. They couldn't have known, could they? Mr. and Mrs. Młotek didn't have any grandchildren because their own children had died in that Katyń place, and Pan Apanowicz probably didn't realise girls of my age no longer played with cuddly animals.

I looked up at Mrs. Młotek. Her ankles seemed glued together and her bottom was so close to the edge of the sofa that one nudge and she'd fall right off it. Two wrinkles she'd had between her eyebrows earlier had now become one fat one. She was rubbing her knees through her skirt and gazing at me the same way people look into the sky, waiting for sun rays between the clouds. I checked that Mum and Dad weren't listening.

"*Dziękuję bardzo*," I said. "It's the best present I've ever had."

Mrs. Młotek's hands flew from her knees to a clap, then to a prayer which she put to her mouth. Her smile spread to her sparkling eyes and into her rosy cheeks. "Ania, look! Look at the cord."

I hadn't noticed it. I stood Bugs Bunny on his legs – he was nearly the same size as Iwonka – and pulled the plastic tab on his back.

He said, "What's up, Doc? I love carrots."

I pulled it a second time. "Of course, you know this means war?"

Mrs. Młotek was nodding her head at me to do it again, her eyes all shiny and glittery like a stream. I did.

"Gee, ain't I a stinker?" Bugs Bunny said.

Yes. That was one way of putting it. I probably was. I had to try to start being nicer to old people, even Granny.

*****

Mum said it was a good idea, so on Boxing Day after *obiad* and *Woman of the Year* with Spencer Tracy and Katharine Hepburn, I unzipped the best present

I'd *really* ever had and rolled in a piece of paper.

In Polski I typed:

Most respected Panstwo Mlotek, (which was a bit rubbish because my typewriter didn't have the right Polish letters and Grandad's only had Spanish ones like ¿ and ñ).

On behalf of my esteemed brother and sister and myself most sincerely I thank you for the gift of the miraculous presents. May God reward you – Granny was always saying that, so it must be grown-up.

Comma. Carriage return.

Now what else?

From the deepest depth of our humble hearts, we thank you for joining us in sharing our wigilia feast and most sincerely I cordially invite you, respected Panstwo Mlotek, to return to join us in our celebration again next year. God willing – another one of Granny's,

I bow to you – one of Dad's,

Most respectfully yours,

Miss Anna Beata Walewska Esquire.

On the bottom I typed Manchester, December 25 1966, like our family in Poland did on Christmas cards, except they put Warszawa or Wrocław.

I slaved for two full hours what with thinking up the right words, working out the sentences, and trying to remember whether it was ż or rz, or ó or u, except I only had z and o anyway. Writing stuff for grown-ups seemed to take forever, so many decisions. Maybe I should be a Hollywood film star, after all. In *Woman of the Year*, Katharine Hepburn played a famous international newspaper lady. She got to boss everyone around. Maybe I could be like her?

To finish I drew little Christmas trees on the corners of the paper because Mrs. Młotek might like the professional touch.

When it was done, I showed it to Mum to check for spelling mistakes. Something was wrong with her because she started coughing.

"It's very good, Ania, very good," she said and sort of snorted like a horse. Then she quickly opened a cupboard, where she must have seen something funny. I looked into the cupboard too, but there was nothing there except the usual cups and saucers.

"No spelling mistakes?" I asked.

"None. It's perfect." Mum laughed and that's when I knew she was lying. I *had* made a mistake somewhere, but she didn't want to tell me.

"Taken you a long time, hasn't it, love? But don't you think you should thank Pan Apanowicz too?"

I returned to my Olympia Splendid 33 and started all over again.

Most respected Pan Apanowicz,

Thank you for the present. Please join us next year.

Most respectfully yours,

Miss Ania Walewska.

I compared the two letters and they seemed to say the same thing in the end. Why couldn't I have thought of that in the first place? Writing was dead easy.

*****

In preparation for the New Year's Eve Dance at Kombo's Mum and Dad went shopping together for a frock for Mum. They were gone all day. They came back with two, both floor-length and short-sleeved, equally beautiful.

Mum laid them out on the bed for us to see. The first was a white and lilac creation with a waistband pin-tucked into fine stripes. The second was made of black flowing chiffon with a split skirt. It had a midriff-wide, white satin waistband and a roll-over collar, both of which were studded with diamantés. They were heavenly. Manuela would love them. Two gorgeous dresses to pick from. Lucky Mum!

She smoothed the bodice of the black dress over her knees and ran her fingers over the diamantés.

"It'll be all right," she said.

Iwonka's mouth was open so wide I thought her tongue might fall out. "It's so beautiful, like Petula Clark's dresses."

Mum made a soft hmph sound. "I'm not Petula Clark. Your father is mad."

Late in the afternoon Mum came back from Mrs. Ptak's house where she'd had a shampoo and set. She was bouffed up and two inches taller. She looked so much prettier than Manuela's mum with that skunky stripe of hers.

Leaning back against the front door, we waited for the great reveal.

"Are you ready?" Dad called.

He came down first, one step at a time, as usual. He was wearing a tuxedo and bow tie and his shoes were shinier than I'd ever seen. He looked gorgeous, a movie star like Fred Astaire, but much more handsome, like James Dean. Iwonka clapped.

Then it was Mum's turn and Iwonka's applause stopped.

Mum had chosen the black dress, but the top part – all those glittering diamantés, everything that made it spectacular – was covered by a black woollen shawl. Apart from her face, she looked boring as an old nun in a potato sack. On the sixth stair, the shawl slid off, showing the scar that ran in an angry, jagged line from her shoulder down her arm.

In one deft move Mum rearranged the folds and pulled them together, tucking her hands underneath.

"Wandzia?" Dad stood with one foot on the bottom stair. His arm was out-stretched towards her, as if she was Ginger Rogers lightly tripping down a wide, golden staircase.

Smiling, he turned his face slightly sideways and looked up at her out of the corner of his eye. "Wandzia...?" He began to sing. "*Ven dey begin de Beguine...*"

Mum was at the bottom now and he slipped the shawl back off, kissed her scar and, holding both her hands at her sides, kissed her in the corner of her neck. Then he gave her a really long kiss on the lips. Not like the one I'd had with Stevo. This was more like Simon Templar or James Bond. It went on for *hours*, like they'd forgotten we were there. Iwonka snuggled into Dad's bottom and hugged him. I had to go back into the kitchen because I wasn't feeling so well and Janek followed me. He was probably queasy too.

*****

Granny turned up. After the door had closed behind Mum and Dad, I went to their bedroom. Mum's other dress lay on the bedspread, begging me to try it on. Her bedside table drawer hadn't been pushed to. When I saw what was inside, I completely forgot about the dress. A new addition – Mark Eden Bust Developer. Wow! I read the instructions. You had to rub your breasts regularly in an upward motion, which seemed easy enough, and they would expand into 'fulsome roundness'. But maybe you had to have some breasts in the first place. Manuela had *something*, but I didn't have anything at all. Still, I couldn't wait to tell her about it and ask if Mrs. Karageorgis used it because her bosoms were big enough to stand a goldfish bowl on.

I went through the rest of the drawer. Mum's manicure set, odd buttons, a prayer book, *Angelique Loves Again*, bits of paper, two cotton reels. Nothing much.

In Dad's drawer I found receipts, ointment of some kind, three cassette tapes of Polskie songs, Dad's driving licence and a few metallic pouches with the words *Durex Gossamer* and 'sensitol, protective and lubricated' printed on them. I ran my fingers over the ridge inside which felt like a really thick elastic band. So, also nothing much.

Then I noticed Dad's wardrobe was ajar. Strange. He always locked it with a key when he left. I'd seen inside it often, but this was the first time I had an opportunity to explore it properly.

The wardrobe was two-sided – suits, trousers and jackets on the right, and three shelves and underneath two deep drawers on the left. I pulled out the top drawer to find nothing but socks, and two spare lifts for Dad's shoes, one in brown leather, the other black. The second drawer, nothing but white vests and underpants. Was that all? Why lock your wardrobe with a key? I mean, who would want to steal your clothes unless they were exactly the same size as you?

But I wasn't ready to give up. The bottom shelf had nothing of interest either, just sweaters. I inserted my hands down the sides to make sure I wasn't mistaken. The second shelf contained folded shirts. The interior of the top shelf was beyond my grasp even on tip-toes, so I pulled Mum's dressing table stool over and climbed onto it.

There were light wool scarves at the front, and behind there was a huge paper bag full of something and a carved wooden box from Poland. In between the bag and the box, a thick buff envelope. I pulled out the envelope carefully and lifted the flap. It was full of pound notes. I flipped through the wad as if it was a deck of cards. There must be hundreds of them. Hundreds. Where had he got them from? Wow.

"Ania! What are you doing up there?" Granny yelled from downstairs. I nearly jumped out of my skin and fell off the stool. "If you want to watch Hogmanay, it's starting."

"I'll be down in a minute." Janek and Iwonka had probably fallen asleep on the sofa by now, and I wasn't that fussed about Andy Stewart. Besides, I had something better to do now. Should I or shouldn't I borrow a pound or two? Would he notice?

On the one hand, Dad was precise with money, I saw that often enough at the factory when he did his sums with his machine. He probably knew exactly how much he had.

On the other hand, this wasn't the factory…

Sitting on the bed, I pulled off the two brown elastic bands, flattened the notes straight and began to count. In all, there were one hundred and thirty-two. Wow. No, I wouldn't take any though because, when I thought about it, there was only one way this could finish. First, he'd kill me, then he'd make me kneel on dried peas for the rest of my life and I didn't fancy that. Doing the best I could, I rolled the notes back up and replaced the elastic bands exactly as they were. I reinserted the wad tightly down into the corner where he'd written a name, POSK, in capital letters. POSK? That wasn't a Polski name. Maybe it was a casino or something.

The envelope went on the side while I checked out the carved box. It caught my eye because when Stevo and me had whittled, no matter how hard I tried to make patterns, what I ended up with was just a skinnier stick than I started with.

But this box was gorgeous. The edges were carved, the first layer into tiny S shapes with two circles inside both curls, then a line of spirals, and another of triangles within triangles. On the lid was a coat of arms, the letters *Warszawa,* and a mermaid with masses of curly, long hair. In one hand she held a shield with an emblem, in the other a sword raised above her head. Silver threads outlined the shapes. A scroll was unfolding the letters *Semper Invicta.* Latin probably.

I opened it. Typewritten papers, some with a photo of Dad's face, most without. Some in Polish, some English, and a few in German with the two dots above the vowels like in *All Our Yesterdays.* Underneath the papers, a knife with a horn handle, some medally metal things, a pearly-coloured pair of cufflinks and a pendant. And underneath those a fabric pouch which contained a tatty piece of fabric with a six-sided star like two triangles on top of each other, a watch, and a badgey kind of pin with some weird writing on it – a code or letters in a foreign alphabet, like Chinese, except it wasn't Chinese. They seemed to be written sideways with a calligraphy pen. As well, there was a photo of two boys, aged ten or eleven, in a rowing boat. They were bundled up in knitted jumpers that looked dead scratchy. And here they were again, somewhere covered deep with snow, this time with woolly hats and boots. They were perched halfway up a lop-sided tree, the fair-haired boy higher than the dark-haired one. Behind the tree to the left stood a black horse attached to a sled. I thought the blond boy might be Dad, but I wasn't sure. I returned all the items to the pouch.

Nothing special there either. Why did Dad always lock the wardrobe? Was it the money? I put the pouch in the box.

The brown paper bag held a squashed sombrero, a gun and holster and a little furry black thing. Also, a small cellophane bag like Mr. Edzio used for the WT 799 wallets – who were all these people in the yellowy photographs? The women wore long, elaborate dresses and tight bodices, and the men had moustaches, bushy ones curled up into a point at the end. They sat in groups or on their own, either in front of painted country scenes or against a plain background. Exactly the type of people I'd imagined at Spooky when I first saw it.

Next, a blurry photo of a teenager in a cassock who looked like Dad, except couldn't be because Dad never went to church. Then, definitely Dad in a scout uniform, which meant the altar boy *must* be Dad after all. Dad, looking really skinny, with other scouts. Dad in army uniform with two other men standing outside a building called Queen's Arms and pointing to a sign saying Glasgow. Why weren't these photos in the albums downstairs?

The last picture was smudged and grainy and had been folded over in the past. Two men on a stage, both holding canes, wearing bowler hats and wide trousers. As I peered into the picture I realised the Charlie Chaplin on the left was Dad. The man on the right – Sławek Kardasz. So at one time they must have been good friends. Curious.

I put all the stuff in the bag and returned it and the box to the wardrobe.

CHAPTER TWENTY

DAY SIX

I feel a storm surge.

Mieczysław Fogg's rendition of *'Mały Biały Domek'*, The Little White House, streams out to me as I tidy Dad's medication into unnecessary piles on the dining room table. I didn't know that was on the CD when I inserted it two songs ago. His eyes were closed within moments.

Ever since I got here the memory of *Shoah* has been rising and ebbing like a semi-diurnal tide. Slightly lower water when I've thought of Ossie.

I look through to the conservatory at Mum. She's pairing Dad's socks, accompanied by the strains of *The Bold and the Beautiful*. She'll be there a while.

I return to Dad's room to sit and force myself to do it – recall what I felt then in order to give myself courage now.

It's over two years since I watched *Shoah*, two years of lying about being too busy to come and visit until I absolutely had to. The opening scene showed two men in a boat. One stood punting; the other, middle-aged with curly, silver hair, sat at the front, singing the same song in Polish. The lament in his voice and a profound sorrow behind his eyes made me want to hug him, kiss the head of the boy he'd been, the boy who sang there during the war.

As I watched the boat flow down the tree-lined river, I recalled the photograph in Dad's wardrobe; two children, same landscape, same bucolic, peaceful atmosphere.

The following shot was trained on the silver-haired man as he walked silently through a track in the forest. After a cough, he stopped at a clearing. *"Schwer zu erkennen aber das war's hier, da waren gebrannt Leute, viel Leute da waren gebrannt,"* "Hard to recognise, but it was here, they burnt people here. A lot of people were burnt here," he said.

I was expecting footage from the Holocaust next; nothing. No frightened little boy in the cap and short trousers beneath his coat, his hands up, being marched through snowy Warsaw streets; no images of the corpses the Allies found when they liberated the camps. Just testimony and shots of steam engines trundling through Polish countryside, using tracks that once transported Jews to their death, the camera panning across pastures covering the remains of unidentified victims who will never be claimed.

The director of the film put forward queries, gently phrased, as if not seeking answers to the biggest question of all. Some Polish interviewees sobbed, still grief-stricken, unbelieving. That was the story I thought I knew, the one I felt.

Then the interpreter asked a fat-bellied farmer who'd watched the transports roll in, "Were you afraid for the Jews?"

The man replied, "If you cut yourself, it doesn't hurt me," and smiled. He *smiled*.

Nausea rose to my chest.

More farmers, laughing, cheerful, simple people, replying as if immunised against the magnitude of what happened there. They could have been shot for helping the Jews, they said. Another man added, "But our people gave them the water nevertheless."

I began to tremble, overwhelmed with an undefinable recognition.

Our people. *Our* people? Were those Jewish people not *our people* too? Part of *our* human race? In my head a voice whispered, "If you prick us, do we not bleed?"

Did these Polish peasants not see the parallels? Even then in the 1940s they must surely have known *our* Catholic people had been forced on similar journeys to the labour camps in Siberia. Granny told me about those cattle wagons, people packed upright, nothing to drink; women scratching each other, fighting over icicles to melt with their hands to provide water for their parched and hungry infants. And poor Pani Jeleńska, barely in her twenties, huddled in the corner, mute after the gang rape. Slavery, starvation, disease; death lurking in every corner. I thought of Granny selling herself for the eggs to feed Mum and Kasia, and how she sang the national anthem in defiance. It wasn't so very different to the Jewish Czech families singing the Hatikva in the face of the Nazis. Was it?

The director probed further. "Did you know they were going to their death? What did you do?"

The fat farmer was still grinning. "I did this." He sliced his fingers across his neck. I thought I was going to be sick.

In the next shot a Jewish man described the *Gebrüll* and *Geschrei*, howling and screaming. He confirmed the farmer's story. "*Er hat so eine komische Geste gemacht, so, am Hals.*" I understood. "He made a queer gesture, like this, at the neck."

First there was unease; it became fear. As if I were sitting on the tiniest island in the ocean and the tide was flooding in, drowning me. I recalled all that drunken ranting at the table when we were kids. Those people hanging by their necks. By ropes from the balcony. The Jewish jokes. Janek sitting there chewing his cuffs. Iwonka on the verge of tears.

And the things Dad used to say. "Through deed and failure to do." He *did* something. Something he couldn't live with. Had he informed on them? It just couldn't be. But it had to be – because there was no other explanation. He was obviously responsible for *something.*

Was that what he meant by *'mea culpa?'* How many times did we hear that – my fault, my fault, my fault. And Yankel – who was Yankel to him?

My fault.

Was that the full story?

It was guilt he couldn't live with. The only conceivable reason why he never sacked the man with the Auschwitz tattoo.

How could I be so stupid? Why didn't I know? The truth fell into place.

The CD player clicks to a halt. No songs left. Silence. Please God, let me be wrong. I look up from my lap and study the face on the pillow. Even now I can't believe I'm thinking these things as I look at this old man who is dying, my dad. My Tatuś.

THEN

Granny had one of her loony moments and insisted we go with her to Alexandra Road in sub-zero temperature because it was good for the constitution, and she'd survived it "in Siberia where a breath could freeze the lungs and noses went black and dropped off " blah-blah.

As soon as we walked into Woolworth's, my glasses steamed up and I had to rely on Janek's blurry shape to guide me to the sweet counter where I waited for my specs to clear. I was trying to focus on the raspberry sherbets when something flashed in the corner of my eye and my heel was kicked forwards. I whipped round to see the back of a familiar head. Stevo. Definitely him. My palms felt as if a hedgehog was rolling round on them and my cheeks were on fire. He turned and winked at me as if no time had gone by, but four months had passed since he left. I remembered my glasses, quickly took them off and put them in my anorak pocket.

His face was fuller and he had both broadened out and shot up a couple of inches. He wore a khaki-coloured parka coat, not the raggedy old brown anorak he'd had at Spooky. His trousers stopped above his ankles, and on his feet were what looked like new broguey shoes. One of them trailed a shoelace.

Next to him stood a lady in a black knee-length PVC coat, with leopard skin cuffs and collar. Back-combed dyed-blond hair, pale, shiny pink lipstick, thick black eyelashes that looked as if they might drop off because they were so heavy, and hoopy turquoise earrings big as half crowns, except they were plastic. She certainly didn't look like someone who lay in bed all day. Not a bit of it. This lady got up in the morning and headed straight for her make-up bag, made an effort, you could tell. No lolling around reading *Angelique* books for her.

Why had he lied about her?

I was about to go over to him and ask him how he was when he shook his head as if to say "No" and put his hand over his mouth. As he pointed to the hardware counter, I took the hint and meandered over. Janek reattached himself to Granny at haberdashery.

"Hi," I said, hoping he couldn't see into my brain and get to the memory compartment where pictures of me kissing my hand kept pinging up like Jack-in-the-Boxes.

"When d'ya get the specs?"

I felt myself blush. "Not long. Don't have to wear them all the time," I lied. "Never mind them. How are you?"

"Yeah, okay," he said. "For now." He glanced at his mum who was gossiping with the shop assistant, deciding if Yardley or Coty smelt more sophisticated.

I shuffled on the spot and put my hands in my pockets. Then, horrified, I remembered the cold sore on my lip. My conversation was exhausted. I picked up a piece of sandpaper from the counter, put it back again when the man serving gave me a funny look and said, "What're you painting, love? Window frames?"

Scrabbling for the right questions, I turned to Stevo. "Did you have a nice Christmas?"

"Went to Eccles to see my Auntie Maureen and her lot. Same as last year. D'ya like my parka?" I said yes, wondering who Auntie Maureen was.

"So you're okay now then? Everything's all right at home?"

Stevo shrugged. "Yeah. S'okay. Suppose. My dad came round."

My face must have shown my surprise.

He went on, "That's who I got the parka from. Bought it for me for Christmas. And a pair of football boots."

I remembered that first day when we found him, and then all the other times I'd asked him questions and as usual none of it stacked up in a neat orderly pile. It didn't matter though, I still wanted to kiss him. "So you're all right then?"

"Yeah. Been going to school. My teacher was dead impressed with semaphore."

School too?

His mum seemed to be getting to the end of her conversation because she handed some money over. I had to hurry. "Are you ever coming back to Spooky?"

"Dunno. Depends."

"On what?"

"How things work out."

His mum finished talking and walked towards us.

"See you. I'd better go now," I said. I looked for a getaway and hurried to Granny's side. Behind me his mum asked, "Who's your friend, Stefan?"

"Someone from school," he replied.

"Come on, luvvie. Time we got home. Uncle Charlie's coming over. Egg and chips for tea?"

He was gone by the time I put my glasses back on to look at the entrance doors.

*****

The bell rang four times, the front door opened and a menacing male voice growled *"Buenos tardes, muchachos!"*

I dropped *Lorna Doone* and jumped off the bunk to lean over the banister and check what was going on.

There was a very brown, slightly streaky Mexican in our house. He had bushy black eyebrows and a moustache that drooped down the sides of his lips. His red and white checked shirt was open, showing his chest, and around his neck he wore a red bandanna loosely tied in a knot. On his feet were calf-length studded boots with thick Cuban heels.

He spotted me, put a finger to his mouth like for "shh" and called "Wanda, *arriba, arriba*! We go in an hour." He had a peculiar half-Polish half-Spanish accent.

I ran downstairs. Janek came to see what the commotion was about, and the Mexican narrowed his eyes, flicked his gun out of his holster and pointed it at Janek's stomach. "Hands up if you don't vont to die, *gringo*..."

By the time I'd worked out it really *was* Dad, Iwonka appeared, looking bewildered. The Mexican, eyes still slitty, twisted the tip of his moustache, then moved forward, his arms outstretched as if about to grab her.

"Vot a beautiful *chiquita*," he said. "I vill kidnap her and take her to Chihuahua..." Iwonka's eyes widened, her mouth started to tremble and she ran to hide behind Mum.

"Iwonka, child, it's me," Dad said in his normal Polish voice.

Mum laughed. "It's Tatuś – word of honour," she said, turning Iwonka round to face him. Less cheerfully she added, "I'll get changed."

Once Iwonka calmed down, we joined him at the table where he pulled out a huge, fat cigar, rolled and sniffed it, and bit the end off which he spat upwards across the kitchen. This was great!

Chewing on his cigar and leaning back in his chair with his Cuban boots on the table, he introduced himself as the world famous Pancho Villa who, along with his faithful horse, Pedro Ramirez, had single-handedly won the Mexican Revolution. He told us how he stole all the *haciendas* and gave them to poor people who had nowhere to live, like Robin Hood in England, except browner.

"And now I vill tell you how Pedrrrro and I climbed to the top of the highest heel een Mexico city and—" he stopped.

Mum was in the corridor. She was wearing a jester's outfit. The hat was a creation of silly jingle bells dangling from three sagging corners and was glued around her forehead and neck like a nun's wimple. Almost every inch of her from feet to crown was bagged up in white. The sleeves extended to a point and were attached to her middle finger by a loop, hiding the now paler mess of scars on her hands. Her face seemed tiny.

Something inside me shrivelled and died. Last year, when she came down to parade in her outfit, it was obvious she'd be the most beautiful lady at the carnival dance. Nobody could look as gorgeous as my mum in her suede, squaw mini-dress embroidered with beads and shells, and sandals that criss-crossed up her calves. And the headband with three feathers.

Now as she stood in the doorway, feet in flat-heeled, curl-toed jester slippers, I thought of Stevo's mum dolled up to the nines with her make-up and her eyelashes.

Dad said, "You look very nice, love." I knew he didn't mean it.

"I'm ready," Mum said. "Babcia will be here in a minute. Be good."

As she turned round to unhook her coat from the stand, the feeble tinkle from the bells on her slippers made me want to hide under a blanket and stay there forever.

*****

The salt and pepper cellars, still in the middle after *kolacja*, marked out the boundaries. There'd been an invisible wall between Mum and Dad since the dance and here it was at the table too. He was reading the *Manchester Evening News* and she was playing patience, and what with Dad and his paper and Mum and her cards, practically no space remained for me. I joined them anyway to see if Mum was winning or if she was in trouble. This particular game was tricky, it rarely worked, maybe three times out of ten. I sat on my haunches on the chair, put my elbows on the table and leaned forward.

"What are you playing for?"

"To find out if you'll be a good girl for the rest of your life."

Very funny.

"Feet off the chair," she said.

I moved sideways to let my legs dangle over the edge, propped my chin on my hands and bent forward to see if I could help.

"Look at Altrincham," she said to Dad. She flicked my right arm out of the way and dealt another row. I straightened the cards in my reach because she hadn't lined them up properly, they were all over the place.

"We are staying here," Dad said.

She slapped a queen of hearts on the king of spades. "It's a good area."

No, please, no. Now I understood what the atmosphere was about and it couldn't happen. What would I do without the gang? No Ossie to chat to through the window… What about Granny and Grandad? What about *cheese and onion crisps* and the black handbag? I'd be without pocket money… Who would get Grandad's Woodbines? And I'd have to go to a new school and no-one would like me because of my glasses. I'd have no friends and where would I go out to play?

I waded in. "No, it isn't, it's disgusting."

"Anka, find something to do. We have things to discuss," she said without lifting her eyes from the cards.

Dad said, "Too far."

Mum lifted the ace of spades from the bottom of the row and slapped it down at the top. "For what? Dom Kombatanta?"

What did Kombo's have to do with it? My rib cage stiffened tight as a washboard. Dad folded the paper over, ran his fist over the crease and looked up.

He spoke slowly. "What does that mean?"

Mum was collecting and stacking a row onto the ace of diamonds, a card went up with each word. "It means…" *stack* "that…" *stack* "you are never…" *stack* "here." The last one she slammed down.

He folded the paper again and stood up. "Don't exaggerate. I'm going for a shave."

She turned her face to the window. It was only just seven o'clock so even I knew he planned to go out again tonight. Mum swept the cards towards her and shuffled them first by cutting the pack in two and flipping them into each other, then by sliding the bottom layers to the top. She did this five times, getting noisier and noisier.

Another patience went down on the tablecloth.

We couldn't leave here. Just couldn't.

"I don't want to live in Altrincham. I won't know anyone," I said, trying not to whine so she wouldn't start slamming again.

"Me neither," she replied, hunched over, cheeks in her hands, gazing into the cards.

I changed to Dad's chair and knelt up on it, watching her thinking about her next move. It looked like the aces were trapped. It might work if she put the six of diamonds on the seven of clubs, and then she could put the four of clubs onto the five of spades…because then…

But no! She could flipping well find it herself if she was going to make us move!

Please God, don't let her make us leave Old Trafford. Please. "Are you doing this one to see if we'll live in Altrincham?"

She rubbed her cheek and looked into the distance, way beyond the pear

tree. "No. This one is for the absence of wars."
What was she on about now? "What wars?"
"Global and domestic."

*****

In the morning Mum had been agitated and sharp with us, and looked as if she hadn't slept much. Now I was back from school and her face was puffy and sponge-like – she'd been crying.

As I walked past the sitting room to get changed out of school uniform, I saw the ashtray on the arm of her chair was overflowing and three crumpled hankies were about to slip down the side of the orange cushion. No books anywhere.

By the time I came back down, the ashtray had gone, Mum was in the kitchen banging about in the cupboards and voices from the radio were discussing events in Vietnam.

"*Kolacja* is early today," she said.

"Can I have—?"

She waved me away. "Watch television." Her throat was gloopy with something as if she'd been gargling semolina. It was better to say nothing – asking might make it worse, whatever it was.

In the sitting room, Janek whispered, "What's the matter with her?"

"No idea." Maybe someone had died, or maybe Mum and Dad had rowed about bills or Kombo's again? Or maybe…Altrincham, a subject I'd rather not mention in case I accidentally made it happen, like when I wanted one of those purses the man with the tattoo was putting into frames.

Granny and Grandad's arrival confirmed it. Something serious *had* happened. And when Granny closed the sitting room door so us three wouldn't hear, I told the others to shut up and re-opened the door an inch.

I caught the end of Grandad's sentence, "…Karbowski too?"

Mum said, "And Jurek. Jacek as well. Four of them."

Somebody was pouring water from the tap into a pan or something. It must have been Granny because then she said, "Tea?"

"How bad is it?" Grandad asked.

Mum's voice was hesitant. "They wouldn't tell me. Only about Witek."

Granny said, "What time are you going?"

"Six thirty. But what should I tell *them*? I can't. You'll have to tell them."

"Not yet. Wait."

A long silence. I wondered what they were doing. Eventually Granny asked, "Did they say how long?"

Mum sighed loudly and began crying again, each word a separate little puddle, "Weeks, maybe months. That is if—" She broke off, and began another sentence. "I asked him not to go. Why didn't he listen? Why doesn't he *ever* listen?"

233

"Yes, well..." Granny's tone was harsh. "And the police? Did they say what happens next?"

"They won't be coming back here. They have all they need to know."

The police? Here in our house? It was beginning to make sense. The wad of money I found in Dad's wardrobe – where did he get it? Had he stolen it? Had he done something bad again with this Karbowski and Jacek, whoever they were, and Dad's poker friend Jurek from Kombo's? They must have robbed a bank. And what about the time he came home and told us to choose a pocket? Where did *that* money come from?

I myself would have to explain everything to Janek and Iwonka, tell them Dad was in prison, if Mum couldn't.

As soon as we finished *kolacja*, Mum put her coat on then while she was looking for something in her handbag, I sneaked a peek into the vanity case she'd put by the door. I saw Dad's dark green pyjamas. I couldn't bring myself to tell her they'd be no use and I knew that for a cast-iron fact because of the film.

In the Christmas holidays me and Dad watched the *Birdman of Alcatraz* which was about a man who kept thousands of birds in his cell. But the Birdman wore black and grey pyjamas with horizontal stripes – all the prisoners did, that's prison for you. Same ones, day and night.

Mum said he might be there for weeks. Months. But supposing they made him stay there for forty-three years like the Birdman? Would Dad remember how he repeated the Birdman's words and told me to memorise them. "A man ain't vipped until he kvits." He had to stay strong. What had he done?

Grandad went home and Granny did the washing up.

I didn't know where to put myself in the evening. Brownie Law Number Four again, like when Mum fell into the window. I'd have to tell Janek and Iwonka. I was the eldest, up to me to break the bad news.

But with Dad in prison, who would pay for food and everything? Mum didn't go to work, so how would we manage? And, would we be allowed to see him? Then the next thing – everyone at Polska school would find out, and Mrs. Piotrek with her mean, skinny lips would broadcast it in the Polski deli queue. People would stare at us in church because Dad was a bad criminal. Oh no – Krysia Nowicka. She'd go all holy and smirk at me.

I thought about all the children I knew. Apart from Stevo, everyone else seemed to have a dad or step-dad (like Gianni) who lived at home with them. Stevo! Was that why Stevo's dad was never there? Maybe he'd been in prison too. Maybe *all* dads who came out of prison hit their children with slippers and hot pokers.

The hours wore on, my imagination went through a thousand scenarios, each one grimmer than the last. Granny put Janek and Iwonka to bed.

I decided to hold fire. I hadn't found the right moment or the right words.

I don't know what time Mum came back home, but she was there in the morning, same as usual, in her armchair, coffee and Kensitas at her side. She looked worn out. I sank into the sofa opposite her and did up the buttons of my dressing gown.

"Darling," she said, with a weak smile, "It's good I've got you on your own. I need to talk to you." My feet felt itchy, wanted to run.

"It's Tatuś," she said. I waited for her to tell me he was in Strangeways. "He's been in a car accident."

A car accident?

Not in prison?

Mum took a long drag of her cigarette, and in the time it took her to inhale and exhale, I came to a horrifying conclusion. "Mama...is he dead?"

Perching her cigarette on the edge of the ashtray, she said, "No. No, of course not." She sat next to me and hugged me into her chest. I felt her heart beating against mine. "He's not dead. But he is very poorly. And we all have to do our best to be good and kind to each other while he's getting better. I'm relying on you to help me."

*****

Mum had a quick look at Mrs. Markham's desk and then told me to come with her. Although she knew most of the Polish people, or as Granny called them 'Godless heathens and communists' because they didn't go to mass, I knew more of the English people because I came to the factory more often.

Some of the workers were at their tables and machines, most of the O'Hanrahans and MacGraths. I followed Mum around the factory floor, and when people greeted her and asked after Dad, I could see she wanted to get back to the office really quickly.

The man with the numbers tattoo patted me on the shoulder, smiled and said, "Good morning. I hope your father gets better soon," which was very kind considering Dad had been so mean to him that time. So I said, "Thank you, Pan Maniek."

Eventually, we returned to Dad's office where Mum sat in his chair, at his desk and, with her elbows on the blotter and hands on her cheeks, softly moaned.

"I have no idea what to do. What does Tatuś do when you come with him?"

"He walks round, checks crates, mends machines, makes patterns and does sums," I replied. "Sometimes he phones people," I added because she might have to do that too.

Mum looked at me blankly. "Oh, dear Lord. I have to get a grip on things."

She shuffled papers, read letters and lined invoices in neat piles just as Dad would have done, but she kept sighing.

When the door bell sounded, she jumped back and gripped the edge of the

235

desk then took a deep breath and smoothed her skirt as she stood up. She went to open the door and exchanged a few words with a male voice. I couldn't make them out. As they approached the office, I heard her say, "I can't buy anything, Mr Baumzweig."

A short, bearded man, even older than Grandad, wearing a suit underneath a heavy black coat, followed Mum into the office. Mum motioned I should give up my chair for him. "Ania, go and sit in Dorothy's office – take your book."

I pulled out Mrs. Markham's chair from under her desk, just far enough for me to have a good view of them.

Mum offered him a cup of tea which he declined. Her face flushed, she said, "I'm so sorry. I forgot."

"Not to vorry, Mrs. Vitcher. I don't vont a drink. Really, nothing to do with kosher." He rubbed the tops of his thighs and chewed on something in his mouth. "Accordink to your people, He rests on Sundays, so He's puttink his feet up." I think that was supposed to be a joke because Mum sort of half-laughed.

Will McGrath knocked on the door, and apparently mistook me for Mrs. Markham because he excused the interruption and asked to speak to Mum. I waved him through. He wanted to know if he could leave early because it was his grandmother's birthday and they were having a family get-together. For a second Mum looked as if he'd asked her the capital of Borneo.

"What would my husband say?" she said.

Will reddened and stared at his huge brown lace-up shoes. "I don't know, Mrs Whitcher."

"Yes, go," she said and turned back to Mr. Baumzweig who'd been watching her face.

"It vont be easy," Mr. Baumzweig said. "I heard from Itzek. I think everybody knows now. They say he may—" he stopped. "How is he?"

"Still in intensive care, Mr Baumzweig."

Mum gazed everywhere but his face, finally finding a focus in her thumb cuticle which she scraped with her nail.

His voice was soft. "Mm. Mrs. Vitcher... Mrs. Vitcher, have you examined the accounts? Ver do you stand? You have three children?" He bent forward and put his hand on her knee.

Why was this man asking how many children she had? What business was it of his? Why was he speaking so gently to her? I pushed my knuckle into the twitch that pinged in my left eye. I definitely wanted to slap his hand away from her leg.

"You have money?" he said, leaning in to her.

Mum didn't reply immediately, as if she was choosing her words. "I spoke to Dorothy and I can't pay you. We have deliveries going out this week, but Dorothy said it could be a long time till the customers pay up."

"Has anyone else been to see you? Vee can come to an arrangement." What did he mean by that? He sat back in the chair, taking his slimy hand with him. I felt more comfortable.

She said, "The frame supplier. He wants to be paid now. And Johnson's said no more cardboard until we pay in full."

As Mr. Baumzweig splayed his legs and sank further into the seat, his trouser hems rolled up. He put his hands together and interlocked his fingers, his thumbs tapping against each other. "Brownink vont give you more frames? Anyvon else? This is not good," he said.

Mum swallowed and a smile flitted across her lips. "It's early days, Mr Baumzweig. And I don't know what I am doing. And you know what they say," she stifled a sob, "business is business."

The background hum from the sewing machines and presses ceased abruptly, as if the world had come to an end. The clock above Dorothy's desk showed 1.00 pm.

Mr. Baumzweig said, "You get your leathers from Rappaport?"

Mum nodded.

"Plastics from Rosen?"

"I think so."

"Maybe I vill have that cup of tea."

Mum stood up. "Of course," she said. "I'll be back in one moment."

"May I sit at the desk? I must write a few things."

"Please do. I won't be long."

As she walked past me, Mr. Baumzweig watched her, then inclined his head in my direction and put on a cheesy grin for my benefit. I returned it – I knew Mum would want me to be polite even if he was revolting – and pretended to read my book. He removed a tiny crocodile skin notebook and pen from the inside pocket of his jacket, tried to block my view with his back and wrote something down. From the corner of my eye, I saw him flick through the papers on Dad's desk, the ones on the left of the blotting board, and then the ones on the right. He stroked the underside of his nose for a few seconds, used the machine that Dad sometimes did his calculations on. A line of paper came out of the top which he ripped off and inserted into the notebook. He pushed his sleeve up to look at his watch.

By the time Mum came back, Dad's papers were all where they should be and Mr. Baumzweig was idly looking up at the eagle on the wall, and pulling at hairs in his beard. He resumed his place in the other chair when Mum handed him the cup. As I glanced at them both, he gave me another fake smile. "Is it interesting the book you are reading?"

"Yes. Thank you." I knew he was trying to make me think he was nice.

He took a sip of the tea and a bite of the digestive Mum had unearthed from somewhere.

"Witek is a good man," he said, and then something in Yiddish which

237

sounded like "*Gotnemt mitenthand*" and some other words. "You don't have to worry. I vill speak to Frankel, all my people. You vill see. You vill stay in business. You have my personal guarantee. Vich hospital?"

Mum said, "Manchester Royal Infirmary."

"I can visit?"

"I don't think so. Even I'm only allowed two hours. Not yet. Maybe next week?"

It seemed to me the conversation should be over, that he could go now. But Mum seemed to want to keep him there because she asked after his family. He told her about his grandchildren. The eldest grandson, Simon, who'd studied economics was now working in the family business. The middle one was at Oxford studying mathematics and youngest had started in Manchester doing medicine.

Mr. Baumzweig said, "Simon – he vill leave, Mrs. Vitcher. The vorld is a big place. Maybe America. *Gotgit mitenthand…*"

Finally he slid forward in the chair, bracing his knees to get up, and said, "You promise not to vorry?" As he stood, he put his hand into the same pocket that he'd inserted the notebook.

Mum said, "Yes. Thank you."

"Johnson's and Browning…" he pulled his hand out of the pocket "this is enough, I think." He handed her a fat envelope.

She looked aghast and pushed it back at him. "I can't take it. Witek would never forgive me. Supposing I can't—"

"Vee talk about that later," he said. "For now – the problem is solved. I vill visit Witek next week." He patted her knee again. "*Alles gut.*" I knew what that meant, but everything wasn't good at all. It made me want to be sick when he touched Mum, even more than when Dad kissed her like Simon Templar.

After he'd gone, I told Mum what I'd seen while she'd been making the tea. She wasn't even angry that he'd spied in Dad's papers and said we should count God's blessings.

CHAPTER TWENTY-ONE

DAY SEVEN: LATE MORNING, EARLY AFTERNOON

"Tatuś, who was Yankel?"

Dad's features don't move. "My friend."

"You talked about him often when we were little…"

"Did I? There were things I didn't understand then."

"Like what?"

"Forgiveness."

I'm not sure what to ask next. It seems as if Dad has stepped from A to somewhere in the middle of the alphabet with nothing in between. Drawing back to B as casually as I can, I say, "What happened to him?"

Eyes shut, Dad sighs. "He was a good friend. My best. He lived in my building on the second floor. Janek's father took me fishing…" Dad pauses. "We played football…" His eyes have wrinkled at the edges in a smile or a wince. I can't tell.

Josie said this might happen though, the disorientation, possible hallucinations. He's been quite compos mentis so far. I suppose he's confusing this conversation with Janek telling him about the match.

The radiator rumbles, reminding me how long the window hasn't been opened. I remove my jumper and adjust my T shirt. The under-wiring of my bra digs into the sweat.

Gently I say, "I don't understand. We were talking about Yankel."

"Yes, Yankel. His parents called him Yankel, to us, Janek."

"And?"

"It's such a long story, child." Shifting his legs slightly under the duvet, he adds, "Why is it important to you?"

My tone is neutral. "I don't know. I've always wondered."

"It happened so quickly. When they started rounding up the Jews to put them in the ghetto the Bielinskis took the Perlmanns in. I knew where he was.

239

My Ciocia Kazia used to take spare food." He breaks off. "A drop of water…"

He's leaning on the sit-up contraption at a thirty degree angle and I don't want to disturb him. I pour a glass of water, bend an expanding straw and put it to his lips so that he has control.

He continues, with a barely perceptible shake of his head. "I made a terrible mistake, child. Terrible. Janek's sister was ill, so ill she needed medicine. My Ciocia Kazia was distraught. Ciocia loved her so much – she was her favourite pupil." Dad sighs. "You should have heard her play Chopin's Nocturnes…"

"What happened?"

"I asked a boy in the Grey Ranks if his uncle – a doctor – would help. I…well, I trusted him. We had made the same oath."

I can see this is wearing him out, yet I continue. "Tatuś, was it the Perlmann family on the balcony?"

"Yes…" Dad shudders. "I think you knew him. He died in the eighties."

I knew him? "Sorry? Who did I know?"

"Sławek Kardasz."

My heart pounds. What does this mean? I'm awash with uncertainty, shifting sands beneath my feet. Pictures race through my brain. Mum throwing knives in the sink, Granny in her scarf with her "I'll say no mores", photos of Charlie Chaplins and funeral banners, Ewa, Kinga, Stevo.

Dad carries on, "Even then I knew it was him. Immediately. He admitted it later." His voice strains on the sentence, getting quieter.

I blurt, "Are you saying *he* informed on them? Not you?"

Dad moans. "Me? You thought I—"

I haul back the rope of my words, frantic. "No. I meant that…" Can't think how to change "not you" into something else, give it another connotation. Help me, God. It wasn't Dad. Help me. My feet want to run down the drive, onto the street, my mouth wants to shout "It wasn't my Dad!"

Help me. He's dying. What have I done?

Dad says, "Give me your hand. Is that what you thought all these years?" He breathes like he used to when he was trying not to get cross, in, wait, out, wait. Three times. Can he see inside my brain?

I put my hand in his. "Of course not. Never. Only, you said you made a 'terrible mistake'…I thought that's what you were going to tell me. Just now." Does he sense the lie through my skin? Iwonka said let it go. I wait a moment, praying he can't feel my tremor, then ask, "What did you mean about forgiveness? You forgave Kardasz?"

"Him? No, I never forgave him for that. Myself. I made a terrible, terrible mistake, but that is what it was…the mistake of a boy. In the same way I overlooked your mistakes." Dad groans, his mouth contorting. "Did you look over the papers in my desk?"

"Yes. I know what to do about the banking and shares."

"Look in the bottom drawer in the box at the back. The one with the mermaid. He's in there. There are two photographs and a watch Pan Perlmann gave me."

"Yankel?"

"Janek, Yankel. Ania, child, I've been thinking about it. Janek's rowing club pin is in there too. Give everything of his to the Jewish museum in Warsaw. They will know what to do with it. The rest to the Museum of the Uprising. You don't need it." He pauses, agony written on his face. "Child, I need more morphine. Call the nurses. It's not strong enough."

I draw the Oramorph into the pipette, place it into his mouth, and gently squeeze the teat. I watch his lips, his tongue probing inside his cheek, then he swallows, grimacing with the effort.

Blurred images mingle with hazy recollections of time frames that make no sense. Somehow Dad must have made his peace with Kardasz too, at some point.

"Give me another, child. Not much longer. No consulate."

I repeat the process.

"Let me sleep now," he says. I move to give him a kiss on the forehead. With difficulty he lifts one hand to the back of my neck, with the other he smooths my cowlick, then puts his lips on mine, holds me there a moment. "Look after your mother. Get her a higher interest rate."

I phone the doctor, the district nurses and Iwonka.

At 2.30 Sarah and Tom arrive. In the dining room they begin to prepare the equipment for the intravenous medication while Mum and I watch.

Iwonka enters through the back. She draws Mum to her in a hug and locked in the embrace, Mum presses her cheek into Iwonka's chest. She's acknowledging, I think, what we all know. Soon.

With Sarah and Tom leading the way, we follow to Dad's room.

While Dad moans, unable to speak, Sarah attaches a morphine drip to his hand, quietly efficient in her work. We watch.

I appreciate how they don't dress up the situation with unnecessary comforting platitudes. They are merely polite, considerate; it's business as usual for them.

Back in the dining room, Sarah addresses Mum with a tender smile. "He'll be more comfortable now. He may not seem conscious, but keep talking round him, speak to him too." Turning to Iwonka and me, she nods. "He can still hear you."

THEN

The whole world was upside down. People visited in the evening and whispered in the kitchen. The ladies brought cooked food in heatable containers, the men just came and talked. Mum didn't offer sandwiches or any drinks other than tea. And when Mr. Franek asked for a drop of cognac, Mum said he must have fallen off a bull and damaged his brain. I'd never heard Mum say anything like that to a guest before.

All I gleaned from hanging over the banister and being in the right place at the right time was that Dad had been on the way from Kombo's to a casino in the city centre, and Mum told Granny he'd promised her last summer that he'd never go there again. Granny grunted like a camel and said he was an expert at making promises. "I'll say no more."

*****

Mum was wearing black, top to toe: blouse, cardigan, skirt, even her tights and shoes, like everyone who went to the general's funeral. My heart leapt to my mouth and stayed there. Dad was dead and she hadn't even told us. All the time she visited him in hospital, she said he was getting better. How could she lie like that?

Granny bustled in, and I immediately knew it wasn't Dad. She was wearing her headscarf and an apron with a reddish stain, and a wide ladder in her American Tan stockings ran from ankle to knee. She wasn't going to a funeral. Dad was alive.

"What time is it?" she said, tone hard as tarmac, hanging her brolly on the coatstand.

Mum replied, "Mass is at 10 o'clock. Moston cemetery, not Southern. And the wake…I don't know if I'll come home before the hospital."

Granny deposited the tin of plum charlotte by the cooker, ran the hot water tap and squeezed out a dishcloth.

"So you are going to the hospital tonight?" she said, swiping the breadcrumbs off the table in fast strokes.

"I'll be back by eight. I have to tell him about it."

I dared to speak. "Who died?"

"Nobody you know," Mum said. "Coats on. Time to go or we'll be late. I don't want any more letters from Miss Moscrop."

Some piece of information was missing, something I hadn't been told about, hadn't managed to overhear. I had to wait till after school to find out the rest.

*****

Granny scribbled over a word in the crossword puzzle in the *Dziennik Polski*. It didn't seem to be going too well for her. Nevertheless I broached the subject and asked who Mum was talking about earlier.

Granny slammed down the cup from which she'd just taken a serene sip onto the saucer. It shattered and scattered all over the tablecloth leaving a spreading brown puddle. "No surprise. I told her not to marry him. Silly girl with her romantic 'he was a hero' notions."

"Who?"

She walloped the top of her thigh liked it belonged to someone else. "No-one." She jerked up, quickly brushing the saucer fragments with the side of her hand into a mound.

I persisted. "No-one died?"

"Jacek Sadkowski died."

What was it that Mum had said when I thought Dad was a bank robber? Karbowski and Jurek. And a Jacek.

"Why did you tell Pan Sadkowski's wife not to marry him?" It didn't seem right that Granny was entitled to an opinion, even though she had one about everything else.

"What? He had no wife. What are you talking about?"

I reran the reel of the conversation and, even on the second hearing, I understood nothing. Granny threw the bits into the rubbish bin under the sink, and went back to the puzzle. "That's enough talking. What did I say? I'll say no more."

I waited for her to calm down, let her fill in a few more answers, because it wasn't done with for me yet. And that "I'll say no more" was just a minor Granny obstacle that could easily be negotiated if I put my mind to it. I took the brush out of the cupboard and pretended to sweep the floor for a few minutes.

"Good girl," Granny said.

I returned the brush and joined her again. "Who is Jacek Sadkowski, Babcia?"

She was only half-listening. "Three letters... tree... Oak. The man who was driving. Drunk. He killed the young couple in the other car."

*****

While we waited for Dad to get better in hospital, the sky didn't fall down, we didn't have to live in cardboard boxes on the streets and food appeared in the fridge same as always, so "in Old Trafford when we ate nothing but mice caught with our own hands..." blah-blah didn't happen.

Mum was different somehow, as if she'd been wearing thick socks and army boots for years but now had sandals. She got up later but washed and dressed immediately, no Kensitas, *Angelique* or Jim Reeves for an hour. And she applied lipstick and looked like a proper lady boss when she went to the factory.

Easter was early with the same egg-making, horrible fish all day on Good Friday, going to Kombo's for the blessing of the same chewed-off, legless sugar lamb in the traditional manky old Easter basket. All the same, except no Dad.

Before the ball Mum had asked us what we were giving up for Lent. I said

Brussels sprouts, Janek said mushrooms, Iwonka said beetroot. Dad had said no. Without him there we stuck to our resolutions, and the 'Oh no, it's nearly six o'clock' feeling never happened. But Groucho hardly moved from his bed at first, and when we threw balls for him to fetch or teased him with an old tea towel, he sloped off miserably. Then that happened to us too. Nobody to watch the Hollywood musical with, no noisy guests, no Helen Shapiro or Bink, no rooting in pockets for five pound notes, no Mexicans. It was dead boring really.

*****

"Ania, look at this," Gianni said. "Must've come round and posted it through our letter box." He handed me a folded-up piece of notepaper. All it said was 'Here' with a drawing of a circle and the letters O, M, A, G, D, S around the perimeter.

I leaned against Ossie's wall, trying not to let Gianni see I was busting with joy inside. Stevo was back.

I re-folded the note. "Have you told the others?"

"Give me a chance. Be here in half an hour."

I dashed home, grabbed whatever I could find, dropped my glasses on my bunk, and returned to the wall.

Stevo was back! The misery of the winter months, what with Mum falling through the window and Dad's accident, evaporated. Spring was here, summer would follow, we were a proper gang again. Hurray!

Gianni gathered the troops and we were in Old Spooky yelling *Torta di Mellay Jenno Vazay*, as if no time had passed at all.

Stevo was in the den on the window seat. His bike leaned against the wall. In January when I saw him with his mum, he'd grown and looked bulkier somehow. Or maybe just happier. Now, his hair was longer and greasier and a few pimples huddled on his chin. The new parka coat he wore on that day was grimy, zip broken, its crooked teeth bared like an angry dog's.

"Blimey, all of ya at the same time, eh? Hand it over then," he said, a half-grin playing on his face as he put his hand out to Gianni.

Manuela tried to hug him. Stevo squirmed and wriggled away. "Give over! Missed me or summat?"

Gianni gave Stevo the bag from under his arm. Stevo unfurled the top and took out a chunk of thin salami, and we stood watching in silence as if a boy eating Italian sausage was as fascinating as a solar eclipse.

He bit into it ravenously. "What ya been up to, eh, you lot?"

Dermot remembered to close his mouth then opened it again. "Nowt much. You?"

Still chewing, Stevo said, "Back t'shit at home."

"What's happened?" Manuela cocked her face to the side in an expression of concern.

Stevo shook his head. "She's got another one now. I'm fuckin' sick of it."
A piece of salami jetted out of his mouth and landed on Dermot's cheek.
"Sorry, mate. She's a bloody tart…that's what she is. A fuckin' whore."

Manuela's eyebrows vanished under her fringe as she turned to me.
Meanwhile, my blinkers crashed to the floor. I'd never heard him swear like
that before. How could I have been so stupid? Had the others realised? Was I
the only one who hadn't understood?

The uncles, they weren't uncles or even husbands of Stevo's mum's
friends. She had *fancy men*.

When Mr. Baumzweig had put his hand on Mum's leg, my veins felt as if
termites were marching down them, so how could Stevo stand it? I shuddered
to think.

"Any road," he growled, "I'm fuckin' never going back there again. That
was her last chance." His face coloured up in pinky blotches like he'd been
holding his breath for weeks. This time he meant it.

The air weighed a ton, loaded with none of us knowing what to say and
Dermot sniffing and wiping his snot on his sleeve.

Finally Ossie broke the tension. "Who's up for Cluedo?" Dermot went to
get the box. It had lain for six months at the back of a cupboard in the
basement.

We stayed for roughly two hours during which the subject of his mum
wasn't touched on again. Stevo won.

At bedtime, I resumed kissing practice. Just in case.

*****

Gingerly, with the help of his crutches, Dad lowered himself into the
armchair. Underneath his clothing his chest was still bandaged where his ribs
had snapped and punctured his insides and outsides, but his face was healing
from the cuts he received when he was hurled through the windscreen.

Iwonka perched herself on the arm of the chair. "Are you feeling better?"

"Much better, treasure. I've been through far worse." He grimaced as he
leaned back. "After the war I spent a year and a half in hospital, child. This is
easy."

Dad's Kombo's days were temporarily over. He couldn't drive and Mum
refused point blank to take him. She was the boss now.

*****

Where the heck was Stevo?

Dermot yelled *Torta di Mellay Jenno Vazay* for the third time and there was
still no sign of him. He'd promised he'd be here because we were all going to
ride our bikes up to Seymour Park.

Ossie tried again. "TORTA DI MELLAY JENNO VAZAY!"
Nothing.

245

B. E. Andre

"Maybe he's asleep," Manuela said.

All of us traipsed upstairs to see if he was in his cubby hole, but he wasn't there.

"He's not gone again, has he?" asked Gianni.

"He could be on the roof," said Dermot. "TORTA DI MELLAY JENNO VAZAY!" he shouted upwards. Still nothing.

Gianni said, "Let's wait for him in the den. If he's not here in half an hour, we'll go without him."

We trudged back to the den and kicked our heels. It seemed so much colder in there than usual, as if the wind had been howling through the rooms. I lay on the window seat and tried to warm up in the sun. Where was he? He couldn't have gone home because he always left a note, and besides he'd said he was never going back again. Perhaps he'd gone off to nick something from the greengrocer's. Manuela remembered some custard creams she'd left in the basement and skipped off to get them. The door slammed on a draught as she left, and the Greek eye clinked against the rosary beads.

First there was a scream. Then there was screaming, screaming, screaming. This wasn't normal Manuela girl-screaming. It echoed through the corridors, up the stairs to the rafters and into my bones. She sounded like the devil was trying to kill her. We pelted out of the den and down to the basement to see what had happened. She was rooted in the door frame, scratching furiously at her cheeks, unable to stop. Ossie covered her mouth with his hand then pulled her closer.

I looked over Ossie's shoulder and saw.

Stevo lay face down on top of a pile of crumbled plaster and bits of floorboard. The back of his parka was covered in a thick layer of dust and one of his shoes was missing. I looked up at the hole in the ceiling. The day when Manuela trapped her leg in the room above flashed through my memory. Ossie had said, "There's something wrong in there. Like evil."

My legs buckled.

Manuela sobbed in heaving gulps. "What the matter with him?"

Ossie nudged her towards me, his voice a whisper, as he inched forward into the room and knelt in the debris. "Stevo...Stevo...come on, mate. Stop messing. She's having a fit." Ossie poked his arm. "Oh my God, oh sweet Jesus...wake up!" But Stevo didn't move.

Then Ossie put his hand round Stevo's wrist, padded with his thumb, his gaze fixed on us. "He's cold. I think...I think he's dead."

For a few moments we were still, watching, as if someone had stopped a film.

Ossie tried to heave Stevo sideways but he seemed locked into place, tensed up. "Gianni, help me." Between them they shifted Stevo so that his face was visible. It had gone a deep purple, his nose was almost black, his mouth crusty.

I gasped and looked away. Manuela screamed again, pushing her face into the top of my arm. What had happened to him? Why was he that weird colour? My breath felt trapped in my lungs. This wasn't happening. God wouldn't do this. It was just a nightmare. That's what it was. Everything would be normal soon.

Gianni was saying something. His lips moved, his eyes were fixed on me, but I couldn't hear him because I was at home, waking up to a new day, Iwonka climbing into my bunk with me, Mum calling us for *śniadanie*. This nightmare wasn't real.

"Ania! Get a blanket!" Gianni's voice battered my thoughts down.

Ossie said, "How will that help?"

I didn't stay to hear Gianni's answer. Desperate to be anywhere else and taking the stairs two at a time, I ran to Stevo's little room at the top, and still panting, leaned against the wall and stared at his nest of ragged bedding. The pink candlewick bedspread and pillows stank of mould, piss and mildew. How did he even sleep on it?

I sank down, trying not to cry. I'd never been so sad before, so scared, so worried, miserable, so wretched, jittery, frightened, so everything, and all of it tangled together like messed up knitting wool with no end or beginning. Breathe, breathe, breathe. My vision blotched out into coloured blurs, I had to focus. Blinking, blinking. Until a piece of white took shape. The candle stub on the plate. Blinking. A piece of notepaper creased into a card, like the one Stevo dropped through Gianni's letterbox. Blinking... clearing...

On the front was a pencil drawing of an old-fashioned airplane with no cover on the cockpit. The person behind the windscreen had a lop-sided fringe, hair flowing out into the breeze and glasses on. I unfolded it. Inside it said,

"Bet you dont get this one, Speccy.

YYUR

YYUB

ICUR

YY4me

But I bet you arnt."

It could only be for me. The blurry shapes swam behind my eyelids again. I put it in my pocket.

Footsteps were coming up the stairs, then Ossie shouted, "What're you doing? Get down here, will you?"

"I'm coming."

His footsteps retreated. I bundled up Granny's smelly bedspread and returned to the basement where Gianni sat cross-legged by the wall, waiting on his own.

"They're in the den," he said, getting to his feet. "Give it here. Take the other side." Keeping my eyes on Gianni's face as he flapped the bedspread over Stevo, I caught the other end then dropped it.

"I can't," I said.

Gianni pulled the edges straight on his side. "All right. Go. I'll bloody do it myself."

*****

Twirling the rosary beads he brought in after that time the crow flew in, Dermot huddled in the corner. His hands were trembling. Manuela, knees pulled up to her chin, and Ossie, hunched over, sat side by side on the window seat. I joined them and stared into the mess of bramble further down the garden. The sky was blue and clear apart from two trailing ribbons of see-through cloud, and the sun shone as if it was ignoring what had happened.

When Gianni returned, he took control of the situation. "We have to think. What're we going to do?"

"Call an ambulance, or the police..." Manuela's words tumbled out in strangled hiccups.

"No, I don't think that's a good idea..." Gianni pinched a corner of his lip and rubbed it with his thumb. "Suppose they—"

"We could say we were exploring and found him," Ossie said.

"All of us? They'd ask more questions. They'd want to speak to our parents...probably."

"We have to tell his mum...write her a letter," Dermot said.

Manuela blurted, "Why? Why do we have to tell her? She doesn't even know he was here and since when was she ever bothered? "

"Well, I don't know where she lives, do you?" Ossie was looking at me as if I had some magic power to solve this. I slid my hand in my pocket to touch the note so it would help me decide what Stevo wanted us to do.

Gianni turned to Ossie. "Who's going to call the police?"

Ossie shook his head. None of us dared. We needed to tell a grown-up, but who would tell their parents? None of us wanted to do that either. For a few moments we sat in silence, alone with our thoughts, certain we had to do something, we couldn't just leave him there.

At last Ossie spoke. "We'll have to bury him."

*****

"Stop pacing about. Either sit down or go to your room," Dad said. "What's the matter with you?"

Stevo was dead, tomorrow we were going to bury him, and I mustn't tell anyone.

I went to lie on my bunk. I'd already forgotten what he looked like, and no matter how many times I read his card and tried to remember, the only image in my mind was his purple face and tons of ashen dust. It clogged my throat, choking me. I scrunched my eyes and tried to kaleidoscope the lines and colours from deep in my temples into his living shape. It was no use, they just collected into his dead body on the floor.

We didn't have time to do it today, Gianni had decided. And because the trowel and seaside bucket and spade we had at Spooky weren't strong or big enough to dig a proper grave, we needed something more suitable.

Ossie had suggested I borrow Grandad's big garden fork which I knew would be impossible now because when he wasn't using it to sow vegetables, he stored it at the back of his shed. And he was always in his shed. Mum had nothing at our house of any use, except her trowel. She got everything else from Grandad.

Thoughts of tomorrow spun in my head. The boys seemed to have a plan, but I hadn't been listening properly. We go to Spooky, we dig a grave, we bury Stevo, we come home. Was that all of it? It couldn't be. I wanted to tell Mum, but I was too scared they would all be mad at me. Ossie was bound to say I was a traitor.

Iwonka hopped into bed and I put my pyjamas on. Groucho was hovering in the doorway, so I picked him up, carried him up the ladder and tucked him in beside me.

We go to Spooky, we dig a grave, we bury Stevo, we come home.

Thousands of shabby people were pounding on the doors and windows of my house, only it wasn't my house, and I was alone. Faces squashed against the panes, skinny purple finger-tongues jabbed through the glass and covered my cheeks in slimy trails of hot saliva. The tongues pointed at something next me, and shouted "You did it!" I gripped my ears against their throbbing howls.

My eyes snapped open. Groucho was licking my face and whining to be put down on the floor.

Please let it be over. Get me to the end bit. When we come home.

B. E. Andre

CHAPTER TWENTY-TWO

DAY SEVEN: EVENING

The phone rings; Mum answers in the kitchen.

"No. They gave him a morphine drip today." Pause.

"If you want to." Pause.

"No. Don't do that, don't be silly." Pause.

"At this time of night? No. I won't hear of it. Get ready. Ania will come for you." Mum gives me a limp wave. "Will you fetch Ciocia Teresa?"

"Now?"

Mum raises her palm either to stop me asking questions or to hear what Ciocia's wittering on about.

I nod.

"She'll be there in half an hour." Mum replaces the receiver. "She wanted to call a taxi. It's all right, isn't it, Ania? You don't mind?" She doesn't wait for me to reply, opens the bread bin and pulls out a sliced rye loaf. "See if we've got any gherkins. The *sopocka's* on the bottom shelf."

I open the fridge; I guess I'll have to eat all that cheese myself.

Buttering the bread, Mum says, "She hasn't been well this past couple of weeks. She wants to see him to say…" She's facing the other way, but I can see her back expanded just now as though she took a huge breath.

Say goodbye, I finish the sentence in my head. "Do you want me to slice these before I go? She won't want to eat, you know…"

"It doesn't matter. If she does, I'll have something ready. Make them thin, I'll fold them over."

I slice enough to feed four people several sandwiches each and ask Mum for the address.

"Edge Lane. The red brick block across the road from Longford Park. You know it? Flat 16."

I've never been to Ciocia Teresa's sheltered flat; I know the park, I'll find it.

Bloody Washway Road. Bloody traffic lights. Bloody Chester Road. Bloody traffic lights. I turn right into Edge Lane.

I can't remember when I last saw her. Five, maybe ten years ago. Not good.

Through the glass door I spy her in the lobby, coat and hat on, sitting bolt upright on a high-backed chair, her walking stick tight against her knee. I want to laugh. Where the hell did she get that from?

In the car when I stretch over to fasten her seat belt, she smacks my hand. "I can do it myself, thank you, dear."

I switch on the ignition and ask about her fabulous walking stick.

"This? Pah. It was a gift from the girl who sets my hair. She comes every week, you know, and only charges five pounds. From the new Polonia," she says. "Magda, nice girl. Not a great deal of taste sadly...but very, very kind. I have others in the flat."

A miracle occurs and most of the traffic lights let us through on the way back. At home, Mum's cleared the crap off the kitchen table, open sandwiches are in the middle on a Christmas serving platter. She's used up some of the cheese, thank goodness, although I doubt Gorgonzola and pickled beetroot is an ideal combination.

Ciocia Teresa allows me to help her remove her coat, but the hat – a tired confection with two purple feathers – stays firmly on. She notices the sandwiches. "Is this for me? Oh, Wanda. Why?" Guess I'll have to eat those too.

Although I'm tempted to leave Mum and Ciocia, switch on the news, see what's going on in the world outside this stifling little house, I still have a job to do. I search for an opening as they talk; the chat is brief.

Ciocia stands. "May I go to him now?"

"You do understand he's not responding?" Mum says.

"That's not what I'm here for."

While they're gone I read my Kindle; Saul Bellow's words swim into each other, so I shift to the larger font; no change. I flip from *Herzog* to *Gone Girl* and still can't concentrate. This heat is killing me again; I go outside, breathe some fresh air then come back in.

At 8.15 they return to the table and Mum makes tea.

I'll just spit it out. "Mama, can I ask you something?" Remembering her reaction when I was child, I quickly add, "But don't get angry."

"Why should I be angry? Go ahead."

"Dad mentioned Sławek Kardasz earlier."

Ciocia Teresa sniffs, picks up her first sandwich, rolls the gherkin slice between her fingers then pops it into her mouth. Overhead the light bulb sizzles like a wet finger on a hot iron, flickers and dies, but it can wait; I'll change it later.

Mum unstiffens. "Why bring that up? It's such a long time ago."

Ciocia Teresa is eyeing me. "You know, if I asked Magda I'm sure she could find a good colour for you, dear." She runs her pale pink nail through my hair, making a parting, as if checking for nits. Wily old buzzard. She reminds me of my Babcia.

I turn to Mum. "He worked with Dad, didn't he? Something happened?"

Mum's explanation is brief, just facts. Yes, they worked together. Mum and Dad's wedding was coming up, Dad already had his business. He let Kardasz come in as a partner. Dad was broke, wanted to buy up-to-date machinery and Mr. Baumzweig loaned him a substantial sum, in cash. And Kardasz, instead of depositing the loan and getting the wages, withdrew the payroll, went to the casino, blew the lot on Black Jack then disappeared off the face of the earth for several weeks. Grandad bailed Dad out.

"They were very difficult times..." Mum adds, which I imagine is the understatement of the decade.

Ciocia sits mute throughout this, nibbling at the doughy centre of the sandwich, avoiding the crust. Now she speaks. "Liar, thief, philanderer... Wanda, when did Jasia Wróbelska have the baby? 67? 68? And the shame... He was always a bad one."

Astounding. It slips out. "Someone from the *Armia Krajowa* a bad one?"

She shoots me a look suggesting 'you aren't too old for a good slap', sits back in the chair and pulling her hat off, says, "My goodness, it's hot in here." Her hair, what's left of it, is an iridescent pale aubergine. I won't take her up on Magda.

She places her hat on her lap then plumps out her backcombed coiffure making it look like a clown's party wig. "And your *stupid* father—"

Mum gasps.

"I'm sorry, Wanda. We both love him but you know it's the truth..."

Mum lowers her eyes and fingers her wedding ring ready to twist it; it doesn't budge, stuck in the groove of a lifetime's marriage.

Ciocia continues. "Your father was stupid. He imagined he owed him a debt of honour. But how long can these things go on? How many times does an idiot return for more?"

"Teresa, he's dying, give it a rest, I beg you."

"We're all going to die. I'll be next, no doubt. Pull yourself together."

I want to move to the other side of the table to give Mum a hug, to protect her from Ciocia's default tell-it-as-it-is mode.

But Ciocia imprisons my hand under hers. "The Germans were everywhere and we had to get back to the centre of Warszawa. Your father was wounded, leg bandaged, he could hardly walk. You know that? The only way was through the sewers. *O mój Boże.* Oh my God, the stench, the *gówno...Piekielne szczury.*" At the thought of that shit and those hellish rats, she stops and presses a finger and thumb deep into her eyelids, as if to blot out what's behind them. Under her breath, she says, "*Krótko i węzłowato*" – get it over and done with.

She opens her eyes and continues. "I got separated from him and had to go ahead. You understand – I had no option?" I'm not sure what she's asking me here. My forgiveness? For what?

"Your father and Sławek were at the back of the group. Witek had a fever – his wound was infected. In and out of consciousness, he told me later. It was the one decent thing Sławek did in his entire life…"

I'm getting a picture, focus sharpening. Two teenage boys in scout uniforms, one dark, the other fair. Pitch-blackness, sewage up to their chests, turds floating past their faces as they stumble. A labyrinth of tunnels, fear, death threatening at each turn, distant German voices from above or Polish whispers echoing down the passages. Feet, legs, dragging through the filth. Rats scurrying, gnawing the boys ears as they try to rest. Witek Walewski can't go on, Sławek Kardasz pulls Witek's arm over his shoulder, grips his hand, his other arm supporting Witek's back.

Dear God. "He saved Dad's life," I say.

"He saved his life," Ciocia repeats with as much emotion as a paving slab. My brain reeling with this, I swallow. My larynx feels as if a marble's lodged in it. Ciocia lets out a tiny snort.

"Oh, don't be so romantic," she says and I stare at her, bewildered.

"This was Sławek," she says. "Who knows why? He didn't have a single noble drop of blood in his veins. It was war. There was no acting, only reacting. Often we had no idea what we were doing, why we were doing it, we just did it. Open your eyes, dear. During the Uprising I stole a dying man's money out of his pocket. What use was it to him?"

I gaze at her ninety-plus old face, try to meld it with the young woman who survived into old age, and realise she's made of steel – no, diamond – this doddery lady with iridescent hair and a red and white pin stripe walking stick. I got away lightly with her, she could still rip me to shreds.

"Anyway, I ought to go. Wanda, dear – about the funeral…" she begins.

Dad's still alive, I want to remind her.

Mum says, "I'll call you. Can you phone the scouts…and whoever else has to be informed…when the time comes."

Ciocia says, "Of course, of course." I assist her with her coat and she doesn't seem to mind my helping her this time. As we walk to the car, Iwonka pulls up. She winds down the window. She looks shaken. "I had a sen—I think…I don't know…Ania, I need to sit with him through the night."

THEN

Manuela had to go to the dentist first thing, so we'd agreed to meet at ten o'clock. Ossie knocked on my bedroom window just after eight. I'd already been awake for two hours, looking at Stevo's note, crying, trying to work out what would happen if I told Mum or Granny. But if I told them, it wouldn't be just me in trouble, it would be all of us, and I'd have to own up about everything I'd stolen for him in the past year, too. But…we could just say we found him there and didn't know him. Except I knew Mum would get the truth out of me in the end. It was all so confusing.

A faint drizzle caught me as I leaned out the window to find out what Ossie wanted. I was to meet him in the secret passage at five to ten.

"Don't forget about the clothes," he said. I knew something was missing from the list.

The laundry basket was full, but it didn't take long to find my crimplene trousers and a mucky blouse and cardie. I'd not get my legs filthy, navy wouldn't show the dirt and Mum wouldn't ask any questions.

Feeling as if I was carrying three coal sacks on my back, I trudged to the garage to search for Mum's trowel. How were we going to do this? We should tell someone, shouldn't we? This wasn't right. Stevo should have a proper funeral with lots of flowers and a long black car.

In the garage, I spotted Grandad's fork leaning against our old armchair. Now what? I could hide a trowel under my anorak, but how would I get a garden fork past the window above the kitchen sink and across the road in broad daylight? And also how would I get it back again? But if I managed to get it to Spooky, the grave wouldn't take so long to dig, would it?

I looked through to the window to check if anybody was about and seeing no-one ran back, grabbed the fork and carried it as far as the lilac bush by the gate where I hid it behind the wall.

At five to ten, with my clothes from the laundry basket rolled in a bundle, I met Ossie in the passage across the road. As promised, he had a spade.

"What've you brought?" he asked.

"You'll have to get it. I was too scared."

"Nothing?"

"Grandad's fork. Only I haven't got it."

"Well, where the hell is it then?" He looked as if he wanted to punch me one. "Fat lot of use you are."

I wiped the tears from my eyes, doing my best not to fall apart altogether, and this wasn't helping. He didn't seem to think it was such a big deal when I told him where I left it. I watched from the bushes as he crossed the road, found the fork, checked no cars were coming and ran back. It was all over in less than a minute.

We were halfway down the passage when we heard whispered voices behind us. Gianni and Dermot were on time too. We clambered over the crumbling wall and stood in the garden.

"Where's Manuela?" I asked when they caught us up.

"I called for her. Her mum says she's ill and can't come out today," Dermot replied.

Was that the truth? She probably couldn't face it, same as me, and she'd worn herself out yesterday with all that screaming and crying. Or maybe Manuela's non-appearance was more Mrs. Karageorgis's fault than hers. I wished Manuela had come.

Gianni immediately set to making decisions. While the boys discussed where we should dig the grave, I removed my glasses, wiped away the drizzle that had collected into drops on the lenses and tried to push away the picture of the bedspread lying over Stevo.

"Over there by the trees." Ossie pointed to the left of the garden.

"Or over there by the steps," Gianni said.

"Not in front of the steps. It'll be obvious. And not in the trees either..."

"What's wrong with the trees? Nobody will find it there."

"Roots."

Gianni put his hands to his temples then dragged them over his hair and locked his fingers behind his neck. "Where then? Where?" He looked as if he hadn't slept all night either.

Like me, Dermot was standing by, useless. He said, "There's one place we could—"

"Where?" Gianni's voice was shivery.

"By the little wall where you said they grew vegetables."

"It's covered in weeds—" Ossie stopped abruptly.

Gianni moaned. "Everywhere's covered with something."

Ossie looked to his feet, his gaze moving from side to side. "Wait a minute... That would make sense, by that wall..."

I thought I knew the garden as well as everybody else, but I hadn't noticed any wall other than the big one surrounding the property. But it was there, just as they said. It wasn't so much a wall as two layers of bricks like Grandad had in his garden, except his was concrete and painted white.

Between us we had a penknife, two trowels, a full-size spade and a garden fork.

"Here?" Ossie asked, pointing to a patch by the corner of the wall.

Gianni nodded. "Here."

I hid behind the bushes to change into my dirty clothes while they began. When I came back Ossie and Gianni had taken the larger tools, which made sense because both of them were stronger, and Dermot was using the trowel. It would take ages.

But the top soil wasn't too difficult to dig, more moist and crumbly than in our front garden, with fewer clumped up bits, and it came away more easily than I'd imagined. It was still hard work, especially now the rain was worse.

We dug in silence apart from Ossie issuing the odd instruction. Several times he let us swap tools but got exasperated with Dermot and me. And when Ossie and Gianni had the spade and fork, Ossie made it into an unspoken competition between them, heaving two loads to Gianni's one.

Gianni's, I noticed, were bigger.

Dermot put down his trowel and swiped his filthy hand across his chapped lips. "Are we gonna say anything?"

"Who to? The police? What do you mean?" Ossie asked.

"Like a prayer. Our Father?"

"Oh. If you want."

I'd been thinking about it myself. That and the card. "Can I say something too?"

"You do Hail Mary," Dermot replied, wiping his sodden fringe back.

Where did Stevo get YYUR from? I couldn't remember where I'd learned it either. I tried to lock his purple face inside a compartment in my brain and found myself digging to the rhythm of the words going round and round my head. Too wise you are, too wise you be, I see you are too wise for me. But I bet you arnt.

I hadn't taken shoes into consideration. The trousers I might be able to rinse and dry out before Mum saw them, but my shoes and socks were ruined, caked in mud to my ankles. I'd have to think of an excuse later.

The piles of wet earth on the sides were now starting to fall back in, so Ossie, panting and heaving, stood on top and shifted them further out, water and sweat trickling down the sides of his face. We carried on. And on. Until the centre of the hole was above waist-high on Ossie.

At last Gianni said the grave was deep enough. It was time to bring Stevo.

"I can't do it," I said.

Ossie threw me a furious look and shouted, "You've got to. Three's not enough."

"I can't."

"You're in this too."

"I can't. I CAN'T!"

Gianni pulled Ossie's jumper at the elbow. "Leave her. Dermot, you can stop now. Come on."

I traipsed behind them as far as the steps and sat down because my bum was so wet that it didn't matter. I wasn't going down into the basement ever again, couldn't go. Did they even have a plan? How would they get him up the stairs and carry him all the way to the grave?

Rubbing my shoes against each other to get the mud off, I examined the dirt in the ridgy bits where I'd chewed off my nails, and waited. I spat on my cuticles and scraped at them with my teeth. Then I squeezed my hair into ropes to get the water out, and waited some more. I wiped my glasses on my blouse. It was taking such a long time.

Eventually, at the side of the house, the gravel began to crunch and I heard a regular grinding squeak and the boys' hushed voices. I turned to look. First came Ossie pulling two lengths of tatty pink rope, then the cart, and last, Gianni and Dermot bent over, pushing at the back. On top, flopping over the edges was Stevo rolled up in that horrible candlewick bedspread which they'd tied at the ends with string. It looked like a giant raspberry sherbet.

As they walked past me, Ossie jerked his head so I'd follow. They bumped Stevo between the bushes, through the weeds, squelching over lumps in the earth until they reached the hole where Ossie let go and sagged onto the ground.

"I can't move," he said.

Gianni slumped down next to him and clapped him on the back. "We've got to." He turned to Dermot. "You ready?"

Dermot's eyes were glistening. He was pulling at the top of each of his fingers, cracking the joints. With an attempt at clearing his throat, he croaked, "Ready."

Together they tried to lift Stevo, Gianni at one of the tied up ends, and Ossie and Dermot at the sides but they failed. Maybe it was because the bedspread was wet, or perhaps they were so tired. I tried to remember what Mr. Skowroński had taught me about pulleys and levers and shifting heavy weights. I couldn't recall any of it.

Gianni shook his head and took a deep breath. "Oz, drag it round a bit further, then we can—" He stopped and motioned towards the grave. They heaved the cart nearer onto the pile of earth we'd taken out, stood next to the cart and, all three lifting one side, tipped it over. Stevo spilled into the hole, the cart on top of him.

Ossie groaned. "*Psha kreff.*"

For a moment, we stared down at it. Then a mewling rasp, like a violin bow hitting all the strings at the same time, seemed to get stuck in Dermot's throat. His teeth were chattering. Then his hand jerked up and grabbed his neck.

"I'm gonna be—" He retched again. The puke jetted out on top of the cart. Bits of it dribbled through the wheel and onto the bedspread. I began to gag too, but nothing came out.

Ossie shouted, "Oh God...shit," and jumped away. He stamped his feet then spun to turn his back on the grave, hands clawed up and squashing into his scalp. "Shit. Shit. Bloody *psha kreff* shit."

Dermot wiped his mouth and nose with his sleeve. "Sorry... Why can't we leave it?"

Fingers entwined at the back of his head Ossie was gazing at something in the sky. What was he thinking? Why was he taking so long?

At last he dropped his arms to his sides and straightened his shoulders. "No, we've got to lift it," he said as he swivelled round. "Give us a hand."

As soon as they'd dragged it out, he picked up the spade again. "It won't take so long this time."

We shovelled, kicked and swept the earth back in with the fork, trowels and our forearms. There was mud all over the place and when the earth in the

257

hole was even with rest of the ground, we still had a ton left.

Ossie and Gianni were staring at each other as if they had a private language, and Gianni was twiddling the corner of his lip again with his black thumb.

He said, "Well, how else are we going to do it?"

Dermot's eyes almost popped out of their sockets when suddenly Gianni and Ossie stepped onto the grave and started stomping it down. I turned away.

"For Chrissake, come on you two!" Ossie barked.

No, I couldn't. Dermot neither. But we passed more dirt under their feet. What were we doing? This was all wrong. How could they stamp on him like that? Like he didn't exist underneath? Like he never existed?

When the earth was as flat as they could get it, Ossie said we had to put the rest of the mud into the cart and distribute it round the garden. It felt as if this day would never ever end, like it would go on for the rest of my life.

After all that was done, Ossie scraped his shoes over the top. "You can still see it," he said. "We need old leaves."

So then we crawled around under the bushes and brought back soggy dead leaves and twigs. Gianni and Ossie trod them in while Dermot and I waited. I glanced at Dermot and realised I probably looked the same as him. Filthy, soaking, hardly a patch of skin visible on his face. What was I going to tell Mum? What would all of us tell our mums?

Gianni and Ossie nodded at each other, they were done. The drizzle had stopped and there were big bits of blue in the sky.

"Shall we say prayers now?" Dermot asked. Without waiting for a reply, he made the sign of the cross. "In the name of the Father, Son and Holy Spirit."

"Amen."

He led us in the Lord's Prayer, which everyone said, and I took over for Hail Mary, which Ossie didn't join in with. At the end of it, I realised something was missing. "We need a cross."

Gianni shook his head. "Can't have that. Someone might find it."

"So? They'll think it's an animal," I said, remembering the time Janek and I buried our hamster.

Ossie yanked my sleeve and thumped me with his voice. "Are you mad or what? Why do you think we've done all this? No cross, Ania."

No cross then. Nobody in the world who cared. Dead, purple, wrapped in that horrible bedspread, thrown in a hole, stomped on, no cross. Just like Mum's sister, buried in that Kazakhstan place that Granny told me about. Granny had said that nobody would even have known her baby was there.

Stevo's life.

I ached from head to toe, my teeth shivered, my toes were stuck together in my shoes and my glasses were so smeared I could hardly see out of them anyway. I took them off. "Can we go home now?"

"Yeah. Nothing more we can do here." Ossie picked his spade up. I took Grandad's fork, Gianni the trowels, and we trudged back to the passage.

*****

Neither Dad's car nor the delivery van were in our drive, so I managed to replace Granddad's fork where I'd found it. I removed my shoes and opened the back door. Granny went berserk when she saw me. Berserk times a thousand. I was so desperate to get home, I'd forgotten to change back into my clean clothes which were still in a bag at Spooky.

"*Psia krew!* What have you been doing? *Psia krew!* It's a good job they haven't arrived yet," she shrieked, pressing her thumb against her top teeth to push them back up. "Don't you dare pull any tricks like this when they're here. How will it look if your grandparents from Poland see you behaving like this?"

Then Granny saw my shoes. "*Cholera jasna!*" and launched into "and I went barefoot all summer in Tarnopol..." wallop on my bum, and from that to "in Siberia, we made shoes out of rags and ice..." blah-blah, another wallop, "God give me strength!" – which He did because the last whack sent me flying into the fridge door. Berserk times a million.

Granny pushed her scarf higher over her hairline, wrist-pinched me, her nails almost drawing blood, then made me strip to my vest and knickers right there. She unscrewed the cold water tap, told me to go and have a bath and said she'd be up in fifteen minutes to check I'd scrubbed properly.

It could have been worse – Mum would have asked a heap of questions, Granny was just on the rant of the century. As she turned her back to rinse my clothes, still spitting swear words, I said I'd wash my shoes myself. I ran upstairs, locked myself in the bathroom, and thought I'd never manage to stop crying.

*****

My eyelids flickered, my lips trembled with the taste of baklava. Stevo was kissing me. I felt his tongue touch my teeth. When I opened my eyes to look at him, his crusty black mouth spread wide open as if he'd unlocked his jaw like a snake. He sucked my face into this throat, and then swallowed the rest of my body. I thrashed against the sides, screaming for someone to come and help.

The eiderdown had twisted around my head. I kicked it away, spread out my arms and legs to cool my skin. Panting, I stared at the black ceiling, too scared to fall asleep again.

*****

Through the glass in the porch I saw Manuela holding a metal box that looked like a biscuit tin. The lid had a picture of some Greeky ruins on it. I

259

hadn't seen her since before she'd lost her nerve, three days now. I opened the door.

"I'm…sorry I didn't come. I've seen Dermot. He said…" She was trying to avoid looking in my eyes.

I said, "You weren't really ill, were you?"

I shut the door behind me so no-one would hear and sat down on the step where she joined me. She hugged the box in one hand and with the other kept running her finger over the ridge of the lid. I waited for her to speak.

She began, "How did… Was it awful? Did you cry?"

Half of me wanted to be kind because I sort of understood why she chickened out, and the other half refused to forgive her because she'd let me down. I didn't feel like a heart-to-heart about it and had no intention of going through the details. They were too horrible. When my daytime thoughts started to creep to the edges of them, I wanted to curl up and hide with the fluff balls under the bed.

"What's in there?" I asked.

"It's for Stevo."

"Bit late."

She cowered as if I'd slapped her. "I thought we could put in special memories and stuff, like from us, all of us."

"And then what?"

"Bury it next to him."

"Bury it next to him? I'm not going back," I said, making her look me in the eyes. "Are you?"

She sobbed. "Ania, I'm sorry. Maybe Oss—"

"Getting everyone else to do the work again? Where were *you?*"

Her sob multiplied into more sobs. Why was I making it worse? My stomach churned and I felt the same as when I thought I'd jump out of my bedroom window, just because I could, even though I didn't want to, just to see what happened.

Manuela fumbled for my hand. "Don't stop being my best friend. Please." I let her hold it. No, she'd always be my best friend forever and ever, even if I was mad at her now.

"It's a good idea about the box," I admitted. "I'll see what the boys want to put in. Maybe they'll go back if we ask." My other clothes were still there. I'd ask them to bring those back too.

*****

We met behind Ossie's garage to give our contributions. Four marbles, a set of jacks, an old paintbrush, a Hotspur comic folded in four because we couldn't squash it in, a sugar lamb, a wooden coloured egg, and another blue eye like the one inside the den.

Dermot dropped in a tinny blue medallion of the Blessed Virgin. "We won't go back ever again, will we? After this?"

No, we wouldn't. How could we play at Spooky knowing that Stevo lay beneath the soil?

*****

"They'll be here in three hours," Mum said, replacing the receiver then picking up the duster.

Since morning she'd been scrubbing places I didn't even know existed in our house. She cleaned the windows, moved all the furniture to hoover underneath, wiped pictures and straightened the general and his moustache who'd gone a bit wonky of late. She also brought out the crocheted doilies Polish Babcia sent us (they clogged up two drawers), washed, starched, and ironed them until most were hard as frisbees and put them on every single surface upstairs and downstairs, including on top of the telly. Which was a bit annoying because that one trailed onto the screen. And me, Janek and Iwonka had been polishing things for hours too because Mum said we'd have to go to bed at six o'clock if we didn't. The sitting room smelled of clean laundry and roses.

Unfortunately, the kitchen didn't. Granny's tripe soup was bubbling on the cooker.

Mum bent over to open the fridge. "According to him they had pristine linen table cloths with never a crease on them," she said to Granny. "And she speaks French. And two silver candelabra."

Mum removed all the Polish sausage, *Krakowska, Wiejska, Myśliwska* and the rest, the ham, the hard-boiled eggs in horseradish sauce, the various salads, gherkins in brine, gherkins in vinegar. There were another two gherkin jars on top of the fridge, as if she expected to feed my new grandparents gherkins for *śniadanie, obiad,* and *kolacja.*

When just about everything else was out on the cupboard surface, Mum retrieved a Pyrex dish of Granny's pigs' trotters in jelly. She'd need to tie a rope around the fridge to get it closed again.

Granny took the dish from her. "Pah, French! What's French? I can do better than that. *Jambo. Mr. MacDonaldo. Please nie mnoszko fish na tarylku. Muchos gracias.*" She lifted her chin and swatted a nothing in front of her hand.

"They had servants," Mum said glumly.

I interrupted, "What was that, Babcia?"

"Russian, Swahili. Spanish, English, Scottish."

"What does it mean?"

"It means anybody can speak French." She turned to Mum. "*Psia krew.* One! They had one! What are you getting so upset about? Does she have a servant now? No. Everything will be fine. Candelabra..." She shook her head.

Granny dipped the dish into the hot water in the sink then slid out the jellied trotters upside down onto a plate. Please God, don't make us have to eat them.

"We're as good as they are, Wanda," she said. "I may not have had shoes when I was a child, or servants, but I survived it all. Siberia, Persia, India, Africa, England. And so did you. Remember that. She sat on her *dupa* in the same house."

"Mama, children…" Mum muttered.

What was all the fuss about? It wasn't as if we hadn't had guests before, even posh-ish ones, so why was everybody in such a stew?

Janek slumped in the chair, put his elbows on the table, chin in his hands and sighed. "When can we be normal again?"

Granny tsked and Mum smoothed Janek's hair. "Oh now… Tatuś hasn't seen his parents for over twenty years. He wants to be proud of us. He was eleven when he left home for ever, so—"

Janek interrupted. "Were they mean to him?"

I hadn't thought of Stevo properly for at least ten minutes, he'd gone into the wavy bits at the edges of my mind. Now he moved back into the middle.

Mum said, "Mean? Ah, no. It's complicated. The town he lived in was German—"

"Tatuś is really *German?*" Janek's eyes widened and his voice rose in disbelief. He could be such a twit at times.

"No, no." Mum paused, a smile loitering in the corner of her mouth. "When the war broke out, the Nazis annexed his town, and after that all teaching was done in German. It became their territory. You see your Dziadzio was an officer in the Uhlan regiment stationed there—"

"What does Uhlan mean?" Janek asked.

"It's the cavalry," I said. I knew that from a song the guides and scouts sang.

"Like in cowboy films?"

Granny finished slicing the trotters into segments and arranged them upside down on a bed of lettuce. She passed it under Mum's nose with a swipe. She was definitely in a strop about something.

"Will her almighty highness with the candelabra be satisfied?" she said.

Mum scowled. "You can stop that now," then turned back to Janek.

Grunting, Granny whipped round on her heel and strode down the corridor to the dining room.

Mum continued. "What was I saying? Your father wanted to speak Polish, not German, and learn Polish history."

Dad had obviously been a loony since childhood which would account for his massive looniness now. Why would he actually want to learn about King Tanglefoot and What's-his-name Crooked Elbow? Why would anyone want to? Maybe he was like Krysia Nowicka, hand flying up first for every question, "Pick me! Pick me!" A proper swot. That didn't seem like him though.

She went on, "So he stayed with his Ciocia Kazia. You've heard him mention Ciocia Kazia, haven't you? She taught him how to play the piano. In Warszawa children were still taught in Polish. It was a huge sacrifice. How would you feel if you had to go and live somewhere else without Ania and Iwonka. Or me, or Tatuś?"

"I'd want to stay with you," Janek said.

"Exactly."

I was still reeling from learning that Dad could play the piano and realising what a lucky escape I'd had not to have lessons, when something else stirred in me, a jumble of reasons about why Dad was so peculiar and angry at us most of the time. But I couldn't work them out. It was to do with the way Mum said "huge sacrifice". I'd never thought about it that way before. That must be why he went on and on and on and gave us ear flicks. Because he wanted it and couldn't have it. Because those obnoxious Nazis took it away from him, all of it, his mum and dad, his friends, his town, his language, his history. And they'd killed all his nice neighbours. Maybe that's what it was all about.

But how? I tried to work it out differently. If I wanted to go Carnaby Street…and Mum and Dad said no…but Mrs. Karageorgis promised to take Manuela…I'd be jealous. But if Manuela said she didn't want to go, how would that make me feel? Probably jealous and cross. I'd think she was a complete idiot, and actually, I'd be furious with her because if I couldn't have it, at least she'd tell me about all the pop stars who went shopping there when she came back. Was that what Dad felt?

Before he drove to London to fetch the new Polish Babcia and Dziadzio, he made us line up in front of him by the door. His list of requirements gave me a monumental headache because there were so many to memorise.

no English *at all*, anywhere, never mind just at the table

no fights

no slurping or eating with mouth open

no sliding food around the plate, making scraping noises with knives, or burping

NO SLOUCHING! (that was definitely for me)

no nose-picking (that was for Janek)

no lying on the carpet in front of the telly

no moaning about homework (me again)

no nail-biting (also me)

no socks left on the floor in the sitting room or upstairs in the hall

no speaking unless spoken to and especially no interrupting when grown-ups were talking (me)

no whining about going to church or Polish school OR ELSE (all of us)

no noise in the morning until both grandparents were up

My job was to offer regular cups of tea, and if we were sitting on the sofa when they walked in, we had to get off and let them sit down.

I thought nothing could be worse than Dad's last instruction, for which he handed me a rota – clearing the garden of Groucho's poo before *śniadanie*. Except it wasn't the last or the worst.

"Learn this, please," he said, handing me a piece of paper. At least he said please. He'd typed it up on my Olympia and pencilled in all the Polish letters. I had to recite the dorkiest poem I'd ever seen for this new Polish Babcia and Dziadzio.

And they were going to stay six full weeks. That was nearly forever.

CHAPTER TWENTY-THREE

DAY EIGHT: AFTERNOON TO NIGHT

Of all the senses, Josie said, hearing is the last to go. So we keep talking, Mum, Janek, Iwonka and I. Trivial nonsense about the weather, what we'll eat later, the children, just to let Dad know we're here with him. It provides comfort, Josie said. Mum holds his hand, her fingers on his wedding ring.

He's been unconscious for several hours, the gentle rattle in his throat persistent, his breathing irregular. He looks skeletal now, the skin underneath his cheekbones sunken in. The Vaseline Iwonka smeared on his lips glistens, incongruous against the pallor of his skin.

Iwonka's phoned the priest; he'll be here soon to give the Sacrament of Extreme Unction. I don't expect it will take long, Dad took Holy Communion the other day.

We start when Dad suddenly draws a loud hacking breath then doesn't let it out; the rattle stops, no movement in the room. Iwonka's chin is quivering. She, Janek and I exchange glances, acknowledging it's over, ready to deal with whatever Mum's reaction might be. She heaves a long stuttering sob, her eyes in shock.

Dad exhales and we relax. It's a discomforting feeling – the desire for the end, and it's not only to do with his suffering. This sense of limbo, inactivity, reminds me of the urge to get rid of needy friends when I'm preoccupied with a stack of things requiring attention. "Yes, yes. We all have pain-in-the-arse children, hopeless husbands, the menopause, but I haven't time to revisit the usual complaints in your Groundhog Day." I'm not proud of myself.

Father Moczek arrives, his face grave, and greets us with "May Jesus Christ be praised". Amen. He asks us to stand. With the holy oil he makes a sign of the cross on Dad's eyes, ears, nostrils, lips, hands and feet. "Through this holy unction may the Lord pardon thee whatever sins or faults thou hast committed." And we join him in prayer.

We stand for another two minutes then he apologises to Mum because he must hurry; someone else is dying in Stretford.

It's 4.39. Dad's rattle stops. We fall silent, waiting for him to exhale, not allowing ourselves a reaction this time. We wait a little longer.

Mum drops her prayer book and wails, "No. Witek! Witek, beloved," as if the past few months and this week haven't prepared her in the least. "Witek, not yet!" She's standing over him, helpless, her face inches from his, dripping tears on his cheek.

I feel her panic at the closing of this chapter called their marriage. Their life together, the emptiness of the house, lack of human warmth in every room, and waking to silence with no plan to fill her days other than television soaps to act as the hours' markers from morning till night.

Don't worry, Mum, you have us.

Iwonka and I glance at one other, sensing we must let her get through the next couple of minutes on her own, the time for comfort postponed for the moment; we are here, a family, yet this is a private moment we children can't even begin to understand. Almost sixty years of loving and dancing through good times; loathing, wading, half-drowning through bad; suppressing anger; making allowances; adjusting. They made it this far, together. I have no idea how.

I cross myself. After a short while, I put my arm around Mum while Iwonka removes the cushions from behind Dad's back then lowers him flat and presses his jaw upwards to close his mouth. Janek, for want of knowing what to do, smooths out the duvet over Dad's feet. He's let a few tears go, too.

It's been two hours now since Dad died; he hasn't left yet though. Mum's saying the rosary, weeping on and off by the bedside. She gets to her feet, opens the window and stands to the side of it, still holding the handle, her gaze fixed on Dad. Then she starts to close the window, dithers, opens it wider again.

"I'll be back in a moment," she says. The hinges of the door squeak as she leaves the room. Psiuńka pads out after her, tail down between her legs, ears flat.

Grateful for the icy air, I gulp it in and whisper to Iwonka, "What was that?"

"I think she was releasing his soul."

Mum returns with a tea light. "Lay his hands on his chest, please."

I lift Dad's arms and do the best I can to put his hands, chilled already, together. Mum strikes a match and puts it to the tea light which she places on his hands. She takes a step back. Observes. Then she weaves the rosary beads around his fingers.

Iwonka hugs her. "Are you ready, Mama? Shall I make the phone calls?"

It's the usual undertaker in Chorlton. We had the same one for Granny and Grandad, for most of the Poles in Manchester; they know the routines. Iwonka discussed a few things with them yesterday, she says. She speaks to the doctor first to get the death certificate.

I never visited Granny or Grandad in the Chapel of Rest because I couldn't cope with it. Mum said she understood. I realise Dad and Stevo are the only people I've seen dead.

The children...Sam and Rachel – I ought to call them, but I can't face them yet, and besides, better they get some sleep tonight; tomorrow they'll have an entire day to come to terms.

It's 11.30. The funeral directors have taken Dad away, just Mum and I left in the house now, and she's in bed, still in the guest room, probably also awake. Reading the Bible or *The Consolations of Philosophy*, no doubt.

I lie in bed longing for sleep that refuses to come. The strangest sensation creeps into me, as if someone's prodding my back. Aware of Dad's instructions, I rise, go to Mum and Dad's bedroom and close the window which we forgot, then switch off the hall light, and also the one in the bathroom which Mum left on. He's gone but not gone. He'll leave when he's ready, I guess. There's something else he wants me to do. I walk round the house trying to fathom what he's telling me, until I find it – the thermostat. I lower it by three degrees.

Get her a better interest rate.

It's no good; I may as well stay up and check if Rachel and Sam have added a status on Facebook that indicates all is well in their world. It's the only reason I joined – to keep an eye on them. Rachel laughed and asked if I was spying; I told her a mother can't help being concerned.

I get through the passwords; Comet for Google, Mata Hari for Facebook. The kids are fine.

Idly I search for Manuelas and Emmanuelas in the UK. I'd recognise her anywhere, even now; so unless she's hidden behind those blue and white cameo profile pictures, she's not here or she emigrated. No Emmanuela Karageorgis. Manuela wasn't even with us, I realise; she had nothing to do with it.

I log off Facebook and check my work emails, knowing I'm prevaricating.

Finally, I return to Ossie on Google. As I scan his entries I come across papers he's written and societies he belongs to. Was Ossie that smart? I missed it. Fellow of this, fellow of that. Loads of abstracts about phytoplankton and calcifying coccolithophores, whatever they are, in the world's oceans. I remember him imitating his mum, "me restin' me chilblains", telling us how she put her feet in her own wee-stew. It doesn't seem possible. He's attached to the Marine Biology department at James Cook University in Townsville, Australia. Where is that? I pull up a map and find Townsville down the road from Cairns by the Great Barrier Reef. That wasn't so difficult.

Gianni comes up instantly in LinkedIn. Never in a million years would I have imagined *that*. He teaches salsa and flamenco in Sunderland of all places. Is there much call for Latin American there? I imagined him as a solicitor.

I'm half expecting Dermot to be a dancer too what with those lessons at Mrs. Delaney's Academy of Irish Dance in Chorlton. It seems not. By the looks of it, Dermot must have beefed up in the end, not that there's a picture from then. He ran youth rugby clubs in Cork for a few years. Then he entered a seminary in Kilkenny at the age of 28. Father Dermot O'Donnell has had an interesting career doing missionary work in Rawalpindi, Ecuador and Lesotho, Wiki says. I'll be able to track him down.

I've traced everyone who needs to know. Depending on what's happening over the next few days, I'll send them emails. We buried Stevo together then. Together we must decide what to do now.

THEN

It wasn't so bad when Dad returned with Babcia and Dziadzio from Poland. Grandad arrived in his suit and Granny (minus her kerchief) kept smiling at them with her gold tooth. She didn't say *Psia krew* or *Cholera jasna* even once, and – thank goodness – she didn't have any skin bobbles with threads hanging down on her face.

Over *kolacja*, Polish Babcia watched Dad like he was Jesus, all moony and lovey-dovey. And he was extra nice too. He'd never keep it up for the whole six weeks.

Granny asked Polish Babcia whether she'd like to come with her to church on Sunday and Polish Babcia said she rarely went to church these days because she wanted to eat. Which was a bit strange.

"They know who goes to mass, the NKVD," she added. "And I don't want any more trouble. It's hard enough trying to buy food."

I knew she meant the Communists and the secret police.

For a moment Granny looked as if she'd swallowed a grapefruit, whole. "Without God we would never have survived Siberia—"

Mum interrupted. "Shall we sit more comfortably now?" and Granny gave her a filthy look sideways so that no-one but me could see. Mum pushed her chair back quickly and led the way to the sitting room.

In the hall, Dad whispered in my ear. "Are you sure you know it?"

"Certain." I'd been dreading the poem since he'd handed it to me.

When everyone parked themselves, Dad, who was still standing by the door, said, "Ania has a special surprise for you." He nodded at me then jerked his head towards the telly.

I stood in front of it, to attention, and recited the questions and answers in two different voices.

Who are you?

A little Polish girl.

What's your emblem?

The White Eagle.

Where do you live?

Among my people.

On which soil?

On Polish soil.

What is that soil?

It is my motherland.

How was she won?

With blood and scars.

Do you love her?

I love her sincerely.

And what do you believe in?

I believe in Poland.

What are you to her?

Her grateful child.

What do you owe her?

The gift of my life.

Polish Dziadzio beamed, Polish Babcia dabbed at her eyes, Dad nodded again, Janek smirked and I wished the ground would open and let me slide down.

CHAPTER TWENTY-FOUR

DAY THIRTEEN

Mum, Iwonka, Janek and I sit in the chief mourners' limousine. I turn to look at their spouses and all our kids in the cars behind, only half-convinced Rachel and Sam will stand up, sit down, kneel, regardless of whether they believe any of this stuff, which they don't. No, they'll do it for Dad though, out of respect. I hope Rachel hasn't been mawkish and put up a Facebook status. Sam won't let me down, he's a good lad.

At the Polish church people have gathered outside and approach us to express their condolences, among them old soldiers, medals on their chest, sitting in sturdy wheelchairs which someone will have to heave up the steps. The scouts, both middle-aged and young, stand by the gate holding the Gdynia standard.

We walk inside and sit in the front pew. I gaze at the altar and at Christ on the cross now hovering overhead, like something from *Close Encounters of the Third Kind*, suspended at an angle by wires from the ceiling. In the place where He used to be, at the back of the altar, is a gaudy painting of Jesus that looks as if it was commissioned from a GCSE student.

Feet shuffling behind us, whispers, the opening and closing of handbags and hymnals. I want to turn round and see who's there in the echoing fidgets. The church sounds surprisingly full.

The pall bearers carry Dad in, followed by the altar boys, the priest and scouts. Dad asked for no flowers, just donations to the fund for Underground Army veterans in Warsaw which provides medical care for those still holding on to life. It seemed a reasonable request. Iwonka ignored it somewhat; she wanted seven red poppies on the coffin, but couldn't find any that wouldn't droop, so Dad's got radiant artificial ones.

Mum didn't mind. I glance at her. She's bearing up, though in a daze.

I look at the coffin, my feet seem rooted, my memories wandering.

Iwonka takes a tissue from her pocket and dabs at her nose then Janek takes her hand. On the pew to the left sits Ciocia Teresa and the four surviving members of the Underground Army, the PW in their lapels, walking sticks perched beside them. Ciocia Teresa, it seems, has brought one of her sensible ones today. Magda's been round for the shampoo and set.

The requiem mass begins; the Polish words haven't evaporated despite my church-going days being limited to weddings and funerals since I left Manchester.

Eulogies. Mum left Ciocia Teresa to organise those because she knows everyone who would want to be here. We elected not to speak; Iwonka's too shy, I'm hopeless at it, and the last time Janek tried public speaking was for Mum and Dad's fiftieth wedding anniversary. His voice broke and he couldn't carry on, sentimental fool.

First up is one of the older scouts, the son of Mum and Dad's friends.

I don't entirely recognise the dad he's describing; the man who with many others saved up to buy this church, the man whose name is on the boards at POSK, the *Polski Ośrodek Społeczno-Kulturalny* in London, as one of the first benefactors, the tents he bought for the scouts, his donation to refurbish the building in Penrhos when it was falling apart.

Seventy-five grand. Bloody hell, Dad. You kept that quiet. I'm sorry, so sorry – how could I have doubted you?

Out of the corner of my eye I look at Mum; she's really not with it. Did she hear that? Does she know about it? I wonder whether Iwonka knew that bit about the Polish Social and Cultural Association? I glimpse myself as a child, ferreting about in the secrets of Mum and Dad's bedroom. There was an envelope with POSK on it in your wardrobe. Casino money, I thought.

The scout mentions your frequent contributions and support, adding that you funded the new Gdynia standard. No wonder you want me to get Mum a better interest rate – is there any money left? Oh God, I'm sorry. No, I'm sure you've provided for her.

Next there's a slim young woman I've not seen before, somewhere in her early thirties I'd say. She wears a navy suit, and as she passes through the altar rail I notice her skirt's a bit tight, size 12 would look better. In a whisper I ask Iwonka who she is. She doesn't have a clue. "New Polonia probably?" she says.

The young woman talks about yet another dad; the one who sent a monthly contribution to some home for disabled children outside Bydgoszcz and who collected spectacles and surplus medicines to send to the charity clinic for elderly veterans in Warsaw.

Sam rises. I didn't know of this plan. I feel nervous for him among all these Poles. His will be the first English words spoken in this service. I watch as he squeezes his ear lobe, a little trick I taught him to calm down when Reverend Mother insisted he play 'The Brightest Star' in the nativity play in junior school.

He says he's here on behalf of all Dad's grandchildren. The story he tells is about his Year 6 school project for which he got an A+. I remember it now. He spent hours with Dad looking at the papers and identification cards from the war. They kept on disappearing into town to get photocopies every time Dad unearthed something new. Sam says how kind Dad was and how honoured all the grandchildren are for having known him. There's a murmur of appreciation from the crowd. Sam waits a moment then continues. Had it not been Dziadzio giving him *God's Playground* to read, Sam says, he wouldn't know of Poland's rich history. I'm embarrassed, realising that ought to have been my responsibility. Sam says he's proud and grateful to have Polish blood in him. Someone sniffles in one of the pews on my left.

As Sam returns to sit, there's a shuffling on the far right of the second pew. I turn my head. A young woman and an old man stand. He looks a hundred, at least. She puts a Zimmer frame in front of him. The congregation waits and waits as he inches forwards, the woman at his side. When they reach the altar steps, she puts the Zimmer frame on the top one and almost lifts him over the others. He carries on with the Zimmer frame to the podium. We must have been waiting five minutes.

The woman moves the Zimmer aside and guides him nearer the microphone. He says something we can't hear and she adjusts the mike towards him.

His voice is thin like crumpled tissue paper. He says, "Witek Walewski was my dear friend. I worked with him for over forty years." He doesn't appear disrespectful when he pauses and allows himself a little laugh. I still don't recognise him. Who is he?

He carries on. "And in each of those years I almost got the sack at least twice." His voice catches and the young woman puts her hand under his forearm. He nods at her and bends forward into the microphone again. "Witek was a good man, a righteous man."

With her help it takes him several minutes to get back down off the steps and into his seat.

The pall bearers lift Dad and the organ plays a note, a second, third. I don't know the tune at first, then I hear the middle section of Chopin's *Marche Funèbre*. The organist skipped the beginning; I'll ask Iwonka to drop him or her a well-deserved extra tenner.

While we prepare to leave for the crematorium, outside by the gate Mum accepts more I'm-sorry-for-your-losses from people.

Mrs. Nowicka takes Mum by the elbow, comforts her, saying she must phone and come round for *herbatka* whenever she wants, chat about the old times – a cup of tea I realise won't ever materialise unless I pull my finger out and drive Mum there.

An indefinable anxiety rises within me, filling my ribcage. There's something I must do, now, no other time will be the same.

I say, "Mama, I'll be back in a second. I dropped my glove inside."

I dash up the steps. It's the columns I really want, that's where it all lies: the history, the resilience, the suffering that supported us all. But I resist and re-enter on the left. Thank God, there's no-one here. I'd do it on the floor if I could be sure nobody would enter. I look right, travel down all the stations of the cross on the walls, past the statue of the Virgin Mary, where the old confessional used to be, across the altar, over fluorescent Jesus, past the painting of the Madonna of Częstochowa, along the other stations of the cross— Where? Where shall I do it? Dad's waiting.

There's no time. It must be here in the back pew. I turn my back on the altar, raise my arms up, press my body against the wall, and kiss the white paint. I feel them sending their current through me; the Pani Jeleńskas, Pan Skowrońskis, Edzios, Widzowskis and Kucyks. I hear Granny's *Psia Krew*, smell the peardrops she stashed in her coat pocket so we wouldn't find them, taste her apple charlotte. I inhale Grandad's Woodbines and the sawdust from his shed. I want to climb into the wall, feel their embrace forgiving me for everything I never understood then. On the back of my head, there's tugging, a twirling, an irritating twiddling in my disappointing grey hair.

Ciocia Teresa's voice has the insistence of a power drill in my ear. "Pull yourself together."

I draw back. Exit.

Sam's coming up the step, concern on his face. "Mum, are you okay?" He links my arm, bends into me.

"Oh, you know." I can barely speak. "There's so few of them left. Your dziadzio, my babcia and dziadzio..." My voice catches. Pull yourself together.

"I do understand, Mum," he says. How can he? Bless him.

In the limousine I'm still trembling as we inch towards Southern Cemetery. Iwonka asked the undertakers to take the old route down by the 53 bus stop where the unfortunate Catholics used to wait in the rain. At Brooks's Bar she points right. "Look down Shrewsbury Street. Quick! Look!" Kombo's is still there, now a ruin, never to be reclaimed.

Iwonka's gaze is far away for a moment. She giggles. "Do you remember that time Dad came home as a Mexican? I nearly wet my pants I was so scared."

I watch Janek's crooked smile as he laughs. "Yeah... Do you remember the first time he took me fishing in Scotland? I nearly drowned. He hired a cruiser – with a cabin – the works, said I had to catch six pike by the end of the day. So there I am with the fishing rod, while he's lying back smoking his pipe, doing bugger all."

He turns to Iwonka. "Did I ever tell you that? He yelled at me to put my life jacket on and I didn't want to. So in the end he says, 'It's your decision.' Guess what – the line caught in some reeds and I fell in trying to yank it out."

"He never," Iwonka says.

"He did."

"Did he jump in after you?" I ask. I've never heard this story either.

Janek's snorting with laughter now. "Did he hell! What a *dupa*! I was doggy-paddling like mad and he leaned over the side, me drowning – did I mention that, *drowning*, and said, 'What did I tell you? Are you a *zuch* or not? Be prepared!' I swallowed half of Loch Doon and three trout before he pulled me out."

"Are you ever going to swim the Channel again?" I ask.

"He-he. Are you mad? It was an early mid-life crisis. Once was enough."

He's still chuckling as we drive along Upper Chorlton Road. I sense Janek, Iwonka and Mum look right at our old house, but I glance left down the passage that took the gang to Spooky and Stevo. I think I know what I'm going to do about Stevo, almost sure I've made a decision. I'll let things settle down then I'll sort it out.

Once at the crematorium we pray that Eternal Rest is Granted Unto Dad and that Perpetual Light shines upon on him, then watch him glide off behind the curtains in the cheapo pine coffin he insisted on. His ashes will be ready for dispatch in a few days, according to the undertaker.

Back at the parish hall, the tables form a huge cheerful patchwork of squares. Soon the place is buzzing with standing room only, so Iwonka and I ask the ladies in the kitchen whether they can stretch things out more. Of course they can; no problem, they say, there's always enough to go round in a Polish home.

The priest leads us in grace and another prayer and shortly after we drink a toast of wine to the Repose of Dad's Soul. Three courses follow: various *surówki* arranged like tiny Interflora creations with their bright pickled-veg colours, then pork fillet in a creamy sauce, potatoes – naturally – red cabbage, bigos if anybody fancies a little extra; and finally several types of cake.

I'm lifted when I hear periodic ripples of gentle laughter from around the room. I've kept an eye on Rachel and Sam throughout and I can't fault them; they've surpassed themselves, as if they've always belonged here in this transported Poland. Sam's working his charm on all the old biddies; Rachel's managed to keep her mobile in her bag – we must thank the Lord for small mercies.

Three hours later and that's it; Dad's had his penultimate send-off.

At home, Mum refuses offers of tea and doesn't join the rest of the family in the dining room and kitchen. She says she needs to lie down for a while.

Now all we have to do is sneak a Tesco's carrier bag and contents through Ryanair.

You're a pain in the arse, Dad. Do you know that?

THEN

We were sitting in the round on our circle, all of us, singing 'Yellow Submarine' at the tops of our voices. An empty wrapper of milk chocolate digestives lay discarded by Dermot's legs and dappled sunlight played on his face. One by one, Stevo, Dermot, Gianni, Manuela and Ossie began to change colour. I watched the purple spread into their hands, travel up their necks into their faces. Their noses, lips and cheeks scabbed up like they were lepers, then their faces melted into a blackish sludge. As the gunge dripped down, rats poked their snouts through my friends' eyeholes and began attacking each other. Everyone was screaming, screaming, screaming.

Someone clapped a hand on my mouth. I woke. Mum was standing by my bunk in her nightie, wiping the sweat off my forehead, saying it was just a dream, a nasty dream. I wanted to tell her everything, from the moment we met Stevo, right until the very end. But I knew it would be a mistake. All I admitted was that I'd wet myself. She held me close for a second then told me to get out of bed so she could remove the sheets. After I took my pyjamas off, she wiped me down with a cloth, all down my legs, around my private parts and bum like I was a little baby. Overcome by shame, I couldn't stop sobbing.

New Polish Babcia pushed my bedroom door open.

"What's wrong with the child?"

Mum replied, "She's troubled. Please, it's fine now. Please go back to bed." Bundling up the sheets, Mum said, "Get into bed with Tatuś," and went downstairs.

I climbed in on Mum's side.

"Do you want to tell me what it was about?" Dad asked.

I lied and told Dad about a film where a lady was stabbed, that her face appeared in strange places, and I couldn't get that picture out of my mind, not even when I slept.

Dad stroked my cheek. "I used to have bad dreams too, about things I'd seen." He paused and kissed the top of my head. His hand moved to my earlobe, rubbing and twiddling gently. "I learned a trick to stop them. Close your eyes. I'll put my hand on your tummy and when you breathe in, make sure you stick your tummy out. Breathe in." This made me feel silly – I was eleven now and in the space of one hour I'd become younger than Iwonka.

But I did as told, breathed in and out ten times. Stevo was behind my eyelids. "The lady is still there. She won't go away."

"Make her small. Smaller. Is she tiny yet? Blow her to the corner of your eye." Dad waited. "Tell me where you feel happy."

"On the swing, upside down," I said, but even that was a lie because I hadn't been happy for ages.

He chuckled. "What can you see in your happy place, child?"

"Our house. Grass. Groucho's poos. Those pink flowers Mama planted.

275

Ossie's house."

"Can you lift your head? What do you see?"

"The sky and the sun."

"Anything else?"

"A white puffy cloud." I heard his breath come out of his nose.

"What can you smell?"

"Air and grass. And the pear tree."

"Anything else?"

"Leaves."

"What can you hear?"

"Just birds. And the cheer at Manchester United."

"Has she gone?"

"Yes." Stevo was still there in the corner, but only just, like a floaty thing in my eye.

Dad pulled the eiderdown over my shoulders and cuddled me, his arm over my waist. He breathed into the back of my hair, and even though it was only Dad, it was like having a guardian angel on my shoulder, making me warm and safe.

"Did you always have nightmares when you were little?" I asked.

"Not when I was really small. Later. So I learned the trick."

"What's your happy place?"

"Sleep now, Ania." I thought he wouldn't tell me. Then, very quietly just above a whisper, he said, "I'm lying in a boat on a lake in Poland with my friend, Janek. It's cold. I'm watching the sun and white clouds in a blue sky. I hear the birds and the water lapping against the side of the boat. For one hour all is peaceful."

So that's why he kept the photo I found in his wardrobe. To keep it safe. It was Dad's happy place.

*****

The six weeks were almost up and Polish Babcia and Dziadzio would soon be going back to Warsaw. I hadn't disgraced myself again and now found it easier to nudge Stevo into the corner of my eye. But he still showed up at least three times a day.

Granny stopped being snippy with new Polish Babcia who was very nice because she'd brought me a watch from Poland. The face was a kind of reddish gold which, she said, was all they had in Russia and that's where Polish watches came from. She added that no matter how hard Polish people worked, whatever they produced in factories or whatever they grew in their fields, the Russians stole it, and so it had been for centuries. And that's why you couldn't buy any white toilet paper, not even school Izal, only crinkly brown stuff. The Russians had stolen all the toilet paper too. Granny agreed with everything that Polish Babcia said.

With three days left of the visit, Granny invited Polish Babcia and me to go to Alexandra Road. Polish Babcia wanted to buy presents for her other grandchildren in Poland, so we went to Woolworth's where my two babcias linked arms, like candelabras were no longer important.

I wandered off to look at things on my own.

Then I saw her – Stevo's mum. Was it her though?

Yes, definitely her. But she looked nothing like the colourful lady from January. Only her clothes were similar. Make-up-less and piggy-eyed, her hair flat and scruffy with dark roots, she seemed smaller, as if her outsides had turned inwards.

I breathed in deeply, deeply, deeply just like Dad taught me, trying to chase Stevo's purple face from my mind's screen. An invisible magnet drew me towards her. For some stupid reason, a desire to touch her overwhelmed me.

As I inched in her direction, a bald-headed man approached from behind. He tightened the belt on his mac.

"Are you done yet or what?"

She started and turned round. "Yes, Bill. Sorry. Won't be a sec." She looked at him for less than an instant before lowering her eyes. "Nearly finished."

With browny-yellow fingers like Grandad's she passed a ten shilling note over the counter.

"Mary! Get a move on," the man said. "I won't get to Maine Road on time."

The assistant dropped the change into Stevo's mum's outstretched palm.

"Ta, love," she said. She was still adjusting the shopping bag on her arm when the man grabbed her elbow and propelled her out of the shop. His shoes tapped on the floor as if they had metal heels.

I watched her through the window, wanted to follow her to find out where she lived and tell her what had happened. She must have loved Stevo a bit. Mustn't she?

That night, trying to get to sleep, I blew Stevo into the corner, just as Dad taught me, and hung upside down on the swing.

In my dreams though, instead of Stevo, I saw his mum standing naked in front of a mirror. In the reflection her face was white, except she had no mouth or nose, only eyes trickling tears.

CHAPTER TWENTY-FIVE

DAY SEVENTEEN

Rachel and Sam left the day after the funeral, both declaring they'd like to spend Christmas here with their Babcia which strikes me as somewhat morbid; it won't be remotely happy-clappy. I told them they don't have to, but they insisted. Maybe they've matured. At last.

I'm staying here.

There's a pile of unopened letters from Poland on the hall console to tackle with Mum this evening. I'll write the replies; she's not up to it. She nearly went to Tesco's this morning, got as far as the traffic lights, she said, and came back. Her eyes had looked puffy. We'll have to make her drive beyond there, otherwise she's stuck for life.

It's taken her forty minutes to write me a list for Barbakan, including the real Matjes herrings, not the *à la* Matjes ones.

"Not the fake ones. You hear?"

"Yes, Mama. I hear."

She's told me that at least half a dozen times. Not the fake ones.

Pani Nowicka, God bless her, is coming for a *herbatka* shortly – still driving, apparently.

"I'm going now," I call to Mum, opening the front door then seeing she's parked me in even though there's plenty of space next to my car. I grab her keys and back out of the drive.

Amber. Red. More red. An eternity of red. Will they ever change? Yesterday the *Manchester Evening News* said Manchester's population stands at two and a half million. And they're all here in front of me, every single last one of the inconsiderate buggers on the sodding Washway Road. Last minute Christmas shopping, I expect.

I switch on the CD player; it's Katherine Jenkins. Singing 'O mio Babbino Caro'; that's all I need. Cheers. That must be why Mum came back. It's like

278

that pregnancy thing: before it happens, you've never noticed a single pregnant woman. When it happens to you, the whole female world waddles with a belly as huge as yours.

Radio Two, much better. Golden oldies. Lynne Anderson – 'I beg your pardon, I never promised you a rose garden'. Shit – Dad wanted me to buy Mum some flowers after he was gone. I forgot. I drop into the florists opposite Chorlton library and ask the assistant to make up a bouquet. I'm surprised they have any lilies at all at this time of year, but they've even got calla lilies. She's always liked those – they were in her wedding posy. That's what he must have meant about 'no petals'.

I leave the flowers on the back seat of the car.

At Barbakan I sneak through the people drinking hot chocolate on the veranda and enter the shop. My scarf pulled up to my ears, I mingle in the throng, keeping an eye out for anyone who was at the funeral who might want to talk about it. Fortunately there's only Chorltonites and New Polonia.

Not the fake ones – the real ones, I hear Mum saying. Not that I've ever tasted much difference. Herring is herring, isn't it?

I place my order for the fish, two caraway seed loaves, two rye, a bottle of *barszcz* concentrate, a couple of *kiełbasy* and a packet of sesame seed bites for me.

"Anything else?" the assistant asks.

Just one more thing, I think. But not here.

From the Wood Road end, I enter Whalley Road; still beautiful, even in the winter, even though many of the 19th century buildings are no longer there, replaced by soulless apartment blocks and two nursing homes by the look of them. It's the trees that matter; in the clear blue sky of this frosty day the sycamores and horse chestnuts tower almost leafless above, their girths fattened by the last fifty years of comings and goings. The foliage of holly bushes and rhododendrons spills over garden walls of the houses that are left, taking me back to the moment when I gazed, wide-eyed, at Old Spooky's splendour. The car windows are closed and the only smell is lemon air freshener wafting through the vents. Maybe it will come to me when I get out.

I park beyond Sylvan Avenue, trying to figure out exactly where Spooky stood. Almost directly opposite Whalley Avenue.

This place must be it; four storeys with some parking at the front, not enough clearly since they're extending the car park at the back where they found him. Will the police cordon be down yet?

He's no longer here, I know that, his soul set free from the earth like Dad's through the window. I walk down the side of the building nevertheless; the same route Stevo travelled on the go-cart. At the other end of the garden the car park's abandoned; still signs of work going on.

At the bottom where we used to climb into the secret passage a rock

279

garden nestles in the corner, compact as an exhibit at the Chelsea Flower Show. I sit on the bench beneath the rowan, listening to the birdsong and remember the crow that scared us witless with all that demented flapping, Dermot spouting Devil's spirit nonsense.

How would I even begin to discuss Stevo with the police? I'd have to tell them his surname, although I'm not sure what he said was true. Maybe it was his wishful thinking, or his mother's. Did his mother assume the surname for both of them? Kardasz wasn't a 'good' man, but he did buy Stevo the bike and the football boots. And Stevo's mother... I don't know how I know it, but I'm sure she's dead too. She seemed so much older than Mum and Dad.

I open the sesame packet and bite into the biscuit. A robin lands on the edge of the pond and dips his beak in the water; then he trips over the large ornamental pebbles and lands on the arm of the bench. We watch each other for a moment. He doesn't seem bothered by human intrusion. I break off a piece and slowly place it a foot away from him. He accepts my offer.

So I am left with Ewa and Kinga. Ciocia said Kardasz was a 'liar, thief and philanderer' – did they ever suspect? Did they know about Pani Wróbelska's child? He could also have been a halfway decent father whom they remember with affection. I shouldn't ruin that. No, I won't open that Pandora's box. None of them need to know his secrets now.

I look at the sun, then close my eyes, wondering if there is anyone up there to listen. In the orange hue behind my eyelids I see Gianni, Manuela, Dermot and Ossie sitting in the round, singing 'Paperback Writer'. From the corner of my eye floats an indistinct shape; it fills out with colour. I see his sandy hair, his green eyes, the mouth that gave me my first kiss.

Grant unto him Eternal Peace; may Perpetual Light shine upon him.

When I take the rosary beads out of my pocket, the robin hops onto the back rest. I put the crucifix to my lips then lower it into the water, watching as minuscule ripples engulf the crystals.

My shoulders loosen and I feel lighter. The pictures of these last few weeks seem to be receding.

I lean back with my hands in my pockets and think about summer. My ISA matures in three weeks time – there's over six thousand pounds in there, enough for the three of us. Would Sam and Rachel fancy coming with me though? They would if I told them it was Goa. And I don't mind – I expect there are elephants all over India. I might even write some travel articles.

As I stand to leave, the robin skips to the pebble as if to have a look in the pond. With a high-pitched chirp, he puffs out the feathers of his splendid red breast.

Thank you for reading With Blood and Scars. I hope you enjoyed it. If you'd like to help other buyers make a decision about purchasing it, please leave a review at http://hyperurl.co/obt81i Or, if you prefer, please drop in a few lines at www.goodreads.com.
On Facebook you can find me under B. E. Andre, Author. http://on.fb.me/1E77xjn
I will be pleased to answer any questions.
My email address is b.e.andre@hotmail.com

Acknowledgements

Many people, organisations, and Facebook groups have helped to create this book. I am extremely grateful to all of them. The novel was conceived when I did an MA in Critical and Creative Writing at the University of Winchester, supported by my tutor, Carole Burns. To write my dissertation I went to Poland where my Stryjek Jacek and Ciocia Danusia housed me and let me get on with it. Serdecznie dziękuję. After that, for a while, the embryonic novel languished. Then my Portuguese family, Tuxa, Paulo, Rita and Marianna offered me a writer's retreat in Mem Martins to finish my first draft. Muito obrigada.

Thank you to Sarah Dobbs, my editor, who guided me through the changes that had to be made and who was always available to offer support and advice.

http://www.sarahdobbs.com/

Thanks also to my two writers groups, Chester Writers and South Manchester Writers, who offered advice, support, friendship. I am particularly indebted to those who critiqued sections or beta read: Stanley Salmons, Michelle Rimmer, Clare Dudman, Fliss Newson and Rebecca Sowray at Chester, and David Beckler, Mark Thomson, Beverley Proctor and Andy Smith at South Manchester.

http://www.stanleysalmons.com/
http://www.claredudman.com/
http://www.davidbeckler.com/

Several Facebook groups and friends have also been superb sources of information and inspiration. In particlar, I'd like to thank Urszula Gacek, Wanda Fabbri, Jaśmina Krupa Slater, Ren Behan, Christina Małkowska Żaba, Agnieszka Sheppard, Danuta Gajewska, Marek Lange, Les Michałczyk, Roz Ryszka-Onions, Andre Bielecki, and George Cieślik.

I am also obliged to John Guzlowski and Danusha Goska.

http://lightning-and-ashes.blogspot.co.uk/
http://save-send-delete.blogspot.co.uk/
http://bieganski-the-blog.blogspot.co.uk/

A special thank you goes to Maria Jastrzębska for allowing me to use her poem, *Think About It,* and to Katy Carr for allowing me to reference her creative and outreach work within the story.

http://mariajastrzebska.wordpress.com/
http://www.katycarr.com/
Many friends and family believed in me when I didn't, inspired me, put up with me when I talked of nothing but writing, and added snippets from their 1960s lives. Thank you, all of you. Sally-Ann North, Sheila Blair, Sheila Clancy, Ann Bailes, Anna Hagan, Juliet Ellis, Joan Madden, Betty Clancy, Sue Godwin, Bernie Carney, Basia Sheeran, Becci Hey, Su Lewis, Carol Meredith, Sue G, Belinda Bekker, Chris Best, Die Booth.

The family house I wanted to write about is now inhabited by Mrs. Surjit Kaur Singh and Mr. Karnail Singh. Mrs. Singh very kindly let me wander round the house and garden, and she shed further light on how it was for other immigrants in the 1960s. Thank you.

Finally, thank you to Mariola, David, Janusz, Ellen, Rafi, Alex and Owain, but especially Owain. I'm sorry it took me so long.

Should you ever want to visit the Barbakan delicatessen, I can highly recommend it.

http://www.barbakan-deli.co.uk/

Book Club Questions

Characters

How does Ania's attitude to her father change throughout the course of the story?

What do you think is the truth about Stevo's parentage? What is your view of his mother as a parent?

Ania often allows herself to be led by Ossie. Why do you think this is?

How might the relationships of the gang members have changed after the burial? Were the children initially brought together or driven apart?

Even though Ania says she managed to lock away the memory of Stevo, would it have affected her subsequent relationships?

How do you think the other children dealt with the disposal of Stevo's body?

What do you feel about the group dynamics of the gang?

In adult life Ania seems to be prepared to let Iwonka take the lead. Why might this be?

How has Ania's relationship with her mother developed?

Who is your favourite character and why?

Themes

What do the portrayals of Mr. Kucyk, Mrs. Jeleńska, Mr. Skowroński and Auntie Teresa tell you about their history and the way they have adapted to living in the UK?

How would the sight of Yankel's family hanging from the balcony have affected a boy of Witek's age?

How is it possible that Witek can look for the good in all nations despite everything that he saw? Would you be able to forgive?

At the bus stop when Ania rescues Mrs. Jeleńska what feeling is she describing? Have you ever felt this way?

What do the scenes at Polish school and Polish church show about ethnic communities?

Discuss the race issues presented in this book. Was Witek ever antisemitic? Why do you think the gang stick together even though there are plenty of other children to play with in the avenue?

What insights has the novel given you about what it means to be a refugee in a strange land? How would you cope with living in another country?

Author Biography

B. E. Andre was born in Manchester, England, the child of Polish post-war refugee parents. She was educated at Stretford Grammar and Loreto College, read French, German and Swedish at U. C. W. Aberystwyth, and completed an M. A. in Critical and Creative Writing at the University of Winchester, United Kingdom. She worked for Reuters News Agency in London.

She is the proud mother of three grown-up sons who left home when they were supposed to. She lives in Northwich, Cheshire.

Among her many interests is the study of wood cabins and garden sheds. This is her debut novel.

13258614R00174

Printed in Poland
by Amazon Fulfillment
Poland Sp. z o.o., Wrocław